NIGHT'S FAVOR

A WEREWOLF SUPERNATURAL THRILLER
ADVENTURE

NIGHT'S CHAMPION
BOOK ONE

RICHARD PARRY

CONTENTS

NIGHT'S FALL

Night's Favor

Valentine Everard is a nice guy with a drinking problem and nothing to lose. That was yesterday.

Today, he wakes up with a **splitting headache, a blank space where last night should be, and a kill squad kicking down his door**. Biomne, a ruthless megacorp, wants him gone—**no questions, no witnesses**. If that wasn't bad enough, a **murderous Russian psychopath** is also on his trail, and he's not the type to leave loose ends.

Something inside Val has changed. He's faster. Stronger. His wounds heal before his eyes. But power like this comes with a price —and the more he uses it, the harder it is to hold onto himself. **It's not a gift. It's not a curse. It's something worse.**

To survive, Val must **master the monster inside him before it consumes him completely**. If he fails, he won't just lose his life— **he'll lose himself. And when that happens, everyone he cares about dies with him.**

YOU'RE AWESOME

You could have picked any book, but you chose this one. That means a lot.

Your support keeps independent authors like me forging ahead, writing the stories we love (and hopefully, the ones you love too). Whether you're here for the characters, the worldbuilding, or just a little escapism, thank you for being part of this journey.

You. Kick. Ass.

ROLL FOR NARRATIVE

WHERE WORLDBUILDING AND OVERTHINKING COLLIDE

Love stories that linger in your brain long after The End? Ever wonder why some books hit like a natural 20 and others critically fail their way into the 1-star abyss?

Join *Roll for Narrative*, my hub for sci-fi and fantasy lovers. I explore storytelling like a rogue casing a dungeon, review movies, books, and games, and dish out writing tips like a chaotic-good bard with a grudge against bad prose. No spam, just good stuff.

Join the quest:
https://rollfornarrative.parrydox.com

All the things, big and small, that you do — you make my life wonderful.
For my Kitney.

The van stuck out of the wall of Elephant Blues as if it had been thrown there, the skid marks of the tires showing where it had veered before jumping the curb. One door on the back was missing — they still hadn't found it — and the other hung loose on a single hinge, its handle missing. The laminated glass of its single window lay in a spider-webbed sheet on the pavement, a hole torn through the middle.

A hand sat beside it, the pool of blood diluting in the rain. It was a left hand, but no wedding ring — strong fingers, definitely a man's. It lay palm up, fingers curled like a dead insect. The fingernails were carefully trimmed and clean, as if the guy had managed a manicure just before having it torn off. At least it looked torn; not cut, not sawn, but torn. The bones of the arm stuck out from the stump, the stark white ends free of other tissue. Big floodlights kicked back the night, the fingers of the hand stretching tall shadows along the sidewalk. They hadn't found the rest of the body — not out here.

It might be in the pile inside.

"Think he punched through the glass? Maybe got out? Lost his hand that way?" Elliot chewed on the end of his pen.

"Nah." Carlisle shuffled her feet through the puddles on the wet sidewalk, trying to get the bottom of her soles clean. She was getting rained on, and her pants were starting to stick to her. Well, more than they already were — Carlisle glanced at her red-stained knee and clamped down on the shudder. She should have kept her overcoat on, but inside the heat had made her want to retch, the memory of the slaughterhouse reek still with her. She tried to loosen her pants, but they were plastered on — God*damn.* "Knuckles are fine, and that's safety glass. No cuts on the wrist, not that I can see. Almost looks chewed. We've got to find the arm... Jesus, Vince. There's so many people in there." Rain was running down the back of her collar. "And they're all dead. How are we getting on with a witness check?"

"No one saw shit. I swear the only way we'd have less witnesses is if this was a Foundation for the Blind annual meet. Connolly and Malloney are in there too. Somewhere. They were good guys. Fuck's sake." Elliot offered his umbrella to Carlisle. "You're going to die of hypothermia. Take the umbrella."

It was pink, with Hello Kitty motifs in the fabric, a cheap white handle at the bottom. Carlisle snorted. "Where'd you get that thing?"

Elliot tilted it, looking at it as if for the first time. "You know, I really can't remember. It might have been the evidence locker." He shrugged. "I'm not buying an umbrella. Too damn windy around here. I'll call their families."

"Management thinking, buddy. Keep it, it's more your color. Leave the calls to me. I knew Connolly, a little." Carlisle looked inside the van, taking in the straps tethered to one side. There was some kind of harness, big enough for a man, but it was hard to tell with it all shredded like that. "I'd bet you your next night shift that those straps are nylon." She reached into a pocket, rescuing a stick of gum. Chewing, she stepped up into the van, wiping her wet blond — *and just a little gray, right?* — hair away from her face. She used the end of a pen to poke through the remains of the harness. Definitely torn —

the frayed ends of the nylon hanging down from the steel wall, which had been pulled in slightly with whatever force had torn the straps. A bench seat was opposite the harness.

She took in the bullet holes on the wall with the harness. She'd noticed them before, but just how many hadn't sunk in. Lots of them — a quick eyeball said twenty or thirty rounds had been unloaded in here. Someone on the bench seat had fired into the opposite wall, probably into whoever was in that harness. Blood was smeared down the steel wall, with a small puddle on the ground. Not a lot — not enough for a guy with a bunch of bullets in him. Casings lay on the floor of the van, the bright of the brass distinct against the carpet. Two machine pistols shared space with them. No damn bodies though.

They were all inside.

"You need ... just come here." The tone of Elliot's voice brought her out of the van in a rush, almost turning her ankle in the rain. She just missed — *shit* — the severed hand, nearly stumbling head first into the street. Elliot was looking up — above the van, the blood running down its white paint stark even at night. Carlisle followed his gaze to above the overhang of the Elephant Blues. A bronze elephant about the size of a small car sat on top, trunk proudly raised to the sky, one foot lifted. Elliot was staring at the elephant.

A body had been impaled on the trunk, easy to miss in the darkness. No head. Carlisle recovered first. "Different guy."

"What?" Elliot was a heartbeat behind, still shaken.

"Body's still got both hands. Just no head. Closest thing to a full corpse I've seen all night." The ragged ends of tissue, tendons, and the spine stuck out from the torso of the corpse. Blood was being washed down from the body onto the awning, onto the van, and into the street. "I hope Forensics did their thing out here. Our evidence is being rinsed away."

Elliot shrugged, just a little. "They got worse problems. Not one of them is going to see their wife for a week, the amount of reassembly needed in there."

"Probably won't see lunch for a week, either." No way you could have pastrami on rye after spending time in the Blues this evening. Nodding to herself, Carlisle walked over to the squad car. It had mounted the curb, nosing up behind the van, but back ten or fifteen feet. Both doors were still open, lights on, but no siren. It wasn't that the car had done the chase running silent; the siren was missing, the ends of wires sticking out where it had been mounted. The trunk was open, the shotgun missing — the officers had probably left the car in a hurry, but the lack of bullet holes in the car suggested it hadn't been under fire. The patrol unit had made the call in for support a half hour ago; it'd been Connolly on the radio, panic in his voice. A car chase in the center of the city with shots fired, real gangster stuff. No idea on number of people involved, no idea who was shooting, no idea why. Just shots fired — in pursuit — and then silence. They'd tracked the car by the GPS in it, finding it here at Elephant Blues. The engine was still running.

It made no sense. A half hour was a long time. Long enough for two good cops to die. Not long enough for their bodies to be cold. If they could confirm which bodies — *which parts* — were theirs.

The first evidence that Connolly and Malloney had made an armed response came at the entrance to the bar. Two spent casings were on the ground alongside broken glass and wood splinters. The officers had gone in loud. They'd headed into the bar, to be lost in the chaos of whatever had gone down in the Elephant Blues.

Carlisle looked over at Elliot, who was still looking up at the body on the elephant. "Look, stop fucking around over there. Have you found the CCTV system?"

"I found where it was. You know the bar?"

"Sure. I stepped over twenty smashed bottles of spirits. My socks smell of Midori."

"That's not what your socks smell of. But — look. You know it's crazy in there, right? Tables, chairs thrown around. Looks like some kind of Chuck Norris fight remake."

"*Silent Rage.*" Carlisle swallowed as something hysterical tried to bubble through. She hadn't seen that movie in years.

"What?"

"*Silent Rage.* That's the movie with the bar fight. Dan — I mean Norris — was in the bar..." Carlisle trailed off. "Whatever. What about it?"

"Right." Elliot gestured into the bar. "One of the tables was thrown right through the bar. Sort of unlucky. It went through the DVR."

"You're shitting me. Sort of unlucky? Through it? A thousand places the table could have gone —"

"Be fair, sister. The tables did go a thousand places. One of them was through the DVR."

"You're telling me we've got the bloodbath of the century in there, like someone's siphoning the local abattoir through the sprinkler system, and we've got no footage?"

Elliot looked at his feet. "Yeah."

"Fuck." Carlisle remembered her first steps down into the Blues that evening, seeing the tables knocked over, chairs thrown around. Blood, bits of tissue — there, someone's blood-drenched scarf — were everywhere inside the bar. The shelf that held spirits was shattered, the remains of Midori and Galliano and fifty other types of bottled joy mingling with the sea of blood on the ground. Carlisle's non-skid shoe covers had slipped anyway, and she'd fallen heavily on one knee in the gore. The hand she'd thrown out to steady herself had come back sticky with blood, the latex covering red and tacky. It was the first time she'd thrown up at crime scene in years.

She shook herself out of the memory. So her expensive suit would need dry-cleaning; that was just part of the job. "We might need to wait on Forensics then."

Elliot nodded, pulling his jacket tighter over the belly middle age and too much time behind a desk had given him. "Hell of a night."

"Yeah." Carlisle absently wiped water off her face. "Hell of a night."

CHAPTER
TWO

Val felt like he'd been hit by a car.

Curling over the bowl, he retched again, hands shaking. He didn't remember waking up; he didn't remember getting home, or what might have happened after his tenth beer last night. He hoped it was only a night — he had a big meeting with the boss this morning.

It wouldn't be the first time he'd lost days of time down the bottom of a bottle.

"Get your shit together, Val." He spat into the bowl, bracing himself on the edge of the porcelain. Standing up shakily, he felt the nausea rise and curled back over, retching again. He failed to get his tie out of the way this time, and it came back out of the bowl covered in —

How in God's name was he wearing a tie? He didn't even have any pants.

He tried standing again, this time managing to get to his feet. Holding himself up on the walls of the toilet, he controlled the shuddering, awful urge to throw up. He spat into the bowl again then hit the flush button.

Slowly — and quietly — he made his way out of the toilet and into the bathroom. He caught a glimpse of stubble in the mirror on the wall and felt confident it was only a night gone. Maybe if he could just get in to the office before nine — *God, what time is it now?* — it'd be okay.

He pulled back the mirror, his fleshy reflection pushed aside as he exposed a collection of white bottles set against a backdrop of tired cardboard boxes, tubes of expired ointment, and half-empty boxes of Band-Aids. The bulk pack of store-brand acetaminophen came away disturbingly light — *I bought that just last week* — and he tossed the empty hundred box to the ground, hand trembling towards the Pentazine. Expensive gold, he dry-swallowed four of the tabs. Motion sickness be damned; the drug would take the edge off wanting to throw up his feet. He chased it with some ibuprofen, a generic brand in a white box of fifty.

He started up a good lather to get rid of the stubble. It was then he noticed that his left arm's shirt sleeve was missing, ripped off by the looks of it. The shirt wasn't in great shape overall; it had that creaseless arrogance that only came with being rained on. The sleeve was missing from the elbow down, give or take, the frayed end of a blue thread trailing to wrist level. He'd been laying in a pool of good Merlot unless he missed his guess, the sleeve and side of the shirt a gentle pink. The thought of Merlot almost made him heave the pills back up, so he stripped off the shirt and let it drop to the floor alongside the empty box. If he just left all that crap there Baitan would sort it out later.

His belly wasn't an admirable sight, the booze and the desk job leaving their toll, the flab hanging out over his underwear. John kept nagging him, saying he needed to get back to the gym, do some exercise. There was time for that later — it was important to get more drugs, and maybe shave, if he was going to get to work today.

Focus, Val.

BREAKFAST WAS a mash of overly bright post-dawn light and harsh jarring sounds. He'd choked back some dry white toast, using black coffee syrupy with sugar as a chaser. After he kept that down, he brushed his teeth twice before leaving the house, jacket slung over his shoulder. He was already sweating through his shirt by the time he almost made his bus, watching it pull away from the stop as he rounded the corner.

The driver of the next bus was a man sitting proud behind the wheel, stamping with binary control at the gas and brake pedals, lurching and cursing his way through the crowded morning streets with nausea inducing irregularity. The only blessing was that no one wanted to sit next to him — even Val could smell the Bacardi sweating through his skin.

He spent his time before his meeting surfing the Internet and drinking bad coffee and stale water. He avoided his co-workers, taking refuge in his cubicle. The office hummed with the gentle background of cloistered productivity, phones and conversations overlaying each other into white noise. All except Werner in the cube next to him; that man shouted into his phone like he was trying to raise the dead. Maybe he was — he worked the marketing angle of the project they were on.

By the time he had his meeting with Davies, the shaking in his hands had stopped, the world returning to normal levels of brightness and color. He was still sweating through his shirt.

"Sit, Val." Davies' tailored suits were a thing of office legend, fitting a frame that spent a lot of time eating healthy food and doing whatever it was they did down at Gold's Gym. He stood behind a baroque desk, a screen, keyboard, mouse, and phone laid out just so.

Val's personnel file was open on the desk too, a couple pages marked with cheerfully colored Post-its. A gold pen, Cross brand embossed on the clip, sat ready on a legal pad.

No notes, yet.

Val shut the office door behind him and settled into a chair designed for thinner men. "Hey, Pete. Look —"

"Hear me out, Val. It's not what you think." Davies shuffled a few of the pages of the file, as if he hadn't already read each page twice. "You've been with the company a while."

That was a bit unexpected. "Uh, sure. Since —"

Davies held up a hand. "Almost five years. Done some good work for us. Really saved our asses in that coding war with Unisys." He chuckled to himself, as if it was some beachhead victory they were remembering together. "Top performer three years in a row."

Val shifted a bit. The padding on the chair was worn thin, and he felt like was sitting on raw plywood with sackcloth nailed over the top. "...Right."

"There's not really a delicate way of talking about this." A smile that was more a grimace sat on Davies' face. "Since Rebekah passed, well, we've noticed some changes." Davies looked at Val's gut, then picked up the Cross, tapping it on a paragraph in the file. "Fact is, we still need you." The clock on the wall ticked by a few more seconds, the sounds of the city outside the open windows gentle. "But we need the old you. You're a wreck—"

"Hey Pete, c'mon. I crank out the code like you need. I'm the first guy to punch in every morning..."

"And the first guy to hit the Blues at lunch. After lunch, you're back at your desk, but you're thinking about your next drink. When was the last night you didn't knock back even just a few?"

"Everyone has a beer after work, Pete. Be serious. We work in computers. And our clients are assholes." Val tried for some easy camaraderie. "Who wouldn't drink on a government contract?"

"It's not like we work in the ER, Val. And if it was the work that was the problem, we could fix that. You work in a team of what, ten guys?"

"Yeah, and they come down for a beer at lunch too!"

"They don't all go down. With you." Davies examined a perfectly manicured nail. "At the same time. Fact is, they're going down to make sure you're okay. A few of the guys — and I'm not naming names, it's confidential — are worried about you. They said they want to keep an eye on you. They've come to see me, to ask me to ... intercede."

He grabbed a sheet from the file — this one suspiciously laid out in corporate style — and spun it on the old wooden surface towards Val. "It's a leave form, Val. It's on the house. But it's got conditions."

Val didn't lean forward to look at the form. "You're getting rid of me. Gardening leave. I don't know if I should be flattered or pissed off."

Davies tapped the paper again. "Maybe you should just be ... well. I think we both know 'happy' is a bit of a stretch, considering. Get your house in order. Drive up the coast. See some friends." He paused, as if the idea had just occurred to him. "Get some help, Val. See someone."

Val reached forward to get the sheet, seeing his hand shaking with either anger or the memory of the hangover. *Maybe a heavy salting of both.* The form was straightforward — a month of leave, but with a small catch.

"The company wants some return, of course." Davies looked down in carefully constructed abashment. "We want the old Valentine Everard back. We want you a productive member of the family again. We're going to ... invest, shall we say ... a few weeks. What's a few weeks? That's on us." Nodding, Davies replaced his expression, looking Valentine right in the eye with an affable smile. It was like watching a super marionette, as if all those management courses had taught him which emotions to try to fake, and when. "But you've got to do your share. A part of the bargain."

It was there in black and white. They'd even supplied a phone number and a website — 'they' was probably one of the narcissists in HR. Those fuckers thought of everything with their saccharine sincerity. They wanted him in an alcoholics group of some kind. "If I don't sign?"

Davies swapped the grandfatherly smile for a look of grandfatherly reproach. "Well Val, then things might have to get formalized. You know how it is." As if it was out of his hands. Just one of the boys, Val and him in this thing together. "But we — well. *I* don't want it to get formalized." He handed the Cross to Val.

After he'd signed — *like there'd been a choice* — he walked out to collect his jacket. He felt as if the entire office watched his walk from Davies' office to his cube, the air heavy with the silence of funerals. The Burlap partitions were covered with the same old crap, charts jostling for supremacy next to Dilbert cartoons. The odd slice of fake humanity was shown with photos printed in cheap color on the office laser — corporate functions, team building. Outside his own cube, he saw a photo of himself peeking out from under layers of project charts and productivity estimates. It was like growth rings on a tree, those layers — the closer to the heartwood of the Burlap backing, the older they were.

He remembered that shot. The photo showed him sprawled on the ground, the thick rope for tug-o-war draped over him and his team buddies. He'd been thinner then, the grin cracking his face one of delight.

It was probably about the time when Rebekah had first told him she was pregnant.

CHAPTER
THREE

"We've got the prints back." Elliot banished the serenity with practiced ease.

Carlisle looked up from her computer — *fucking thing* — and gave her partner a stare. "Prints? From what? The meticulously clean van? Or from inside the bar with the ten thousand other prints? No — you've got good news, I can see it from your face. Something from the shotgun?"

Elliot's smirk was almost unholy. "You work too hard. Maybe you should just take the rest of the day off. Shoot some pool. You're clearly not made out for the long hours of real police work." He had a manila file, CONFIDENTIAL in faded red ink on the front. He tapped on it with a finger. "Leave this one to us."

"You're just sore you lost the bet."

"I didn't lose the bet. It's just been... deferred."

"Deferred my ass." The murderer had been meticulous enough to stack the bodies in a single location, but had left two things out of place. One, a body impaled on an elephant — sans head — and two, a severed hand. The body had printed easily, ex-military records describing a man better off dead. Sealed file, no name, but the memo from Defense Overlord HQ had described an SAS officer deployed into Afghanistan, then dishonorably discharged. The only thing longer than the crimes against noncombatants was the list of heroic missions. The memo had politely suggested they contact Ebonlake Associates, a private security contractor known to pay good rates for men with moral flexibility.

It was on her to-do list.

No, the bet was all about the hand. Elliot thought it had simply been misplaced, that they'd find a matching right hand, or maybe an arm. Carlisle didn't think so — the killer was too particular. Forensics had done a pretty good job of assembling near complete cadavers from the remains, only a few pieces still out of place. Smart money was on the hand belonging to someone who got away.

So far Carlisle was in the lead. The hand hadn't matched any of the bodies. Sure, it was possible that it was all that remained of someone, but the killer hadn't seemed to take trophies. Complete corpses remained, albeit disassembled. It wasn't conclusive, but it wasn't looking good for Elliot.

"Prints from the hand on the sidewalk. Valentine Everard, works in computers. Haven't been able to track down his boss yet. Everard's on file — we got him for DUI a couple years back." Elliot flipped a page in the file. "Here it is. Vehicular homicide."

"Let me guess. He's not turned up at the hospital yet?" They'd thrown up nothing but dead ends at the ER when they called from the scene, the staff harried and unhelpful. Yes, they were sure that they'd have noticed someone coming in without a hand. Of course they'd call if something turned up.

"*Nada.*" If anything, the smirk grew wider. "So why's a guy missing his left hand not turn up to the ER?"

Carlisle turned off her screen, grabbing her jacket from where it hung in a crumpled mess over the back of her chair. "The only reason I wouldn't go to the hospital is if I'd just killed twenty guys." One arm through her jacket sleeve, she scrabbled around the clutter on her desk for a notebook. "What I don't get is why you're so happy. This is only going to prove that I've won the bet."

Elliot nodded. "I just took your view, opened an office pool. I might lose to you, but I'm going to win against — so far — five other fine detectives."

"Even if you lose, you win?"

"Yep."

~

"Officers. Please. Try and understand my position." Carlisle and Elliot were seated on two small, uncomfortable chairs in front of a hideous desk. The man had no courtesy and worse taste.

Carlisle sipped her coffee — say what you will about the man, but his PA made a good brew. Better than the slurry at the station by a long shot. "Mr. Davies. We just want to ask him a few questions. It's in relation to multiple homicides. People with families aren't going to see their kids tonight." Something about this Davies guy made her skin crawl — for some reason a lot of guys who made it in management were like that.

"We could always come back with a warrant. It's just easier on you this way." Elliot hadn't touched his coffee. He'd eaten the chocolate that came with it, marks of brown still muddy against the white china. He loved his role as the bad cop, said it was one of the things that gave him job satisfaction.

Davies put down his cup — little finger out — and tugged at his cuff, straightening it. "It's not that I don't want to help. Really. I do. I've got the file right here." He patted a manila folder closed on the desk, opened it. Scanned the first page, closed it again. "Mr. Everard and I had a meeting just this morning. Legal's advised me not to divulge any information without the appropriate paperwork. For the company's protection."

"That's his file?" Carlisle was faintly surprised. She wasn't a great believer in serendipity.

"I can tell you — because it's an item that the company tabled — that Mr. Everard is on leave for a little while. I really can't comment further though."

"Medical leave?" Carlisle sighed. "That figures."

"I'm sorry?" said Davies.

"The accident. His hand." Carlisle held up her left arm.

Davies looked between the two of them. "I'm sorry, Detective. I'm not sure —"

"You disgust me." Elliot stared hard at Davies, his tone suggesting he'd just stood in something unmentionable. "You're worried about your clerical process when people are dead? I've half a mind to just take the damn file." Elliot started to rise from his chair. "You know—"

Carlisle already had a hand on Elliot's shoulder, making a show of pulling him back to his seat. "Thank you for your time, Mr. Davies. You can be sure we will be back with a warrant. If you change your mind — here's my card." She flipped the small rectangle onto the desk. "C'mon Elliot. Let's leave the man to his day. Thank you for your time."

On the street outside Elliot rounded on Carlisle. "Why'd we leave so soon? We'd barely got started. He would have given us something."

"Two reasons. First, because the guy was a cockroach and I didn't want to breathe the same air for too long. Second reason? Because I know where Everard is."

"Fuck off. How can you possibly know that?" Elliot didn't get many opportunities to be the bad cop. He'd be grumpy until lunch, like a kid who'd missed his chance on the roller coaster.

"Well, okay. I know where he's going to be."

"Tell me you didn't steal something. We're cops. We can't steal shit. You're always stealing shit."

"That was one goddamned time. Give it a rest. Anyway. You really should learn to read upside down."

Elliot grinned. "The file. You got something from the file."

Carlisle patted Elliot on the shoulder. "The first thing on Everard's file was an HR note."

"So tell me, oh *sensei*. Where's our suspect going to be?"

"They've put him in an alcoholics program — Everard still has a problem with the booze. I think we should turn up for the bad coffee and stale biscuits, and then ask him a couple questions."

FOUR

"I'm telling you, Davies is not that bad a guy." John chewed while he talked, a couple of fries in his hand. It was hard to tell if he was serious through his Ray-Bans.

Val snorted, reaching for the bowl of fries. "He's an asshole. He just put me on gardening leave for a month."

John was checking out some women a couple tables away. They were checking him out right back, giggling and talking to each other. "Look man. He just gave you four weeks' paid vacation. To do with what you want. Sure, you've got to go to a few meetings. Talk some random shit with the AA. It won't kill you."

"They don't want *you* to stop drinking. That might kill me. Can you imagine a week in this town without a beer? Oh for Christ's sake, stop showing off."

John stopped, mid stretch, then rubbed at his designer stubble. He'd been flexing in his ever-so-slightly too tight shirt. "Just playing to the crowd, man. I'm getting digits before we're done here." Val turned to look at the ladies. "Don't be like that."

"Like what?" said Val.

"Like, I don't know, some kind of animal nerd. You're cramping my style. You don't look, man. You *glance*."

"You were the one ogling. Besides, aren't those two a bit young for you?"

"No such thing." John looked at the table. "Well, okay. Maybe there is."

"A pretty boy like you wouldn't last ten minutes in prison," said Val.

"Christ, what are you, my mother?" John changed tack. "Tell you what, since you've got a week with nothing going on, why not come down and do a session or two with me?"

"A session?"

"A session."

"At the gym?"

"At the gym."

"You can't be serious. I work in IT." Val looked down at his belly. "This body is built for comfort, not speed."

"You're going to die fat and alone. I'm saying this for purely selfish reasons — I don't want to be one of your pall bearers." Their waitress — a pretty young thing with a perpetually harassed expression — arrived with their meals. Val's order was a pasta number named *An Oblivion of Cream*. John had some sort of hunter-gatherer diet meal of grilled turkey breast on a tasteless buckwheat slice. Val didn't care what it was called — knowledge like that might lead a man to accidentally ordering it.

"See, that's what I'm talking about." John pointed at Val's meal with a knife. "There's about a billion calories in that. And they all hate you."

Smearing some cream sauce around on his shirt with a napkin — *stupid restaurant napkins have the absorption qualities of plastic bed sheeting* — Val looked at his belly again. "You're just jealous. There's a whole lot of playground here."

"No really, man. It's no joke. Come on down, we'll put you through something light. Maybe get you on a regular program. It's on me — and I even promise we'll have a beer after. You probably shouldn't, but you'll have earned it."

Val looked as his belly again. *Hell with it.* "Okay. Sure."

"What?"

"I said let's do it."

John swallowed his mouthful, then took a foamy sip of beer. "I just want to check. You just agreed to come down to the gym with me."

Val thought back to when Rebekah had admired his body, their youth and passion for each other the most important thing in the world. He knew he'd been sliding ever since, knew she'd have been disappointed. He grabbed almost savagely at his beer, taking a strong pull. "Yeah man. Tomorrow?"

"Tomorrow. Yeah right. Tomorrow you'll have forgotten about this. Let's do it this evening. My last client's at five. Come on in after, grab me at reception, then we'll grab a beer and a bite."

"Tonight?" said Val. "Really?"

But something inside him relished the freedom of the unexpected and wanted to —

Run free.

—escape the shackles of shitty bosses and fat and aging bodies. Too many expectations and demands, and not enough time to just... be. It was an unusual thought, a touch of surprise following just a footstep behind. A younger, still-married self might have had those more often, had someone to just *be* with—

"You all right?" said John, the women at the other table temporarily forgotten.

"Oh, sure man." The lie came easily. John spent too much time worrying about him. "I was just mentally checking my schedule."

"Your schedule? What in God's Earth is on there except going to a bar?"

"Exactly why I was checking it. You never know. But I think we're good. Tonight sounds great."

John turned on his megawatt smile. "Outstanding. Now if you'll excuse me, I'm off to get a number."

~

HE FELT STUPID, of course.

The last time he'd tried to exercise was longer ago than he cared to remember. Val still had workout clothes, fitted for a younger — *and thinner, Christ, so much thinner* — self. His shorts were uncomfortably tight, his shirt stretched over his belly. The Nike Swoosh over the left breast was wider than it should have been, distorted by the stretched cloth.

He was already sweating into the armpits of the shirt.

One thing was for sure, he wasn't getting a number; there wasn't a single glance, let alone a second, from any of the women here. Not that he wanted to try his luck — how sleazy would it be to try and pick someone up at the gym? He couldn't imagine a woman being happy with that kind of approach — they were all here, sweaty and uncomfortable, just trying to get the job done. Then some overweight asshat comes along and breaks into your zone?

It had fail written all over it.

John slapped him on the shoulder. "Great to see you, man." He waved a piece of paper in the air. "This slice of fun here is our workout for the day. We're going to get manly."

"I really don't feel manly." Val looked down at his shirt.

John snorted. "You're a machine, brother. Don't forget it. You're at the gym, about to be manly. Keep that in your head."

"Manly. Got it." Val experimentally flexed his shoulders. "I can try."

"There is no try. Only do, and do not."

"Did you just try for Yoda?"

"I didn't try. Weren't you listening? There is no try."

"Whatever. Manly. Hooah."

"Right on. We're not doing any shitty cardio. We're going to start with manly exercise number one. Your new temple: the bench."

John led the way to the bench. In Val's eyes, it looked more like a medieval rack. Sure, it had a bench — a padded slab not quite long enough or wide enough to get comfortable on, the foam cover torn in one corner. It wasn't tired, just well used: clean steel struts rising from the upper area of the bench to support a bar lying horizontally on supports. "That looks horrific."

"Get in there, buddy." John was pulling out weight plates, the slabs of metal painted black, their edges chipped in places. He dropped a couple of larger plates onto the ground, selecting some smaller ones and fitting them on the ends of the bar. "We're going for something my grandmother can do to start with." He patted the top of the bar. "We'll have you curling this shortly."

"Curling?" Val hadn't moved to lie on the bench. "What's curling?"

"Seriously. Get in there. It won't kill you. We haven't had a bench death in at least three weeks."

Val moved forward, slipping in under the bar. The smell of metal was strong laying here surrounded by the steel of the mechanism. The bar, knurled for grip at shoulder width, was a clean line of stainless steel across his vision.

John stepped into his field of view. "Okay, grab it here, and here. I'll be right here at the top, so if you drop it on your face I'll try to stop it knocking your teeth out. We'll just do a few warm up reps."

"Thanks man. I appreciate that." Val felt a tiny thrill. He was *here*, actually *doing this*.

Running free.

He gripped the bar, pushing it up and off the rests — it didn't feel that heavy. He brought it down to his chest and pushed it back towards the ceiling with ease. Val looked up at John. "Look man, I appreciate this going easy on the new kid thing. But that's made of plastic or something. An infant could lift that."

"It's like that is it?"

21

"Hey. You said manly. All I'm saying is that's not manly right now. It's a far way from manly."

"We'll step it up." John shuffled around at the top of the bar, taking the smaller plates off the bar and attaching bigger ones. "Give it a shot." Val gripped the bar again, brought it down, pushed it back up. "How was that?"

Val thought for a minute. "Did you make it lighter or heavier? I can't tell."

"That's it. We're bringing the pain, right here." John slapped on some more plates, the clunks and clangs of meeting metal. "Okay Mr. Banner, let's see how you go with that." Val pushed the bar — it was definitely heavier this time. He could feel the knurls against the soft skin of his palms. He brought it down to his chest then thrust back to the ceiling with a small exhale. "Not so chatty now are you?"

In his peripheral vision, Val could see a couple people glancing their way. He felt unaccountably self-conscious, the whale beached on the bench. "Well, I mean, it's hea*vier*. I can tell that. But it's not heav*y*."

"You're not serious."

"I'm serious." Val paused. "How much is on there?"

"Two twenty."

"Is that a lot?"

John stared at him, the megawatt smile not coming so easily this time. "It's a lot. For a first lift, it's insane. I reckon we should maybe pull up here. I don't want to do you an injury on your first day."

The stares of the other gym goers lay heavy on Val. "No way, man. Let's go heavier. I could be out drinking right now — this needs to be worth my time."

"You're the boss."

More plates slotted on the bar. A man walked up, one of John's fellow trainers dressed in staff colors, the green and black making them stand out amongst a sea of haphazardly dressed fitness buffs. "Who's the new guy?" His voice was deep.

John was talking over his shoulder as he checked the bar. "Hey,

Emilio. This is a friend of mine. Finally talked him into coming down."

"First time?"

"Yeah."

"He's a friend of yours? Not an enemy?"

"Friend. I think."

"This I got to see." Emilio sat down on his haunches beside the bench.

John stood above Val's head. "I'll be right up here. If you feel like you're going to drop it, just shout and I'll help you up."

"Thanks man." The bar definitely felt heavier this time, and a creak came from the bench underneath him. He brought it down, pushed it clear to the top with a quick exhale, racking it again. The metal clanged to rest, the frame of the bench juddering slightly with the weight of it. "How am I doing?"

"He doesn't look like a lifter. I don't get it." Emilio hadn't moved. "No offense my man, but you've got no muscle tone. Well, not a lot anyway. I picked you for a desk jockey, soon as I saw you come in here."

Val turned his head to look at him. "Computers."

"Exactly. Computers. So tell me, computer man. How did you just bench three hundred free and clear?"

John was silent. A couple other trainers had drifted over to stand at the foot of the bench, their arms crossed, appraising. "I don't know what you mean. John got me down here today. I figured it couldn't hurt."

Emilio said nothing for a heartbeat or two, then he broke into a laugh, a throaty comfortable thing. Lots of teeth, clean white against his dark skin. "My man. It most definitely could hurt. But not you. You keep lifting like that, we're out of a job." He laughed again, no malice in it. "You do your thing." He gave a little nod to John, who started placing more plates on the bar.

Val could feel it now — the weight of the bar resting against the bench. It moved slightly and he could feel the small shudders and shifts through his back as John put more weight on the ends of the bar. One of the watchers from the foot of the bench — there were six now, some gym customers amongst the trainers — tossed in, "You can't be serious."

No megawatt smile came from John. Val said, "Holy shit. You're actually worried."

John leaned down, close to his ear. "You're doing great. But this thing, this is heavy. I've put on close to four forty for this press. At my best, when I was competing? I couldn't do that. Anything feels weird, you sing out. We got you."

Swallowing, Val gripped the bar again, lifting it clear of the rests. His hands trembled slightly at the weight of it. John's hands hovered above him, ready to catch it. The bench creaked underneath him again as he brought the bar down to his chest. He breathed out as he pressed it to the ceiling, slower this time — *Damn, it feels like I'm pressing the roof up.* He racked the bar, a bead of sweat now on his forehead. "That's ... that's pretty heavy."

Emilio laughed again from beside him. "No shit, my friend."

A voice from the small crowd at the foot of the bench spoke up. "I got five bucks says he can't do five fifty."

"I'll take that bet. But only for fifty." It was John. Standing tall — he had his back, like he always did. John patted the bar companionably, letting his left his hand rest on it. "Five's not worth getting out of bed for."

"Five-oh?"

"Five-oh."

"You're on."

"What the fuck, man." Val spoke up from down on the bench. "No pressure, right? I'm feeling a little exposed here."

John squatted down. "Don't worry. You just do your thing. You got this."

"I'll double down on that." Emilio — still at the side of the bench — stood. "I've got a hundred on the new fish benching clear to five fifty."

Some muted conversation broke out from the foot of the bench. "I got twenty," was followed by, "Okay, yeah, I'll back that too." And so on, pooling up the cash. Val swallowed again — they were betting on his *failure*.

More plates went on the bar. "Everyone happy that looks like five fifty?" John spoke to no one in particular, his eyes on the bar, checking it again himself.

"Sure. I can feel that hundred already." Some excited clapping of shoulders came from the foot of the bench.

He unracked the bar, forearms trembling with the effort. The muscles in his arms burned and his chest was on fire. Val could feel the sweat pouring off his face. The bench underneath him creaked and groaned, the metal squealing in protest as he pressed against the bar. Val dragged in big gulps of air as the bar rose slowly to the top. It was almost there when he started to falter. The shaking in his arms was really bad and the bar started to swing a little.

Then John was there by his ear. "You can do it buddy. You got this. Just a little further. It's like an inch. What's an inch?" He talked Val through it. "See, that's it. Push it up. Nice. Rack it!"

The clank of the bar against the rests was loud inside the gym.

Val's belly heaved, his breathing ragged. John slapped his chest. "Yeah! That was... That was some serious shit."

Even in his exhausted state, Val noticed the silence. The crowd at the foot of the bench were looking at each other. Someone said, "That's bullshit man. Five fifty? That's not five fifty. Bullshit."

John brought out his megawatt smile. "I think someone owes me a hundred bucks."

"I'd owe you a hundred if that wasn't bullshit."

John looked surprised. "Val, get up." He helped Val off the bench, the vinyl wet with sweat. "If you think it's not five fifty, you hop in there and press it. As you can see," and he tugged at his skin tight uniform, "There's nothing up my sleeves."

There was some chuckling, the tension bleeding out of the room. "Nah, it's okay man. Here's the hundred."

John nodded to Val. "Grab a drink, get your breathing back. This last press is going to be killer." He started putting more plates on the bar. Now he was upright, Val could see the bend in the middle of the bar, bowed by the plates on either side. Someone in the crowd was videoing it with a phone.

Val looked at John. "What's all this about? Some clown over there is shooting video." He gestured down to the shirt stretched over his belly. "I'm not exactly a figure for cinema right now."

"It's cool. I'll tell you in a little while." John tightened the clamps at the end of the bar. "You're good to go. Hop in."

Val lay on the bench again and wiped his hands on his shorts. He needed to put some real effort into it this time as he cleared the rests and hoisted the bar above his chest. It was already a bit unsteady, swaying a little to and fro before Val got it centered right. There were a few excited intakes of breath from the crowd — *Christ, there's like fifteen guys there now* — as they waited for him to drop it.

Down to his chest. Exhale.

Once as a kid Val had lost a ball behind the family refrigerator. It had escaped his grip, fleeing in asymmetric hops and bounces out of his clutching hands to hide behind the fridge. He'd been six years old, give or take. He'd tried to move the refrigerator to get the ball out, but the wall of iron and plastic of the old Frigidaire hadn't budged. This bar felt like that — no matter how hard he pressed, his arms trembling, it didn't move. Not an inch.

A snicker came from the foot of the bench, and white hot rage flared up. It burned bright inside him. The video would be on YouTube, just another gym wannabe failing in front of the world.

They jeer at us.

A yell of exertion came from him. His hands gripped the bar as if they'd tear it in half. Val powered the bar back to the ceiling in one smooth motion, racking it clean with a shudder and clang from the bench beneath him. He breathed in great ragged gasps, the sweat pouring off him.

He sat up on the bench, leaned over sideways, and threw up on the ground. The room spun around him as his heart thudded in his chest. *Christ, I'm going to die, I'm going to have a heart attack, Christ —*

It started to seep in. People slapped him on the back and wanted to shake his hand. Water was pushed into one of his hands and someone — *John* — was handing him a towel.

The person with the phone was asking him something.

"What?" He was still breathing hard and couldn't hear right.

"I said what's your name?"

John answered for him. "This is my good buddy Val. Valentine Everard." He winked at the phone's tiny camera. "If you're watching from home, he could use a beer — come buy him one tonight. Elephant Blues. We'll be there from six." He helped Val to his feet. "What do you reckon? Time for a beer?"

Nothing had ever sounded so good, but... "Maybe a shower first."

CHAPTER
FIVE

Carlisle knocked on the door again. "You sure this is the place?"

Elliot nodded. "Yeah. It's on his sheet. We can always stick with the plan and wait for him at the AA." The sound of cicadas was heavy on the air.

Carlisle looked around. Come to think of it, Everard didn't have a bad place. It was a little small, but cheerfully painted and nestled in amongst the trees. The driveway that led up to the house was the stark white of bleached concrete, and the sound of insects and birds was clear. You wouldn't have thought a place this alive was right on the doorstep of the city, just a short drive from the main business district. "Nah. I like being more proactive. Besides, I can hear someone in there."

The door opened a little, tethered by a chain. Part of a face — eyes, the side of a face, dark hair — were visible in the gap.

As if on cue, Carlisle and Elliot both manufactured smiles. Carlisle showed her ID to the gap in the door. "Good morning, ma'am. Detective Melissa Carlisle." She nodded to Elliot with a tip of her head, putting away her ID in a practiced motion. "Detective Vincent Elliot. We're here to speak with, uh, a Mr. Valentine Everard."

Elliot nodded cheerfully at the woman. No response, just those eyes looking back and forth between the two of them.

"Uh. Ma'am. Is this Mr. Everard's address?"

"Meestar Balentine not home." The Filipino accent was clean and clear, first generation but softened by time away. She made to shut the door.

Elliot put his hand on the door, still smiling. "Ma'am. Do you mind if we ask you some questions? About, Mr, uh, Everard?"

"What queestions? Poleece queestions? I hab no poleece answers. I clean for meestar Balentine."

"Clean? So you're not his wife?" Carlisle's smile remained firmly in place. Sotto voce to Elliot she said, "Put your damn arm down."

"Wife! Meestar Balentine always bery proper!" She tossed her head, the motion visible through the crack in the door.

"Ma'am, I didn't mean to suggest —"

"But you deed. As eeb I am *puta*! *Anak ka ng puta* yourseelf!"

Carlisle had seen enough bad movies to know when she was being insulted in a foreign language. *Ignore it and move on, Carlisle.* "Ma'am. We believe Mr. Everard may be in some trouble. We're trying to get to the bottom of it, hoping he might be able to help with our inquiries. It would be tremendously helpful for Mr. Everard if you could answer a few questions for us."

The other woman's suspicion was starting to wane. After all, police didn't lie to you, did they? Not in this country, anyway — it wasn't like the Philippines. She nodded, just once, and unlatched the chain to open the door wider. She had a mop in one hand, an obvious if unromantic weapon if they'd turned out to be mother rapists or whatever she else had imagined them to be. It'd take some time to get over that natural distrust. Her apron was well worn but spotlessly clean. Maybe Carlisle should get her details to clean her place?

Good cleaners were hard to find and Lord knew it'd been many years since it'd seen a professional touch.

"Thank you ma'am. We do appreciate it. Maybe if it's not too much to ask, we could get acquainted. As I said, I'm Melissa Carlisle. Here's my card. And this is Vincent Elliot. We're with the Police, working on an investigation." The offered slip of white card was taken, scrutinized and then whisked away to a pocket under the apron.

"I eem Baitan." And then she put her suspicion away, tidied out of sight as if it had never existed. Smiling a signature Colgate smile, she led them through the small house chatting over her shoulder at them. Carlisle made encouraging noises in all the right places, taking note of the photos on the walls. There were only a few of them — what was presumably Everard with a woman, pretty in a youthful way, dark curls and an impish grin. He was definitely a reacher, batting outside his league on looks alone. Carlisle was never quite sure how plain guys with no obvious physique managed it — maybe he was comedy gold. *Here's a funny one: I kill people.*

The inside of the house was cool without being cold, the heat of the day left behind with the cicadas outside. The place had plenty of windows, light from the surrounding trees brought in and diffused with softer greens. Those photos on the wall looked slightly faded, exposed to the light of years — they hadn't been updated to change with the times. Everard's life had stopped, time marching right on by a couple years back. Probably after the accident.

She snorted to herself. *Accident.* She hated how they had to describe things without attribution of blame, as if accidents just happened. In Carlisle's experience, there were no accidents. Just a series of actions with consequences. Mostly stupid actions, or stupid people, and bad consequences, to an unlucky few.

Elliot was writing in his notebook with a black pen, attentive to Baitan's words.

They arrived in a small living room of sorts, a couple of couches pushed up against the walls huddled around a too-large TV. Some DVDs were lying around the TV on top of some red Netflix envelopes. A garbage bag sat on the ground next to a vacuum cleaner, likely evidence of Baitan's industrious efforts to make it look habitable. Chinese takeout containers vied for space with beer bottles in the bag. There wasn't a lot else. The cleaner had thrown the windows open to get some air in the place, but it still smelled musty.

Baitan was sparing them no detail now she'd decided to open up to them. She continued to bustle about the room, tidying here and cleaning there, occasionally disappearing into an adjoining galley-style kitchen. Where the lounge was messy, the kitchen was positively austere, not a utensil out of place — Everard probably never used the thing. Baitan cleaned every surface anyway, but spent some special attention on the microwave. It reminded Carlisle of her dorm room days; she'd ignored the cafeteria, living on take-out and beer. The only kitchen necessity was a microwave, the only tool needed a fork. She'd managed almost an entire semester on frozen dinners.

It was hard to interrupt Baitan's stream of words, but Carlisle managed it. "Have you been working for Mr. Everard long?"

"Oh yees, a few yeers. Meestar Balentine beery good to me, always leabes money on table." She gestured to the small kitchen table, a vase in the center of it amongst some cut flowers. "He know I been, I take money and leabe him flowers. Since accident, he needs more habby thoughts."

"Do you ever see Mr. Everard?"

"Yees, yees, a few times a yeer. And he write note to me, I write back." Again, a gesture to the table.

Piece by piece, they got a picture of Everard. A man who ate nothing but take-out, whose fridge was full of beer. He'd hadn't actually hired Baitan himself — a 'Meestar John' had arranged for her to start, Baitan's daughter one of his clients at some gym downtown. She was proud of her daughter, beaming with stories of her living in everyday happiness.

31

Everard spent almost no time here, or at least Baitan never saw much of him. He paid well, always leaving twice their agreed rate on the table. "I tried to leebe him money on table, next week he leebe me four times money!" And because of this Baitan went a little further for him than for her other clients, tidying rather than just cleaning, washing clothes, doing a little ironing, leaving him the flowers. She was full of the tiny details — she knew he drank, not just by the bottles but by how many empty boxes of pain meds were in the trash. She knew he wore the same five shirts to work each week — and had thrown one out this week, the sleeve torn.

"Ma'am? The left sleeve?"

"How you know? Yees. Left sleeve. Here." She fished a super-sized plain white shirt out of the trash bag from somewhere near the bottom, offering it to Carlisle. The shirt itself was unremarkable, a simple cut available at any menswear store. The left sleeve was torn, irregular lengths of cotton hanging from it. All of the left side of the shirt was tinged a gentle pink, as if Everard had spent some time lying in a pool of his own blood.

It was dry. Curious. Carlisle balled it up, ramming it into a plastic bag before tucking it under her jacket.

Baitan continued, as if the shirt was of no consequence. By her reckoning Everard spent time in just three rooms in the house — a home office with a computer, the bedroom, and here in the lounge drinking beer and eating frozen foods. She knew this because there were beer bottles by the computer and the bed had always been used — same side every time, the other untouched — and the trash pile here in the lounge. The lounge was where the worst of the drinking happened — she tidied up red wine and whiskey bottles here, a few each week.

Her description pegged Everard as a lonely man, perhaps even a recluse. Came back here each night, worked a little from home, and then probably drank himself to unconsciousness. What she didn't paint the picture of was a psychopath. Psychopaths could be lonely recluses, but they didn't have cleaning ladies. If they did, they didn't

pay them extra to poke about their affairs and go the extra mile —
killers needed places to hide the bodies. Carlisle lacked hard
evidence either way but her gut told her that Everard wasn't the guy.

Psychopaths didn't really go in for cut flowers, you know?

They made their exit from the house — Baitan's chatter
following them out to the gate — and walked down the drive back to
their car. Elliot was tapping his pen on the cover of his notebook,
deep in thought. Back in the car, they both stared ahead, rows of
parked cars and the clean lines of prefab housing stretching out
ahead of them.

"He's guilty as sin." Elliot punctuated this with another tap on
his notebook.

"Are you cracked? He's as innocent as a schoolyard virgin."

"He's got all the signs. Lonely recluse. Drug problem. Woods to
stash the bodies in."

Carlisle snorted. "What, with the cleaning lady to wipe up the
blood stains? And it's not drugs, it's Jack Daniels. C'mon. We're
getting out of here." She put the keys in the ignition, firing the big six
to life. A satisfying grumble came from the car, deep as the growl of a
wild beast. "You might have forgotten, but we've got his arm on ice
at the station. It's hard for a guy to unzip his fly with only one arm,
let alone disassemble a bar full of people."

"She's in on it."

Carlisle turned to face Elliot in the seat. "You can't be serious.
She's like four feet tall. She's not the best assistant for a killer.
Where's her motive? Hell, where are the bodies? The thing is, Everard
is likely to be one of our vics. We've got his hand, that's pretty much
it. We haven't got his body, a weapon, or a motive. Poor bastard is
probably dead in a ditch somewhere. The best we've got," she said as
she pulled the plastic bag from under her jacket, "Is his shirt, with
DNA all over it."

"It's probably wine, not DNA." Elliot was silent for a moment.
"Nah, girlfriend. Remember I said it. There's something funny about
Valentine Everard."

"Okay Matlock. How you figure it?"

"My gut says he's guilty."

"Your gut needs some work." Carlisle looked at Elliot's growing paunch. "Get the shirt down to the boys in the lab. Then we'll talk. Your gut and me, I mean."

CHAPTER
SIX

"I'm still sweating." Val pulled his wet shirt away from his skin. Much as he had to admit that transparent shirts on a fat guy looked bad, he'd carried his jacket rather than putting it on. A light breeze was nudging against the fabric. "I thought a cold shower after the gym would help. This isn't selling it for me."

"That's a mark of pride, buddy. Just don't get too close to me." John grimaced. "Did you use deodorant?"

"Wait. I can't remember." Val sniffed under his arms. "Yeah. Smells like Axe. I'll probably sweat it off, but my intentions were pure."

"No doubt. You did good today. Really good." John seemed distracted — he wasn't checking out the women on the street, and he wasn't really paying attention to where he was walking. His phone had rung a couple of times, and he'd just ignored it. John, the man whose digits were in more single women's phones than anyone else alive, was *ignoring his phone*.

It was uncanny.

"You don't sound like I 'did good.' You sound like we're

discussing my funeral." When he'd been a kid, Val had come off his bike. He'd fallen a long way down a bank, rolling a couple times before the bike had caught up with him. The tumbled images of earth and sky along with the taste of green grass and dirt in his mouth stayed with him. He remembered the clank of the bike following him down, banging its way through the brush. He'd wrenched his shoulder pretty badly. Nothing serious, the doctor had said. Rest it, it'll be fine. They say you don't remember pain, but he swore his new after-gym arm felt the same. Wincing, he rubbed his shoulder. "Damn."

"Well, shit. Okay. Give me a minute. I think I need to break this down for you." John continued on a few more paces, then stopped. A couple of women almost walked into him, veering at the last minute. One gave him a look over her shoulder as she passed. John didn't even notice. "Look. So you benched a lot today."

"Dude. You just got a hair flick."

"What?" John looked around, but she was long gone. "Was she hot?"

"I dunno. I guess. It felt like a lot. Man, I've never hurt this bad." A memory came, stark against the mundane street around him. She'd been bleeding so bad. He could remember that damn headlight shining in his face through her shattered passenger window. "Except maybe after the accident."

John didn't seem to notice the reference, focused on something different. "Do you know how much is 'a lot?'"

"I dunno. You said it was more than you could bench, but I figured that for a sort of motivational speech. So I guess maybe less than you, sure, but a lot, right?"

John just stared at him.

"What? Say something." Val looked around the street. "What!"

"Okay, stupid, we'll play it your way. Today, you benched around six hundred and fifty pounds. Maybe a bit more, a bit less." John slapped the mixed roll of cash his back pocket. "It's what's buying the beers tonight. That six fifty press."

"I guess that sounds like a lot. But it's all Smurfberries to me." Something else was hurting in his back. Val arched, trying to work the kink out. *This is why exercise isn't more popular — it hurts too damn much.* You could read it in the papers: man killed while jogging. You never read about a man killed sitting on a couch.

"Smurfberries? Are you on coke?" John looked him in the eye. "You can tell me."

Val snorted. "I've only got a thirst for Jack. There's this iPhone app, Smurf Village."

"I don't see where you're going with this."

"Give me a sec. I'm trying to play your six fifty pounds game. Trying to get it in my head, okay? So in this app—"

"Smurf Village."

"You got it. In Smurf Village, you can build houses, go fishing, whatever. I don't know, bang Smurfette, whatever you want." Val frowned. "Okay maybe not that, it's for kids. But the game's free, except it's not."

"Smurfette's a hooker, right?"

"You're on the right track John, but it's a kid's game for fuck's sake. You need to work that out somehow, it's creepy. You can play the game, but you can sort of ... I don't know, incentivize your Smurfs. Buy them Smurfberries. And Smurfberries come right off your Mastercard."

"So what's a Smurfberry get me?"

Val clapped his hands together. "Exactly. We know how much a Smurfberry costs, because those thieves charge your Mastercard for them. But before you go in, before little Johnny —"

John winced. "Jemima, please."

"Sure." Val nodded. "Before little Jemima gets hooked on the game crack that Smurf Village is, you've no clue as a consenting parent what a Smurfberry costs. So when Jemima comes in and bothers you in front of the big game, asking for twenty bucks for some more Smurfberries, what do you do?"

"I dunno." John rubbed his chin. "The big game. Is it half time?

Does she leave me alone for another half hour? I might pay twenty bucks for that."

"Sure you might. But that's the thing. You just don't know. It's like any other arbitrary measurement, like—" Val waved his hands in the air. "Like, I guess, a megawatt hour, or a megabyte maybe."

"I know what a megabyte is. I work in a gym, but I'm not prehistoric."

"Okay wise guy. What's a megabyte?"

"It's, well..." John trailed off, then tried to man up to the challenge. "It's a bunch of emails."

"How many?"

"A lot?"

"Is six hundred and fifty pounds a lot?"

"You fucker."

Val nodded. "You see, I know what a megabyte is, and I might even be able to work out what a Smurfberry is worth. I know cheese comes in pounds. I can maybe imagine a six fifty pile of cheese, but I don't know. Is that a lot?"

"Seriously, you're an asshole." John turned away and started checking out the talent, looking for the next hair flick.

Val dragged him back with a pat on the shoulder. "Can an ordinary dude lift six fifty pounds worth of cheese? I mean, it's not something I've tried."

"Fair enough. Okay. You got me." John walked on a few more paces. "Here we go. You know a guy called Scot Mendelson?"

"Does he work with you?"

"I wish. Scot holds the current world record for the raw bench."

"Raw?" It'd been a while since meals. "Like, uncooked?"

"Raw, like unassisted."

Val gave John a blank look. "How can you assist a guy on the bench? Are there two guys pushing up? One pulling from above?"

"It's not important. Well, it's a little bit important, because you strap on a special shirt, and you can lift more. But the raw bench is where it's at, okay?" John watched a woman walk past, head tracking as she sashayed past him. "Ah. So Scot, he's the world record holder."

"I know you're dying to tell me. What's his record? A thousand?"

"Not even close. You need to think much, much lower."

"Eight hundred? We can play this game all day. You should just tell me, since I made you famous on YouTube today."

"We should probably get you a beer first. Make sure you're sitting down." John patted the wad of cash in his pocket again. "You're going to need to be lubricated for this one."

"Now you're scaring me. What's his fucking record?"

"Seven hundred." John paused, every so slightly — *damn drama queen.* "And one. Seven oh one pounds. Dude's been powerlifting his whole life, he's a real significant piece of machinery, and he benches just fifty pounds more than you."

Val stopped so suddenly the guy behind him on the sidewalk walked right into the back of him. He turned and stared at John. "You're just trying to make me feel better for throwing up at the gym."

"I'm really not. I had to clean that up." John rubbed the designer stubble on his jaw. "Look, you did an amazing thing today. Really, truly amazing. So amazing, you shouldn't have been able to do it. I'm sort of impressed, but I'm wondering when the guy from Candid Camera is going to come out. What you did, well, it's a bit like the Coyote finally catching the Road Runner. It breaks all the rules."

Val laughed, a slightly weak and hysterical sound. "You know me. I just keep breaking rules." He swayed a little, then leaned against a parking meter.

John slapped him on the arm. "It's okay. You did good. I just — I just can't really believe it. Even now. I think I need that beer more than you do."

"There's one thing I don't get."

"Just one thing? What is it?"

"Your friend, the guy who was there?"

"Emilio?"

"Sure, I guess. Why'd he back me to six fifty?"

"Emilio's crazy."

"He bet a hundred bucks — our drinking money — that I'd bench six fifty. Just fifty shy of Scot Wosshisname's record." Val stared into the sky for a second, then back to John. "If I was a judge of character, I reckon Emilio's rigged this."

"Maybe. He's coming down to drink with us tonight, so you can ask him then. Since we're sharing though, there's one thing that *I* don't get."

Val stood up, pushing his bulk away from the parking meter. "What? I'm really thirsty. It's kind of inhumane keeping me out here like this."

"How do you know what a Smurfberry is?"

Val chewed the inside of his cheek for a moment. "That can't be what you want to know."

"No, I really want to know. You've got no kids—" And there was that damn memory again, burning as bright as the headlight through the shattered passenger window. Rebekah was looking right at him, grasping his arm. She was begging him to not leave her, *What about the baby*, she'd said. "—but you know what a Smurfberry is."

Val shook off the memory. *Just a dead relic.* "Let's get that beer."

"Now that's something you don't see every day." John stood with arms akimbo, surveying the scene. "Tell me you weren't here last night."

A bright yellow line of police tape marked out the borders of the scene, *DO NOT CROSS* in commanding letters. Officers moved about, talking to each other, hurrying pedestrians along, shouting at reporters. It had started to rain again, heavy cold drops promising a downpour. Val shivered, tugging an arm through a sleeve of his jacket. At least he'd stopped sweating. "Fuck it's cold."

John nodded. He wasn't really paying attention, focused on the scene outside Elephant Blues. "What do you reckon went down?"

"Went down? What, like a mob hit?" Val hunched his shoulders against the rain, shuffling his feet a little. He needed to get inside with a beer. Preferably more than one beer.

"Look." John's arm pointed to each item. "Six ambulances. But the lights aren't on, no one's rushing. Medics are just wandering about, comparing notes. No hurry there. Whatever they came for, it's happened and moved on. There's a billion cops but they don't look worried — see those two? Talking like they're out for a Sunday stroll. There's reporters everywhere. It's like Al Capone stopped by for a whiskey."

"I've got it." Val slapped his hands together. "Al Capone came down here with a friend for a beer. But they spent all this time fucking about on the sidewalk talking about the weather, he went nuts, shot his friend in the face, then killed all witnesses. Seriously. You never want to get between a man and his beer."

John snorted. "Yeah all right. I get it. Let's go." He was about to lead them off when a couple of guys, *CORONER* stenciled big and yellow on the back of their jackets, came back out. They had a gurney, stark steel rails a contrast to the black zippered bag on top. They were having some trouble wrestling the gurney up the steps of the Blues. The black bag jostled unevenly. "Shit, is that a body bag?"

"You watch TV, not me. But I'd say so." Val held thumb and forefinger of each hand touching in front of his eyes, framing the scene. "Say. If that's a body bag, there should be a body. But that bag isn't full of a body."

"How can you tell?"

"Lumpy." Val lowered his hands. "Look, it's all wrong. Too fat in some places. Too thin in others. Bits sticking out. I mean, you ever seen a guy with an elbow where his stomach should be? Seriously though, I don't care. I care about beer. We can actually find out when some helpful reporter puts this on the news tonight."

Leading them off, Val let his feet wander away from the crime scene, the chaos and lights falling further behind them. The rain was getting heavier, the drops becoming a shower. Sensible people were pulling up hoods, raising umbrellas, bowing their heads against the rising torrent. It felt ... familiar. Val rubbed his left forearm. It had begun to ache, adding voice to the chorus of other twinges and pains in his chest and shoulders. They walked a couple of blocks before he stopped, wiping some of the rain from his face.

John pulled up beside him. "Where we going?"

"Hm? Oh, I dunno. How about in here?" The faded wooden sign above the door read *Presence Unlisted*.

"You been here before? It looks too classy for you."

"It's a bar. I'll fit right in." Val opened the front door, the brass handle fitting comfortably in his hand. The inside came out to greet them as he pulled the door back, air smelling of warm food and good conversation. They hurried in, shaking drops from their jackets. A couple of stools were still free at the back of the bar. Val moved through the crowd, a practiced conductor through an orchestra of close bodies.

Her name tag said *Danny*. "Get you boys something?" Despite the busyness of the hour, she still had a spring in her step and gave them a genuine smile.

"Oh God yes. Peroni." Val looked to John.

"Sure. Make it two." Settling into the stool beside him, John took out the roll of notes from his pocket, peeling off one and handing it over.

"Thanks." Val started to peel off his jacket, trying not to elbow anyone in the face as he wrestled with the — *God dammit* — clingy thing.

"Okay, so what's on your mind?" John played with a coaster on the bar.

"What? Nothing. What makes you say that?"

"Since the Blues you've been pushing through the crowd like a man possessed."

"Thirsty." On cue, Danny arrived back with two bottles, the

green glass perspiring. She dropped them on the bar with their change, and headed back down to another customer. Val reached for one and took a strong pull. "Oh man. That's good."

"So you don't know what happened at the Blues? I'm surprised you weren't there." John took a more measured sip from his beer. "You're right. That is good."

"Didn't say that."

"You were there? What the fuck happened?"

Val rubbed his left forearm again. "Well, shit. I don't *know* if I was there."

"How can you not know?"

"I had a few last night." Val's forearm was really aching now. "Christ. This exercise thing will never catch on if it hurts like this after every session."

"Harden up, Tinkerbell. You got so wrecked last night that you can't remember where you were?"

Val took another pull from his beer. Damn, but those Italians knew how to brew a good lager. "John, I woke up without pants, all right? I like to think I must have had a good time somewhere. Orgies don't just start themselves, you know?"

John laughed. "I'll drink to that." They clinked their bottles.

"Still." Val hesitated.

"Still what?"

"Something about it seemed real familiar."

"What do you mean? Of course it's familiar. You drink there seven nights a week."

"No, not like that, like—"

"Hey, it's him!" The shout came from just to the right, a couple of fit looking young guys crowded around a phone. "Check it out!" They came over. The one with the phone held it out towards Val and said, "My *man*. Is this for real?"

The phone's screen showed a frame of Val, on a bench. An impossibly large amount of weight was on the bar above him. The guy pressed a button on the phone and the movie played forward, showing Val pressing that weight down and up — and then throwing up on the floor afterward. Val turned away. "Shit."

"Nah man. That was awesome! Hey, what's your name?" And — impossibly, simply — like that, Val was the center of the group, being clapped on the shoulder, his hand being shaken, young guys high-fiving around him. He looked to John for help.

"Hey, don't look at me. You deserve this." He cleared his throat. "Guys, this is my friend Val..."

The crowd around Val started to grow. People shared the phone with the video. Someone worked out how to put it up on the screen behind the bar, showing Val's massive lifting effort from earlier in the day. People bought him beers, clapped him on the back like old friends. They wanted to know how long he'd been lifting for, what his secret was. There were cries of disbelief when he admitted it was his first day in the gym.

"So it's a fake then?" The guy with the phone looked crestfallen. He looked down at Val's belly. "Figures".

John stepped up then, putting a hundred dollar bill on the bar. "No fake. I'm confident in my buddy here. So confident that I reckon he'll take anyone here in an arm wrestling match. Right now. So confident that I'll put up this hundred against your fifty." The crowd quietened then.

Val looked around. "John, what are you doing—"

"I'll take that bet." Working his way towards the back of the bar, the newcomer was young, cocksure. He was muscled, lean, and moved like a wrestler. A table was quickly cleared, and Val found himself very alone in the center of a crowd, his opponent already with his elbow on the table.

"What..." Val swallowed, feeling panicked.

John came up behind him, put his hands on Val's shoulders. Leaning forward, he said, "Don't worry. You got this. Just grab his hand, take it to the table."

Tentatively, Val reached out, putting his elbow on the table. It was slightly rickety — one of the legs must have been shorter than the others. The top was coarse, veneer roughened by the passing of glasses and plates and God knows what else over its surface. He looked at his opponent, taking in the bulging bicep and muscled forearm. The predatory, mocking grin.

Something inside Val — something hungry — made him reach forward, and they clasped hands. He answered the mocking grin with one of his own.

Val's opponent wanted the win — that grin said he knew he was going to get it. He tried a vice grip on Val's hand, applying pressure before giving a savage wrench and slamming Val's arm to the table-top. At least, that's what he thought was going to happen. As soon as he used that pressure, trying to crush Val's hand in his, the game changed. That hungry thing inside of Val noticed the change, felt the point where this stopped being a game and started being a fight. Instead of his arm slamming to the tabletop in defeat, it stayed upright.

Val's arm didn't move an inch.

Val's teeth were still showing over the top of their clasped hands. He began to apply pressure of his own, inexorably pushing the back of his opponent's hand towards the tabletop. The motion was slow and smooth, no trembling of exertion.

Like that, it was over. The back of his opponent's hand touched the table. Val hadn't realized how quiet the bar had become until people started cheering, clapping him on the back. A beer appeared in front of him, and he chugged it thirstily. His opponent kicked back his chair, pushing savagely through the crowd. Jeers followed him to the anonymity of the night outside.

John reached forward. "Another fifty. It's going to be a long night."

CHAPTER
SEVEN

"What?" Her head cocked at him, the small bar having become so loud that it was hard to hear yourself think, let alone get an order across.

"I said — hell — sorry! Peroni!" Val was almost shouting at her across the small bar top. The place had become almost rowdy, but in a jovial way — *good people, good times*. Val's kind of crowd. At least, this was how he imagined his crowd was, if he could remember it in the morning.

She held up two fingers, head tilted to the side. Val nodded. "Sure!" And then those amber curls jounced away to the frosted door of the beer compartment. Val watched as she pulled the beers out, and with a practiced swipe pulled an opener from her back pocket. Two quick motions and the caps were tossed somewhere behind the bar, thrown in with the litter of another busy night.

Danny. That was what the name badge said. "You running late for work this evening?"

She leaned closer. "What?"

Val pointed to the badge. "Your badge. You swipe it from one of your pals?"

She looked down at it, then laughed. "Nah. My Dad always wanted a dog named Daniel. Wait a sec!" And like that, she was off down the other end of the bar for an order. Val watched her go. There was something about her, a feistiness in her grin — *and dimples* — that spoke out to him.

He stared down at his Peroni, watching the perspiration bead on the glass, then took a pull from it. He was sure he'd drunk his body-weight in beer, but he only had a long smooth high, like the bottle couldn't touch him. Not tonight. If only his left arm would stop aching.

"Why the hangdog face?"

He looked up to find her back. He dragged up a lopsided grin. "Sorry. I've been trying to teach myself Italian all night, can't seen to get past 'superior beer.' At least, I'm pretty sure that's what it says."

Danny grinned at him. "Where's your friend?"

Of course. None of the pretty girls really wanted to talk to Val. It was John they were usually after. "Hell, I don't know. I think he went to the..." Val looked around. Come to think of it, he hadn't seen John in a while. He'd been swapping manly stories about a Russian tennis game last time Val had seen him.

"Hey, wait a sec!" And like that, she was gone again. No surprise really. Like he thought, they were usually after John. Val didn't mind, he wasn't jealous of John — after all, John had the looks and the body to match. That body took effort, and Val was honest enough with himself to know that didn't come for free. You needed to earn it, work for it, really want it.

He looked up at the TV behind the bar. There was some story on about the Blues. Or at least, the backdrop for the scene was the Elephant Blues, yellow Police tape flapping in the rain. The sound was either turned down or too low for the noise in the bar and he couldn't hear any of the details, but a bold banner marched across the bottom of the screen proclaiming, "MASS MURDERER LOOSE IN CITY... POLICE HAVE NO SUSPECTS... EYE WITNESSES BEING SOUGHT..."

She knocked on the bar in front of him, startling him. "Oh hey! I didn't think you'd be back."

"Why not? I said I would be."

"It's nothing! Say, want a beer?" The second beer for John was still on the bar, untouched.

"I'm working! But thanks! Maybe later." She was leaning forward over the bar again so they could hear each other.

Val tapped a finger in the ring of water left by his Peroni, tracing the circle. "Okay, I'm confused about something."

She looked back at him. "Shoot."

"Actually, it's three things."

"Three?" She grinned at him again. "You can have any answers without numbers in them."

"Fair enough. So, three questions. First, what's it short for? And secondly, why not just have the whole thing on there?"

"You said three things." Danny tilted her head to the side, her cheeks dimpling.

"We'll get to the third thing in a second."

"All right. Well, you've got to trade me. Shit. Wait a second." She went back down the bar to get another order.

Val watched her go. Picking up his Peroni, he finished it off. It had been a little while since anyone had bought him a beer, his moment of stardom fading out as the alcohol blurred the sharp edges of the afternoon into unfocused memory. Stories had been shared, they'd all sworn to stay in touch, he even had a couple of numbers on his phone. He'd probably delete them in the morning. It just wasn't really his style. This whole thing, it was more John than him.

They were a great team that way. John made a great front man, Val brought the brains. Just like at school.

"Okay, so I've got three questions." Danny had arrived back, wiping her hands on her apron. "What would be on your name badge? And what do you do when you're not warming that bar stool?"

"You said three!"

"So did you. So we'll trade our third one later." She grinned. "It's only fair."

"Sure. It's only fair. Okay. I have to go first?"

"You don't have to."

"Yeah, yeah I do. There's a rule about it somewhere." Danny nodded in mock solemn agreement. "Okay. My name badge? It'd say Val. And right now, I guess you could say I'm on a sabbatical."

She nodded in exaggerated slowness. "Sabbatical. You're not a musician?"

Val snorted. "Shit no. I can't even dance."

"Thank God. There's that many dead beat musicians arrive in here, they all try and hit on me."

Val sensed a trap. "I guess it's lucky for me I can't play. After I decided to leave Juilliard, I became a software engineer."

"A what?"

"I write programs. On computers."

She wrinkled her nose. "I think I prefer musicians."

"Shit. Would it have helped if I said I was a tax accountant?"

She thought about it. "I think so. I think I know what one of those is. Are they — do you scrape those off your shoe sometimes after it rains?"

Val laughed out loud. "I think so, yes. Now your turn."

Someone called down the end of the bar. Danny gave him an apologetic look, and headed off again. Val reached for his second beer, starting in on it. Sure, his arm still hurt, but at least his chest and shoulders had eased up. The alcohol was good for something at least.

She arrived back, wiping the bar in front of him. "Got to look busy. The boss just asked me if I was wasting time down here."

"What did you tell him?"

"It's too long."

"What?"

"My name. It's too long for the name badge."

"You told your boss your name was too long?"

She threw the bar cloth at him. He got his hands up, fending it off. It landed on the bar top, where she scooped it back up. "Lucky. I'll get you next time."

"I consider myself reprimanded. Your name's too long? So what's it short for?"

"I don't think I want to tell you that."

"What'll it take for you to tell me that?"

"Is that your third question?"

"No. My third question is why are you still talking to me?" Val gestured around the bar. "I'm no one."

She looked sideways at him. "Seriously?"

"Seriously. I'm not even a musician."

"Will you come back tomorrow?"

"Is that your third question?"

"That's my third question. You come back tomorrow, and maybe I'll tell you what it's short for. I finish earlier." She left again, this time replaced at this end of the bar by another guy. Val nodded at him, held up his empty bottle. Another round couldn't hurt.

Yeah. He'd come back tomorrow.

EIGHT

When they stepped out of Presence Unlisted, it was well on the wrong side of midnight. The streets were empty of people; it wasn't a hard Friday or Saturday night, and the big crowds were saving their money to buy happiness on a more popular evening. The cool of the early morning was an old friend, reminding Val of the comfort of bed to come. He probably should have been there hours ago. They wouldn't even find an open MacDonald's at this hour.

John leaned against a lamppost, head down. He groaned. "I think I'm going to throw up."

"I'm not going to hold your hair back." Despite them both having drunk the small bar out of Peroni, Val was still buoyant. The alcohol just couldn't touch him tonight. Sure, he was a bit unsteady on his feet, and he'd probably feel like John looked closer to arriving at home in a few hours. Right now he just felt—

"No really, I'm going to throw up." John's back curled a little.

—happy. He looked back over his shoulder at the doorway of the bar. The details of the evening were losing clarity, their sharp edges blurring and becoming indistinct through overuse. All except the conversation he'd had with Danny. He knew he'd be back — nothing would stand in the way of that. That memory wouldn't fade, and he knew however drunk he'd become he'd remember it in the morning.

His train of thought was interrupted by the sound of John throwing up into the gutter. "Shit man. Don't get it on your shoes."

John retched again, then turned and gave Val the universal gesture, middle finger extended upwards. He looked gray, eyes slightly unfocused.

"Yeah, fair enough. I'm betting you've got work tomorrow too." Val chuckled. "Let's find you a taxi." He helped John upright, half carrying, half steering him as they walked away from the bar.

Typical. Any time you didn't need a taxi you'd find the taxicab stands full of them, eager faces imploring you to take the easy route and just hop on in. Right now there wasn't a taxi in sight, the rain slick tarmac free of almost any traffic at this hour. A lone street cleaning machine was trundling away from them, the howl of the brushes muted by distance. Now that was a shitty job, stuck in a tiny cab and scrubbing the streets of people's waste, day after day.

Still. The guy was probably warm in that cab.

An empty bus passed them, the lit sign proudly proclaiming, "NOT IN SERVICE." The two of them stumbled further afield in search of a ride home. John mumbled something.

"What?"

"I said, if we're — wait, I need to throw up again."

"Christ. I've known schoolkids who can hold their beer better. How do you even get drunk on beer anyway?"

"You know schoolkids? We need to —" The rest of this was cut off as John retched again. He straightened, wiping his mouth on his sleeve. "Hell. We probably need to find a side street or something."

"Thanks, Socrates." Val shrugged. Statistically speaking John was probably right — there were less taxis where there were more people, so if they found a quieter area of the city they'd be more likely to get that elusive ride home. He steered their steps in a different direction. They stumbled past a vagrant, wrapped up in a dirty blanket and some newspapers.

"Fuck. We're idiots." Val started to pat his pockets down.

"What are you looking for?"

"Well, we could just call for a taxi. Beats walking the entire city looking for one. Fuck. I can't find my phone."

"It's cool. Uncle John's got his." John offered Val his phone, who took it and started tapping in a number. "I haven't been this drunk since I was last in Vegas. Tomorrow's going to be hard work. I've got clients. You know what a hot gymnasium is like with a hangover?"

Val noticed them first as he hung up the call with the taxi company. It was the way they walked that hit him first, the over-arrogant swagger of those with something to prove. It was a group of perhaps ten young men, looking for trouble to belong to them. The usual warning signs were there, plain to see. Hoodies, drawn up over the heads. Baseball caps underneath. Too-loose jeans hanging low, underneath hunched postures. A couple of them were smoking. He looked at John. "We should probably go somewhere."

"What?" John was slurring.

Val handed the phone back to him. "Taxi will be here in ten." He pointed to the group with his chin. "Those fools."

John squinted. "Ten minutes? A lot can happen in ten minutes."

Val nodded, the look on his face saying it all. They both turned to cross the road, to get some distance. It was too late, of course. A whoop came from behind them as they were spotted, and the group ran in a haphazard clump towards them. Very quickly they were surrounded, ringed to prevent easy escape.

Val hadn't been in a fight. Not since school, and those didn't really count. John had always been there to sort it out. True to form, out came the signature Miles megawatt smile, ever so slightly loose from too much beer. "Guys."

They were young. Just kids, really. Val could see that now: through the collection of mismatched clothing and wannabe gang patches, there wasn't one amongst them over 22 years old. Damn.

Kids always had something to prove. One of them stepped forward a bit. It was hard to see his face under the hood, the peak of a baseball cap poking out from underneath. His breath puffed in the cold, and he flicked his cigarette stub to the ground.

"You guys trying to," and he glanced for the reassurance of the crowd to those around him, "get away from us? You cunts trying to run?"

John's smile didn't fade. He wasn't trying for eye contact, and he was still swaying on his feet a little. "Run? Shit no. We just called a taxi, man. Thought we'd wait over here." He gestured at a bus stop nearby, brightly lit advertisements surrounding an area of dry seating.

The leader nodded, as if agreeing. "That's good. We don't like it, do we boys? We don't like it when they run." Jitters and nasty laughter rippled around the ring.

Someone behind Val — he didn't see who — pushed him hard on the back. He stumbled forward towards the leader, who pushed back again from the front. "Hey now. Watch your step. You almost ran into me." Val felt nervous, a sick wet feeling in the pit of his stomach.

John stepped in front of Val, hands up. "Hey. No need for that. We—"

The leader broke in. "You a fag? This your queen bitch here? Well. You've got to pay. A fag tax." More laughter. Someone pushed Val from the side, making him stumble again.

"Well, see now lads, there's a problem—"

John was interrupted again, this time the leader's voice angry. "Ain't no problem, cunt. I said you got to pay. You and your fag pal here." He seemed to consider. "Want to see my blade?"

Someone kicked the back of Val's leg, and he went down on one knee. As he started to rise again, one of them punched him hard in the kidney, and he cried out. He could hear the heavy, eager breathing of the group around them.

John moved then, swinging with a boxer's grace slightly muddy with alcohol. He was good enough though and he hit one of the thugs in the face once, twice, before wrapping the kid up in a hold and slamming a knee into his gut. The youth fell back, and John turned around and delivered another jab followed by an uppercut to the one who'd hit Val in the kidney. One of them stepped in to try and grab John, but he was too slow. John batted the kid's hands aside, grabbed his hair, and slammed his fist into the youth's face. They stepped back a few paces, watching as John turned slowly in place. Waiting.

It was as John reached a hand down to try and help Val back up that they caught him from the side, a punch Val didn't even see coming hitting his friend in the jaw. John staggered, and the leader stepped in to deliver a punch to his gut. They grabbed John from the sides, held his arms, and delivered more punches to his face, his stomach.

Val was still on the ground, a clump of them landing kicks in on his body. He'd got his hands up over his head somehow, but their boots hit his body over and over. All of this was done without words, an efficiency of violence as the group used fist or foot against flesh.

The leader lost interest in John when he passed out, his head lolling loosely. They let go his arms, his body hitting the pavement like a sack of meal. Stepping around John, he approached Val, crouching down to be closer. The group stopped their beating, stepping back to catch their breath.

"This is it, see? See it fag? I said look at it!" He reached and slapped the side of Val's head. He'd drawn a small, thin blade. Tapping the point against his palm, he said, "Got this from my bro. Every week, I cut someone with it. Every week. And this week? No one's been cut yet."

With that, he stabbed sharply down, the blade cutting into Val's leg. Val's cry of pain seemed to galvanize their leader, who stabbed again and again, going into a frenzy. The little blade entered arms, legs, chest, stomach.

The leader paused then, panting, and looked up at the group around him. They were standing in silent vigil. "What?" Blood dripped from the end of the knife, and was all over his hands, his jeans, and his boots. He looked down at the body, and seemed surprised to see Val dragging himself away.

Val was whimpering, a small animal noise of pain and fear. A slick of blood, dark red leaking out around him, marked his progress across the sidewalk. He was pulling himself towards a small alley. Some animal instinct goaded him, making him seek the safety of a cave to curl up in.

It was a long way to the alley.

FOR A MOMENT, the group lost interest in Val, and turned their attention back to John. They rolled his unconscious body over, looking for a wallet, a phone, anything of value. They weren't gentle, cuffing and shoving. One found John's phone, and then with a shout he raised a fist full of paper: the remainder of the money won on Val's achievements of the day. The notes were crumpled in his fist.

The leader nodded, the peak of his cap bobbing up and down. "Damn. These fags must have been working hard tonight. Turning tricks." He giggled, a slight edge of hysteria creeping in. "Say. Where's tubby? He must have something." The knife in his hand moved as he remembered the surge of power as he'd stabbed the life from Val. He moved towards the mouth of the alley, following the trail of blood.

"Don't run away!" he called into the alley. It was dark in there, and he couldn't see much. There was a dumpster and a few trash cans. He started in, his knife held low. "Don't make me look for you!" As he got deeper into the alley, his eyes adjusting to the low light, he was able to see the blood trail. It moved around the trash cans, behind the dumpster, and then ... stopped.

"The fuck?" There was no body, no sign of his victim. Easy money lost. "Shit!"

Once when the thug had been smaller, he'd been taken to the zoo by a concerned uncle. Trying to sort his life out or some shit like that. They'd seen the tiger pens, the large cats pacing inside their too-small enclosures. It'd been close to feeding time, and the tigers had growled at the crowd as they paced back and forth, back and forth. If only they weren't caged up, they seemed to say, all those people would have been lunch. Their growls had been full of urgency, and the part of him that wondered whether he should run or fight had screamed to run and never stop.

This growl was the same, primal sound. It came from his left, and he found himself frozen, the hairs on the back of his neck standing up. He turned slowly to his left and saw it. It was crouching down, half lost in the darkness and trash. He couldn't make out the details, but he could tell it was big. No, not big.

It was huge.

It was as big as two large men together. His gaze was drawn to the eyes. Lambent and yellow, they stared at him, full of hunger. The knife dropped from his loose grip, his hands trembling.

His scream was cut short almost before it began, his body grabbed like a rag doll and dashed into the side of the dumpster, life snuffed out with a snap. The creature held up the broken body, and shook it once. Then it roared its rage and defiance at the corpse, and threw the body into the street with the same ease a child would discard a toy.

It moved fast, powerful muscles underneath a shaggy coat. From out of the alley it surged into the loose circle of youths, knocking a few of them aside with casual ease. It crouched over John's unconscious body, muzzle bent close to his head. The beast sniffed once, twice, then placed a clawed arm on either side of him, crouching low.

It raised its muzzle to the sky and roared. The sound was pure animal rage, anger and challenge bound together in a song as old as life itself.

A couple of them broke and ran then. The rest stood, caught between fright and flight, unable to move. Just one decided to fight.

He pulled an old revolver from his jacket pocket, pointed a shaky arm at the creature, and fired.

He managed just two shots before it was on him, batting the gun aside as if it were no more concern than a baby's rattle. It seized him in two giant clawed fists, one at the thug's shoulder and one on his leg. Raising the youth from the ground as if he weighed less than a cardboard cutout, it brought its muzzle close to his face. Breath puffed in and out as it sniffed again. Muscles bunching across its back, it tore the youth in two in a single quick motion, tossing the pieces aside.

That's when the rest of them ran. Away from the creature, some blind instinct taking over as they sprinted down the street.

Not one of them was fast enough.

CHAPTER
NINE

The stack of magazines was full of the usual suspects. Faces of the rich and famous smiled with candied sweetness. From the outside they seemed so perfect, and yet so many of them fell into lives of addiction and neglect.

He absently tapped at the small plastic box in his pocket. Val figured it was far better to be ordinary.

The faces in the waiting room were a fair mix of that ordinary. A kid was there, snot streaming down from his nose while he played with a small collection of septic-looking toys. His mother talked in low tones as he bashed plastic blocks against a small fire engine, the red paint chipped in so many places it looked as if it had been in multiple accidents. An old woman sat quietly, head bent over her cane. A young man, the very picture of health. Now that one, he looked nervous.

Maybe an STD check?

"Mr. Everard?" Val looked up at his name, grabbing at his coat. Dr. Phillips was standing at the edge of the waiting room with a manila folder in his hand. He nodded at Val, then led the way down to his rooms. He closed the door behind them, then shook Val's hand. "What can I help you with today?"

Val tapped the plastic box in his pocket again, then sat down. He draped his coat over a spare chair. "I think I'm sick."

Phillips chuckled. "Well sure, Val. I don't get too many healthy people in wanting to pay for a chat."

"Sure. Well, okay, check this out." Val stood again, patting at his waist. "See?"

"My wife does this to me all the time, Val. I'm not sure. Have you dyed your hair? Clinically, I'm not sure I can advise you on the right color."

Val laughed. "No, Barny. Check this out." He undid his belt and pulled his waistband out. If he hadn't been holding his pants up with his hands, they would have just fallen down.

Barnaby Phillips' face crinkled into a well-used smile. "That's great, Val! You're losing weight? When did you start?"

Val wasn't smiling. "This morning."

"Come again?"

Val did his belt up again. The hasty extra holes he'd punched in this morning weren't as clean a look as he might have liked, but at least his pants stayed up. "I wore these pants last Tuesday. All my pants are the same though. Same size waist. I wear this same damn belt day in, day out. I woke up this morning and they were, well, I guess they were too big all of a sudden."

Phillips pulled the stethoscope from around his neck. "Let's check you out. I'm not sure I believe in this sudden weight loss, but there's no harm in running a few tests. Anything else?"

Val reached into his pocket for the plastic box. It was a Tupperware container; Rebekah had been *big* into those and they were all over his house in all kinds of shapes and sizes. There was nothing special about this one, except that inside it were some teeth instead of a leftover salad. "These." He tapped on the small blue lid with one finger, then left the box on the desk in front of Phillips.

"Jesus Christ, Val. Are those teeth? Whose teeth are they?"

"Mine."

"These are your teeth?"

"I think so, yeah."

"You think so?"

"I'm pretty sure."

Phillips puffed out his cheeks. "Maybe you'd better start somewhere that makes sense."

Val nodded. "Yeah. When I woke up this morning, I was naked."

"I sleep naked too. Mrs. Phillips likes it that way."

That prompted a smile from Val. "I'll bet. Well, naked's no big thing. Except that I wasn't in my house."

"Someone else's house?"

"No. Well, I was at my house, right, but I was outside. On the porch."

"You woke up outside? It was below zero last night!"

"It was? Okay, whatever. I woke up on my porch. And there was a small collection of teeth next to me. And like I said, I was naked."

Phillips paused jotting notes down. "Anything else?"

"I was sporting wood."

"I'm not sure if that's medically relevant. I meant, do you know how you got there?"

"No clue. I think John and I went for some drinks after the gym—"

"You went to a gym?" Furious scribbling in the notebook. "That probably explains the weight loss."

"First session yesterday."

"You had your first session yesterday?"

"Yeah. John took me for some drinks—"

"I can't believe you went to the gym. I mean hell, Val. We've known each other for years. I keep telling you to get some exercise. Take a walk maybe. How did it go?"

Val paused for a moment. "I'm not sure. Good, I guess. John said I benched a lot."

Nodding, Phillips continued writing. "Great, great. He's a good man, your friend John. You said you went for some drinks?"

Val smiled. "I met a girl." He remembered those bouncing curls, the easy grin.

"Is that why you woke up naked?"

"I don't think so."

"You don't think so?"

Val looked down at his hands. "I don't actually remember."

This time Phillips paused. "Did you have a lot to drink last night?"

"I don't remember that either."

Phillips nodded. "We'll say yes, then. What's the last thing you remember?"

"I remember leaving a bar, Presence Unlisted."

"That where you met the girl?"

"Yeah. But she wasn't with me when I left."

"You're sure."

Val nodded. "I don't think I'd forget something like that."

"What next?"

"That's all I've got." Val reached out and tapped the Tupperware box. "Except for these."

Phillips picked up the box, turning it around in front of his eyes. "They don't look broken. Nothing wrong with them as far as I can see. Except for the obvious, of course. They're not in your head. Let me see where they came from."

Val held up his hands. "Wait. We haven't finished."

"There's more?"

"Not a lot more. I mean, aside from having to break into my own house."

"How'd you do that?"

Val looked at him sideways. "I'm not sure that's medically relevant."

"Touché." Phillips chuckled. "I'm curious. This is the most interesting story I've heard this year."

"I leave a key with a neighbor."

"You..." Phillips looked down at his notes. "I don't think I need to know any more."

"Right." Val had blushed a little. "So after I'd got inside, I grabbed up the teeth, right? They were all lying about next to where my face had been on the ground. That's why I guessed they were mine. I went to check myself in the mirror."

"You guessed? But you're not sure?"

"That's the crazy thing. I've got all my teeth."

"In your mouth?"

"Where else?" Val looked at the plastic box again. "Okay, that was a fair question. Yeah, in my mouth."

"So whose teeth are these?"

"No, really. I think they're mine."

Phillips snorted. "Val. You don't just grow new teeth. It's impossible."

Val nodded. "I know. It sounds crazy. But I was thinking about it, about the teeth inside the plastic box, and about how I still had all these teeth in my head. Then it came to me."

"What?" Phillips had stopped taking notes, his pen held only loosely in his hand.

"My teeth have fillings."

"I'm not sure I follow."

"My teeth," and here Val shook the plastic box, "Have fillings. My teeth," and here he tapped his jaw, "don't have fillings."

"Let me see." Phillips leaned forward with a tongue depressor, looking in Val's mouth. "Hm." He threw the wooden instrument into a small trash can by his desk.

"See? No fillings."

Phillips put his notepad on his desk and placed his pen on top of it, straightening the edges with deliberate care. "Val, I think we'd better run some tests."

"What kind of tests?"

"I don't want to get you alarmed at this point, because none of this makes a lot of sense to me. But if we run some tests, we get a little more information to work with. I'd like to run up a complete physical on you. Draw some blood, get that looked at. Is that okay?"

"Can't you just give me a pill?"

"What for? There's nothing wrong with you. And that's got me confused all to hell. Been practicing medicine for forty years now, this is the first time I've seen someone who claimed they grew their teeth back."

Val rattled the box of teeth. "I'm not claiming anything. I've got the teeth right here."

"Like I said. First time. I'm sure you believe it too, but it's just not possible. I'm not ... this might be a bit out of my league."

"You can't help me?"

"Oh hell Val. Of course I'll help. You're my patient." Phillips rubbed his chin. "I'd say your health is improving. We doctors don't usually try to cure those who aren't sick, but I'll give it my best shot."

CHAPTER
TEN

"Mr. Miles?" The voice was a woman's, but not a bedroom voice. Usually he'd expect a bedroom voice when he was in bed. "Mr. Miles? Can you hear me?"

There was soft light hitting his closed eyelids. He felt tired, although he must had slept for an age. It was unusual for him to sleep until it was light. Early to bed, early to rise, hit the gym for a workout, that's how he started his day.

"He's coming around." He became aware of a soft, rhythmic beeping to his left. Must be his alarm clock. Someone should really turn that thing off.

He tried to open his eyes and failed. It felt like they were taped closed. "Mr. Miles, you're in the hospital. You've been in a bit of a fight. Don't try to open your eyes. They're quite badly bruised and swollen, but that should go down in a couple of days."

He tried to speak, but nothing came out except a croak — he was parched, his tongue thick in his mouth. "I'm going to place a straw next to your face, Mr. Miles. It's just water." He sucked on the straw. It was warm and flat, and nothing had ever tasted so good.

John tried again. "I said, 'Where's Val?' Have you seen my buddy Val?"

There was a pause, then the voice answered. "You were admitted alone. There were ... there are some police officers here who would like to take a statement, if you're up to it."

This time, a different woman's voice. "Thanks doc. Mr. Miles, I'm Detective Melissa Carlisle. My partner Vince Elliot is around here somewhere trying to get us some coffee. Garret and McNamara are on the door. You're safe here. How are you feeling?"

John chuckled, the sound wheezing and cracking through chapped lips. "How do I look?"

"Honestly?" The cop — *Carlisle?* — paused. "You look like you've been beaten half to death."

"Only half? I feel like it was most of the way there." John scrabbled around. "Any chance of some more water?"

"Oh, sure. Hey doc, I got this. Why don't you take a break?" Footsteps moved around to John's right, the sound of leather soles softly shuffling across the floor. Water gurgled and sloshed into a cup. "How the hell do I ... oh, I see. One sec, John. Can I call you John? I'm going to raise your bed up." His bed lurched under him as the whirring of electrical motors started, raising him slowly up. "Right. I'm going to put this cup in your hand. It's mostly full. I've taken the straw out, because you're not a kid at a birthday party."

John's first sip was cautious as he found the water level in the cup, then he drank it all down quickly. He felt Carlisle steady his hand while he refilled the cup. "Oh man. It's the weirdest thing."

"What's that?"

"I feel like I've got a hangover too."

There was a scraping sound a little further away to his right. "Christ. These hospital chairs aren't meant to make you feel welcome, are they? I've sat in church pews with more padding."

John chuckled again. "Sorry, Detective. You can have the bed if you want."

"The bed? What? Oh, right." There was the sound of fabric

rustling, then pages turning. "Just call me Carlisle. You say you feel like you've got a hangover?"

"Yeah. I mean, I've had a few. It feels just like that."

"They've got a drip in your arm. I'm no doctor, but water's the thing, right?"

"How long have I been here?"

"Clock says it's a quarter to two. You were brought in about six in the morning, so a little less than eight hours."

John coughed out on the sip he was trying to take. "Eight fucking hours? And you don't know where my buddy Val is?"

There was a pause. "This buddy of yours, Val. What's his full name? I can check with the station. See if he's come in somewhere else."

"Valentine. Valentine Everard. He's a big guy, about—"

"Valentine Everard?"

"Yeah, that's what I said." John hitched himself up in bed a little more. "You've heard something?"

"I'll be dipped in shi... Sorry. Pardon my language." The voice was new, coming from John's left. He turned his head towards the noise.

"Oh, hey Vince. John, this is Detective Vincent Elliot. He's the hero of the hour, because he's just brought me coffee. Vince, I love you. Give me one of those."

Elliot's voice still came from John's left. It didn't sound like he'd moved. "You know Valentine Everard?"

John turned his head between the two of them. "What's going on? Where's Val?"

Carlisle cleared his throat. "John, Mr. Everard is a person of interest in one of our inquiries. We can't say any more at this stage, but we've been looking for him for a couple days now. Any information you have—"

"A couple of days? I was drinking with him last night! Well, this morning. It started last night. I mean." John tried again. "We were out last night, after I finished work. It turned into a bit of a thing. You know."

The sound of footsteps moved across the floor as Elliot bussed the coffee over to Carlisle. "Yeah, I think we know."

"What the hell is that supposed to mean?"

Carlisle started in before Elliot could. "Vince, why don't you see if you can find me some more sugar? This tastes like swamp water."

"You want sugar?"

"I want you to go away. You getting me sugar will help with that."

Elliot laughed. There was no hurt in the sound. "Sure, boss. Sugar. Be back in a bit." His footsteps shuffled towards the left, fading out with distance. There was a mumbled conversation at the door as Elliot started to talk to the door guards. John tried to pick out their voices, wondering which one was McNamara and which one was Garret.

"It's not just an excuse."

"What?" John wished he could just open his eyes.

"This coffee really is terrible. Getting sugar, it's not just an excuse." There was a slurping sound, followed by a cough. "Elliot's a great partner, but he lacks subtlety."

John thought on that while he took another sip of water. "Something about this needs subtlety?"

"Sure. Do you remember anything from last night?"

John's hand touched the side of his face, the motion light. He winced anyway. "Christ. Yeah, a little. We were looking for a taxi—"

"You and Mr. Everard?"

"You should call him Val. Every time you say, 'Mr. Everard,' I keep wondering who you're talking about."

"Sure. You and Val were looking for a taxi? How was he feeling?"

"What? How was he … what the fuck is going on?"

"John, you hear that thing about the Elephant Blues? The bar down town?"

"A little, sure. Saw something on the news last night. We actually tried to get in but it was closed."

"Closed. Yeah, that's one word for it." Carlisle sighed. "So, a lot of people were killed at the Blues."

John ran that through his head a few times. "Killed?"

"Killed. Stone dead. It's a bit worse than that, but we don't need to go into that."

"What's worse than being dead?"

"Like I said, we don't need to go into that. Anyway, we've been collecting evidence from the scene."

"The scene being the Blues?"

"That's right." Carlisle paused here, the sound of breath puffing out between pursed lips. "Some of the evidence is ... inconsistent with what you're telling me."

"Inconsistent how?"

"You're saying Mr. Everard — sorry, Val — was fine last night?"

"He was great. We'd had a few beers. Made some friends. He even beat someone in an arm wrestle."

Carlisle started to laugh. "Wait, you're serious. An arm wrestle?"

"He won, too."

"Fu ... sorry."

"What's wrong?" John tried to open his eyes again. *No chance.*

"Our evidence team collected a, ah, a severed limb—"

"A severed limb? Like, cut off?"

"Something like that. The forensics boys say it's a match to Val."

John laughed, loud and clear. "Well Carlisle, there's something wrong with your forensics boys. Val benched over three hundred at the gym yesterday. I think I would have noticed if he only had one arm. Shit, we've been friends since school. I'd have thought he might have mentioned it to me if he'd lost an arm."

"You and Val are close?"

"Close? Like friends close, or lovers close?"

"Whichever."

"Sure," said John. "We've been friends since school."

There was a tapping like pen on paper from Carlisle's chair. "We might not be talking about the same person. Do you have a photo of him?"

"What?"

"A photo. Like, in your wallet. You said you were close."

"I said we were friends close. How many of your girl friends do you carry a photo of around in your wallet? It kind of says the wrong thing, you know?"

Carlisle laughed. "I know what you mean. It's hard to explain, right?"

"Exactly." John coughed, and took another sip of his water. "Wait. I've had a thought. You got a phone?"

"You want to call someone?"

"No. Yesterday, at the gym. Someone took a video of him. Uploaded it to YouTube I think. You should be able to check that out, see both of us there."

"Wait a sec." There was the sound of cloth rustling, then the distinctive clicking sound of an iPhone unlocking. "YouTube?"

"Yeah. I think so."

"What should I search for?"

"Try something like, 'Fat guy benches six fifty.'"

"He's fat?" More clicking as Carlisle tapped in the search.

"He's huge, man. I keep telling him to lose the weight, but since Rebekah..."

"The accident..? Here it is." The sound of yesterday's gym session played out in miniature through the iPhone's tiny speaker. "Christ. That's him."

"See? Both arms, right?"

"Right."

There was a knock at the door. "I've got your sugar."

"Thanks Vince. Check this out." Footsteps padded from the doorway to Carlisle's seat, then the sound of the video replayed again.

"What am I looking at?"

"You're looking at you losing another bet."

"Oh for pity's sake." The other cop, Elliot, sounded pissed off.

"Seriously. See that fat guy on the bench?"

"It looks a lot like Everard. From the file. Except he's put on some weight."

"Yep. This was shot yesterday."

"Wait, yesterday?"

"Yesterday. John, my partner and I are going to go now."

"We are?"

"We are. Because we're going to see Val's doctor."

John broke in. "Why are you going to see his doctor? Shouldn't you be out looking for him?"

"We already are." There was more rustling as Carlisle put on her coat. "This way, we hopefully get some evidence to clear Val of another crime. Focus our efforts, if you like. I've left my card on your bedside table. John — thanks for your help."

"Wait. What about the guys who mugged me?"

A final pause, before Carlisle and Elliot left. "They won't be troubling you again."

"You got them?"

"Someone got them. See you later, John."

CHAPTER
ELEVEN

The big car nosed through the afternoon mid-city traffic. The streets got a bit nastier as the day wore on and people got tired of not getting car parks and being cut off by assholes. Carlisle was running out of patience with it all, the old temptation to fire up the lights a familiar grin-touched craving that wouldn't end in anything but more paperwork. She sighed, her hands tapping in absent-minded rhythm against the steering wheel in time with the radio. Her mind poked through the details of the two cases she had, comparing the details.

Case one, a bunch of happy night-lifers executed. Forensics had completed time of death as near as they were able; most of those people had died within the same narrow window. A homicide on a grand scale, the ferocity of the killings strangely at odds with how the killer — or killers — had stacked the bodies in a neat pile. Carlisle was liking her multiple-killers theory on this, because it just didn't make sense otherwise. You didn't get one guy who killed people that messy, but who also tidied up after himself. If you did, she was going to be famous with a new killer type — there might even be that job promotion at the end of it. The case was bizarre —

no survivors, which meant no witnesses. Except for one Valentine Everard, and there was doubt if Everard had ever been there now, because the man clearly had both hands. Best to assume Everard was a red herring here, guilty only of police procedural error when they initially recorded his evidence details. If it was a simple error, it meant the lab or — *God* — a cop had mixed up results. Untangling that mess looked ugly, but it'd be someone's job well below her pay grade once they had their hands on new prints.

What really gnawed at Carlisle was that she didn't like coincidences. In her experience, there was no such thing. And it seemed an unlikely coincidence that an evidence error on a crime scene had tagged Everard — who turned up related to a case involving multiple homicides.

That case two, now that was equally interesting. A bunch of low life scum killed in the middle of a street. That they were killed didn't really bother her at all — from what was left of them, they'd dragged up some prints and found a collection of crimes that meant the world as a whole wouldn't weep for their loss. All of them were destined to end up in a gang, or prison, or dead anyway — someone had just sped that process up some. Finding out if Everard had been there wasn't a question of prints or even DNA — she had a witness on the scene who placed him there. Witnesses were unreliable, but Carlisle was riding free on a hunch that John Miles wasn't the kind of guy to make stuff up. No, the interesting bit was that there were no witnesses other than her one survivor, who'd been — conveniently — unconscious for the whole thing. So — no witnesses.

Again.

How was it that someone killed whole groups of people without a single witness managing to stay alive? It spoke of a thoroughness that was — in some warped way — as admirable as it was unusual.

The drunk guy on the street didn't count. A homeless vagrant at the scene of case two claimed to have seen everything, and had exuded half truths, lies, and fabrications on breath strong with old booze. Carlisle wasn't buying that some wild man had come busting out of an alley and tore people in half. If the bum had wanted to be taken downtown for a statement and the free hot meal that implied, he might have put a bit more effort into a believable lie. Carlisle had left him to deal with a pissed off Elliot as she'd walked the scene.

Truth be told, both of them were getting pissed off — a good night's sleep would go a long way. Why didn't these assholes have the common decency to murder people in the light of day? Back when she'd been younger, she'd had more fire in her belly and a willingness to get up before the dawn. She'd thought they spoke for those who'd been robbed of their voices by the cold of the grave.

Carlisle sighed again. The longer she did this job, the less clear cut it seemed whom the wicked were. It wasn't often that people got killed who didn't deserve it. Still — it was hard to chalk up a whole nightclub of people as villains. Those people still needed justice. Case two, not so much.

Her phone rang, derailing her train of thought. She dragged the big car to the side of the road, nosing it half into a park and fumbling in her jacket for the phone. She managed to get it on the fifth ring.

"I thought you didn't love me anymore." Elliot's voice seemed subdued, the wisecrack more habit than feeling.

"I hate your voicemails more than I hate talking to you. It's like you leave everything in some ten minute epistle I have to listen to rather than just asking me to call you back."

"I figure you love detail."

"I admire detail. I love brevity. There's a difference." Carlisle rummaged about in the glove box for her notebook and a pen. "What's up?"

"Yeah. So I found a piece of CCTV footage."

"An actual piece of video we can use? What's it got?" The pause drew out. Carlisle tried again. "You still there? Did you hear me?"

Elliot's sigh came through, tinny over the cell. "I heard you. I just … I just don't know if you're going to … shit."

"Vince. What's going on?"

"You'd best have a look."

"This isn't funny, Vince. Just tell me."

"Nah, boss. You won't believe me. I'm not sure if I believe it. I don't want you to think I've lost it. Just ... you need to see this. Get down here fast." Elliot rang off, leaving her staring at her phone.

Carlisle pocketed the phone then looked down at her notebook. The page was blank, and she tossed the thing into the footwell of the passenger seat. It wasn't going to be much use to her without stuff written in it. Rubbing her chin she considered Elliot's words. *You need to see this — get down here fast.* The man was not usually prone to strange outbursts — if anything, Carlisle liked having him as a partner because he was so delightfully unimaginative. Dependable, sure. Loyal, absolutely. Emotional or creative, *shit no.* Whenever Elliot's gut was telling him something, it was a sure sign that was exactly the opposite of what was going on — he had the intuition of a cinder block.

Best get downtown then. See what all this was about. Carlisle tugged the big car into gear, then grinned. Elliot had said fast. Fast it would be.

She flicked on the lights and siren, the big car roaring back into the street.

CARLISLE FOUND Elliot in the video evidence room. He was surrounded by a collection of DVDs arranged in piles, some of the cases open, their contents scattered about. Elliot had fortified his position with empty coffee cups. An old chipped saucer sat on top of a monitor screen, an unhealthy pile of ash building up in there.

"When did you start smoking again?"

Elliot's shoulders were slumped. He looked tired, worn thin. "This morning." He took a couple of gulps from the Styrofoam cup in his hand, grimacing. "Crap. Cold."

"Well, don't let them catch you smoking in here. It's not worth the pain of the paperwork, and you know it." Carlisle looked at the ceiling. "You pulled out the smoke alarm in here? You must have needed that cigarette bad."

Elliot fumbled through his jacket with his free hand, liberating a crumpled box of cheap cigarettes and a lighter. "They can go fuck themselves. If they watched this video they'd be smoking too." His hand was shaking as he mumbled a cigarette into his mouth, lighting it on the third strike from the lighter. He took a deep drag, then blew smoke into the ceiling fan.

"What video?"

"I ... I thought about just throwing it out. Losing the evidence. It's happened before. It'd be easier."

"What video?"

Elliot borrowed more strength from his cigarette. "It wouldn't be good police work, but it'd mean I could just forget about this. Put the case on hold."

"Vince." Carlisle put a hand on his arm. "What video?"

"Yeah. The video." Elliot flicked on one of the monitors, fiddling with some buttons on a remote control. "*This* video."

The scene before them was high up, probably on a lamppost. The grainy black and white footage showed the street where Carlisle and Elliot had spent the early hours of this morning as they'd cleaned up bodies. Front and center was a bus stop, lighting from its panels spilling out into the street. She could see two men — Miles and Everard — crossing the road from off-camera towards the bus stop. The video was time-lapsed, each frame a few seconds from the last, giving their walk across the street all the authenticity of an old stop motion movie.

From up the street a group of thugs — all bodies now, still and cold in the morgue — came onto the screen, running towards Miles and Everard. They were surrounded, the inevitability of the situation clear to Carlisle. She could see one of the thugs pushing Everard, and then Miles stepping up to help. She could feel where the fight of it started, and noted how quickly it was over as Miles was knocked unconscious.

"I'm waiting for this to get interesting." She pushed a pile of DVDs aside, sitting herself on the table.

"Quiet." Elliot's voice was hushed. "It's coming."

They both watched as Everard was stabbed and then dragged himself off camera behind the bus shelter. Elliot gestured at the screen with a remote control. "It's not easy to see here, but there's an alley behind there."

"That's a fucking lousy place to not have CCTV, isn't it? A dark alley couldn't be a more clichéd place to have shit going down."

"I don't install 'em. Wait. Here it is."

One of the thugs broke off from the group. It was hard to tell which one it was through the tumble and jumble of forms but Carlisle suspected it was the one who'd done the stabbing. "This video quality is crap. This is exactly why we can't get prosecutions from these things — I can't tell which one of those fools that is, and he could be carrying a Barbie Doll for all I know."

Elliot didn't reply, his attention fully on the screen. That's when Carlisle saw it.

"What the fucking fuck is that?" She grabbed the remote control from Elliot, jamming a thumb onto the pause button. The image froze, the creature clearly visible. It was holding up one of the thugs by one hand, the CCTV catching a full view of it. It was humanoid, standing taller than the thugs around it. If it'd been a man, Carlisle would have said it was over four hundred and fifty pounds of lean muscle — not something to get in the ring with. Shaggy hair draped its body. But it wasn't — *it can't be!* — a man. No man looked like that. Unbidden, the vagrant's words came back to him from this morning. *A wild man*, he'd said.

"Thank God." Some of the tension seemed to blow out of Elliot. "I was ... I was sure I was going mad." He took another drag from his cigarette. "Even so ... I'm not sure what's worse. Going mad, or having to work out what that—" and he waved his cup at the screen "—is."

Carlisle leaned closer to the screen. "It's some kind of animal."

"That's what I said at first. What kind of animal is it?"

"I. Um." Carlisle stood up. "A wolf?"

"Right. It's the head that makes you think that, right?"

"Right."

"How many wolves you seen with fucking hands, girl? It's got fucking hands!" Coffee sloshed out of the sides of the cup as Elliot gestured, some of it running down his fingers. "I had a friend once, owned a dog. Cleverest fucking dog you've ever seen, could open a beer cooler and bring him a cold frosty. He trained that dog to do all kinds of tricks. One of them was to walk on its hind legs. It could do a few steps before it would fall back over. Dog's got no toes, right? So just remember your wolf theory when you see the rest of it." He took the remote back from Carlisle, clicking a button.

They watched the rest of it in silence. Saw the creature tear through the thugs, the ferocity of it clear even through the stilted images of the CCTV. It was impossibly strong, impossibly fast. Carlisle gestured for the remote. "Lemme see that."

Elliot handed it over. "I've been through this thing frame by frame. It's not a trick, not some guy in a suit."

"No, it's not that." Carlisle fiddled with the remote for a few seconds until she found the rewind function. "Just a hunch. Bear with me."

"Sure, whatever. I'm going to get another coffee. You want one?"

"What? Oh. Yeah." Carlisle hit the pause button, then turned to Elliot. "Vince."

"I know." Elliot was looking at his shoes. "We probably shouldn't talk to anyone about this."

Carlisle nodded. "Not just yet. We want to find out what the fuck that thing is. A story like this, without some evidence better than this Blair Witch shaky cam? We'll get busted back to walking a beat. Also, you've probably had enough coffee." Elliot nodded, shuffling out. The light streaming in through the open door seemed to be from another place — a reminder of just ten minutes earlier, before the world turned crazy.

Pulling a chair in front of the monitor, Carlisle skipped the video back until she found what she was after. She played the segment through three times to be sure. The creature had killed all the thugs without a qualm, that was clear. The really curious part was how it had sniffed Miles' unconscious body on the ground. Carlisle froze the video again at that point. She could see the creature crouched over Miles.

"What the actual fuck." The idea was crazy — as crazy as anything in the last few minutes. But the creature wasn't *attacking* John Miles.

It was *protecting* him.

CHAPTER
TWELVE

Val wished John would answer his phone. He'd lost his own phone somewhere along the way and had picked up a new one this morning. It'd be bad coincidence if John had lost his phone too — what the hell had they been up to last night? He really needed some advice. It'd been a long time since he'd been on a date, but he remembered enough about it to know that turning up at her work around lunch time was a sure sign of desperation, so he was going to leave it a while longer. Beyond that, he was lost. Still, John wasn't answering.

So, coffee.

He knew a little place, run by some Italians — they roasted their own beans, you could smell the place on the air before you got close enough to see it. He hitched his pants up again. It seemed crazy, but he was sure his pants were looser now than when he'd seen Barnaby Phillips in the morning.

No: that was definitely crazy.

Val reached the coffee shop, the door frame chipped and peeling. A little bell rang as he walked in, the smell of fresh brewed coffee hitting him. There were a few smells sent right from Heaven. Baking bread. Mowed lawns. Coffee.

"Oh hey, mister Everard!" It was Tulip, the daughter of the owners. She was running the register today.

"How you doing, Tulip? How's school?" He walked towards the counter, eying up the food displayed in the glass-fronted cabinets. Muffins went very well with coffee.

She made a face, pushing up her glasses. "You sound like my Dad."

"Yeah, sorry about that. Just asking. What about Robby, then?"

"We broke up."

Val looked up from a tray of caramel slices. "No way. I thought you two were going to get married some day. I'm sorry about that too."

She giggled. "Don't be silly. Anyway, it's fine, I've got an exam this week. The usual?"

Val nodded. "Sure. And could I grab one of those slices too?"

"Sure thing mister Everard. Say, have you lost weight?"

"I guess." Val put some cash down on the counter as she bagged up the slice for him. He'd always been interested that food that was bad for you was bagged just like porn — brown paper bags that you couldn't see through. That might be a sign of some kind, but he wasn't going to get philosophical before he'd had his coffee.

Tulip rang up his order then started counting out his change. He held up a hand. "Don't worry about it."

She tilted her head a little. "You sure? You've got over ten dollars in change!"

"Yeah, I'm sure. I know your Dad's allowance doesn't stretch that far these days."

"Thanks, mister Everard. You're the best!"

As Val waited for his coffee, he stared out the small window of the coffee shop. It's possible that John was just busy today and not picking up his phone, but he'd usually get a text from him during a break. Whatever — he'd stop by the gym. He needed to pick up some new clothes anyway, and his usual menswear store was nearby. That way he could talk to John about tonight and get some advice on a good first date dinner venue. He grabbed his coffee off the counter, waved to Tulip, and headed back out on the street.

SHE LOOKED at him over a magazine with a casual disdain he was used to. It wasn't just the way her eyes kept checking out his gut, or the way she chewed her gum, but how she wasn't really paying attention to him. Her name badge said Marcy.

Val tried for a smile anyway. "Is John here?"

The gum popped, a small but perfect bubble breaking over glossed lips. "John who? We got a lot of Johns."

Val kept the smile plastered on his face. "John Miles. He works here."

She glanced up. "John Miles?"

"That's right. You seen him today?"

"No." She looked back down at her magazine.

"Wait. You haven't seen him today, or he hasn't been in today?"

She sighed with the gravity only a late teenager could muster. "Haven't seen him because he hasn't been in. Had a lot of his clients calling up." She looked at Val's gut again. "Are you one of his clients?"

"No, but—"

"Thank God. I am *so* over taking his messages for him." She turned another page in her magazine. It was some kind of gossip rag with too-thin women doing things with too-fat men.

"Well, did he call? Did he say why he wasn't coming in?"

"No." She didn't look up this time.

He was used to people looking past him because he was fat, but today it was important. No one had seen John, he wasn't answering his phone, and this tart was giving him attitude? Val slammed his hand down over the counter on the surface of her magazine, making her start back in alarm. Her name badge jiggled. "For fu—"

A hand clamped down on his shoulder. "Big man." A throaty chuckle followed the hand. "How you doing?"

Val jumped a little, looking around. It was John's friend Emilio. Seeing the familiar face, Val's anger drained away. "Oh hey. Emilio."

"Say. You remembered my name. I wouldn't have thought you had the blood sugar for that after yesterday's workout."

Val smiled. "I don't think we were introduced." He stood back slightly, and pointed at the badge on Emilio's chest. "Your name's right there."

The black man chuckled. "It sure is, it sure is. Say, you here for John? He hasn't come in today."

The girl piped up. "Em! This asshole—"

"What? He did what, Sandy?"

"Well, he banged the counter, and look what he did to my magazine!"

Emilio glanced out the window. "I'd guess you probably deserved it again."

"What?" Her voice was up a few octaves. "Get rid of him!"

"When did you get promoted to be my boss? Besides, big man here—"

"Val. Valentine." Val offered his hand.

"Right." Emilio's return grip was strong. "Val here is going to do a workout with me. I tell you what, Sandy. You go get a glass of water. Calm down some. We don't need to say anything more about this. We certainly don't need to tell anyone you're wearing Marcy's name badge again, do we?"

Sandy looked down at her chest, the movement quick and involuntary. Staring daggers at Emilio, she got up from behind the counter, throwing Marcy's name badge on the desk. She then turned without another word and walked through a door, the sprung hinge flapping the panel behind her.

Emilio chuckled again. "I swear, we never should have hired that one. Got the work ethic of a narcoleptic."

Val laughed. "Sure. Thanks. Say, have you seen John?"

"Well, no. He's not come in today." Emilio rubbed his chin. "Didn't you guys go out for a celebratory drink last night?"

"Yeah." Val shuffled one of his feet. "I don't remember what happened."

"No shit. I've had nights like that too. Ain't no thing, Val. John, he'll be throwing up into whatever he can find about now. You, on the other hand, look like you could use a workout."

"A workout?"

"Is there an echo in here? A workout. My client canceled last minute, so I've got a slot. On the house."

"Well, sure. But on one condition."

"What's that?"

"I need some advice too."

That booming laugh again. "Uncle Emilio will help you out, Val. Come this way. You can ask as many questions as you like, if you can still breathe."

THIRTEEN

Val chewed, thinking about the question that sat fat and heavy between them. It was almost visible to him, like the salt and pepper shakers or the rather excellent steak. He put down his knife and fork, and chased back his mouthful with the wine. It was a good sign they both liked the same wine.

"C'mon. It's not that hard of a question." Danny eyed him over the top of her glass, an eyebrow raised.

"The problem is, it's got more than one answer, and that's sort of like you getting two questions instead of one."

"It's not my fault that your life's so terribly complex you've got two jobs—" A shriek of over-loud laughter cut her off, a table of older women trying to relive their youth through a shared meal and too much wine. "Jesus. Anyway. It's not my fault you've got two jobs."

"I didn't say I had two jobs! I said I had two answers."

"Holy shit." Danny put down her knife and fork.

"What?"

"Seriously. You're embarrassed about it. That's why."

"What? No! Anyway, you were embarrassed about your name."

"You totally are!" Danny grinned, picking up her knife and fork again. She sliced into her steak — she'd ordered the rib eye, leaving Val impressed that she was unafraid of getting steak caught between her teeth on the first date. "I don't even care anymore. You said you liked my name. It's you who hates your name."

"Danielle? I love your name. It's you who cuts it down to a bite-sized portion. You try being a boy named Valentine at school — that'll redefine your perspective." Val puffed out his cheeks. "Okay. Here it is. I'm a bum."

She laughed at him. "Val's not bite-sized? I like Valentine better. I thought you said you worked in computers? Anyway, I said I don't care anymore."

"You burned up your question for an answer you don't care about?"

"I get a refund on that question."

"I gave you the answer!"

"You gave me *an* answer, after I didn't care anymore." She pointed at him with her steak knife. "Doesn't count."

"You're changing the rules?" Val tried to drink from his glass and found it was empty. "Hell. This is thirsty work. I'm up against the Stasi."

"The Stasi wouldn't let you have such a fine Pinot gris." Danny nodded at him. "Well chosen. I'm not changing the rules."

"Wine lists are the language of my people. You so are changing the rules. One question each."

"I'm just making some refinements."

"You're a contracts lawyer?"

"No, but I work in hospitality. The contracts there will make a lawyer out of anyone."

Val nodded. "Fair enough."

"Fair enough that I get another question, or fair enough that I work at a bar?"

Their waiter returned. "Sir. More wine?"

Val nodded. "Thank Christ. Same again?"

86

"Very good sir. It will be just a moment. Your." The waiter tried again. "The second steak should be here momentarily as well."

As he walked off, Danny pointed with her chin at his back. "That guy really didn't like you ordering two steaks."

"Yeah." Val glanced down at his belly. He was *sure* it looked smaller than this morning. "I've never done that before. Is there a rule against it?"

"I don't think so."

"I mean, I've ordered two breakfasts before."

"For yourself?"

"Yeah. I was at this little place uptown. I'd never been there before. Can't remember the name of it. Anyway. The breakfast they made was amazing. Truffle fries on the side of eggs and bacon. That kind of thing."

"Wow."

Val grinned at her. "You bet. So I finished my breakfast, and I realized that I could probably go another round." John called him the *Mike Tyson of eating.* Always ready to go another round. "So I went to the counter, and ordered another breakfast."

"No way."

"Woman behind the counter looked at me like some kind of alien." Val shrugged. "It was good the second time too. I live by my decision."

Danny nodded. "I had a customer last week." She stopped to chew another mouthful.

"Just the one?"

"You're not as funny as you think you are. Anyway. He kept ordering plates of fries from the kitchen."

"I see nothing wrong with a good plate of fries."

Their waiter arrived with a second bottle of wine, offering it label first to Val. He nodded. "Yep, that's the one. Thanks." He pushed his empty plate away from him, watching as the waiter refilled his glass.

"I can't remember if it was after his fourth of fifth plate. They were these big bowls, you know, chunky fries, probably a good two or three large potatoes in each bowl."

"Sounds like a good bowl of fries. Do you reckon it would have been too low class for me to ask for fries with my steak?"

She giggled. "It's never low class to have fries with steak. It's what fries are *for*."

"Dammit all. I should have got fries." The waiter was back, delivering a second main course of steak in front of Val. "Thanks buddy. Say, can we grab a bowl of fries between us?"

The waiter looked down his nose at Val. "Fries, sir?"

"Sure. Thanks."

"I ... very good, sir."

Danny looked at the waiter's retreating back. "I think you're getting special sauce with your fries."

Val looked back over his shoulder. "You think so? I'm not sure it's that kind of place."

"It's always that kind of place. Anyway, this guy with the fries."

"Right. Five bowls of fries." Val sipped his wine.

"So I bring him his fifth bowl of fries, and he just starts chowing down like he's starving."

"That's a little unusual."

"And so I ask him, 'Can I get you anything else?'"

"Like another bowl of fries?"

Danny nodded. "It's what I was expecting. He looks at me, right, then pushes his chair back."

"Like he was going to get up?"

"Except, he then just bends over at the waist, and throws up all over his feet."

Val clapped his hands together in front of his face. "Oh man! That's nasty. I thought you only got sick people in medicine."

"So I'm standing there, this guy's just thrown up literally into his shoes. There's bits of fries everywhere."

"You're standing in it?"

"I'm standing in it. And the guy turns to me, and get this, he says, 'Can I get another bowl of fries?'"

Val swallowed another mouthful of steak. "What did you do?"

"I got him another bowl of fries. Customer's always right."

"I don't think I want to know if there's another end to this story. So your turn."

"Hey! I got a refund on my question."

"You squandered it, the penalty shot only stays open for so long. Like I said. Your turn."

"What's the question?"

"Same question."

Danny looked at him over a fork of steak. "I picked you as more original."

Val lifted the bottle. Danny nodded as she chewed, and he topped her up. "Seriously. What do you do?"

"You met me at my work."

"That's where you work." Val chased a piece of steak through his blue cheese sauce. If she was ordering steak, he was going for the cheese sauce. "It's not what you do."

"This is really good steak."

"No kidding. My favorite steak place."

"When you told me to meet you at a steak joint..? I figured ten dollar steaks with a garden salad. Like you had no class."

"I never said I had class, but damned if I'll eat bad steak. Stop avoiding the question."

"I'm a sciences major."

"That's what you're trained in. Still not what you do."

"You realize you're getting three answers for the price of one?"

"It's legit. You're avoiding the question."

"I swim."

The waiter returned. "Your ... *fries*, sir. The kitchen took the liberty, I hope you don't mind. Truffle oil, sir."

Val nodded up at him. "It's like you knew what we were talking about. Thanks to the chef." The waiter walked away, back stiff. "That man's going to give himself a prolapse just walking around."

"My question now."

"No way. You've told me what you do. You swim. Sciences major. And you work in a bar."

Danny looked down at her plate. "It's not that bad a combination."

"Didn't say it was. Sounds... eclectic."

"Now you're saying I'm crazy."

"Eclectic, not eccentric."

"Same thing."

"I sense a trap."

"You're not as stupid as you are funny looking." Danny grinned at him.

"I'm touched. Let me guess. Bar work pays the bills? But your sciences major — it's in something to do with water. Chemistry?"

"Close. Marine biology."

"I work in computers, so I might be wrong here, but that doesn't sound close."

"We're all just bags of chemicals."

Val swirled some wine in his glass, then took a sip. "And we can add more chemicals to the mix at any time..."

Danny snagged the bottle from the table, swirling it around. "We're hitting this one pretty hard. Sure you can keep up with me? Remember, I work in a bar."

"Last time I heard a challenge like that, I woke up chained to a lamppost." Val thought for a moment. "You're on."

Danny giggled, then poured them both more wine. "Yeah. We're all a chemical mix."

"What about love? What about poetry?"

"It's from the chemicals. Trust me, a few more bottles of this wine and you'll sing, dance, and write the best sonnet of your life. You'll also hate yourself in the morning."

"Personal study."

"What?"

"You've got a degree in chemicals. Marine biology. Whatever." Val waved his wine glass. "You work in a bar. Only reason you'd do that is if you want to learn something you can't learn somewhere else."

"I could just be another sciences major who can't get a job."

"A bum?"

"I'm not like you."

"I can tell. No really — sciences majors get jobs just fine. It's lawyers who can't get jobs, especially if they've got morals."

"Ouch."

"Truth hurts. Yeah. You're studying something."

Danny nodded at him, her smile fading a little. "Funding's hard to get."

"What is it?"

"Viruses. Bacteria." Danny swallowed another mouthful of steak. "Things that go bump in the night in the ocean."

"Fish get sick?" Val tried the fries.

"Everyone gets sick. Fish don't have government health care."

"I'm not sure government health care is all it's cracked up to be. You're trying to work out how they get sick?"

"They get sick a lot like we do. I'm trying to work out how to make them better, especially when we keep shitting in their ocean and killing them all."

Val looked down at his plate. "I'm glad I didn't order the fish special."

Danny pointed at him with her knife. "You'd never get to second base ordering fish around me."

"I'm not sure we're at first base yet!" Val looked into his wine glass. "Or do I just not remember? I'm sure I'd remember something like that."

Danny pushed her plate away. "I'm stuffed."

"No room for dessert?"

She looked at him, head tipped sideways. "Are you crazy? There's always room for dessert."

～

THE NIGHT WAS chilly around them. Danny hugged his arm. "I've had a really good time tonight."

"Me too." Val grinned into the darkness. "A really good time."

She looked up at him. "Feel like walking me home?"

"I'd like that." Ahead of them, a small group of people — men — were grouped around a young woman. Val watched them without really paying attention. "You got work tomorrow?"

"You see those guys?"

"What? Yeah."

"I think that girl doesn't want to be with them."

She is not Pack.

Val looked at the group again. "I'm not sure."

"How can you not be sure? Fine. Look, I'll show you." Danny detached herself from his arm, striding towards the group.

"Fuck." Val followed her, an uncertain two or three steps behind.

"Why don't you leave her alone?" Danny looked up at them, fists clenched on hips. The line was so clichéd as to be laughable, but no one laughed.

The biggest one of them, a tremendously ugly man sporting a green Mohawk, leered down at her. "Look what we have here!"

One of his friends snickered, the chains joining the piercings in his ears to his lips jingling. "First time I've seen a guy hide behind his girl." Chains sniffed.

Val reached to put his hand on Danny's shoulder. "Maybe we should—"

She shook him off. "What, it takes four of you to handle a girl?"

Mohawk looked at her, then at Val. "Man, you should get your bitch under control. Someone might get hurt."

"Uh, yeah—"

Danny held out her hand to the young woman. Now they were closer, Val could see the tracks of tears down her face. "Come on. We'll take you home."

A man behind the girl, decked out in ripped denim, grabbed the young woman's shoulder. She struggled against his grip. Denim gave a small, ugly laugh. "She's not going anywhere with *you*."

The fourth man, the hair on his arms curling out from under the sleeves of a faded Metallica T-shirt, looked at Mohawk. "This is taking too long. This part of town? We'll get seen. C'mon."

Danny tried to shoulder through the group to reach the young girl. It was such an unexpected movement that it almost worked. If Val could have picked the part where it all went wrong, it was right *there*, the moment in time where her hand touched Mohawk's chest, where she turned the motion into a shove. It wasn't much, she was barely brushing past him, but Mohawk was already pumped.

Val was just two or three steps behind her — such a short distance. He started to move forward, but he was never going to make it in time. He knew that. On his first step forward, he could see Mohawk's expression change from confusion to anger. On his second step, he saw Mohawk's raised arm swinging. His third step was too late.

Pack.

Danny's body staggered back as Mohawk's backhand hit the side of her face. Val couldn't be sure but it looked like the blow caught her on the jaw, her head whipping around. She didn't make a noise as her body slammed into wall of a building, the back of her head hitting the old bricks.

Mohawk's body pinwheeled away, rising up through the air and slamming into the same brick wall, a stream of blood and teeth following his short flight through the air. He hit the wall with an audible crack, one of his arms caught up between his body and the wall, and bounced back off onto the sidewalk. Val looked down at his fist, the blood on his knuckles bright in the street lights. He hadn't remembered swinging his arm.

Danny had started to slump down the wall. Val's lips curled into a snarl. Two more steps took him to Chains, who sidestepped Val's wild swing with a boxer's grace. He returned the volley with two quick body rips to Val's ribs. Val grabbed the lapels of Chains' jacket, the muscles of his forearms bunching like big, fat cables and yelled in his face. Then he brought his forehead down with a crunch onto the bridge of Chains' nose. The man was still jerking uncontrollably as Val let his body fall to the ground.

Metallica looked between Val and Mohawk. One glance was all it took to take two more steps. "Hey—" Whatever he'd been about to say was lost as one of Val's fists slammed into his stomach, doubling him over. Val's other fist hammered into his back, and his body hit the pavement so hard his head bounced against the ground.

Denim had the young woman — barely a teenager, really — in front of him as a shield. He had her hair gripped in one hand, a tiny knife in the other against her throat. "Back off man! Just back off."

Val caught himself. Something inside him wanted to step forward, to crush this puny man who'd hurt one of his—

Pack.

Val shook his head. He couldn't think straight.

"That's right man! Now I'm just gonna walk out of here. Don't follow me!" Denim's eyes were wide and wild, darting to the bodies of his friends.

Val looked down at them, then back up to the girl. She wasn't much older than Tulip. Her eyes were screwed up tight, the runs of mascara stark against her cheeks. She was babbling something that sounded like, "Please please please please please..."

Saliva streamed down Val's chin. He didn't notice. He took a step forward. Denim's knife hand jerked closer to the girl's neck, and she let out a small cry. "Back the fuck off!"

What if it were Tulip? How would he explain it to her father?

She is not Pack.

Val wiped his chin with his arm. It came away slick with drool. He brought it up in front of his face, staring at it as if it was someone else's arm attached to his shoulder. It hit him like a slap, and he shook his head again. He stared down at the bodies around him. *Did I do that?* He looked back at the girl. Her eyes were screwed up tight. She was so young. *What was I about to do?*

He lowered his arm, tried to speak.

"What?" Denim's knife was shaking, bright and darting like a moth around a flame.

"I said, 'What then?' When you walk out of here."

"I'm gone, motherfucker. I'm out."

Val nodded. "Right, right." He sighed. "Look, I don't know about you, but I'm really tired. We all just want to get home."

"What the fuck you talking about?" Denim stepped backwards, dragging the girl with him.

Val took a step forward, his eyes on the knife. "Well, when you get out there," and he gestured to the empty streets behind Denim, "It's going to look funny you dragging some teenage girl around by the hair. If I saw that, well, I'd probably call the cops or something."

Denim looked at his hand in the girl's hair. He let her hair go, then grabbed the back of her dress. "See? Doesn't matter. I still got her."

"You think that's better?"

"What?"

"It's not that you've got her hair." Val nodded at her. "It's that you're a thirty-something guy with gang tats holding a teenage girl and a knife. I don't know how far you've got to walk. You can't really call a taxi. If you've got a—"

"I've got my own wheels, asshole."

"If you've got a car around here somewhere, how you going to drive the car with a screaming girl in it? It's not like the movies, she can just get out at a set of traffic lights or something."

"Bitch!" Denim shook the girl. "You do that, I'd cut you—"

"Hey!" Val's voice lowered again. "You don't have to cut anyone. You can just walk away. By yourself, well, you're mobile. Nothing holding you down. No one notices you. Even if you're running, you're just some guy late for his bus."

Denim looked at the knife. "No one notices me?"

"That's right. A block away, there's nothing to tie you to this. But take the girl—"

"If I take the girl, everything goes to shit."

Val waited it out. He wanted Denim to make up his own mind.

"Okay." Denim licked his lips. "Okay. Just be cool."

"I'm cool." Val looked at his hands, turning them over in font of him. He wasn't even shaking. "When you're ready."

"I'm going to walk out of here. You're not going to follow me."

"That's right. I'm not going to follow you. As long as you let her go."

"Right." Denim looked at the knife in his hand. "But I'm taking the knife!"

"Sure. It's your knife."

Denim pushed the girl at Val, then turned and ran. Val caught her, then held her at arm's length. "Are you okay?" She was sobbing, great gasping breaths coming in between the tears. "Shh now. It's going to be all right. Look, let's go over here and check on my friend—"

Two squad cars burned down the street towards them, lights on but sirens silent. He watched them come. "Thank Christ. The good guys."

CHAPTER
FOURTEEN

The room was not particularly large. Val had expected something different, maybe with a mirror on one wall. Instead, aside from the peeling paint, all it held was a crummy old table bolted to the middle of the floor. Coffee rings stained the surface. He could see a camera high up in the corner behind the officer, red light watching them.

"Mr. Everard, do you know why you're here?"

"I'm a little confused to be honest." Val traced a line through one of the coffee rings on the tabletop in front of him. He looked up at the cop. "What did I do wrong?"

The other man sighed. He flipped open a folder in front of him. "Let me see. We've got a broken jaw, concussion, spinal fracture ... okay. Broken nose, severe concussion. This one might not wake up. And a ruptured spleen." The folder flipped closed as the officer spun the file away from him on the table. "Want to tell me what happened out there?"

"What?"

"I said, what happened? In your own words." The officer looked at the folder that sat between them. "Take your time."

"You going to write this down?"

The officer blinked. "What?"

"You don't have a pen. Or paper." Val waved his arm at the table-top. "There's not even a, what the hell are they called, a Dictaphone."

"Do you want me to record this?"

Val blew his cheeks out. "Actually, I don't care. I just want to know what's the point."

"The point?"

Val nodded. "Sure. I've seen the cop shows. How are you going to use this as evidence if you don't record my statement?"

The officer looked at him for a couple of heartbeats. "You think we need to use something you say as evidence?"

"For fu— Look. I tried to help someone tonight. I thought maybe I might get a thanks. The last thing I figured on was ending up locked in a cell."

"You're not locked in a cell, Mr. Everard." The cop tapped the table between them. "So you admit you were engaged in ... something earlier this evening?"

Val looked at the officer without blinking. The moment stretched between them. The officer cleared his throat. "Mr. Everard. I think we've got off to a bad start."

Val said nothing. The officer reached for the file on the table between them. "When we picked you and Miss..?"

"Kendrick."

"Of course. Miss Kendrick. Well. You were pretty insistent at the scene that you be able to go to the hospital with her." The officer taped the file with this forefinger, deliberate and slow. "She's a subject of some interest to us."

Val leaned forward. "Danny? Why would you ... she didn't do anything!"

The officer leaned back in his chair, shrugging his shoulders. "You know how it is. If we can't get what we need from you, well, we'll get it where we can. Her situation is ... delicate."

"'Delicate?'" Val looked at the other man like he was something he'd just found on the bottom of his shoe. "She was out cold, going to the hospital. You took her to the hospital, right?"

Another moment stretched between them, neither man speaking. Val broke the silence first. "I said, you took her to the hospital, right?"

The officer let out his breath in a sigh. "Mr. Everard. It's a bit more complicated than that—"

"How can it be complicated? You had an unconscious woman who needed help!"

"As I said before, we need some information. There are other ways of getting that, should you choose not to cooperate." The officer showed too many teeth in his smile. "Now, shall we start again?"

"Just answer one thing. Did you take her to the hospital? Yes or no?"

"Well. Let's just say that she's safe for the moment. And will continue to be so, if all goes well here. Now, onto my first qu—"

Val swept the file off the table, papers scattering across the floor. He slammed both hands on the table between them, getting out of his seat. The officer scrambled back, his chair knocked to the ground behind him. "What have you done to her?"

"Mr. Everard!" The officer was trying to back away, scuttling like a crab. His hand scrabbled at his holstered sidearm.

"You motherfuckers!" Val grabbed the table, tearing it from the bolts mounting it to the floor, and flinging it into the wall. "If you've hurt her, I'll—"

The door slammed open. Val and the officer both froze, looking at the doorway. "What," said the newcomer, "exactly is going on here?" Her voice was mild, almost casual.

Val looked at the gun in the newcomer's hand. It wasn't pointed at him. His gaze was drawn by the gun's angle to the officer on the ground.

"Thank Christ. I was just—" the officer on the floor started to get up.

"Don't." The newcomer waved her gun towards the ground. "Just stay there."

"What? Look, I'm—" The officer tried to get up again.

"Maybe I'm not being clear. If you move again, I will shoot you. How's that?" The newcomer's eyes flicked to Val, then down to Val's left hand. "Mr. Everard? You're a hard man to track down."

"I." Val tried again. "What?"

"Detective Melissa Carlisle. I'm assigned to a … murder investigation, in which you are a suspect. That's why you're being held here." Carlisle's gaze flicked to the officer on the ground. "I've been working at this station for twelve years. I like to pride myself on my good memory for faces. Names too. And you sir," and now she pointed the gun at the officer, "Do not work here. Who the fuck are you and why are you here with my suspect?"

"Go to hell."

"It's like that is it? Let's play a different game. I know who Mr. Everard is, because I've got a file on him. I also have his left hand down on ice." Carlisle's eyes flicked back to Val's left hand again. "Which isn't his left hand, clearly, but I'd still like to talk to him." She reached inside her jacket with her free hand, and pulled out a leather wallet. She flicked it open to an ID. "Look. Mine's all official. Government issue. Says I'm a cop. Let's see yours."

The officer on the ground sat silent.

"Mr. Everard." Carlisle's eyes didn't leave the man on the ground.

"Yeah?"

"I appreciate this evening's been highly unusual for you, but I'm going to have to ask you for some help. You see this guy's jacket?"

Val looked at the chair on the ground, then the jacket lying near it. "Sure."

"Can you grab that and find me some ID?"

Val shuffled over and grabbed the jacket. "There's no ID."

"What?"

"There's no ID. There's … yeah. Like three hundred dollars in here in cash, and nothing else."

"No driver's license? What about a credit card?"

Val looked up. "Look. What's going on? Where's Danny?" For just a second, Carlisle's attention left the officer on the floor as her gaze flicked to Val. The man on the floor lunged up towards Carlisle, grabbing for the gun. The two went tumbling into the corridor. The shot rang out, hard in the confined space.

"Fuck." Carlisle pushed the man off her. "I wanted to know who he was."

Val stared at the two of them lying on the floor. "I think I need a beer."

Carlisle started to laugh. "You and me both. Hey…" She stopped, looking at the man lying beside her. "Outstanding. He's still breathing." She shook her gun, red splatters hitting the ground. "Why do they always go for the gun?"

"Should we get him a pillow or something?"

"A pillow?"

"Or a blanket. You know. You just shot the guy."

"Sure. Look, in about ten seconds this place will be crawling with cops. One of the guys will grab him a blanket. Probably a nice cup of coffee and a danish. Don't worry about it." Despite her words, Carlisle began moving the man's arms and legs. She looked up at Val. "Recovery position. That make you happier?"

"I guess. Detective..?"

Carlisle got to her feet. "Just call me Carlisle."

"Carlisle, am I under arrest? I don't know what's going on, and my … my girlfriend, I don't know where she is."

Carlisle sighed. "Yeah. About that—"

The lights went out. A half second later, the keening of a fire alarm started from somewhere in the building. Red emergency lighting flickered into life. Val and Carlisle eyed each other. Val tried first. "I guess this isn't a usual day for you either."

"You could say that. Where on God's green Earth is Vince?"

"Who's Vince?"

"My partner. Actually, it doesn't matter. Where's everyone else?"

"I've been in this room since I got here. I only saw this asshole." Val nudged the man on the ground with his foot. "I didn't know you cops had such strong corporate politics."

Carlisle laughed. "You know Val, you're okay. This guy here's not one of us."

"What?"

"He's not a cop."

"He's not a ... well, what's he doing here then?"

"Beats me. Look, can we cover this later? I'd like to know how someone got into the station and started in on my..." She looked at Val. "My witness."

"I'm a witness?"

"Something like that. My gut tells me you're not a murderer." Carlisle stepped a little closer to Val, looking him in the face. "Heck if I know what you are though."

"What the hell's that supposed to mean?"

The sprinklers burst into life, drenching them. The smell of stale water filled the air. Val reached up slowly, wiping his face. "This is turning into a pretty shitty day."

Carlisle stared at the water running off the barrel of her gun. "Something's really, really wrong. Come on."

"Where are we going?"

Carlisle looked at him over his shoulder as she stepped towards the door. "Anywhere but here. Maybe we'll grab Vince, and then get you that beer."

A muffled popping sound filled the air. Val cocked his head to one side. "What's that?"

Carlisle broke into a run through the door, rebounding off the wall outside and dashing down the corridor. Val poked his head after her. "Wait! What's that noise?"

Carlisle kept running for the door at the end of the corridor. "Come on!" She kicked the door open with her foot. Her gun was held in both hands, pointing into the stairwell beyond. "It's clear. Val. Let's go!"

"What's that noise?"

Carlisle looked at him. More popping filled the air, a little louder this time through the open stairwell door. "Unless I miss my guess, that's a firefight."

Val stared at her for a moment, then lurched down the corridor after her. He needed to get the hell out of this crazy place. And he needed to find out what had happened to Danny.

THE GUNFIRE WAS UNMISTAKABLE NOW. The sound was harsh and brutal, a hammering of heavy weapons. Val hadn't heard anything like it before in his life. It had become more sporadic as they'd descended through the building. He didn't want to think about the implications of that. Someone was winning, but he didn't know if it was the good guys or the bad guys.

Come to think of it, he didn't know who the good guys were. He wiped face again — the sprinklers were still bucketing water everywhere. The emergency lighting washed the color out of everything. "What's the play?"

Carlisle nodded at the closed door. "Behind that door is the muster room. We should find someone in there who knows what's going on." She checked her phone. "Still nothing. You wait here." She patted the top of the table they were hiding behind. "This won't stop anything except you being seen, so stay the fuck behind it."

"Got it." Val looked around the break room they were crouched in. A cup of coffee stood, diluted by the sprinklers, overflowing tan water onto the table.

Carlisle reached the door, gripping the door handle. Very slowly, she turned it, pushing it open a crack. Her shoulders slumped, and she slowly pushed the door open wider as she lowered her gun.

Val joined her at the door. "Holy fuck." The room was a mess, the desks in fragments, wood chunks scattered about the room. Chairs were tumbled haphazard through the room, sometimes with holes through their backs. And there were bodies. "I think I'm gonna be sick."

Carlisle walked into the room slowly, turning around to take it all in. She crouched down beside one officer. "Christ. I went to Evans' birthday drinks last week." She checked for a pulse, then tapped Evans' chest armor near the hole in the front. "They're not using guns you get from eBay."

"Why's that?"

"Chest armor'll stop a standard round, say from a pistol, right? This one's right through. I'd bet some kind of armor piercing round. Assault rifle."

"Carlisle."

She looked up from beside the downed officer. "Yeah?"

"What's going on?" Val was staring around the room. His voice cracked. "What happened to these guys?"

Carlisle sighed. She looked like she didn't even have the energy to swear. "I don't know Val. Come on. We've got to get out of here."

The door opposite from where they entered crashed open, the wood splintering as the bolt tore through the jamb. A soldier was framed in the doorway, his face obscured by a helmet. Val took in an all-black uniform under a flak vest before his eyes were drawn to the rifle. Something inside him *snarled* at the weapon, and his lips pulled back from his teeth.

The soldier dismissed Val, drawn to the gun in Carlisle's hand. Slowly, impossibly slowly he started to turn his rifle towards Carlisle.

Val barged forward, grabbing a chair with one hand. Without slowing his forward momentum he spun, whipping the chair around and tossing it at the soldier. He didn't even pause when he released it, vaulting a shattered desk between them. The chair hit the soldier in the top of his chest, knocking him clean off his feet. His rifle sprayed bullets as he fell backwards. The bullets seemed to be firing slowly, each one a distinct flash of sound and light. Val could see the shell cases peeling away from the breech of the weapon, cascading as slowly as falling blossoms.

Then Val was on him, tearing the rifle from his hands. He raised it above his head, ignoring the heat from the barrel. He swung the rifle like a club, smashing it into the soldier's helmet. The stock bent with a squeal of metal. Val raised the rifle again, smashing it down harder. The rifle twisted apart as the soldier's helmet crumpled. The man twitched, then went still.

Val dropped the rifle and stood over him, panting. He held his hands up in front of his face, turning them one way then the other. *Did I just do that?*

"Everard." Carlisle's voice was strained. "Everard, a little help."

Val turned to see Carlisle on the ground. Her gun was nowhere to be seen, but a red stain was spreading through her shirt. "Aw, shit." He bashed a broken desk aside to come stand by Carlisle. "What do I do, Carlisle?"

Carlisle beckoned Val closed. "Whatever the fuck—" She coughed. "Whatever the fuck you do, do not point a gun at these assholes."

Val stared at her, then started to chuckle. "Sure. I meant, about, you know." He gestured at the spreading stain on Carlisle's shirt. "Does it hurt?"

"Are you fucking retarded? It hurts like seven bastards. Help me up."

"Look, on my First Aid course they said not to move people who were bleeding."

Carlisle stared at him.

"Seriously. Apparently—"

"Everard."

"Yeah?"

"There's probably a hundred guys in here who want to shoot me in the face." On cue they heard another blast of gunfire. "The station's overrun. I have no idea where my partner is. Do you think I give two shits about a little extra blood at this point? Just help me out of here. Get me to a hospital or something."

"Fair enough." Val reached under Carlisle's arm, dragging her to her feet.

Carlisle hissed at the pain, swaying a little. "Everard."

"Yeah?"

"They ... these are my friends here. Good cops. I know — I *knew* these people." Her hand gripped the front of his shirt. "I —"

"It's okay." Val nodded. "I know."

"You do?"

Pack.

"Yeah. Just one thing though."

"What's that?" Carlisle pushed herself away from Val, steadying herself against a wall.

"Don't get blood on my shirt."

Carlisle tried a laugh, then coughed. "Deal."

CARLISLE LOOKED through the station's entrance. An officer was splayed backward through one of the broken double doors, glass spread out underneath him. A fallen riot shield lay beside him. Carlisle squinted into the daylight coming in. "Shit."

Val was crouched beside her. "I see them."

Two vans were pulled up at the bottom of the steps leading up to the station. The drivers — soldiers by the looks — were next to them, each facing opposite ways down the road. One of them fired at something they couldn't see, a short hammer of sound stabbing down the street. Someone screamed.

They weren't paying too much attention to the front door.

"I tell you what — where the fuck are you going?" said Carlisle.

Val was already heading towards the door. He scooped up the riot shield in one hand, then stepped over the fallen officer and into the street outside. His feet crunched on glass. The two soldiers saw him, turning their rifles towards him. Val held the riot shield in front of him and charged down the steps.

The rifles coughed into life, bullets tearing into the riot shield. Stray rounds hit the doorway. Carlisle crouched low, covering her head with her arm as splinters of wood and glass fell around her.

Val collided with the first soldier, slamming him with the riot shield. The man fell backwards, rifle scattering away. Val grabbed the front of his flak jacket with one hand, lifting the man clear off the ground and above his head. Then he dropped into a crouch, slamming the man down onto the pavement. The soldier's helmet fell free, and his eyes were wide as he clawed at Val's hand.

Val hefted the riot shield in his other hand as if considering something. Then he stood up, lifting the soldier with him, and slammed him against the ground again. The pavement cracked under the soldier, who struggled to draw breath through a collapsed lung and broken rib cage.

The other soldier had almost worked his way around into a firing line where he could see Val. He stood with his back to Carlisle's position and ejected the magazine from his weapon, the black metal rectangle falling to the ground. The soldier grabbed a fresh magazine, glancing quickly at it — the new one was painted red — before slapping it into his weapon, stepping around the front of the van to bring his rifle to bear on Val.

"Watch out!" Carlisle put all her strength into the shout. It came out almost as a whisper, the blood loss starting to take its toll.

It was enough. For just a second, the soldier was distracted at the noise behind him. The thrown riot shield caught him under the chin, crushing his throat. He staggered back, rifle firing into the sky. Val was on him in less than a heartbeat, wrenching the rifle from his hands. He swung it like a bat into the side of the soldier's head, knocking him clear off his feet. The body came to rest a few feet away.

Carlisle moved slowly down the steps. "I feel like an old woman. Say. Where do you train?"

"Train?" Val blinked at her. "I take the bus to work."

"No. Train. Like kung fu. You just took out two professional soldiers like a boss."

"I..." Val swallowed. It just seemed—

We are the Night.

—natural. "I don't know."

"You don't know. Fine." Carlisle frowned at him, then pointed with her chin at one of the vans. "I've seen a van like this before. The case I'm working."

"Really?" Val looked at the van. "How can you be sure?"

"Last time I saw it was outside that bar uptown. Elephant Blues." Carlisle scratched behind her ear. "Same make and model. It's probably still in impound."

"You always remember vans?"

"I found your hand outside that van."

Val looked at the van again. Then he looked at his hands. "My hand?"

"Yeah. It's the weirdest thing." Carlisle reached into her jacket pocket, pulling out a bloodied packet of gum. She offered it to Val.

"No thanks."

"I'm not offering you gum. Can you peel me a piece? I can't feel my arm."

"Oh." Val started unwrapping a stick of gum. "Sorry."

"It's okay. You've never been shot before."

Val stared at her. Carlisle looked back. "What?"

"What did you say?" Val offered her the stick.

Carlisle popped the gum in her mouth. "You've never been shot?"

"Yeah." Val rubbed his hand through his hair. "I can't quite..."

"What?"

"Something." Val grabbed his head with both hands. "I can't remember!"

"Everard?"

"What!"

Carlisle gestured to Val's hand. "Can I have my gum back?"

Val sighed. He looked at the crumpled packet in his hand. "Sure." He held it out.

"What can't you remember?"

"I..." Val rubbed his eyes. "I don't think you're right."

"You've been shot?"

"Yes. No. Fuck!"

"Why do you think you've been shot?"

The pistol was pointed at his face. It spat its puny fire. He slapped it aside, then grabbed—

"I remember ... *something*. Someone pointed a gun at me."

"That's not the same as being shot."

"Oh, they shot me too. I ... fuck!"

Carlisle chewed for a moment. "Tell you what."

"What?"

She gestured to the vans. "The assholes — whoever they are — that came out of these vans are going to be getting back in them. I think we should be out of here by then." Carlisle swayed. "I really need a hospital, Everard."

"You got it." Val helped Carlisle into the nearest van. "I figure we'll just borrow one of these."

Carlisle grinned, blood tinting her lips. "Least they can do..." She coughed again. "Least they can do for shooting up the station, is make a donation to the car pool." Her face turned sombre. "They killed my friends, Everard."

Val nodded. "Yeah. Let's get you out of here so they don't kill you too." He shut the door for her, then made his way into the driver's seat. Val shifted the van into gear, driving them down the street and away from the station.

THE MAN STEPPED out from behind the phone booth he'd taken shelter in. He walked slowly towards the front of the station, boots crunching on broken glass and stone chips. His head tilted slightly as he sniffed the air.

He took his hands out of his pockets to pick up the fallen riot shield. Holding it up to the light, he stared at the holes pierced through it. He stuck a finger through one, wiggling it through the other side, then he breathed out a sigh.

"Ah, yes. The one that got away. Careless." His accent was thick. He hefted the riot shield in one hand. "Still. Careless can be fixed." He let the riot shield fall to the ground.

He stood by the body of the man with the collapsed rib cage. He grabbed the front of the man's flak vest, lifting the soldier as if he weighed no more than a child. He turned the body this way and that, then leaned forward and sniffed the dead man. "Worthless. Broken." He let the body fall. "Weak."

He seemed to notice the other soldier's rifle for the first time. He lifted it and fiddled with it until the red magazine came clear. He brought this up to his face, sniffing it again, then jerked it away. "*Serebrom.*" He spat, then let the magazine fall to the ground, wiping his hands against his jacket.

"So." He squared back his shoulders. "This is how we start fixing careless." He walked up the steps to the station and stepped through the shattered doors into the darkness beyond.

CHAPTER
FIFTEEN

Elsie looked at the Ebonlake captain over her desk. The rich wood was polished, clean of usual office clutter — it gave distance between her and the captain, and his failure. Her secretary Barnes was at her right, standing straight as the creases in his suit. Men made better secretarial staff than women; they were easy to read, and free of the petty jealousies women brought to the workplace. He'd been with her through the ups and downs of the company, fifteen years now — he could be trusted. An old grandfather clock marked time against the wall, the quiet *tick-tock* sound the only noise in her office. The damn thing — she glanced at the time on her desk phone — was running slow again. She'd need to get Barnes to see to it. It was always hard to keep up with the details.

She tapped the frame of her glasses against her desk. The situation was impossible, of course. She'd been in tight situations before, but the fact that she might fail — that couldn't be allowed. Too much was at stake. She'd let the company collapse before she'd fail.

The captain broke the silence first. "Ma'am." He coughed, discomfort showing on his face. He'd tried to hide it, an experienced military man. Or perhaps just a typical man. But she could see the pain around his eyes, the slight creasing at the edges. The eyes never lied. "You asked to see me?"

Elsie looked at him a few heartbeats longer, the old habits of boardroom politics as natural as breathing to her. It was rare that a man didn't want to fill the silence with his own voice. This one was different though; he sat in his chair waiting for her response. Her respect went up a few notches — perhaps he wasn't a complete failure. Perhaps he could be used again rather than discarded. "Captain..?"

"Spencer, ma'am. Tim Spencer."

"Of course. Captain Spencer, I'm curious. I'd like to get your personal view on today's operation."

This was the test. Would he blame someone else? It would be easy to do, given the circumstances. It might even be someone else's fault. In Elsie's view, that was never important — blame was parceled out, given and traded like any commodity. But the person who could accept blame was a rare individual. Despite their flaws, people who owned failure could be made into trustworthy tools.

"Ma'am." Spencer shifted in the chair. Either he hadn't taken the edge off with some medication or his injuries were more severe than was apparent. Something internal? "For the record, I've accepted full responsibility for the mission. They were my men, acting under my command."

So. Flawed, but with future potential. She nodded at the captain. "Noted. But I'm not interested in blame right now. I want to know what happened." She shifted her chair slightly towards Barnes, leaning back a little, then made a small gesture with her glasses. "Continue."

Spencer looked at her for a few moments. "Our man Christian—"

"Please. It's better if I don't know too many..." Deniability was important, especially now. "Details."

"As you say. Our, ah, operative, reached the objective. He made the signal. The team went in to extract Volk." The captain cleared his throat. "It wasn't him."

"Your man got it wrong."

Spencer nodded. "It seemed that way to us too, ma'am. Then we lost the team."

Elsie glanced at Barnes, then back at Spencer. "The police were prepared for you?"

"No ma'am. Our man made sure of that. Their comms were down. They had no idea we were coming. As per your instructions, no officers who saw our team were left alive."

"I'm sorry, Captain Spencer. I'm not following you. You said your operative gave the signal, but Volk wasn't there..? How did you lose the team?"

"We followed the likely profile. Long odds reports on the usual channels, police or ambulance. We got a hit. Single male involved in an altercation in the downtown area. As I said, long odds — four on one."

"Four men against one? He had no help?"

"Ma'am." The captain nodded. "Police chatter suggests two women were also involved. We don't find it credible that they had a hand in what happened."

Elsie snorted. "Because they were women?"

"Because three of the men were hospitalized with injuries severe enough to suggest they'd been involved in a car accident."

"I see." Elsie watched Spencer for a few heartbeats. It never hurt to nurture a silence. "You took precautions this time?"

"Yes ma'am. We inserted Chri— excuse me. We inserted our operative according to the parameters that suggested highest success. He was posing as a police interrogations specialist. We think he felt that the contact was good. We believe he thought Volk was there."

"You think? If you lost the team — again — he may have been right."

"We're not sure, ma'am. Our operative was killed before he was able to effect the extraction. Looks like he was shot by the police." Spencer reached into the breast pocket of his jacket, wincing as he pulled out two photographs. He offered these to Barnes, who placed them on the desk in front of Elsie. "Ma'am. The color picture is a still from the interrogation video at the station. The police knew him as Valentine Everard. The second picture — the black and white — is a still from another CCTV in the station. Looks like Volk."

The first photo had a red smudge where the captain's thumb had touched it. Elsie looked at the shot, then tossed the photo back down onto the desk. The man in that photo wasn't who she wanted. But the black and white photo — yes. She'd know that face anywhere, despite the grainy image. It was Volk — no question.

"I want to make sure I've got this clear, Captain." Elsie tapped the first photo. "This was the man whom you thought you were extracting. Your operative went to get him. But Volk," and here she tapped the second photo, "Is who we're actually after. And they were both at the police station."

"Yes ma'am."

"That seems a little far fetched, Captain. What are the odds?"

Spencer coughed — again, the pain showing around the eyes. He caught his breath, then started again. *Good. He can push through when it counts.* "We believe we have a new opportunity. Ma'am."

"How so?"

"Ma'am, if your intelligence is correct—"

"My money should be good even if the intelligence is not. Humor me."

"Of course, ma'am. We believe that the man in the first photo — Mr. Everard — should now be considered a person of interest in your inquiries."

Elsie put her glasses on again, and picked up the first photo. She looked back at the captain. "Are you sure?"

"No ma'am. But I do know that my team encountered resistance from within the station, and outside on the street. Hard resistance, ma'am, but no use of firearms. Despite the lack of firearms, I believe that I'm the sole survivor of the mission."

"You're not sure?"

"Smithson is in intensive care, ma'am. He's not expected to make it."

"Please, no names." Elsie winced. The death benefit payments in the contract would be significant. "If you don't mind me asking, how did you make it out, Captain?"

"I lost consciousness. I believe I was thrown out the first floor window."

Elsie thought about the discomfort the man was showing, then nodded — a drop out a window would leave you uncomfortable. "Very well. I suggest you get together a new team."

"Ma'am?"

"Captain Spencer, you've shown an acceptance of the situation I find refreshing. Your familiarity with the — with both possibilities — will be an asset in the further acquisition of one of these ... contacts."

Spencer looked at her, nurturing his own silence, then nodded. "Of course, ma'am. I'm knocked about, but nothing that some drugs won't fix. They say it may be concussion."

Good — the man knew his limits. Elsie waved with her glasses. "Whether you're on the ground isn't really a problem. And we have medication that can help get you through. I trust you'll be sufficiently ... motivated to get back on top form."

"Ma'am. Yes ma'am. I'm very interested in returning to the field."

"Captain."

"Ma'am?"

"Captain Spencer, get together a team. We'll talk more on this soon. *We need that man.* If the virus is spreading ... well, we need to understand how." She nodded at Barnes, who escorted Spencer out of her office.

The *tick-tock* of the grandfather clock kept pace with her thoughts as she waited for Barnes to return. Captain Spencer was right — this was a rare opportunity. If her information was correct — and it was hard to be sure, the trail of evidence so faint that it needed to be taken on faith — it was exceptionally rare. The first extraction team had been sent to get a virus. The sample returned was unusable, but the team's report had confirmed a single test subject remained alive. A second team was sent to extract the survivor — *Volk*. How did one gulag prisoner survive to carry a virus that made him into a god, yet killed all the other test subjects? She wouldn't have thought the Soviets had developed such effective gene therapy.

Maybe they hadn't. So many test subjects, so many dead. There was but one survivor, who seemed to have given the virus to another. Was there a cofactor they were missing? She tapped her fingernails against her desk, considering the options.

A once in a lifetime opportunity. Well, the odds had doubled. Which was good — she had little time for faith in her life. She preferred numbers. Or people. She could manage either.

BARNES RETURNED A FEW HOURS LATER, carrying a thin manila folder. Elsie was still lost in thought and almost didn't notice him as he let himself into her office. She liked that about Barnes — he was quiet and efficient in equal measure. He came to stand at the front of her desk and cleared his throat. "Ms. Morgan. We might have an opportunity."

Elsie looked at him. "How so?"

Barnes looked down at the folder. "Ms. Morgan, the captain — Spencer — was in pretty bad shape. This made me wonder where other people in similar condition might go."

She looked at the folder. "You have something?"

"I've looked into Mr. Everard's personal details. Nothing much here that we can use. His wife's dead. No girlfriend."

"Dead wife?"

"Dead wife. She passed almost at term — the file's unclear on whether there was a complication during the pregnancy or not. As I said, no girlfriend. He's a known alcoholic, which we can infer started about the time his wife and unborn child died. He was just suspended — with full pay — by his company."

Alcoholic. Full pay. "Mr. Everard is good at his job?"

"Apparently. Something in computers." Barnes waved the folder. "However, his company is close to the Elephant Blues."

The pieces clicked. "Of course. He's been exposed."

"It's slim, but the chance is there."

"There weren't any survivors of the Blues incident."

"Not that we know of. Which means, that the police know of. The surveillance tapes were all destroyed. We don't really know for sure what happened in there."

Elsie went back to tapping her glasses on the desk. "We know that a lot of people died."

Barnes nodded. "Yes, Ms. Morgan. They were killed." Was that disapproval she heard in his voice? "Back to Mr. Everard — if he's been exposed, he might be seeking help."

Elsie looked down at the photos, still on her desk. "He doesn't look like a man who needs help. The captain's right."

"Ms. Morgan?"

"Spencer. He seemed pretty sure that there was a link here. That we had a second host. He's a man of action. Probably lives by his 'gut feeling.' You've got some more evidence that suggests that's likely."

Barnes smiled slightly. "Let's not call it 'evidence' just yet. We're playing long odds on a hunch."

"Sam, we've done this dance long enough that I trust your hunches. Still, there's one thing that doesn't work yet. If he's been exposed, our information suggests he shouldn't need a hospital. That's the point."

"He's not answering his phone at home, I can't get him on his cell, and the police don't have him in custody. There's a chance he's at the hospital. Standard protocol for a disaster situation. You take everyone in for a medical."

"Did the police note anyone matching his description?"

"No ma'am. The police report is ... disturbing." Barnes flipped through a few pages in the folder. "Ah, here. There's a record of a number of firearms-related fatalities at the station. There's also a report that many of the bodies were torn apart. Not all of them — I've run some rough numbers and it's probably just the Ebonlake team. They found a ... a *parts pile*. Like at Elephant Blues."

"God damn it!" Elsie slammed her hand down on the desk, making her phone jump. "He was *there*, Sam. Volk! He was there!" She grabbed the black and white photo off her desk. "This shows he was on there. But that—" and she waved the photo at the folder in Barnes' hand "—shows that he was *invested*."

Barnes closed the folder. "It seems likely. No reports of a disturbance at the station when other disaster relief teams arrived. If Volk was still there, he was taken to another location as well — and didn't resist." He paused. "Bearing in mind what we know of the man, it seems more likely he left the scene before the relief teams arrived."

Elsie considered the color photo, still on her desk. "We need to get a team to the hospital."

"Of course. Shall I release further funds to Ebonlake Associates?"

"Please. And Sam? Tell them we need more men."

"It'll be expensive."

"Whatever it takes. Oh, and one more thing."

"Ms. Morgan?"

"Get someone to fix the clock. It's running slow again."

Elsie sat in silence after Barnes left, staring at the photos on her desk. Finding just one had been hard, almost impossible. It cost a lot, and she was almost out of time. Still, her luck had held. It was like stumbling across a cure — a *real* cure — for cancer.

She sighed, leaning back in her leather chair. *Cancer*, she thought. *If only it hadn't been pancreatic.*

She could have fixed almost anything else.

CHAPTER
SIXTEEN

Danny looked around the ward. It was a big old Nightingale-style number, the beds laid around with curtains for whatever passed as privacy in a hospital. She hugged her arms to herself, feeling cold despite the blanket over her shoulders. The doctor had left a little while ago with a friendly smile, saying she'd be all right — that it was just shock. No signs of concussion yet, but she'd need to stay in overnight for observation.

He'd also said she wasn't allowed to go to sleep. That had to be the most annoying thing, because she was tired as hell. She was damned if she was going to lie alone in her bed, so she'd started walking the halls, stepping between the wards. Her feet had led her here, the view through the big windows more interesting than being alone. There was only one other person in the ward, a man who'd followed her with his eyes when she'd walked in. It didn't bother her; he looked beat up, like an old Buick her father had owned. That was the last thing she'd seen of her father, that Buick driving off in a spin of tires and dust.

She put her phone back in her pocket. At least her mother had been able to stay over to help out with Adalia. Having your mother live close by was great for babysitting. Mom understood how tough it was being a single mother from experience. They didn't need to talk about it, it was a quiet understanding shared between them. She'd rung off with a thanks, her mother promising to bring Adalia with her tomorrow when she came to pick her up.

That guy in the other bed was weird though — he kept staring at her. She couldn't tell if he was familiar or not — she saw too many different faces each night at the bar, and besides, his face was bruised and swollen. He'd had a rough night too.

She pulled her phone back out of her pocket to check her messages for the hundredth time. She'd tried to text Valentine, to see what had happened to him. He hadn't texted back.

She hated it when they didn't text back. It was always the ones she actually liked — he'd been so sweet, and funny with it. She knew he hadn't wanted to get involved in the fight back on the street, but her temper had taken over.

Danny just wanted to know if he was okay.

"Hey." The man's voice was creaky, horse. She jumped at the noise. "You look familiar." It was the guy who'd been staring at her.

"C'mon." Danny was still looking at her phone.

"What?"

"You can do better than that. 'Don't I know you from some-where?' That's how it usually goes."

The man tried to smile, then winced as the expression pulled at the bruising on his face. "It's not like that."

"Sure it's not." She nodded at his bed. "You're probably going to tell me I should see the other guy next."

His chuckle was weak but easy. "To be honest, I've got no idea what the other guy looks like. The police were in here, but they weren't really clear."

"I know the feeling."

"Maybe. I'm just saying, you're sitting up with a blanket, and I'm lying in a stretcher with broken bones."

Danny laughed. "No, not that. I mean, I know what you mean when you can't remember what the other guy looks like."

"Jesus." The man tried to lever himself up on one elbow, but gave up. "Look, could you help me find the — the thing." He was rummaging through the tubes and cords surround him. "I think I'm making the Gordian Knot out of this crap."

Danny walked over. "This thing?" She held up a panel attached by a wire to the bed.

"Yeah, thanks." He took it from her, and fiddled with the buttons. The bed went backwards. "Shit."

"Give it here." Danny took it back from him. "It's this one." She pressed a button with an up arrow on it, and the head end of the bed rose up, elevating the man to a seated position.

"Thanks." He gave her a smile. He'd have had a nice smile if it wasn't for the bruising. "I'm John."

"Danny."

"Good to meet you Danny. Presence."

"What?"

"That's where I know you from. Presence Unlisted. The bar. Now I'm not lying down, I remember now. From a couple nights back."

Danny looked at John a bit closer. "Oh my God. You're his friend."

John's smile faltered slightly. "Maybe. Whose friend? Does he owe you money?" He cleared his throat. "I don't want to be impolite, but you're not..." He gestured at her stomach.

She snorted. "Hell no." She patted her pocket with her phone in it. "He owes me a text though. Valentine."

John's face fell. "You don't know?"

"Know what?"

"After we saw you at the bar — well, Val and I." His voice cracked. "I haven't heard from him. That's where I got all this." He gestured at the bed. "I got ... I was knocked out. I think. The police couldn't tell me what had happened to him "

"Wait. You haven't seen him since you saw me at the bar?"

"Yeah."

"I had a, uh, a date with him this evening." Danny hugged the blanket closer to her shoulders. "He looked fine to me. Well."

"What?"

"Well." Danny shuffled her feet a little, then sat on the edge of John's bed. "You don't mind?"

"Help yourself."

"I was knocked out too."

"By Val?"

"Valentine?" Danny smiled to herself. "He wouldn't do that."

"You've only known him a couple days." John smiled again, relaxing back into the bed. "But you're right. Val couldn't hurt a fly. I've known him since school. Thank God he's okay."

"He's more than okay." She smiled again. "The doctors wouldn't tell me much, but I know he's not injured or he'd be here. With me. Us."

A janitor walked into the ward, a large man with a stained set of overalls, his hair falling in a greasy cascade to his shoulders. The name *Jimmy* was embroidered on to the overalls. He looked up at them, and then in heavily accented English said, "Sorry. I clean floor. *Momute.* A moment." They sat in silence watching as he set up a floor polisher, and began to move the machine back and forth on the ground. The hum of it was soothing, and left them to their thoughts for a while. The janitor finished with the polisher after a few minutes, and — giving them both a smile of perfect, white teeth — shuffled back out of the ward. A few moments later, the hum on the floor polisher picked up again in the corridor outside.

They sat in silence for a bit. John broke it first. "I've known him for years, you know."

"The janitor?"

John snorted. "No. Val."

"Why do you call him that?"

"Val?"

"Yes."

"Because I've known him for years."

"So?"

"He hates his name."

"Why's that?"

"It's kind of a funny story. Like I said, we've known each other for years, right? Well — since school, actually. I don't know, we were young. I was maybe ten. Val's always been smart. Not just a little smart, but a lot. He'd been bumped up a couple years at school, so there's this shrimp of a kid, he would have been eight or so." John scratched the side of his head.

"Right." Danny smiled. "So he was picked on."

"Sure. But imagine. You're the smaller kid in the class. You're the smarter kid in the class. And your name? It's *Valentine*." John looked down at his hands. "It's just not very manly, you know?"

"He doesn't mind me calling him Valentine."

John gave a crooked smile, looking at her for a few seconds, then said, "He must really like you."

It was Danny's turn to look down at her hands. She tugged the blanket close again. "So — how'd you get to know him?"

"I hate bullies." John looked towards the window. "From day one, he was picked on. Maybe one kid here, another kid there. You know what school's like, *Lord of the Flies* shit. He stood up for himself at first, but he's just this little kid, right?"

Danny nodded.

"Anyway, morning recess is on, and I come around this corner. There's one kid holding Val's bag, pulling stuff out of it. Books, his lunch, whatever's in there. There's this other kid holding Val down, just sitting on him. Poor guy couldn't do anything. Smart or not, sometimes there's just a bigger kid." John paused for a moment, then grabbed a glass of water resting on the table beside him. He took a couple of sips. "So anyway, I was a bigger kid too. And I saw this, and I just lost it. I waded in there before I knew what I was doing, decked the kid holding his bag."

"Very brave of you. Beating up a kid."

"Hey. I was a kid too. But it wasn't like that. It was just *wrong*. Two on one? That's just not fair."

"I get it now."

"What?"

"It's this. This is the pickup line, isn't it?"

John smiled at her. "I haven't got to the best bit of the story yet. So Val tells me his name — again, like I didn't know it already — and I tell him mine. And we part ways, he goes off somewhere. Probably to try and sort out his bag or something. But he sees me in class after recess. The teacher is telling us that we're going to have a quiz. A pop quiz. I'm freaking out, because I hate tests. But I really hate tests I haven't studied for. We get the tests, and — thank God — it's multiple choice. But I'm looking down the page, and it's hieroglyphs."

"You studied ancient Egyptian at school?"

"It could well have been for all I understood it. Val keeps looking over at me, I dunno, I'm just staring at my test paper. I haven't even written my name on the top of it. After about ten minutes have passed, Val just stands up, holding his nose, his head back. He's like, 'Excuse me miss! I have a bleeding nose!' Big panic, and Val pushes past my desk to go outside."

"What did the teacher do?"

"Hell if I can remember. But after he's left the room, I look down at my desk. There's his test paper there."

"His test paper?"

"Right. Except he'd written something at the top."

"What?"

"Where it said, 'Name.' He'd written John Miles. My name. And he'd filled out the whole sheet. Every answer. In just ten minutes." John sat in silence for a moment. "That was the first A+ I ever got. It wasn't real, of course. I hadn't worked for it. And Val? He got an F. For not finishing."

"I don't believe it."

"It's true!"

"No, I believe the story. I don't believe that you hadn't worked for it."

"How do you figure that?"

"Think of it from Valentine's perspective. You'd worked really, really hard for that."

"Sure, I guess. Whatever. It doesn't matter. But ever since then? We've been best friends. And no," John held up a hand, "I didn't get him to do my homework for me. It's just — we looked out for each other. I couldn't be there for every fight, and he couldn't be there for every test. But we've got each other's backs."

Danny swung her feet from the edge of the bed. "I never would have ... thank you."

"What for?"

"For the story. Now I can see why Valentine likes you too."

"I could have made the whole thing up."

"You just said you didn't!"

"You don't know that. Say. Can I ask you a question?"

"Sure." Danny tossed her hair back, stretching, then tugged the blanket close again.

"Val really went on a date with you?"

Danny looked back at him. "What's that supposed to mean?"

He gestured with an arm at her. "Seriously. Look at you. And look at Val."

She gave him a flat stare. "It's not going to work."

"What?"

"I don't even want to know the pickup line you're trying. Probably, 'be unique and different, say yes.'"

John laughed. "I've already told you. It's not like that."

"So now I'm not good enough for you?"

The smile didn't leave John's face. "Damn girl. Val's got his work cut out for him. No, I mean, you're — well. You're you. And Val. He's." John cleared his throat. "He's heavy."

"He didn't look so heavy."

"It's okay! I probably shouldn't have said anything. It's just—"

"What?"

John sighed, the smile falling away. "I wish I knew where he was. He keeps popping to mind, like a song you hear on the radio and can't get out of your head."

Danny nodded. "Me too, John. Me too." She pulled her phone out of her pocket. "Let me text him again."

CHAPTER
SEVENTEEN

"Christ, Carlisle. Stay with me." The big van roared down the street. "Carlisle. Melissa!"

Val risked another look over to the passenger seat. Blood soaked through Carlisle's jacket. Her hands had fallen away from the gunshot wound. "Carlisle."

She opened her eyes then. Her voice was faint, hard to hear over the engine. "I'm still here, Everard. You got to promise me something."

Val gripped the wheel harder. "Sure. What?"

"Try not to kill us on the way to the hospital. I," and she coughed, "don't need that on my tomb stone."

They approached the entrance to the hospital. Val stamped down on the brakes, the van squealing sharp and clear. He sawed at the wheel, swinging the vehicle around in an arc, tire smoke blowing black around them. He nailed the gas again, horns blaring around him as he cut through traffic into the entrance to the hospital. He scanned ahead, spotted the big sign touting *Emergency Room*. He lined the van up, keeping the accelerator pressed to the floor, his knuckles white against the wheel. Alarmed pedestrians turned to stare as the van roared towards the hospital entrance. He slammed on the brakes again — spongy with heat, the tires chattering against the asphalt as the van slewed to a halt. Tire and brake smoke drifted out from under the van. Val killed the engine.

"C'mon." He unbuckled Carlisle's belt. "I'll get you out." He jumped out, ducking around the front of the van to Carlisle's side. He yanked the door open, catching her as she rolled from the seat. "Hey!" He looked around for some help, and spied an orderly pushing a man in a wheelchair. "You! I need some help here!"

The orderly took in the blood staining Carlisle's jacket and ran to them. "Put her down."

Val eyed the man. "Now's not the time. We need to get her inside."

The orderly held his hands out. "Sir. If the bullet's still in here, moving her's going to—"

Val shouldered past the orderly and into the entrance to the hospital. The entryway had tired furniture around the walls, filled with the tired faces of the desperate, waiting for the bad news that would set them free. He saw a reception desk, walked up to it carrying Carlisle. She'd passed out, her head hanging loosely back against his arm. "I need a doctor."

The nurse at the counter didn't respond to Val, grabbing a phone from the desk in front of her. "Emergency at the desk. I need a doctor here stat. GSW, female, looks mid 30's. Yes."

"She's a cop."

The nurse nodded at Val, still speaking into the phone. "Possible police shooting. Of course." She placed the receiver back in the cradle, and nodded to the orderly who'd followed Val inside. He'd found a gurney from somewhere. Val laid Carlisle on the gurney, then grabbed the foot of the stretcher. "Where to?"

"Sir—" The orderly clipped the straps together over Carlisle to hold her in place.

"Stow it. You go in front, clear the way. Where?"

"The ER. Through that door." The orderly jogged ahead, Val pushing the stretcher after him.

～

VAL SAT in a chair outside the OR. They hadn't let him in, and Val hadn't wanted to let Carlisle go until a doctor had placed a calm hand on his arm and promised he would take the best care of her.

Pack.

He rubbed his face with his hand. His shirt was stained with blood—Carlisle's blood. He'd been waiting out here for a while. In the TV shows, it always seemed so quick. They didn't tell you that a person could be in surgery for hours. Hospital security had come to talk to him earlier, a fat man in a too-tight uniform. Val couldn't remember what he'd said to the man, but it'd been enough; he was left to wait outside the surgery.

He hated hospitals. Ever since Rebekah's accident—

No.

He wished he could take back time. A thousand times, he'd wanted to trade places with her. There'd been a lot of blood then too—

No.

Hospital security had talked to him then as well, and then the police. So many interviews. Endless questions. He hadn't had good answers then, and didn't have good answers now. If they hadn't been so far from a hospital. If she hadn't been early. If the car hadn't broken down. If he hadn't had those drinks—

No. This memory does not live in the sun.

What the hell?

He stood up, pacing the corridor. His thoughts didn't feel like his own. His body was changing — there was no denying it anymore. He didn't know what was going on, but it wasn't good.

Was it?

He flexed his arm, looked at the muscles in there. Days ago, his arm had been — well, there was no use hiding from the truth of it. His arm had been fat. He turned his hand over; it looked like a stranger's hand, muscled and strong. The nails were clear. He felt his belly — or where his belly used to be. Still a bit fat, but his torso was mostly up and down now, rather than bulging at the bottom.

He didn't feel tired all the time anymore.

Maybe it was good. If only he could talk to someone about it. He hadn't heard back from Doc Philips yet, but he wanted to know what the results of his tests were. Or if he could talk to John. John did this fitness stuff for a living. He'd know what was going on, whether it was normal.

If only he'd answer his phone.

Val wasn't sure how his day had ended up like this. If he was being honest, he wasn't having the best of luck. He smiled to himself — aside from his date with Danny, that is. That had been great, right up until when it wasn't. He didn't know where she was, but that man at the station—

Pack mate.

—said she'd been taken to the hospital. He stopped his pacing, then looked up and down the corridor. Getting his bearings, he headed back towards the emergency front desk. Carlisle wouldn't be going anywhere, and if Danny was here — well.

He grinned. It'd be great to see her again.

"Danny Kendrick." Val looked at the nurse behind the desk, trying to keep the frustration from his voice.

"I heard you the first time. There's no need to bring that attitude in here, young man." Her ID said *Mavis*.

"Sorry." Val gestured at his shirt. "It's been a bit of a day."

Mavis eyed his blood-soaked shirt. "What relationship do you have with Miss..?"

"Kendrick. I'm her..." Val mentally fumbled for the right word. "Friend." *Lame, Val.* He winced as soon as the word left his mouth.

"I see. Well, Mr..?"

"Everard. Valentine Everard." Val stuck out his hand. The nurse looked at it, then reached up and moved a hand sanitizer dispenser closer to Val. He held his hand out a few long seconds, then coughed, pumping the hand sanitizer a few times.

"Mr. Everard, we can't disclose patient details unless you're family."

"Sure." Val tried for a smile. "What if I was her brother?"

"Her brother friend?" Mavis didn't smile.

"You have any brothers?"

The nurse looked at him over her glasses. "Only child, Mr. Everard."

"Right. Brothers can be friends." He mentally smacked himself in the head.

She nodded. "I see. Mr. Everard? If you're her friend, or her brother, why don't you just call her? All you young people seem to have phones these days."

Val smacked himself in the head for real this time. "Of course." He reached in his pocket, pulling his phone out. Fragments of glass fell out onto the waiting room floor, the crack in the glass front showing bits of the phone's now broken electronics. He put the phone on the desk between them. Mavis leaned forward, and they both stared at the remains of the phone for a moment.

"You said you've had ... how did you put it? A bit of a day?"

Val looked up at her. "Yeah. It's really not going quite as well as I'd hoped."

Mavis looked back down at his phone. She sighed. "Mr. Everard. Perhaps you should take a seat."

"Mavis? I don't want this to come out wrong, but have you ever heard of love at first sight?"

She sighed again, taking off her glasses and letting them hang by their chain around her neck. "This isn't much of a place for romance, Mr. Everard."

Val looked around the waiting room. "Oh heck, Mavis. It wasn't here." He grabbed the pieces of his phone together. She reached under the desk, pulling out a trash can. He dropped the pieces of his phone into the can, dusting off his hands. "It was earlier this evening. There was this girl."

"I've heard that these stories start this way."

Val couldn't be sure — was that a slight smile? "She actually asked me out. Can you believe that?"

"Times aren't as old fashioned as they once were. My husband … never mind. Go on."

"It sounds corny, but we met at a bar. I thought she wanted to meet my friend. But it was me, Mavis. I took her to a steak place."

She frowned at him. "Buffet?"

He chuckled. "That's what she thought too. No. This is a little place uptown. Anyway. We were there earlier tonight. After dinner, I was walking her home. And — I guess she saw something. We got in a fight."

"Maybe it wasn't meant to be."

"Oh! Not with each other. We were…" Val gestured with his hands. "Mugged, I guess."

"You guess?"

"I don't think it was a typical mugging. Not that I've been mugged before. She came here. I was taken to the police station. To make a statement. We got separated — I came back here with one of the police. She was shot."

"You came in here with that officer?"

"Yes ma'am. I mean, I guess so. I came in with Melissa Carlisle. Ma'am."

"Don't call me ma'am. That's what I used to call my school teacher. Terrifying woman." Mavis nodded up at the single small TV in the waiting room. "I heard about that business. It's all over the news, something horrible at the police station. You probably saved that brave woman's life."

Val thought on that for a few moments. "It just needed doing. Mavis, you know those guys who never call? You don't hear from them? The old trick where you don't text for a couple days, to show you're not too keen on a girl?"

Mavis pursed her lips. "I certainly do."

"Mavis." Val placed his hands on the desk between them. "I haven't been able to call Danny. To say — to tell her. To let her know. That I'm keen on her. You know." He looked down at his feet.

Mavis flipped through a stack of boards on the desk in front of her. "Mr. Everard, you certainly wouldn't have heard it from me, but there was a young woman brought in here earlier. Head injury, I think. She was taken down that way. Emergency ward. Now," and she held up her hands to stop Val before he could interrupt, "She might not be there anymore. But if she is — you should hurry. Don't keep a lady waiting, Mr. Everard."

Val grinned at her. "Thanks, Mavis."

Mavis looked at his back as he jogged away through the large double doors leading to the emergency ward. She put her glasses back on, pulling her paperwork back in front of her, then looked back up. She smiled to herself, and got back to work.

VAL SAW the janitor pushing the floor polisher. The man's stained overalls were a signature of the trade the world over. He was a bigger guy, which was a bit unusual, but the greasy hair fit right. As Val walked down the corridor towards the janitor, he checked the rooms to the left and right for Danny. Beds filled with accidents, stories of just one too many things gone wrong. Burns, cuts, crashes, broken bones. Just not the injury he was looking for.

For just a moment, he caught the eyes of the janitor. And stopped cold. A savage twist of pain came from his left arm.

Fight.

The janitor's hands held the floor polisher immobile.

Kill!

Val's lips twisted into a snarl, his eyes bright. The janitor's lips pulled back from his teeth. The man grabbed the floor polished firmly in both hands, spun on the spot twice, and with an almost nonchalant ease hurled the heavy machine at Val. It whirred through the air, the cable playing out behind it, and caught him in the chest. Val was bowled to the ground.

Faster than he could breathe, the janitor was on him. Val took in his wild eyes, the name tag. *Jimmy? Really?* A punch caught him in the side of the head, knocking his head against the tiled floor. He heard the hard crack of breaking ceramic. He threw a punch back, knocking the man clear off him. He got to his feet, snagging the floor polisher with one hand. The overhand twist brought it up over his head and into—

The janitor rolled, the floor polisher hitting the ground. Ceramic tiles shattered, the head of the polisher breaking and spinning off. The janitor jumped at him, and they locked together. Val strained, his biceps bulging under his shirt— *fuck, he's strong!* The janitor had Val's left wrist held in his right hand — he bent his head forward, and bit down on Val's wrist. Val yelled, his grip slacking every so slightly—

They tumbled together, crashing through a wall leading into one of the wards' rooms. A woman screamed. Regular beds, curtained for privacy. Machines. People. Plaster dust floated around them, sticking in red and gray to Val's wrist. They broke apart, and Val scrambled through the dust, his fingers catching — *yes!* — something. He held the metal tray in both hands, and swung it edge-first into the janitor. The dust gave him a split second of advantage, the edge of the tray hitting the other man in the side of the head. He swung again and again, blood flecking the curtains around them.

With a hollow gong, the janitor bashed the tray out of Val's hands, reaching for his throat. He roared, the sound primal.

No man should make that sound—

The first gunshots broke out. The staccato of weapons fire sounded like — what had Carlisle said? She'd called it a *firefight*. Val stared at the janitor, holding his eyes for a few heartbeats.

"So." The man spoke thickly accented English. "*Oni prixodjat dlya vas.*" He stepped back from Val, and they circled each other in the dust. "Or for me." He ran a hand, the arm thick with muscle, through his greasy hair. "You and I. We will finish this another time, *da?*"

And then he was gone — running out of the ward.

Fight. Kill!

Val's heart was pounding in his chest. He looked around, took in the frightened faces of the people around him. Listened to the gunshots.

"Fuck. Danny!" He ran back out into the corridor, checking the rooms quickly. More faces had appeared at the entrances to the wards, but he didn't see her — *there.*

Pack mate.

Danny was crouched down behind a bed, a man standing unsteadily in front of her.

"Val?"

The voice made him do a double-take. "John? My God! John!" He stepped forward, grabbing John in a bear hug.

"Easy! Easy, tiger." John pushed him back. "I don't have any underwear on, you know? Also, my ribs hurt."

Val held him at arm's length, the grin coming easy. Then he let go, coming around the bed. Danny and Val looked at each other, then he reached down and grabbed her into a hug. "I'm so sorry." He held the back of her head. "I should have stayed with you."

She hugged him back then her hands pushed — gently — against his chest. "It's okay. Valentine. Seriously. What the hell's going on out there?"

The gunfire was louder now, and they could hear screaming too. They listened as the hammering of weapons came from the direction of the emergency waiting room.

Val held his hands out, palms forward. "Okay. I'll — shit. There's not a lot of time. Short version."

John nodded, fumbling for some crutches. "Short version's good. Where the hell are my pants?"

"I came here. From the police station. Some assholes shot up the place. There was a cop with me."

"Great. Get him—"

"Her." Danny raised an eyebrow at him, but he pretended not to see it. "Carlisle. I'm pretty sure she's one of the good guys."

"Like I said, great." John found some pants, wincing as he pulled them on. "I feel like I've been hit by a truck. Get her, and let's get out of here."

Something very loud exploded from the direction of the waiting room. The could hear the sounds of falling masonry in the brief lull. Then they heard a roar.

"What the fuck was that?" Danny's eyes were wide.

"I ... look, I don't know." Val risked sticking his head around the corner of the ward door. "It's clear. We've got to get out of here." He reached a hand towards Danny. She took it.

"Sure, help the girlfriend. Nothing for your old buddy John." John had managed to get his pants on now, hastily buttoning up his fly.

Val glanced at Danny—

Pack mate.

—then at John—

Pack.

"This is going to sound crazy, but you probably both should stay behind me."

"You Rambo now?" John was looking at the drip going into his arm. "Aw, hell. How do I get this off?"

Danny let go of Val's hand, and moved up to him. "John's right. We need a doctor to get this out."

John started to say something, and Danny grabbed the needles and yanked them out. "Fuck! Christ!" He looked at her. "What did you do that for?"

"Don't be a baby. You're not going to be able to run dragging an IV drip stand behind you."

"Guys." Val looked at them both.

Pack is all.

They both paused, looking up at him. His throat felt tight. "Guys, I'm going … I think something really bad is happening here. We need to get Carlisle."

"She's a cop." John tugged on his shirt, a small yelp escaping him as he flexed his ribs. "She can look after herself."

"Last time I saw her, she was in surgery."

John looked at him. "Fair call. So we get the cop."

"No." Val looked at him. "I'll get Carlisle. After I get the two of you out of here. To the car park, at least."

"You can't go this alone." Danny looked up at him, coming closer. "We're in this together."

Val took a deep breath, then sighed. "Okay. I'm pretty new at this, but — whatever. At least Carlisle should be able to sort out any parking tickets we have after this."

EIGHTEEN

Mavis watched as men entered the emergency room reception. She'd been behind this desk so long it seemed a vocation rather than a job. In this waiting room, she'd seen relief and despair. Anger had sat in those chairs alongside hope. And — like that nice young man, Mr. Everard — she'd seen love. Never before had she seen a group of men walk in *with guns*.

Oh, of course she'd seen guns before. Police carried guns, a part of their equipment alongside their black shoes and badges. Police held guns with caution, the way her husband — God rest his soul — handled the rat he'd found in a trap years ago. Guns, like rats, could be dangerous. These men entering now carried their guns with a practiced ease, as if they were harmless — like they were carrying a stack of towels.

Only one of them didn't carry a rifle of some kind. He seemed a little smaller, but she expected that was just because he wasn't wearing one of those ridiculous jackets. A pistol sat on his hip. She looked over the frames of her glasses at him as he came to the front of the desk. He moved stiffly; she'd seen enough injured people come and go from here to know that he was carrying some pain in through that door with him. Her intuition said he wasn't here to check in, though. He was here to check *on* something. It was the way he looked around, the tilt of his head as he took in the people seated in the waiting room. His glance never sat on any one thing for longer than a moment.

His men stood around him, but facing away, their backs to him — and to her. They stared at the people in the room, their guns held across their chests. Mavis felt a little shiver of — *heavens* — real fear. She'd felt something like that when the police had arrived at her door years ago to tell her about her husband. Still, her husband hadn't chosen a woman to be coddled, and she'd wrapped courage around her like the shawl she'd worn back then. Met the police with their bad news, her head held upright.

She gathered that courage around her again. It'd have made it easier if she'd had a shawl with her now, but some things couldn't be helped. Mavis looked over the rim of her glasses at the man and held up a board with a form attached to the front. She tried to clip a smile to her face at the same time. Mavis leaned forward to offer it to him, covering her press of the silent alarm button. It was always best to get security on to these matters as quickly as possible — nip any unpleasantness in the bud. "Hello. You'll need to fill out a form, and then take a seat. We don't allow guns in here."

"Ma'am." The man didn't look at her, and ignored the board. "We're looking for a man."

"Oh, there are rules. We can't divulge personal information—"

"Ma'am. It's my brother." He looked down at her. "A family matter. You know how it is."

The smile slipped from Mavis' face. She put down the board. "Of course, you must be terribly worried. Your brother's name is..?"

"Everard, ma'am." He pulled a photo out of his shirt pocket and held it out to her. "I've got a recent photo of him."

Everard. Why, that nice young man had just left this very room. She didn't take the photo. "I'm sure we haven't admitted anyone by that name. Do you have some ID, Mr. Everard?"

"He's my brother by marriage. You know how it is." A half smile tugged at the edge of the man's mouth. The smile didn't reach his eyes; those eyes were flat and lifeless. The last time Mavis had seen eyes like that she'd been in the reptile house at the zoo.

Mavis looked up at him. "Honey, why don't you and your ... friends take a seat. I'll see if I can find any information on your brother."

The man didn't move. He looked down at her name badge. "Mavis, is it? Mavis, can I tell you what I think?"

Mavis nodded. "Of course, dear."

"Mavis, I think you're hoping that your hospital security will get here. I really hope — for their sake, of course — that you haven't called them. My ... friends here are very efficient at what they do. Their job is to help me track down my wayward brother-in-law. That's all we want. If we can find Mr. Everard, we can go on our way. There's no need for any fuss." He smiled that dead smile at her again. "We're good at getting what we want."

She felt something cold lick at the bottom of her stomach, her heart beating hard. "I ... see. Mr...?"

"You can call me Spencer."

"Very well, Mr. Spencer. I'd love to help, but really. No one's come in here by that name."

Spencer placed the photo down on the counter, sliding it towards her nice and slow. His voice grew quiet, and he leaned in closer. "My brother in law is a resourceful man. This isn't the first time we've tried to find him. He often uses a different name. Please." He tapped the photo with his index finger, almost gently. "Take a look. A close look. A lot depends on this."

Her eyes left his face, and she adjusted her glasses — Mavis only needed them for close work — as she looked at the photo. It *did* look like that nice young man who'd been in here earlier. She didn't know what men like these would want with Mr. Everard, but it couldn't be anything good. She'd known their type ever since her first encounter with a schoolyard tyrant.

140

She took her glasses off and let them hang by their chain on her neck. "I'm sorry honey. He doesn't look familiar."

Spencer seemed about to speak before two men from hospital security walked through the administrative door behind her. "Sergeant!" One of the — Mavis could only call them *soldiers* — soldiers spun around, his rifle dropping to level at the men from hospital security. They froze, hands somewhere close to their walkie talkies.

Spencer cleared his throat. "Gentlemen. I know those walkie talkies have a panic assist on them. I'd recommend — for the sake of your friends — that you do not send any signal you might regret."

One of the security staff — Mavis remembered him as a man grown especially quiet since the death of his son; she'd taken some baking around when she'd heard — spoke up. "For the sake of our friends?"

Spencer nodded. "My men here and I are here to find a ... my brother-in-law. Once we find him, we'll be gone from here and you'll never see us again. You have my word on that. Sergeant," he said, his attention shifting to the soldier whose rifle was pointed at the guards, "Please arrange for—"

The crash from the emergency room made Mavis jump. She wasn't the only one; a sharp hammering of gunfire blasted past her into the hospital security staff. She screamed, and dropped to the floor, covering her ears. The blast had been so loud! From the ground she could see that one of the security team — well, he'd gone to join his son. It was a relief, of sorts. She could see the other security man fumbling for his walkie talkie; his hands jerked as a round of bullets hit him, spinning him backwards. Splashes of red had appeared against the white paint of the the wall behind him, as quick as you like. She rocked herself on the ground as she watched him fall. She realized she hadn't heard the second blast of gunfire, but she'd *felt* it. *That's how someone dies*, she thought. Mavis realized she was sobbing, but she couldn't hear herself. Had her eardrums burst from being so close to the gun when it went off?

She hadn't even cried when the police told her about her husband.

The administrative door opened again, then shut again as it splintered. The wood rained down around her as she crawled under the desk. Her hands fumbled through splinters on the ground, old age making her slow, her knees scraping on the fragments as she moved across the tiled floor. She was making her way towards the emergency ward. There was an exit at the end of that, if she could get to there and to a phone—

The emergency ward door slammed open. Her head swung up, took in a set of dusty coveralls — *that's not Jimmy!* — as a man ran into the room. She watched from the edge of the desk as he slammed into one of the soldiers, grabbing his rifle as the man fell backwards into his colleagues. The other soldiers were spinning to cover him, but— *My God* — he was so fast. He was already in the middle of them, using the stolen rifle as some kind of club. He flailed around him with mighty swings, knocking a soldier flat to the floor with a blow to the head. Another soldier was tossed backward into the panicking crowd in the waiting room. Spencer had cleared his pistol from his holster, the bright flashes silent as he fired again and again into the man.

Who wasn't there anymore. Spencer's fire was wild, shots hitting the walls, *My God, he's shot people in the crowd*, but not a single bullet hit on the man in Jimmy's overalls.

People in the waiting room surged for the exit to the street outside. They were met by more soldiers who were coming in, their rifles pointed into the crowd. *Please*, thought Mavis, *Please don't*.

One of the crowd tried to duck past the soldiers. That's all it took, the match flare moment where something that was merely tragic became unspeakable. Mavis covered her head with her hands as plaster cracked and crumbled from the walls around her, the gunfire leveling the room.

All those people, she thought. The tears were streaming down her face. *Who are these soldiers? They're not men, they're animals.*

A pair of boots halted her crawl across the ground. She looked up into the flat eyes of Spencer. He grabbed her arm and pulled her up in front of him, the arm around her neck holding her firm against him. She could see his other arm holding the gun out in front of them both. *How curious*, she thought. *There's something red in the bottom of that gun. They always look all-black in the movies.*

The dust was settling. She could feel Spencer's breathing, his chest heaving as he turned her this way and that as he looked around. In the middle of the room, amids the plaster dust and broken furniture, something moved. The man with Jimmy's overalls pushed a body off him, getting unsteadily to his feet. He'd been shot a couple of times, the blood leaking down the front of his overalls. He looked around him, taking in the bodies, and the remaining soldiers around him.

He tipped back his head and laughed, a deep belly laugh. Mavis heard — *my hearing's coming back!* — the happiness in it. How could he be happy in the middle of this?

Spencer spoke behind her. "Get the fuck on your knees, Volk. This one's got silver in it."

The man in Jimmy's overalls — Volk — turned to face them. He looked at Mavis, then at Spencer. "*Tak.* You hide behind old women?" He chuckled, his accent thick. "I am not surprised. *Serebrom?* It will not save you. Your fate is certain."

The soldiers were fanning out around Volk. One of them — well, Mavis thought he looked a little younger. *Wet behind the ears*, her husband would have said. He was holding something that looked like a tube with a drum attached to it with shaking hands. Volk walked slowly towards the soldier.

"Volk!" Spencer's gun tracked Volk. "Get down! I won't tell you again."

Volk looked at him over his shoulder. "I told you. Your fate is certain." With that, he spun and lunged at the younger soldier. The world exploded into light and flames as the soldier's hand spasmed on the trigger of the grenade launcher. The bullet went wide, the ceiling spitting cement and steel through the room. Chunks of shrapnel tore through the soldiers, a piece of the ceiling landing right on top of Volk.

There was silence for a moment. Spencer was lying under her. He pushed her aside, getting to his feet. "Squad! Report!"

The soldiers were getting to their feet around him. There were so few of them left. Spencer reached for the radio at his belt. "Get in here. It's not contained yet."

The growl was deep and low, like a tiger she'd heard at the zoo that time. But it sounded like it was far away, heard from a distance. It was so hard to see what was going on. Why was the room getting dark? Mavis looked down at her hands. They'd come away from her chest sticky and wet, the blood bright and such a *clean* red. The last thing that passed through her mind was, *That's odd. He said, 'Boo,' to that young man.*

CHAPTER
NINETEEN

Val pushed open the door to the emergency waiting room a sliver. He did it slowly; he remembered the police station and what could wait behind closed doors. Through the crack he could see a room completely different to the one he'd left. The room was covered in dust, plaster, and concrete. It looked like the ceiling had fallen in. A hole had been punched through to the level above them. It was charred black.

He also saw — *my God* — that the room was full of people. No — not people. Bodies.

They run in the sky now.

Val pushed the door open slowly, giving it a nudge when it jammed against the cracked and broken floor. He gestured behind to Danny and John, mouthing, "Wait here." He walked into the room, stepping through the ruins. He placed his feet carefully in amongst the rubble and — he swallowed — bodies.

A fragment of color caught his eye. He edged towards it, fishing out a piece of cloth from the concrete and steel. It looked like a piece of heavy cotton, torn. He turned it this way and that, until he could make it out. That was a sleeve, the front zipper here, and there the name tag. Embroidered and clear, it said *Jimmy*.

There wasn't a body. Just a torn and empty set of overalls.

He tossed them aside, looking further amongst the remains. Black flak jackets, rifles, bodies. He found an ammunition belt, a set of magazines in it. The buckle was twisted and broken; it must have come away from someone. There were six magazines, three of them black and three of them red. He pulled one of each out, holding the black magazine up to the light from the windows. He wasn't an expert but it they looked like ordinary bullets. He tossed it aside, and held the red magazine up. These were bullets as well, but the heads of them were a different color metal to the other bullets. Val turned the magazine left and right, fiddling with it until a bullet popped free into his hand.

He yelped in surprise, dropping it to the ground. It burned, the heat like a cigarette against his skin. He shook his hand, blowing on it, then held the red magazine up again.

"What you got there, buddy?" John walked in through the door ahead of Danny. He looked around. "Fuck me."

Danny stepped through the rubble, taking it in. "So many of them." She coughed in the dust.

Val hefted the red magazine, then tossed it through the air to John. "They've got some magazines with weird bullets. Careful. They're hot."

John worked the spring on the magazine, flicking a shell onto his hand. "Hot? Bullshit." He held out the magazine to Danny.

She took it, turning it over in her hands. "I'll be damned. These guys are well funded."

Val looked at her sideways. "What do you mean?"

"Well, that or they're just showing off. You know what these bullets are made from?"

John shook his head.

Val pulled out another red magazine then let the belt drop to the floor. He held the magazine up to his nose, but the acrid stink caused him to jerk the magazine back from his face. "God! They reek!"

John held a magazine up to his nose. "Smells like metal to me."

"Here. Try this one." Val tossed his magazine over to John.

John held it up to his nose. "Nope. Smells like metal."

"Asshole."

"No, really."

Danny spoke up. "You haven't guessed?"

Val reached down to pick up the bullet from the ground. His fingers brushed the tip, and he swore. "It's still burning hot."

Danny walked over to stand beside him. He could smell her hair and feel her closeness. She bent over, to pick up the shell—

Val grabbed her wrist. "Careful. It's burning hot. Look." He showed her his fingertips, already red. "I'm going to have a shitty blister. I hate blisters."

She put her hand on his, pulling free from his grip. Crouching down, she put her hand over the shell, then grabbed it. She stood up, holding it out to him. "See? Cold."

He held his hand out, and she dropped the bullet into his palm. He jerked his hand away, and the bullet dropped to the ground. He held his palm out, the red welt already beginning to show.

Danny grabbed his hand. "Don't be such a baby." She turned his palm to catch the light from the window. "I don't think that's a burn. Looks like allergic dermatitis."

"Aller ... what?"

"Like a chemical burn. An allergic reaction."

"Right. So?"

John picked his way through the rubble towards them. "Yeah. So? Oh — nice burn."

"Thanks." Val waved his hand again, then clenched and flexed his hand a few times. "Let's just keep moving. We've got to find Carlisle."

"It could be silver. Or aluminum," said Danny.

Val and John both looked at Danny. Val spoke first. "Silver?"

"A girl knows jewelery. These bullets. Lead's very dull, a sort of metallic gray, right?"

"I guess." John rubbed the back of his head. "I didn't do very well at chemistry."

"I did," said Val. "She's right."

Danny nodded. "This metal's lighter than lead. It's more, well, silvery. It feels too heavy for aluminum, so ... very high class."

"Wait. These guys have silver bullets?" John held his magazine up to the light to get a closer look. "Shit. What, are they hunting, werewolves or something? We should grab these and melt 'em down for cash. It'd supplement my meager gym wage."

Danny raised an eyebrow. "Gym?"

"I'm a personal trainer."

"You look like a cripple." Danny shrugged. "Maybe your clients are more understanding."

John opened and closed his mouth a couple of times. "Hey. I was mugged, remember?"

"I remember. Anyway, werewolves? What are you, a kid? This is some signature stuff. Like a gang sign." Danny looked out the window. "I'll bet it's all over the news. 'Silver murderers strike again,' or something."

"Maybe." John looked down at his chest. "Really? A cripple?"

Val stared down at the bullet on the floor, then the burn on his hand. He looked up, pointing at a doorway. "Surgery's down there. That's where I last saw Carlisle."

John looked at the door. "The door that's torn in half. That door?"

Val nodded. "Yep."

Danny started picking her way through the rubble towards the doorway. Val joined her, his hand out to steady her. She ignored it. "Easier than walking through the rocks at the beach. There are waves there." She turned to John. "You coming?"

John watched as they walked through the broken doorway, into the flickering light in hallway beyond. He looked back down at the magazine in his hand, then let it drop to the ground. "It's going to be one of those days."

CHAPTER
TWENTY

The hospital was getting quieter, the gunfire reduced to a few brief chatters of noise here and there. The lighting in the corridors was sporadic, the fluorescent tubes flickering. Val pushed open the door leading into the surgery anteroom; the sprinklers were on, covering the floor tiles in water. He looked through the water, wiping his face. His hand came away covered in wet plaster dust; Val held it up in front of his face, watching as the milky rivulets ran and started to turn clear.

He stood in the falling water, turning his face to the ceiling. It felt like rain on his skin. He arched back and—

Running after prey. The rain covers us, the fury of the storm. We call to Pack, shoulder by flank. Tooth and claw, breath steaming in the dark—

John's hand clapped him on the shoulder. "You okay?"

Val shook himself. "Sorry. Lost myself for a bit there."

John's eyes searched his face. "Well, I don't want to belabor the point, but it's fucking *raining* in here. I'm getting cold."

Danny snorted behind them. "You're such a baby."

"Hey. I'm wearing a pair of jeans and a shirt. You've got a jacket."

"You're still a baby. You want to wear my jacket? Really. I don't need it."

Val looked down the corridor. He didn't feel cold. He felt—

We the Night. We are alive.

He looked at his feet, pink water pooling by his shoes. His shirt was running clear, leaving him clean. "We need to get Carlisle. God damn, I hope they've finished sewing her up." Val walked forward, feet sloshing through the standing water. He reached the chair he'd sat in waiting for Carlisle — Christ, it had only been about a half hour ago. The surgery door was closed in front of them. He pushed it open slowly, revealing a small room with sinks against one wall, and another door leading to the surgery proper. He pushed the door all the way open, standing in a room that looked for all the world like an industrial kitchen.

John looked at the sinks. "I've always wanted to say this. 'We need to scrub in.'"

Danny looked at the sinks. "Actually, yeah. If she's in surgery in there—"

"We don't have the time." Val walked up to the door, his shoes squelching with each step. A small glass window was set into the door. Looking through, he could see a bed draped in surgical green, with — *there* — Carlisle out cold. A doctor was using some metal clamps and string. *Stitching* — she was being sewn up. There was no one else in the room. He pushed the door open.

The doctor looked up. "Hey! You can't be in here!"

Val saw the sweat beading on his forehead. "Sir. Do you remember me? I came in here with my friend a few hours ago."

The doctor continued to look at him. "Yeah. I remember you."

"We've come to get our friend and get out of here."

The doctor snorted, the fabric of his surgical mask puffing out slightly. "You and everyone else. My team's run off."

"But you're still here."

"I told you I'd take care of her. I won't leave until it's done."

Val looked at the doctor's hands which hadn't moved. "I don't want to sound ungrateful, but ... I dunno. Are you almost done?"

The doctor looked back down, resuming his stitching. "Almost. And then we need to get your friend to the recovery ward."

Val walked along the edge of the room, taking in the stocks of bandages, linen, and surgical gauze. "Are these..?"

Danny joined him. "Looks like bandages to me. We'll need to get some of these together." The doctor looked up at them, then sighed and got back to his work.

"John." Val gestured. "See if you can find a bag or something."

"A bag?"

"It doesn't need to be Gucci. It needs to hold shit. Plastic, whatever."

John looked about the room, then at the surgical setup. He walked over to a linen bag held upright in a frame. It had a big red logo, the symmetrical biohazard symbol stenciled bright and clean. "What about this one?"

The doctor paused again. "That's surgical waste."

"Right, but it's a bag."

"It's..." The doctor gave up as John upended the bag on the floor. Stained bandages and gauze fell out over the floor. He brought the bag over to where Val and Danny were sorting through the supplies on the shelf. John held it open as they tossed items inside.

"Best I could do."

"It's fine." Val turned his head to the doctor. "Hey. Do we need any medicine?"

The doctor looked over at them. "You're stealing supplies from a hospital, and you want my help? No thanks. I know your friend here is a police officer. That's why *I'm* here. I've no idea why *you're* in here though. I'd have had you thrown out if my staff were here."

John put the bag down and walked back to the doctor. He put on the John Miles megawatt smile. "Sir. I understand."

"I don't think you do—"

"No really. Look at me." He lifted his shirt up, showing the bruising along his rib cage. He winced a little, the megawatt smile dimming a few shades. "My buddy here? Came to get me just before. This place is under siege."

The doctor didn't say anything.

"No, really. That look on your face? That's what I thought too. There are soldiers and police and all kinds of shit out there. Lights are out, sprinklers are on. Your staff have run off." John paused. "Assholes. Really. But I get it. It's not what you thought you were going to get at work when you had your morning coffee, am I right?"

After a brief pause, the doctor nodded.

"I thought so. Look. I'm pretty sure that if we watched the news, this would be a disaster. There'd be police swarming in through the windows on national TV. It's just not *safe*." He gestured at Carlisle. "I don't know this chick. But a friend of a friend. That's how I roll. We're going to get her out to somewhere safe. And to do that? We're going to need a little help. Like some surgical supplies. Can you do me a solid, and help out here? We're not trying to *steal* anything. We're like you. We're trying to *save* someone."

The air conditioner shut off then, leaving the room quiet except for the steady drip of water. The doctor looked at John, then his eyes flicked to Danny, and finally to Val. "Prophylaxis."

"What?"

"You'll need to clean the wound. Antibiotics. They're on the shelf." He went back to his stitching.

"Right." John nodded at him. "Thanks."

"Look for a bottle labeled 'amoxicillin.'" The doctor didn't look up. "Don't forget tape."

Val finished stuffing the sack, then tied it off with the rope at the top. He held it towards Danny.

"Why do I get to carry the diapers?"

Val nodded at John. "Because he's a baby. You said so yourself."

Danny mumbled something.

"What?"

"You heard me."

"I really didn't."

She grabbed the bag from him. "You can imagine it then."

"I can imagine some pretty bad things." A smile tugged the edge of his mouth.

She grinned at him. "Don't get nasty. Wait until we get somewhere private."

John sighed. They both looked at him. "Seriously. Here?"

The doctor cleared his throat. They all turned to face him. "I'm done. Try not to move her. The bullet went straight through, so we didn't have to do too much. But the stitches will tear if she overdoes it." He gestured at Carlisle's unconscious body. "Normally we put them in a recovery ward to wake up easy, but ... well. She'll be out for a while yet. You probably want to grab some tramadol as well."

"Doc." John clapped the doctor on the shoulder. "You got a ride out of here?"

The doctor tugged down his mask, showing a surprisingly young face. The shadow of a tired smile cracked through for a moment. "I bike to work. I'll be fine. Take care of her."

"Great. Look, thanks." The megawatt smile cracked on full. "I mean it. And we will."

"Oh!" The doctor went to a cupboard and opened it, pulling out a small brown paper-wrapped bundle. "Her things. Sorry. We had to cut her out of her clothes. Wallet's there. Her badge, ID. And ... her gun. You better get going."

John took the bag from him, then tossed it to Val. "Thanks again, doc."

Val held the brown bag under his arm. He pushed through the door into the emergency reception with the other arm. "Now, when we get—"

"*You.*" The voice cut him off. Val stopped, John hitting him in the back with the gurney carrying Carlisle. She was still out cold. "Mr.

Everard. This is a pleasant surprise. Ah. And who are your friends? Who is that on the gurney?"

Val looked at the other man, taking in the close-cropped hair. Then he looked at the two men who were with him. Soldiers, dressed in black. "You're ... the guys. From the—"

"From the police station, yes." The man looked Val up and down. "I don't think we've been introduced. Tim Spencer. The police station was regrettable, but our orders were clear. Here? Our orders provide more," and he gestured with his fingers, "wiggle room."

Val looked around the room, taking in the bodies. His eyes noticed a figure near a wall. An older woman, her name badge still attached to her chest. *Mavis.* "This?" Val's arm took in the room around them. "'Wiggle room?'"

"It might be hard to believe, but this wasn't our doing." The man looked the two soldiers next to him, then at the bodies and debris surrounding them. "To be strictly accurate, it was Volk."

"Volk?"

Spencer continued as if Val hadn't spoken. "We thought it was Volk at the police station. Regrettable, as I said."

Danny pushed forward. "This Volk? He carries enough guns to kill this many people by himself?"

A smile tugged the edge of Spencer's mouth, never reaching his eyes. "Volk provoked us, Miss..?"

"Miss Go-Play-Hide-And-Go-Fuck-Yourself."

"Ah. Like I said, we were provoked."

Danny stared at the man. "All these people? They provoked you?"

Spencer cleared his throat. "Regrettable, but I don't want to dwell on the past. Mr. Everard, you have something we want."

Val closed his mouth. "I do?"

"Yes."

"I'm almost afraid to ask. What is it?"

"You."

"Me?"

"You. I'd like to be fairly clear. This is not a request." Spencer nodded towards them. "Squad? If Mr. Everard doesn't wish to accompany us, execute his friends."

John spoke up. "Wait. What?"

"You are?"

"This is not a game of who-the-fuck-am-I," said John. "Did you just say you were going to shoot us if Val didn't go with you?"

That false smile tugged at Spencer's mouth again. "Yes. Squad!" The soldiers raised their weapons, one each trained on John and Danny. Instinctively, Val stepped forward.

We will die before Pack is taken from us.

Spencer nodded, taking Val's step forward for assent. "Mr. Everard, I'm going to have to ask you to put these on." He tossed a set of handcuffs at Val's feet.

"You want me to put handcuffs on myself?"

"Yes. Or I can just shoot your friends. I can also ensure whoever is on that gurney never wakes up. Accidents happen in hospitals." Spencer nodded to his men. "You have five seconds. Believe me, Mr. Everard. You will be leaving with me. Whether your friends are alive or not at the end of it is completely up to you."

"Val, no—"

"You can't—"

Val held his hands out. "Aren't you afraid of hitting me? If you open fire. Don't get me wrong. I don't want anyone to get shot. But if you shoot them, won't you hit me? Maybe?"

"Five." Spencer pulled a pistol out of his holster, and ejected a black magazine from it. He slapped in a red magazine, and cocked the gun. "Four."

"You're going to shoot them with silver bullets?" Val looked at Danny. "You were right. Gangland shooting."

Spencer shook his head. "No, Mr. Everard. I'm going to shoot you with silver bullets. You're perfectly safe from the regular kind. Three."

"Christ! Why me?" Val's hand still burned from where the silver had touched him before.

"You don't know? Curious. I'm pretty certain it won't kill you outright, but it will make you more ... malleable. Two."

"Look man. I picked up one of those bullets before. I got some kind of aller ... derm..."

"Allergic dermatitis," said Danny.

"Sure. I got a burn from touching it." He held his palm out. "See?"

"Mr. Everard, do you know why I haven't pointed this gun at you yet?"

Val thought for a moment. He scanned the room, looking for a way out of this. *This is a really crazy day.* "No clue."

"I see." Spencer lifted the gun, pointing it at Val.

Val's lips pulled into a snarl. He took an involuntary step forward.

"Remember, Mr. Everard. Silver."

It burns.

Kill it. It threatens Pack.

It burns!

Val's mouth opened and closed a few times. No sound came out.

That faint smile touched Spencer's mouth again. "As I thought. We're almost out of time. One."

The creature tore through the wall to the administrative area, showering the room with plaster. Val took a step back as it shouldered its way into the room. There was something — *Christ, that's a body* — held in one massive, clawed hand. It looked at the seven humans in the room, leaned forward, and roared.

"Fire!' Spencer spun on the spot and pulled his trigger, the pistol barking back at the creature. It ducked back, holding the body up in front of it, the bullets thudding into the corpse. Spencer's pistol clicked empty. He ejected the magazine out, reaching for a fresh one. The creature pulled back and threw the body at him, knocking him clear off his feet.

Spencer's men looked at him lying on the ground tangled up in the limbs of a corpse, then at the creature. They turned their weapons from John and Danny, firing into the thing, guns hammering.

Val turned to Danny. "Go! Get Carlisle clear!"

Danny looked at him. "I—"

The creature grabbed one of the soldiers off his feet, holding him up. To the man's credit, he didn't stop firing, the bullets smacking into the thing's face and chest. It roared its defiance back at the man, slapping the rifle out of his hands. The rifle spun across the room, embedding itself into the wall above John's head. The creature grabbed one of the man's arms, and its shoulders bunched. With a bright spray, the man's arm tore free, his screaming shrill. It tossed the arm into the middle of the room, swapping the man to its other hand, then tore off his remaining arm.

The screaming stopped. The other soldier continued to fire. Spencer was shouting something that sounded like, "Red," over and over. The other soldier shouted at him, "I'm out!" and continued to fire.

Val slapped the brown paper bag on top of Carlisle's legs in the gurney. Then he placed a hand on Danny's. "Please. I'll be right behind you. I—"

She looked up at him, eyes wide. "You what?"

Pack mate.

"I—"

John came up behind them. "Look, I hate to break up the moment, but *fucking run!*" He shoved Danny ahead of him, and they started to steer the Carlisle's gurney around the rubble on the floor. "This is like a scene from fucking M*A*S*H."

Val looked back at the soldiers in the room. The creature was still holding the armless torso of the first man. It held the body up — *like a shield,* thought Val — as the other soldier continued to fire. As the man's weapon ran dry, the creature bared its teeth. *Is that thing — Christ, it's smiling.*

Val turned and watched Danny and John. They'd made it to the doorway, they'd made it clear. He looked down at his hands, holding them out in front of him as he turned them over this way and that. They were big hands, strong, and different to yesterday and the day before. He looked back at the creature, which was tearing a leg off the torso. It swapped its grip again, and tore off the other leg. As each leg came free, it tossed them into the pile of limbs in the middle of the room. Four limbs; two arms and two legs.

That is not the hunt. That is not the Night.

The moment hung, a drop of dew caught in a spiderweb.

No man deserved to die like that. Not even these guys. He looked around him, grabbing a hunk of concrete the size of a child's head from the ground. He hefted it in one hand, then threw it with all his strength at the creature.

It swung the limbless torso in one hand — *like a bat* — and swatted the rock aside. The rock crashed through a wall, a shaft of sunlight stabbing through the dust in its wake. Then it tossed the torso on top of the limbs, making a neat pile, and ran at Val.

Christ it's fast, thought Val, a moment before it snatched him off his feet. It grabbed one of Val's arms in a powerful claw, and began to pull.

CHAPTER
TWENTY-ONE

John stared around the hospital parking lot. A tow truck sat abandoned, hitched to a white van. He pushed the gurney towards the van. A quick check inside showed the keys were still in the ignition.

"There's blood all over the passenger seat," said Danny.

"Don't be such a baby."

"I'm not. I'm driving." She looked around. "Where's Val? John! Where's Val!"

John turned around. Val wasn't with them. The sound of gunfire came from inside the emergency room entrance.

"John..." Her eyes were wide.

"I know. Fuck!" He looked at the wheels of the van, snared up in the tow truck's wheel-lift. "Look, get this thing unhooked. I'll get him."

He ran back to the entrance of the emergency room. The sight in the doorway stopped him in his tracks. The creature had Val in one massive claw, and had his arm gripped in the other claw. Muscles were straining in its arms as it tried to pull him apart.

Val was pulling back.

He gripped the thing's claw with his hand, his knuckles white. The muscles in his biceps — *when the hell did Val get biceps? Those are bigger than mine!* — bulged. The creature heaved, roaring into Val's face. Slowly — almost imperceptibly — it was winning. It was starting to draw Val's arm's straight.

Val yelled back at it, jerking his arms, buying himself a little more time.

John looked around and saw a rifle on the floor. He grabbed it. It'd been a long time since he'd last been to a rifle range, but it was like riding a bike. Just point and shoot.

Empty. He fumbled through the wreckage for something, anything — *a magazine, hell, just a bullet...*

The creature roared again, then with a heave tossed Val across the room. John saw his friend go flying into a wall, bouncing off then landing heavily on the ground. The creature flexed its arms wide, roaring in challenge. The soldier who'd been doing all the shooting looked at his rifle, then tossed it aside. The creature came striding through the room towards him, smashing rubble out of its path. The man scrabbled at his belt, pulling out something small and round. The creature lifted him up in one hand, easy as if he was a rag doll, grabbing the soldier's arm with a clawed hand.

The soldier's other hand was clear. His fist opened, showing a small ring with a pin attached—

The wall was blown apart by the grenade's explosion, rubble scattering around. The creature roared in pain — *that thing's still alive?* — as it flailed with its one remaining arm. Blood leaked down its side.

John's eyes went wide as it watched the bleeding slow, then stop. The thing shuffled around, growling, as the rent in its side began to close over.

His hand felt the cool touch of metal. John risked a glance down, catching a glimpse of red through the dust. He picked up the red magazine, holding it up to the light. There were still rounds left in it. He held it under the rifle, fiddling until it slid home with a click. John's hand found the safety, shaking as he flicked it off.

The creature was using its good arm to sift through the wreckage, until it found something, lifting it — *God, it's got Val* — into the light. Val coughed, opened his eyes, and looked at the creature. They stared at each other, the creature chuffing. Val looked down at his waist, held firm, then at the creature's torn side, and finally back up into the thing's eyes.

"Hey, asshole." Val and the creature both turned to look at John. He squeezed the trigger, the gun bucking and kicking like it was trying to escape. John held the weapon down, resisting the rise of the recoil, and watched the creature twist under the fire. It dropped Val, roaring in pain, and — holding its good arm up to cover its head — ran out through the damaged wall.

John let the rifle fall to the ground, then picked his way over to Val. He held his hand out to his friend. "Hell of day."

Val grabbed the offered hand, getting to his feet. "Yeah. Hell of a day. Are—"

"They're fine. They're both fine." John looked around the destroyed reception area, wiping the sweat from his face. "Beer?"

"Best idea you've had all day." The two friends walked out of the waiting room, into the sunlight beyond.

Neither of them noticed Captain Tim Spencer pull himself from the dust.

CHAPTER
TWENTY-TWO

Elsie looked out the window, her back to the room. She ignored the men behind her with — she liked to think she'd cultivated it — a studied indifference. Someone behind her cleared his throat. It was probably Smythe; the man couldn't help himself. Barnes wouldn't have said anything, of course.

"Ms. Morgan, we'd like to discuss the, ah, significant cash sums you've been diverting to your special projects." Yes, it was Smythe. She understood the necessity of having a Chief Financial Officer. She didn't understand why he thought he had a hand in the decisions of the company.

"Special projects, Mr. Smythe?" She didn't turn around.

"Yes. Ah. There's been a significant, as I said, significant cash injection into a private third party."

"Ebonlake Associates."

"Ah. Yes." There was a pause. "So you're fully aware of this?"

Elsie turned away from the window. "There's nothing that goes on in this company that I'm not at least partially aware of, Mr. Smythe."

The man looked down at the folio in his hands, then back up. "Well, Ms. Morgan, the spend doesn't appear to be aligned—"

"Aligned?" She stepped few paces forward. Despite the boardroom table between them, Smythe took an involuntary step backwards. "As the majority shareholder, I have the good fortune to decide what the company is aligned to."

"Ah. Of course." Smythe tried on a deprecating smile, looking sideways at Sam Barnes for support. Finding none, he turned back to Elsie. "It would be much better if we adopted a good governance approach. Flew this up the flagpole with the shareholders, got some support. We might find some alternative ways to, ah, invest."

"Such as?"

"Well. Perhaps if you could tell me what, ah, Ebonlake are helping us with..?"

"I see." Elsie looked at the man's folio, then at his suit, and back to his face. "You've come in here to discuss my expenditure with a private contractor. To offer counsel?"

"Yes."

Elsie tapped her fingernails against the boardroom table in front of her. "You want to offer this counsel without knowing what they do?"

Smythe cleared his throat again. "Ah. Well ... ah. It's just that the expenditure is so significant, I couldn't help but wonder if there was a more—"

"How much is the core upgrade to your finance system projected to cost this year?" Elsie took a seat at the boardroom table. "'Core upgrade.' That's what you called it on the memo."

"Ah." Smythe opened his folio to check the figure. Elsie had no doubt he knew exactly how much it had cost. Men who looked into papers, or their phone, or any other distraction — those men were uncomfortable in their situation. They used their papers as a shield. "Here it is. Ten million dollars capital, with a reduction in operational spending of four hundred thousand per annum."

"Ten million? And how many graduates could we get per year for that, amortized over the next five years?"

"I'm sorry?"

"How many graduates, Mr. Smythe? Ten million is a significant sum. I can't help but wonder if we grabbed another floor in this building, and stacked it high," and here Elsie raised her hand above her head, "With fresh-faced graduates ... surely it would be cheaper?"

Smythe opened and closed his mouth. "Ah. Ms. Morgan, I'm not sure you fully grasp—"

"I beg your pardon?"

"It's just that ... ah. I'm certain, ah, that we could do the financials with sufficient, ah, manpower. But it wouldn't be—"

"The best way of solving the problem?" Elsie looked at the nails on her left hand. "Exactly my point."

"I'm not sure I follow."

"No, Mr. Smythe, you don't. When I give you a job, I trust that you know how to do it. That you're the subject matter expert in that area. Are you?"

"Am I..?"

"The subject matter expert. In corporate finance."

"Of course! My qualifications—"

"Yes, yes. Your qualifications are very impressive." Elsie leaned forward. "They tell me you know everything there is to know about net present value. Whether or not a core system for finance is a good one. I trust that you have done your due diligence on this 'core upgrade.' That it's the best way of solving the problem, and that we can afford it."

"Of course, Ms. Morgan—"

"I haven't finished." Smythe clapped his mouth shut. Elsie nodded. "That's your job, you see."

Smythe sat in silence a few moments. The poor man was ill-suited to this kind of conversation. The trick with keeping people off balance was to do the unexpected. With Smythe — in his comfortable office, with his spreadsheets and forecast models — anything approaching a normal human conversation was unexpected. He tried again. "My job, Ms. Morgan?"

Elsie looked away from him. "Smythe, my job is different to yours. I get to set the strategic direction of the company. I'm in charge of taking risks, promoting change, and deciding which new markets to enter into. I've been successful at building the company. Twenty years, give or take. We know where Biomne was going before I took over. It was almost bankrupt. We had the executives paying company bills with their personal credit cards. We were one month away from not making payroll." She allowed herself a small smile, then turned back to Smythe. "My job is different to yours, as I said. I set the direction. Your job … well."

"Yes, Ms. Morgan—"

She slammed her hand on the table. Smythe jumped. "You get to tell me if we can afford it!"

Smythe's eyes were wide, his lips pressed into a line. "I … I—"

"So, Mr. Smythe. Can we afford it?"

"I—"

"Pull yourself together, man. Can we afford the expense?"

Smythe looked back down to his folio, then back up. "Of course, Ms. Morgan. The company's cash flow is robust. We have significant reserves—"

"I know."

"You know?"

"As I said, there's not much that goes on here that I'm unaware of. But there's much you're not in the loop on. Developments, and strategies."

"If I was—"

"If you were, you'd pepper me with questions about the direction we were taking. If it was in the company's best interests. If there wasn't a better way." Elsie paused. "I don't take kindly to questions about my competence."

"I wasn't—"

"Of course you were. You booked this meeting to challenge expenditure with a private contracting firm. Without knowing anything about it. You saw the figure on the books, and it jumped out at you. You naturally thought that any significant expense needed to be managed. By you."

Smythe rallied, trying the deprecating smile on again. "Exactly, Ms. Morgan. Naturally, as you say."

Elsie nodded. He'd walked right into the trap. "Except only the greatest kind of idiot would think that they knew whether an expense was significant simply by the size of it. The Ebonlake account? I want you to forget about it."

"I ... forget about it?" The smile faltered, then fell away from his face.

"Mr. Smythe, the money we waste here in stationery alone dwarfs the Ebonlake account. These are the things I don't have time for. The details, the tiny incidentals. I didn't hire you to question my strategic decisions." She softened her voice slightly. "I hired you because you're brilliant. At the details. At finding out the small ins and outs. There's an army of people out there who think they can pull something over on me. But not you."

"Not me?"

"No, Mr. Smythe. Because I know how much you care. It's why you brought this to me." She watched the play of emotions across his face. Men were so delightfully transparent.

"I ... of course."

"Sam?" Barnes stepped forward. "Sam, I'd like you to fast track Mr. Smythe's proposal for the core upgrade."

"I'll need your signature." He pushed forward paper in front of her, laying a pen beside it.

She scrawled a signature at the bottom, then handed both items back to Barnes. "Thank you Sam. Mr. Smythe, the reason why I agreed to this meeting at all is because I need your help."

From desperation to salvation, that was the secret. Kick them in the balls, then offer them a way out. No drowning man resisted the thrown rope. Smythe was no different. His smile — God, it was ghastly; the man had children too, what woman could marry that? — brightened. "I'd be delighted. Anything I can do. My office is at your disposal."

Elsie nodded to Barnes. "Sam will furnish you with a list of projects. I want these scrutinized. No stone left unturned, do you understand?"

Sam, efficient as always, was already holding a memo out to Smythe. The man took it, scanning the text on it. "These are ... I mean. There's. Ah."

"Yes. They're projects of significant capital expense. Some instigated by the board."

"Ah."

"Mr. Smythe, do you understand what I'm offering you?" Smythe blinked. Elsie sighed; the man was intellectually brilliant, but as emotionally aware as a stone. "I need a hero."

"A hero, Ms. Morgan?"

"A hero. Something's going on in those projects, I can feel it. But I need numbers, Smythe — hard facts. I need to know where the money's going. I want to know if those projects are delivering. You have the full support of my office. Sam will make whatever you need available."

"I ... of course, Ms. Morgan. At once." Smythe walked towards the door, his chest puffed out with artificial importance.

After the door had closed behind him, Elsie let out a breath she hadn't known she was holding.

Sam nodded at her. "You played a good hand, ma'am."

"I played a bad hand well, Sam. You know that." She tapped the desk again. "Still, it had the desired result. Smythe will leave us alone and he will cause merry havoc amongst the VPs for the next few months. They'll be so busy hiding things and fighting each other that they'll ignore us. A word here, a touch there, and we'll have a clear run at this thing."

"I've booked in the head of HR for a meeting this afternoon."

"Perfect." Elsie looked up at Sam. "I'll need a list of staff. It doesn't matter who. People we can throw under the bus, just like the list of projects. People need to be afraid of the money drying up, and then I need them afraid of losing their jobs."

"It'll impact company performance."

Elsie leaned back in her chair. "I know. Sam, don't I know."

The silence sat, comfortable between them. Sam broke it first. "Ma'am? It's going to be worth it."

Elsie looked at him. "You can still say that? You could ... well, we've talked about it. You could lose your job over this."

"I could go to jail for this."

She allowed herself a chuckle. "Only after me, Sam. I'll be first. But I'll save you a seat on the bus."

Sam smiled at her. "How is your daughter?"

Elsie's smiled faded. "She's..."

"I'm sorry I asked."

"No, Sam, it's all right. You've earned the right." Elsie looked down at the table. "She's not good."

Sam stepped forward a pace, then stopped. "I see. I'm sorry."

"It's okay."

Sam thought for a moment. "There's one piece of good news."

"Thank God. What is it?"

"I've been looking into Mr. Everard. You remember, our second possible host."

"I remember." Elsie waved her hand. "What about him?"

"Biomne conducts blood testing through one of our subsidiaries."

"Yes. The Sanscreen acquisition. Last year, wasn't it?"

"The year before. I put out feelers through our contacts. The usual channels. A doctor, Barnaby Phillips, issued some blood work."

"Why is this significant?"

"The good Dr. Phillips is Valentine Everard's personal physician." Sam held out a piece of paper to Elsie. It was full of numbers with some charts. "The preliminary blood work."

She scanned the page. "My God. It's true. Has this gone back to the doctor?"

"Ms. Morgan ... *Elsie*." Sam sighed. "It's going to be hard to keep a lid on this. It hasn't gone back to Phillips, but we can't be sure what he knows. You know what this means."

"Can we get the blood work?"

"It's done. It's in the lab downstairs."

"What do they say?"

"Mr. Everard is an otherwise healthy man. Perfect health, I'd say. Which is odd — his results are good for someone with an alcohol problem. Exceptional, even."

"That's promising. Can we use it?"

"We've identified a retrovirus in the blood work." Sam looked down. "It matches the original sample we extracted from Russia. But it's completely inactive."

"Inactive? What do you mean?"

"It's dead." Sam rocked back on his feet. "It gives us another channel of acquisition though."

"How so?"

"We can try to clone the virus, but that path has been a bit unreliable to date." Sam turned towards the window. "I have an idea, but we'll need to talk it through with Captain Spencer. There must be some kind of cofactor involved."

"I've thought the same thing. It's why we need Volk — we need to biopsy living tissue." Elsie thought for a moment. "You want a tactical mix of Ebonlake and Sanscreen. How?"

"I've taken the liberty of calling in Captain Spencer. He's waiting outside."

"His operation is finished?"

"Finished? That's a good word for it." Sam gestured towards the door. "If I may?"

Elsie waved her hand at the door. "Of course."

Barnes opened the door, leaning out. Spencer followed him back in, walking with a limp.

"Captain Spencer."

"Ma'am." Spencer stood with his back straight. "Ma'am, our mission was unsuccessful."

"Captain, I'd like us to put that aside for the moment. Sam wants to talk something through."

Spencer's eyes shifted sideways to look at Barnes. "Of course, ma'am."

Barnes walked up to the table, leaning a hand on the back of one of the chairs. "Captain, I have an idea for a potentially lower risk scenario, but I need to talk it through with you. Military tactics are not my specialty."

"I'll help where I can. Sir."

"Excellent. Mr. Everard has a family doctor, and he recently had blood drawn. No, please don't interrupt. What I'm thinking is that we tell the doctor that the blood turned up extremely poor liver function. That should pull Mr. Everard in for a biopsy. After Mr. Everard leaves, your team moves in and extracts the, ahem, fresh sample."

Spencer thought this through for a few moments. "The plan is sound. If I can suggest just a few amendments?"

"It's your ball game."

"Sir." Spencer nodded at him, then winced and rubbed his neck.

"Rough day?"

"Sir." Spencer thought for a moment. "So far, the targets have been resilient to normal means of acquisition. Having said that, I don't think we should abandon traditional approaches just yet. In our most recent operation, I witnessed the efficacy of silver against our targets."

Elsie's breath hissed in. "Captain! Silver is—"

Spencer held up a hand. "Ma'am. It wasn't one of our team — a civilian was caught up in the live situation. As we hoped, both Everard and Volk were at the hospital. There were two companions with Mr. Everard. These two friends of his are unknown to us at this time. However, one of them managed to temporarily acquire the use of one of our weapons and silver rounds. He executed an assault against Volk, and to my eye scored a number of direct hits."

Elsie leaned forward. "Was Volk killed?"

"No ma'am. However, the silver rounds caused him considerable pain. I believe that silver is a viable suppressant method."

"Suppressant?" Barnes rubbed his chin. "How so?"

"Sir. Silver appears to work on them as ordinary bullets do on us. The use of silver weapons should be sufficient to ... I believe they can be weakened. And then captured. My recommendations are to split the team into two. One team extracts the sample. The other team — with silver rounds — acquires the target outside after he's given his sample."

Sam nodded. "It sounds robust to me. Doubles our chances." He looked to Elsie.

She turned her chair to look back out the window. "He won't be killed?"

There was a pause from Spencer. "Ma'am. No."

"You're certain of this?"

"Ma'am. No." She could hear Spencer's wheezing. Was the man motivated by more than the money now? "But I believe it's the best solution for a successful acquisition. Ma'am."

She turned her chair back around. "Captain. Your judgment hasn't been clouded in this matter?"

Spencer's expression didn't change, staring at her with those dead eyes. "No. I just want to get the job done, ma'am."

Elsie studied his face, then looked back at Barnes. "See to it."

Barnes nodded at Spencer. "Of course. Captain, if I can take this offline with you? Firm up the details? It would be most useful to get Sanscreen correctly aligned on this."

Spencer looked at him, then back to Elsie. "Ma'am. Sir. I have just one question."

Elsie nodded. "What is it?"

"How are we handling information leaks?"

"Leaks?"

"The operation is going to be in daylight. Our team will be seen. There will be witnesses."

Elsie leaned forward. "Captain. I trust to your discretion. I don't need the details. But I need silence."

The captain nodded. "I'll arrange it."

Elsie looked at the door after the two of them had left. She checked her phone, looking for her appointment with the head of HR. She still had a few hours. She could fit in a light lunch. And some essential maintenance — she hadn't had time for her facial this week. She nodded to herself — it was important to make time for the little things.

This was going to be a busy week.

CHAPTER
TWENTY-THREE

It was the smell of bacon that brought her around. It wasn't the charred smell of bacon cooked too quickly in a greasy spoon place, but the gentler smell of honeyed bacon cooked slow and steady. She wasn't ready to open her eyes yet, but the images of that bacon — served with eggs, toast, and a good strong coffee — brought her around faster than she would have wanted. It was Sunday, after all. Sundays were for sleeping in. Max always made her bacon and eggs on a Sunday.

Her eyes snapped open. It wasn't Sunday at all, and Max was gone.

Danny threw the covers off the bed, and shuffled around the small room in search of a robe. She shrugged her shoulders into one, finding some discarded underwear — *God, are these even clean?* — to bring about a semblance of decency. She looked at herself in the mirror set in the back of the door, her last minute check spot for the mornings. The marks of not enough sleep stared back at her: bleary, bloodshot eyes. Disheveled hair.

Morning glamour at its best. She held her hand up in front of her mouth and huffed twice, then wrinkled her nose. She wasn't going to be kissing anyone anytime soon. First stop out of the bedroom was the bathroom — the call of nature vying with the call for a quick gargle of Listerine.

She heard voices as she walked towards the smell of bacon. A child's voice — *Adalia*, the smile starting on her face, and a man's voice — *Valentine*. Her smile broadened. Adalia chattered at her usual rate, dominating the conversation. Whatever they were talking about was muffled by the closed door leading into the lounge-kitchen area. Danny leaned her forehead against the door, listening. It'd been a long time since she'd heard Adalia talking like that. It'd been a long time since she'd been woken by the smell of bacon. Her hand rested on the handle.

It's been a long damn time since you let a man stay here. Danny pushed the door open.

"Mommy!" Adalia's yell was accompanied by a mad rush as she darted from the chair to run full on into a hug.

Danny scooped her up. "Ugh. You're getting a bit big for this." She looked around the room, eyes going first to — *Valentine* — the kitchen, then the kitchen table. Scrap paper and felt pens covered it, artwork in various stages of completion. Lastly, she looked at the gurney, so out of place in her lounge.

Carlisle was awake, the gurney propped up so she could look at the room. She was pale, but holding a cup of coffee. A smile flitted across her face for a moment, before she took another sip of her coffee.

"Morning." Val took a step forward, then stopped. "Shit. Wait." He fumbled in the kitchen for a few moments, then walked towards her. He held something out to her, affecting a bad Eastern European accent. "How much for the little girl? I have coffee to barter."

She laughed. "You can have her. I just want the coffee." She took the cup from him, popping Adalia down, who ran back to the table. "God damn. This is good."

Adalia pointed at a jar on the bench. "Ten cents."

"For saying 'God damn?'" She took another sip. "What does Valentine get for saying 'shit?'"

"That's twenty cents now! You just said another bad word. Anyway, he's making breakfast. He said if he had to pay, I wouldn't get any bacon."

Val nodded, his back to them, as he spooned some batter into the waffle iron. "True story. It all started when I found you were out of bacon."

"We're having waffles?" Danny watched Val as he moved about the kitchen.

The back of Val's head nodded. "Yeah. I figured it was a safe option because you had a waffle iron."

"We'll get you a detective's job yet, Everard." Carlisle's voice was hoarse but steady. She looked at Danny, and held out a hand. "I'm Melissa Carlisle."

Danny walked over and shook her hand. "Danielle Kendrick. Or just Danny. How are you feeling?"

"Hungry. I insisted on the bacon." Carlisle took another sip of her coffee. "Also, I feel like I've been shot."

"You were. Shot, I mean."

"Yeah."

"Uh. Valentine said you're a cop? A police officer, I mean."

"I'm off duty. You don't have to hide your dope."

"I. I mean. That isn't." Danny looked at Adalia. "I don't keep anything like that in the house."

That weak smile surfaced again. "No shit. You don't have muffins or chocolate either. Munchies'd be hell without those."

Danny sat down on the couch. "This must seem weird to you."

Carlisle shuffled herself around in the gurney, wincing a bit. "What do you mean?"

"You didn't wake up in a hospital."

"I wasn't sure I was going to wake up at all." Carlisle nodded at Val's back. "I probably wouldn't have, if it wasn't for Everard."

Danny sipped at her coffee. It really was good. "I'm sorry for the state of the place."

Carlisle's hand reached out, covering hers. "Oh. No. You don't have anything to apologize for. You've ... well." She looked over at Adalia. "Everard said you offered your place. Last night. Thank you."

Danny sighed. "There wasn't anywhere else."

"Sure there was. Anywhere your little girl wasn't would have been okay."

"You've got kids?"

Carlisle shook her head. "No. It's not my thing."

"After yesterday ... I needed to be here, Melissa. To make sure she was okay."

"Yeah." Carlisle sipped her coffee. "What's he put in this to make it so good? It's unholy."

Val's voice came out from the kitchen. "A little of this, a little of that."

Danny smiled. "Cinnamon. Chocolate." She sipped again. "Cream."

Carlisle stared into her cup. "That seems like hard work. How do you know?"

"It's how I make it too."

Carlisle nodded. "He's quite the chef. I've been waiting for my breakfast. The smell is killing me faster than the internal bleeding."

"It ... it does smell really good."

Carlisle sat quietly for a moment. "Not too bad for a job for a wanted felon."

"I can hear you guys. I'm right here." Val carefully teased the waffle iron open, then tossed the hot waffle from hand to hand before slapping it on a stack already in the warming drawer of the oven.

"It's on the news." Carlisle nodded at the TV, the picture playing but the sound off. "Apparently I'm dead. That's ... news to me."

Danny looked Carlisle up and down. "That's very sad. Did they find the body?"

"Beats me." Carlisle rummaged among the blankets in the gurney, and pulled out a phone. "My partner's still not getting back to me."

"Your partner?"

"Vince. Lost him at the station, when…" She looked at Val's back, then at Adalia who was still coloring in her pictures. "Anyway. I haven't heard from him."

"Is that unusual?"

"Very. He's not original, but he's reliable." Carlisle thought for a moment. "I last saw him going over some evidence. Footage from a murder we're working on."

"Is that how you know Valentine? Is he, uh—"

"Everard?" Carlisle snorted. "Everard's clean. He was a person of interest for a while, but we've squared that away. Mix up at the lab."

Danny let out a breath she didn't know she was holding. "So what now?"

Carlisle looked at her. "First order of business is breakfast. We just need—"

There was a knock at the door. Val wiped his hands on his apron — *it's a secure man who wears a Little Mermaid apron*, thought Danny — and said, "That'll be John."

Danny stood up. "I'll get it."

"No, it's good. Sit. Enjoy your coffee." Val walked down the hall.

Danny sat back. "I don't often get waited on in my kitchen."

"No Mr. Kendrick?" Carlisle held up a hand. "Sorry. That was a bit forward. I'm used to asking questions. Part of the job."

"It's okay. Her father's still…" Danny looked over at Melissa, then sighed. "Her father's a waste of good oxygen."

"I've dated men like that."

"You have?"

"Yeah. All of them." They were chuckling together as Val entered in front of John.

Val looked between them and started to say something. John clapped a hand on his shoulder. "No."

"No?"

"You don't want to ask."

"I do. I really do."

"You really don't." John pushed on past — the lounge wasn't huge, a stretch to do a dinner party for six, and the gurney was two or three people's worth of real estate. He walked into the kitchen. "You finished with the waffles?"

"Yeah. In the oven." Val started rummaging through cupboards.

"The plates are over there." Danny pointed to a drawer.

"Thanks." Val grabbed out some plates, and started dishing out hot waffles and bacon. "Did you get me a new phone?"

John tossed a small white box at him. "Next time, we're using *your* credit card to buy a new phone. Seriously, how do you break them so often?"

"It wasn't my fault. Did you get the syrup?"

"Do bears do it in the woods? Of course I got the syrup." John worked beside his friend, pouring a generous dose of syrup on each stack. "Everyone's getting syrup."

Adalia jumped out of her chair, holding up a doll. "I need extra syrup. For Madeline."

Val crouched down to look her in the eye. "Madeline?" He looked across at Danny, who nodded. "I guess that's fair enough. Extra syrup for Adalia and Maddy."

"It's Madeline!"

Carlisle looked at the plates of food. "I hope no one's a diabetic."

CHAPTER
TWENTY-FOUR

They'd eaten breakfast seated on the floor, plates on their laps — except for Carlisle, who'd had *breakfast in bed*.

Val held up his phone. "The question is whether I should go."

John scooped a final stray line of syrup from his plate with a finger. "Those waffles were damn fine. I can go to my death happy now."

Val snorted. "I don't think a medical test is quite like going to your death."

Carlisle looked over at Val. "The message was from your doctor? You're sure?"

"I've known Barny for years." Val shrugged. "Sounded like Barny. Sure I'm sure."

Danny leaned back, smelling her coffee. It got *better* on the second cup. "What did he say, exactly?"

"Something about poor liver function. They need to run some more tests."

"So don't go."

Val looked down at his phone. "I need to know."

Carlisle cleared her throat. "I'm with Danielle."

"It's just Danny."

"I'm with Danny. Don't go. Doesn't feel right."

Val spun his phone in his hands. "Look, guys. We need more information. And ... well. That asshole at the hospital seemed to want me for something. I'm not a great believer in coincidence."

Carlisle snorted. "Exactly. It's no coincidence that they want you in for tests."

"This is different."

Carlisle stared at him again. "Walk me through it."

"Okay." Val checked points off on his fingers. "One. My doctor is not involved in a grand conspiracy. He played golf with my Dad on Sundays. Two. I need to know what's going on with me."

Danny put a hand on his arm. "Like what?"

Val tapped his phone's screen, then held it up beside his face. The photo on it was him, but much fatter. "Like this."

"So. You lost some weight."

"That photo was taken last week."

The room fell quiet, the only sound the light scratching of Adalia's pens against paper. John spoke up. "It's true. He's lost a heap of weight."

"I bought new clothes."

"He bought new clothes." John nodded.

"That's not all." Val looked down at his hands. "There's ... other stuff."

Danny searched his face. "Like what?"

He stood up, walking to the window. "Your neighbors are having a fight. About the rent."

"What?"

"I can hear them."

"The boundary wall is soundproofed." Danny coughed. "You're imagining it."

"Her name's Jasmine. He's an asshole."

"You're not imagining it then." Danny frowned.

"There's more." Val turned to face them. He started to tap a rhythm with his finger against his thigh. "There's this."

John looked at him. "White men can't dance?"

Val ignored him, finger still tapping. "Can you guess?"

Carlisle spoke up. "I can. It's not possible."

Val's finger kept tapping, speeding up a little now.

"Christ. Stop it." Carlisle watched his finger.

"What is it?" Danny looked at Val, then at Carlisle. "I don't get it."

Carlisle turned away. "It's my pulse." She took her hand away from her wrist. "Perfect time. How—"

"I can hear it."

"Bullshit." John put his cup down on the table.

"Ten cents!" Adalia piped up from the table.

John felt around in his pocket for some change, then dropped a coin into the jar on the bench. "It's racketeering, is what it is."

Val stood up. "Guys. Look. I. Well." He put his hands in his pockets. "I haven't been drunk in days."

John looked at him. "You on the program? Nice work buddy! When—"

"No, John." Val's smile was sad. He walked towards the kitchen. "I've tried to drink. Last time, when I took Danny out. It doesn't do anything. But there's one other thing."

They watched him as he fiddled about in the kitchen, pulling open the waffle iron. "I've left it on. For a second helping. Anyone want more waffles?"

Carlisle shook her head. Danny didn't move. John said, "I could go another round."

Val popped a dollop of butter on the plate of the waffle iron. It hissed and sizzled as he moved it about the plate, coating it. He ladled some mixture into the waffle iron. The smell of cooking waffle started to waft into the room.

After a minute, Danny spoke up. "I don't get it. What's the other thing? You can make waffles?"

Val kept looking at the waffle iron, then popped the cooked waffle out of the iron and onto a plate. "That's the thing. I discovered it this morning." He smiled that same sad smile again as he put some more butter on the waffle iron, then turned to Adalia. "Could you head to your room for just a sec and see if you can find Maddy a friend?"

"It's Madeline!"

Val tousled her head, then sent her off with a pat on the back. "She probably shouldn't be here for this." He turned back to the waffle iron.

Danny looked after her daughter, then back to Val. "What? She shouldn't be here for what?"

He took a few deep breaths. "This." He put his hand in the waffle iron, shutting the lid. The searing sound was audible above his hissed breath.

John leapt out of his seat, running to the kitchen. "Motherfuck-er!" He wrenched open the iron, tossing it aside, and flipping on the faucet's cold tap. He reached for Val's hand.

Val held it up and away from him, towards the rest of them in the room. The burn marks were clear, the hash pattern of the iron stark and red against his palm, blisters already forming. They watched as the marks faded away, leaving his hand smooth and clear.

John stared at him for a few moments, then slowly turned off the faucet. "I'm not hungry anymore."

Val flexed his hand. "You sure? It's good as new."

Carlisle whistled low. "This is an, ah, interesting development."

"You're telling me." Val pulled out his phone. "So yeah. I think I need to go see Barny."

Adalia came back in carrying a small sheep. "I've brought Shawn."

Val smiled at her. She didn't seem to notice the strain around his eyes as she sat back down at the table, putting Shawn next to Madeline.

John leaned against the kitchen bench. "At least take one of us with you."

"What for?"

John stared at him. "To help."

"I don't think Barny needs help doing more tests. He's got nurses and shit for that."

"Ten cents!"

"Christ." Val pulled out his wallet, dropping some notes into the swear jar. "There. I'm in credit now."

"He's right." Carlisle shifted in the gurney. "Everyone needs backup."

Val's finger hovered over the dial button. "You're going to come? You've been shot."

"I'll go." Danny stood up from the floor.

Pack mate.

"Absolutely not." Val cleared his throat. "I couldn't—"

"Couldn't what?" Danny rested her hands on her hips.

John held up a hand. "I think a team approach is best."

"Exactly. I'm on the team."

John smiled. "Look, we've got a bed case here—"

"I'm a science major. Just because I've got breasts I'm the nurse?"

"I don't need a nurse." Carlisle started to get out of the gurney, then fell back. "I wouldn't mind a hand up. I need to take a leak."

John's megawatt smile came out. "It's not like that. What I was thinking is we split up."

Val looked at him. "Where are you going with this? I don't want to put Danny in danger."

"Relax. Work with me here. The way I see it is, there's some weird shit going down. We've got a missing cop," and he nodded to Carlisle, "your partner, right?"

Carlisle nodded back.

"Right. Missing cop, weird shit number one. Number two, the police station was busted up by soldiers. I don't know about you guys, but I've never heard of that one before."

"Terminator." Danny was looking out the window.

"What?"

"Terminator. Arnie movie. You must have seen it."

"Sure. I've seen it. I didn't see any freakin' robots though."

"Ten cents!"

"I said 'freakin'," not 'fucking.'"

"Ten cents!"

"Oh for f... fine." Coins clinked into the swear jar.

Val spoke up. "Three, they need a sample, when I feel the best I've felt in years."

"That's medicine buddy, not weird. But we'll include it. Right?" John patted Val on the arm. "Chin up. Number four, you can heal major burns and hear heartbeats. And that's not the weirdest thing."

"It's not?"

"No. Five, the soldiers have silver bullets. Right? Silver," said John, "bullets."

"Okay, I'd agree that's weird, but not the weirdest thing. Me hearing heartbeats is pretty weird."

"I haven't got to the weirdest thing."

"What is it?"

John scowled at him. "No showmanship, that's your problem. Okay. Six. There's a freakin' werewolf out there."

"Don't be silly. Werewolves aren't real." Adalia looked up from her coloring to Danny. "Are they, Mommy?"

The silence sat heavy in amongst them, like another person in a chair. Adalia looked between them all. "Werewolves aren't real."

Danny scooped her into a hug. "Of course not, honey." She kissed the top of Adalia's head.

Carlisle sighed. "Labels aren't important, but I know what I saw."

"What? You were unconscious when we pulled you out of the hospital."

"There was a werewolf at the hospital?" Carlisle sat up.

"Wait. What? Yes. Where did you think we were talking about?" John looked around the room at the rest of them.

"I." Carlisle looked down at the blankets on the gurney. "Seriously, I need to take a piss."

Val stepped forward. "Where, Melissa?"

Carlisle sighed. "Vince — my partner — was showing me some surveillance footage. From across from where you guys got mugged."

"We didn't get mugged."

John nodded. "Yeah. Yeah we did."

"I'd remember something—"

It spat its puny fire at his face. He batted it aside, reaching for —

Val sat down slowly on the kitchen floor.

John crouched down. "You okay, man?"

"I ... when was this?" Val looked up from the floor.

"Couple nights ago. Remember, I was in the hospital? You came and got us out." John gestured at Danny. "You met *her*." He wiggled his eyebrows.

"I don't remember."

"Hey." Danny spoke up. "You don't remember meeting me?"

"We'd been drinking pretty solid." John smiled. "See? It's not all bad. The booze still gets you. It's just got to be enough."

"It's not that. I remember Danny. How could I forget?" A smile darted across his face, then was gone. "That was ... it was the morning after that I went to get the blood work done." Val thought for a moment. "I think some of my teeth came out."

"Definitely mugged." John helped him up.

"I don't think—"

Danny broke in. "It's all fine that you don't remember meeting me—"

"I remember!"

"But I want to know." Danny turned to Carlisle. "What was on the tapes?"

Carlisle shrugged. "I don't know."

"You don't know?"

186

"Something big. Fast. I remember that. Tore a bunch of guys apart." Carlisle looked at the window. "I really need to take a piss."

Danny held out a hand, helping her up. "Bathroom's down the hall. Somewhere here ... ah, here it is. The hospital gave us a bag of stuff. Bandages." She handed a bag with the biohazard emblem on the side to Carlisle.

Carlisle took it, looking at the emblem. "They gave it to you?"

"It's probably best not to ask. Bathroom's the first door, toilet's the second."

John looked after Carlisle. "She's saying, uh. She's saying that where we were mugged, that thing was there? And we survived?"

"The thing at the hospital?" Val rubbed his left wrist. "No wonder I got some teeth knocked loose."

"You did okay in there."

"I didn't really. You were there. You shot it." Val looked at John. "You've always been there."

"Don't get all mushy on me. Anyway, weird shit number six, am I right?"

"Okay, six weird things."

Danny joined them in the kitchen, swirling the coffee pot. They both nodded, and she rummaged for more cups. "So. What do we do?"

John leaned back. "Like I said, team approach. First, we need to get Adalia somewhere. They found you pretty quick at the station, Val. God knows when they'll next come for you, but..." He broke off.

Danny nodded. "Okay. Thanks. Yeah." She handed them each a cup. "I've got a friend."

"Nice." John raised his eyebrows. "You got a number?"

She punched him in the arm. "We're like sisters."

"Even better."

Danny sighed. "Adalia can stay there a few days."

"Great." John broke out the megawatt smile again. "We'll have this nailed in a few days. Second. The cop."

Pack.

187

Val looked at him. "Carlisle? What about her?"

"She stays here. Mans the base."

"The base?"

"Yeah. Here."

"My house is not a base." Danny looked around. "It might not be much, but—"

"The base. Carlisle mans the base." John stared at them both. "You're like a couple of kids. Third. The tests. Val goes in. I'll wait around the corner, in a car. If anything cocks up, if we get to weird shit number seven, Val runs on out. I'll have the engine running. We'll jet."

Val sipped his coffee, looking between Danny and John.

Pack is the reason for living.

"I—"

"Val. Look." John set his cup down. "When have I ever let you down?"

Val thought for a moment. "There was that time with Lucy Smith—"

"Besides that."

"Never."

"Who's Lucy Smith?" Danny looked at John.

"I'll tell you later. Like I said, I've never let you down. The plan is solid. It'll work."

"What plan?" Carlisle moved back in, slowly lowering herself into a chair.

"The one that means you don't need to leave that chair. Except to take a piss."

"Excellent. Let's do it."

Val nodded. It was a good plan.

TWENTY-FIVE

Val looked across at Barny. "So, doc. You need to run more tests."

Phillips smiled at him. "It just procedure, Val. Your sample showed something unusual."

"So you think I've got something?" Val leaned forward a little. "Like what?"

"Oh hell, Val." Phillips rubbed his chin. "I didn't mean that. No, if I had to judge, I'd say you were doing great. Say, why don't you hop on the scales here for me."

Val stood up, walking to the scales in the corner. They were an old style with sliding weights at the top. He climbed on the weight plate and Phillips fiddled with the sliders.

"Hm." Phillips rubbed his chin.

"What is it?" Val looked at the weight scales, then back at Phillips.

"I didn't say it was anything. I said, 'Hm.'" Phillips walked back over to his desk and poked at his computer keyboard a few times. "Damn thing. Here it is ... say, Val. Can you read that weight out to me?"

"Do I have to? You know I hate this bit."

Phillips looked over his glasses at Val. "Humor an old man."

Val sighed. "Uh. Looks about, what's this, two hundred, that's a ten, so two ten. Wait. What?"

Phillips beamed at him. "You've lost weight."

"That's more than losing weight. That's amputation. What was I before?"

"Three ten."

"Three hundred and ten?"

"And change."

Val looked down at the scales again. "These aren't busted?"

"Janice Henson was in here before you. They're not busted."

"Who's Janice Henson?"

"Let's just say I diagnosed her last week with diabetes."

"Ah." Val thought for a moment. "I've lost a hundred pounds?"

"And change, as I said. And ... I'll be honest here. I was pretty sure I was going to have the same conversation with you as I had with Janice."

"What conversation?"

"Stop eating or you'll die."

"Christ, doc." Val cleared his throat. "But ... how is this possible? I mean, I've bought some new clothes, but—"

Phillips gestured at a chair. "Take a seat, Val."

"Okay." Val sat, shifting around in the chair to make himself comfortable.

"There's a couple of possibilities that I can think of for weight loss, but not of that magnitude. The honest truth is none of them are really good. We'll need to get a biopsy. If you're okay with it. And then, well, maybe a scan."

"What kind of a scan?"

"Let's cross that bridge when we get to it." Phillips stood, arching his back as he looked out the window. "Damn back."

"What's wrong with your back?"

"There's nothing wrong with it." Phillips looked down at Val. "I'm old, Val. That's all."

"Sorry."

"Hell." Phillips sighed. "No need to be sorry. It's just age."

"So ... what's the bad news?"

"Could be nothing." Phillips looked out the window again. "Could be alcoholic liver disease."

"That sounds bad."

"Could be worse."

"What? How?"

"Could be liver cancer too."

"Cancer? Christ."

Phillips chuckled. "I'm just messing with you, Val. It could be cancer. You kids, you always look up a diagnosis on the Google."

"It's just Google."

"What?"

"It's not, 'the Google.' It's just Google. There's no, 'the.'"

"Okay. You look up a diagnosis on ... Google. Come in here with a cold, convinced it's cancer."

"Is it cancer?"

"That's why we want to do a biopsy."

"Because it could be cancer?"

"Because we don't know."

"Oh. Right." Val stood up. "Let's get it done then."

"It's going to hurt."

"Can you use some anesthetic?"

"Everyone hates biopsies, Val. Five year olds cry about it."

Val stared at Phillips. "When did you get to be so cranky?"

"When I realized I was getting old. Hop up on your back on the bed."

Val watched as Phillips moved around the small room, grabbing a few shining steel instruments. He lifted Val's shirt. "Jesus, Val. Have you been working out?"

Val looked at his stomach. "A little."

"Right. 'A little,' he says, and wonders why he's been losing weight."

"No, really. Only a little."

"Sure. How's that feel?"

"What? Christ." Val saw that a needle was in his upper abdomen. "You're some kind of medical stealth ninja."

"Age is one thing. Experience is the flip side. That should numb the area so we can sidle up to the liver, stabbing it before the patient notices." Phillips picked up a scalpel.

Val looked away. "Stabbing? I want to hear less about stabbing."

"Don't be so squeamish. Are you a child or something?"

Val looked back in time to see Phillips hold up another needle, and he looked away before he could see it slide home. After a moment, Phillips started write a label with neat handwriting. "I've always wondered about that."

Phillips looked up at him, his speech unclear because of the pen cap in his mouth. "Wha?"

"You've got neat handwriting." Val drummed his fingers against the bed. "You're not a real doctor, are you?"

Phillips removed the cap from his mouth. "You're onto my secret, at last. Okay, we're done. I just need to find some tape. Here, hold this." He put a piece of gauze over the biopsy site.

Val held the gauze as Phillips rummaged in a drawer. They both looked up as crash came from outside. They heard a woman's raised voice saying, "You can't go in there!"

The door slammed open. Val and Phillips stared at the man at the door. Val took in the—

Enemy.

—black combat vest, helmet, and rifle. The rifle was leveled at Val's chest.

It must die.

He'd jumped from the bed before a heartbeat had passed, stepping forward to grab the back of a chair as a handle. He spun in

192

place, dropping forward into a crouch as he let the chair fly with a heave. The soldier's gun went off—

Useless, dead meat. It wastes its chance to live.

—the bullets shredding the wall behind Val. If he'd still been standing—

Prey is always slower.

—he'd have been shot. The chair hit the soldier in the chest, splintering with the force of the impact. The man pinwheeled back from the doorway, the plaster wall caving behind him as he fell into it. Val was through the doorway and on the soldier before—

The dead gather all around us. They are many. We have no Pack.

—he could get to his feet. Val grabbed the front of the soldier's vest, hauling him up and spinning him around to face the small waiting room. He crouched, using the man as a shield; bullets hit the man from the other soldiers in the waiting room, his body tugging in Val's grip as each round hit. Val could smell the cordite, so strong he could taste it, and the sound of the guns was sharp and clear in the closed space. He risked a glance around the body, taking in the over-turned reception desk and the men in the waiting room. He dropped the lifeless soldier and ducked back through into Phillips' room.

Strike the deer in the flank. By tooth and claw.

"Doc! Stay down!"

Phillips looked at him, his mouth open. "I—"

"Down!" Val grabbed him by the shoulders, pushing him —

Friend. Wise one. Guardian.

—gently to the ground. He swept an arm across Phillips' desk, scattering notes, books, and the computer to the ground. Then he grabbed the desk in both hands, the muscles of his arms and shoulders bunching under his shirt. Leaning back, Val turned around and—

Strength. By rock and stone and the ground that shakes.

—heaved the desk at the wall. It punched a hole through the wall, lodging half-in, half-out of Phillips' office. Val took two steps towards it and — keeping his momentum up — put a foot against it, kicking it out and through the wall. Sun broke through, catching dusty motes as they drifted through the air. He turned to Phillips.

"Doc. You've got to run."

"I … of course." Phillips got up, and started to walk towards the door to his office.

Val grabbed the back of his shirt. "Not that way, Doc. Through the wall." He nodded at the hole in the building.

"What about—"

"I'll get them." Val guided him to the hole in the wall. "Just go. Get away."

"Where will I go?" Phillips looked lost. "What—"

There was a scream from the waiting room, cut off by a blast of gunfire.

Val looked at him. "There's no time. Call the police."

"Of course." Phillips started through the hole in the wall. "What about you, Valentine? What about you?"

Val flexed his hands in front of him. He could see the feet of the dead man in the corridor outside Phillips' office. He looked at the hole in the wall, and the sunlight streaming in. A smile lit up his face. "You know? I don't think it's cancer, doc. I think I'll be fine."

He waited until Phillips was clear, then turned back to the doorway. He took in the crack in the wall opposite. This would need to be done quickly; Val didn't want to get shot. Not today, not ever, and not—

Burning.

—by anything that fired silver bullets. He backed up as far as he could against the exterior wall of the building, facing the door into the corridor, then got into a sprinters' crouch. He took two deep breaths, then launched himself, his legs pumping.

On his first step, the noise from outside the room seemed to fade away. He could hear a gun firing, but it seemed to come from a long distance away. On his second step, he could only hear the sound of his heart and the puff of his breath. On the third step, he was in the corridor, and he risked a glance into the waiting room. He saw the

194

flaming blossom of a rifle firing, felt the scorpion's kiss of the bullet as it tagged his leg. Then he was through, the wall tearing apart as he fell into the room behind it. His eyes scanned quickly, taking in the basin, the stalls — it was a toilet. His leg felt like it was on fire, the blood flowing freely from the nick in his calf, but there was no time for that now.

Val reached for the door handle, then paused, looking up into the mirror hanging over the basin. Lambent golden eyes stared back at him, no white surrounding the iris. *What the hell?*

Bullet holes popped chunks of wood and plaster into the room as they stitched a line across the wall. He dropped to the ground, hands over his head. The rain of bullets seemed to go on forever. Val yelled, the noise tearing out of him as he pulled himself across the tiled floor.

Be still.

He paused, looking around him on the floor. Val saw the pipe from the sink leading into the ground. It had a straight metal section, connecting from the floor to the S-bend below the sink. Two large rings joined the straight section. Val grabbed the first of these rings with one hand and twisted. It released easily, spinning freely. A few drops of water came out as he unclamped it, then he unlocked the second ring.

The firing had stopped. Val got to his feet, pushing himself up by the fingertips of one hand. He hefted the drain pipe; Val could see his reflection, warped in the curved stainless steel surface. He made no noise as he came to stand by the door. It would open inward, giving him some visible cover from the men outside. Val could hear their—

The prey stumbles about, making enough noise for a whole herd.

—footsteps as they walked towards the door. The steps were slow, almost methodical in their approach. The handle on the door turned slowly, creaking a little. The door opened. Val could hear the breathing of the man on the other side, rough and ragged, the heart—

Wet, salty. Bloody.

—pounding a fevered pulse. He saw the tip of the rifle as it came into view around the edge of the door. Val reached out, grabbing the rifle and yanking it into the room. The man came with it; Val held the muzzle away as the man's reaction fire blasted into the room. He kicked with one leg, slamming the door shut, and then swung up and under the man's chin with the pipe. The man dropped to the ground, boneless. Val tossed the rifle aside, the stench of the—

We must not touch it.

—silver filling his nose. A few more rounds punched through the wood of the door. He waited a few moments then stepped in front of the door. The handle started to turn again. Val took a step back, then launched a kick into the door. It splintered against the frame and pulled free, weakened by the holes from the bullets. He threw the pipe through the gap he'd made, catching one man in the chest. Dropping his shoulder, he rammed through the gap.

There were three of them, the one he'd hit with the pipe still recovering. The other two opened fire —

Move.

—but he stepped forward, bringing himself behind the man he'd hit with the pipe. *How did I know how to step like that?* But there was no time to think as the guns tracked his movements, but slowly, so slowly.

Faster.

His punch hit the man in the spine, and he heard a crack. The man started to fall—

Through the gap.

—and he'd moved on already, hands brushing the barrel of the rifle aside as he came face to face with another soldier. He dragged the man forward, delivering a head butt into his helmet. The man's visor cracked as he stumbled back, grip slackening on the rifle—

Make him toothless.

—as Val tore it from his hands, throwing it into the remaining soldier. The thrown weapon knocked the other soldier's rifle aside and it spun away. He turned back on the man he'd head butted, twisting him around and lifting him above his head. The man screamed—

Finish the hunt.

—before Val dropped into a one-kneed crouch, bringing the man's back down on his raised knee with a crack. Val was off again and moving, his shoulder coming up and into the stomach of the final man. He could feel a rib give as the soldier's rifle fired — *so loud!* — next to his ear. The soldier fell back to the ground and Val was on him, his fists slamming down into the helmet, knocking it again and again into the ground.

Val could feel his heart pound. He got up, looking around him. The sound of sirens called in the distance. *Time to go, Val* — he walked through the waiting room, eyes taking in the bodies scattered about, then he stopped, leaning down. A young girl was half underneath a chair, blood soaking through her shirt. He thought it had a Disney Cinderella on it, but he couldn't really tell. Not anymore. He could hear her heartbeat, fluttering. She looked at him with big blue eyes.

Weak.

He pulled the chair off the girl. One of her arms was stretched out towards a woman's body, face down on the floor. He brushed a strand of hair from the girl's eyes. "Hey, sweetie."

Her eyes were wide as she tried to gulp for air. "Is it over?"

She is not Pack. We must go.

He started to stand.

We must go.

"I will not go!" He fought it, kneeling back down next to her. "It's over. I promise."

The girl tried to move, then stopped. "Who were you talking to?"

He shook his head. "No one."

"I talk to myself too sometimes." Her eyes looked up at him. "It's my birthday."

"Thats..." Val's voice cracked. "I'm Val."

She is not Pack!

He tried again. "How old are you? Today, I mean. It's your birthday."

"Six." She coughed. "My name's Amy. I couldn't have my party because I'm sick. Mommy said so."

"That's too bad, Amy. Did you get any presents?"

She tried to nod, reaching around on the floor. She held up a mangled My Little Pony. "Her name's Prancer. I think she's broken."

"That's a lovely name." Val stroked the girl's head. The sirens were louder. "We'll get Prancer fixed up, don't worry. She'll be better in no time. Did you have cake?"

"Not yet. Mommy said," and she coughed again, "that I would have cake this afternoon. She and Daddy would sing me, 'Happy Birthday.'"

Val nodded. "No one's sung you, 'Happy Birthday?'"

"No."

"Would you like me to—"

This will not leave a memory that lives in the sun. It will burn forever inside you, and you will never be rid of it. We must leave.

"—sing you, '*Happy birthday?*' I'm not sure ... I'm not sure I remember the words, but I can try if you like."

She nodded. Val sank onto his haunches and started to sing. His voice was flat and untrained, cracked in all the wrong places. Val could hear her heartbeat begin to stumble, and his voice broke a little. He'd heard a second verse somewhere, someone had thrown in at an party for him, and he started in on that, trying to keep singing.

Until the end, at least.

Her pulse fluttered to a stop, her dead eyes starring at the roof. He picked up the My Little Pony — *Prancer*, she said her name was — and held it up in front of his face. Val reached forward and closed Amy's eyes, then got to his feet. He walked out, his steps slow, leaving nothing behind.

Except for a biopsy sample, forgotten on Barnaby Phillips' floor.

And two tear drops, staining the dust by Amy's body.

CHAPTER
TWENTY-SIX

The room was unlike any hospital room Elsie knew of. The bed had no metal or plastic; it was a four-poster wooden bed, complete with a tester. The tester had colorful designs painted on it so that a person lying in the bed could see them when looking up towards the ceiling. The designs were of fairies, and dragons, and a princess against a night sky. The curtains around the bed were a thin gauze. They served two purposes — first, to provide some privacy for the bed's occupant, and secondly, to provide some sort of defense against disease.

They needed to be very careful about contaminants. At this late stage, anything could act as a tipping point. Gauze wasn't much, but it was better than nothing.

The bed itself was large, a genuine king-size bed. The bed's single occupant shared space alongside a collection of toys, stuffed animals mostly. Buried in there somewhere was a remote for the TV set against the wall, a large panel that could be seen clearly even through the gauze. Elsie was sure that a computer of some type lay in there too, so that the bed's occupant could stay in touch with friends. Skype was a poor cousin to human contact, but human contact couldn't be tolerated.

The risk was too great. At this late stage, everything was a risk.

Elsie looked down at the bright yellow sleeves of her hazmat suit. They'd been painted — perhaps by one of the staff, who'd become so attached of late — with rainbows. She thought she could see the head of a Care Bear peeking out next to her glove, but it was hard to tell. The suit's bulky material didn't allow her to pull and tug it as easily as if it were a shirtsleeve. The radio of the suit let her hear everything in the room — the slow sounds of sleepy breathing, the muted tones of the television turned down low.

Last time she'd had to wear a hazmat suit regularly, Elsie had been a junior member of an exploratory team. They'd been researching a new virus. She'd taken the clothing seriously. Three men had died conducting that research, the seals of their suits not correctly fastened. Elsie knew the benefits of a correctly fastened suit; she had taken meticulous care with her own suit before walking into the room.

Elsie didn't need protecting. Cancer wasn't contagious.

It was — of course — so she didn't infect the bed's single occupant. She wished she could wipe her eyes. The suit air made her eyes tear up. It made seeing a little more difficult. She didn't remember her last suit doing this, but she was younger then. A younger body was more tolerant, more capable. Still, that younger self wouldn't have had the resources to try to achieve what she was working towards. It must be possible. It had to be possible. She had invested so much.

So much was at stake.

She walked closer to the bed, careful to set her feet down gently. A level-A hazmat suit had steel toes, heavy cumbersome things not built for quiet places. Then again, the sound of the respirator was audible outside the suit; she just wanted to keep avoid any sudden noises. Unexpected noise could be startling, and — well. At this late stage, everything was a risk.

A squeak sounded by her foot. She'd stepped on a small toy, a stuffed animal of some kind. It had a noisemaker inside it, the air causing the squeak. It looked like a mouse, but picking it up with the hazmat suit on would be difficult. The cylinder strapped to her back only gave her about a half hour in here, but it was heavy all the same.

The bed's occupant stirred at the noise, a thin arm moving upwards in a waking stretch. She didn't appear to be startled, so she'd probably been aware of Elsie on some level already. It was Elsie's usual time to get here; she wasn't unexpected.

"Hello, love." Elsie knew her voice would sound a little harsher, a little less familiar through the radio. It couldn't be helped.

"Mommy." The girl sat up carefully, toys tumbling aside as she moved. Her skin had a sallow, waxy look to it. She'd lost so much weight her eyes were sunken in her small face. None of that seemed to dim her enthusiasm. "You came!"

"Yes." A smile tugged Elsie's mouth. "I'll always be here, Birkita. Every day."

The girl wrinkled her nose. "I wish you wouldn't call me that."

"Birkita? It's your name."

"I want to be called something glamorous. Like Brigitte. I was reading about her today."

"Brigitte Bardot?"

"Yes. Or Raquel."

"Brigitte sounds a little like Birkita."

"It's totally different!" Birkita's skinny arms thumped against the mattress. "Sheesh."

Elsie looked at her daughter for a few moments. "It was what your father wanted to call you, you know."

"Brigitte?"

"No. Birkita."

"Oh." Birkita thought about that for a moment. "What did you want to call me?"

Elsie walked the hazmat suit over to a chair by the bed. The chair was large and sturdy; she'd needed something appropriate for her visits that wouldn't break with the extra weight and still be comfortable. She sat down. "I wanted to call you Scarlett. Red is my favorite color."

"I could handle Scarlett." Birkita searched amongst the toys on the bed, surfacing with a laptop. "I'll update my screen name. My friends can call me Scarlett. Why did Daddy want to name me Birkita?"

"Your father was Irish."

"I know that."

"I suppose it meant something to him. We didn't talk much about it." Elsie shifted in the chair. She tried to avoid talking about Birkita's father too much. It could lead to questions, questions with uncomfortable answers.

"The Internet says it means, 'Strong.'" Birkita spun her laptop around to show Elsie. "See? I'm supposed to be strong."

Elsie looked at the screen, then leaned back. "You've been very strong, though. Perhaps he was right."

"Who?"

"Your father."

Birkita looked at the laptop, then closed the lid. "You don't like talking about him, do you?"

"Who?"

"Daddy."

Elsie pushed herself out of the chair, and walked to the window. It was thick, strong glass, sealed to stop anything getting in or out. The room was on bottled air, clean, safe. Secure. She looked at the woods outside the window. Water was dripping down the leaves of the trees. It seemed so peaceful here.

It should; it had cost enough. *It must be the best hospital you've ever built*, she'd told the architect. *It must not be like a hospital at all.*

"Mommy?" Birkita shifted in the bed. "We don't have to talk about him, if you don't want. I'd like to ... what happened at work today?"

Elsie smiled in spite of herself, still staring out the window. "The usual, honey." She turned back around to face her daughter. "We got a little closer today."

"Closer? What do you mean?"

"We've found a ... man. Who's going to help us."

"I thought you'd found one of those already. The man who was traveling from overseas to see me. Because I couldn't go see him." Birkita gestured to the bed around her, the tiny prison of her life. "I'd like to travel. Someday."

"You will. I promise." Elsie walked back to the chair by the bed, settling herself in again. "The man from overseas is still here. We've just ... lost him."

"Lost him?" Birkita giggled. "He's not a watch or a Barbie. You can't lose him."

Elsie smiled. "Perhaps. Maybe he just wanted to lose himself."

"I'd like to get lost. Someday, like I said. Be somewhere I don't know, and get totally lost. Like an explorer. I watched *Tomb Raider* yesterday."

"The movie?"

"With Angelina. She's got a nice name." Birkita pointed at the television. "She punched a shark! She's terribly brave."

"Not as brave as you."

"Is the new man who's going to help me ... is he brave?"

"Why do you ask? What an odd question."

"I want to be brave and strong. You said that the man from overseas was going to give me a piece of himself, and I thought that was brave." Birkita rubbed her arm above where the IV drip was. "If he gave me his brave-ness, I would be braver. I don't feel very brave. I'm scared."

Elsie sat quietly for a little while, the hiss of the respirator going in and out, in and out. "You're the bravest person I know."

"I'm not braver than anyone!"

"Yes."

"Yes I'm brave?"

"That. But yes. I think the new man is brave." *And foolish*, thought

Elsie. *He resists, when it's useless.* "Bravery can also be a weakness, love. It can make you think silly things. It can make you stupid, even reckless."

Birkita thought that one through. "I still want to be brave. Or at least, I don't want to be scared anymore."

"Soon. Soon, you won't have to keep being brave. The man will give you what you need, and you'll be strong again. Like your name. Birkita."

"I'd like that. Can my friends visit me?"

"Oh honey. We've talked about that. It's too—"

"It's so lonely here!"

Elsie sighed. "I know, baby. It has to be that way."

"Why?" Birkita pushed the laptop further away, falling back into the pillows. "I'm dead anyway."

"Birkita!" Elsie was on her feet before she knew it, the weight of the hazmat suit forgotten. "You're not going to die. Why would you say that?"

"One of the nurses said it. She thought I was asleep. She said that it was sad, because I wasn't going to see Christmas. That means I'm going to die, doesn't it?"

One of the nurses? Elsie sat back down, carefully arranging herself inside the hazmat suit. "Sometimes nurses can be wrong."

"I'm going to die, and I'll be dead and ugly."

"Ugly? What?"

Birkita pulled the bandanna off her head. "I don't have any hair! I'm ugly! I want to be brave, and beautiful. I want to travel. I want to meet boys." She sniffed, then continued so quietly that Elsie almost couldn't hear, "I don't want to die."

"Birkita." Elsie's voice was sharp. "You're not going to die. I'm fixing that."

"You can't fix death, Mom!"

"Yes. Yes, I can. It's what we do at Biomne. And we'll do it with you. At least, with the help of one of these men."

"But how?"

"It's … complicated."

"Like when you meet your best friend's boyfriend?"

"More like science-complicated."

"Because they have to give me something?"

"Yes." Elsie didn't say anything else.

"Can you give me a hint?"

"Like a puzzle?"

"Like a puzzle."

"Okay. When I'm gone, you can use your computer to look this up."

"Look what up?"

"'Lysogenic cycle.'" Elsie sighed. "You should probably look up the lytic cycle too."

"What are those?"

"Methods of viral reproduction."

"Viral what?"

"Like I said, it's science-complicated."

"What's it mean?"

"Well … okay. Lysogenic replication is kind of like a secret agent. A virus comes in, and — sort of like a secret agent — injects its DNA into the host's cells. Then, at some point — pop! — it uses it for its own ends."

"A secret agent?" Birkita's look was doubtful. "In bacteria?"

"Virus. In this case, a virus."

"What's the difference?"

"Uh. That's complicated. To us, viruses are … well, viruses are very useful. For lots of medical applications. We can engineer them to do all sorts of things."

"Like fix my cancer?"

"Like fixing your cancer." Elsie thought for a moment. "One of these men has a very rare virus."

"You want to give me a virus?"

"Maybe. What do you think about that?"

Birkita sat in silence for a moment. "Will it make me sick?"

"It will make you better. You won't get sick ever again."

"I don't want to be sick anymore."

Elsie nodded, the movement shrouded by the hazmat's hood. The respirator clicked in and out. "I might be able to get you a friend."

"Oh! Which one? Rachel?"

"Not Rachel." Elsie had no idea who Rachel was. No doubt one of the vacuous girls on Birkita's Skype contacts list. "A new friend."

Birkita felt about for her bandanna. "I don't like meeting new people. I don't want people to meet me when I'm ugly."

"You're not ugly, love. You're beautiful."

"I don't have any hair! Angelina had beautiful hair."

"Hm." Elsie thought for a moment. "You know, I don't think she does."

"What? How can you say that, Mom? Her hair is gorgeous."

Elsie held up a gloved hand. Definitely a Care Bear. "I agree, she looks gorgeous. I don't think it's her hair."

"How come?"

"Hollywood." Elsie gestured at the television. "It's all fake. I'll bet it was a wig."

"Wigs don't look like that!"

"Well, what do they look like?"

"They're," and Birkita gestured at her head, "for old people!"

"I have an idea. Why don't I get you a wig?"

"I don't want to look old."

"You won't look old. You'll look gorgeous. More gorgeous. Like Angelina."

Birkita's look was skeptical. "I don't want it curly or anything."

"It won't be curly or anything. If I get you a wig, will you meet your new friend?" Elsie looked at the bandanna in Birkita's hands. "I expect it'll make you look even better than her. She only has ordinary hair. It won't be Hollywood hair."

"I guess that would be okay." Birkita shrugged. "What's her name?"

"Adalia." Elsie smiled. "And she's going to help us get our new man here."

~

"I WANT HER FIRED." Elsie looked the head of staff in the eye. "I don't care what her excuse is. No one says my daughter is going to die."

"Ms. Morgan. Uh. The truth is—"

"The truth?" Elsie stared the man down. "The truth is she's not going to die. I appreciate we're on a clock, but we've got it in hand."

The head of staff shuffled his feet. "I'll make sure she's dismissed."

"You're skeptical."

"Ms. Morgan, your daughter's tumors have metastasized. She's immunocompromised. The odds of a recovery ... well. As part of your medical staff, I can't lie to you. The odds aren't good."

"I'm not playing the odds." Elsie crossed her arms. "I'm not *playing*. This is my daughter's life! And she will not *die*. Now get out of here and do your job."

The man shuffled out. Sam Barnes watched him go. "We could replace him as well."

"What? Oh. No." Elsie fiddled with the pen in front of her. "He's trying to do his job. And he's one of the best. We made sure of that."

"Yes." Barnes checked the schedule laid out in front of him. "Would you like me to send in Spencer?"

"Please." Elsie turned the chair back and forth. Visits to her daughter always left her distracted. What was the point of owning one of the world's most successful — and wealthy — pharmaceutical companies if she couldn't help her own daughter?

Spencer walked in. "Ma'am. We have a partial success."

"How so?"

"We have the sample." Spencer nodded at Barnes. "Sam's been quite an asset in helping set this up. He deserves much of the credit."

Elsie looked up at Barnes. "Yes. He's very ... thoughtful. Sam, what has the biopsy given us?"

Barnes didn't look down at his notes. "It's a virus, like we thought. This one's got viable DNA, and we're trying to replicate it. It's a tricky little monster though."

"Can you do it?"

Barnes sighed. "My recommendation would be to continue to track down either Volk or Everard. The captain indicated in his report that Volk was injured, so we've got the word out to our affiliates — healthcare, hospitals, the usual — for a man matching his description."

Spencer nodded. "It makes sense. No bites yet, but we'll keep an eye out. You wanted to see me about something else?"

Elsie flipped through the papers in front of her. "Captain, you mentioned that Mr. Everard had some companions with him."

"That's right. A man and a woman. They wouldn't give their names."

"Yes, of course. As Sam said, we have affiliates — healthcare, hospitals. In this case, the hospital that you, ah, engaged in your recent operation was one of our subsidiaries."

"I'm sorry ma'am. The damages—"

Elsie waved a hand. "The damages are inconsequential. Some reparations to families of the deceased is likely. Nothing we haven't anticipated." Elsie found the photos she was looking for. "Here we are. Are these people familiar?"

Spencer took the two stills, a couple of grainy shots taken from overhead. "You got these from security CCTV?"

"Yes."

"They're the ones." Spencer tapped the picture of the woman. "If I remember correctly, this one was a bit spicy."

"Spicy?"

"Not many civilians keep their wits about them when looking down the barrel of a gun."

"Details, Captain Spencer. I don't want the details. Barnes has done some looking into the two of them. The man is useless to us. A nobody. Works locally in the city."

"No leverage?"

"Not that we can tell. We're not quite sure why he was there, but we're digging into it."

"Everard was very protective of them both."

"Really?" Elsie tapped her glasses against the table. "Maybe ... that could be useful. Right now, the woman may have immediate, ah, tactical value."

Barnes spoke up. "She's a waitress in a bar down town. Presence Unlisted."

Spencer looked at him. "I don't know the place. Sir, I don't go to bars very often."

"That's all right, Captain." Barnes gestured at the woman's photo. "Her name is Danielle Kendrick. And she has a daughter."

"A daughter?"

"Yes. Adalia Kendrick. Father's whereabouts are unknown at this point, but he doesn't concern us. Estranged." Barnes checked his notes. "We'd like your team to extract the girl. Bring her to one of our facilities."

"Extract a child?" Spencer shifted his weight from foot to foot. "That's a little outside of my expertise."

"Captain, we're pretty confident it should be within your capabilities." Elsie sighed. "I must insist that you limit your use of firearms this time. She is valueless to us unless she is alive."

"Leverage?"

"Yes." Elsie smiled. "I don't know of any mothers who wouldn't do everything they could for their daughters."

Spencer smiled that dead smile. "Of course, ma'am. What about Miss Kendrick?"

"She must also be alive. It's a necessary step. It's our hope that Miss Kendrick carries sufficient, ah, weight with Mr. Everard."

"To bring him in?"

"To convince him to help us."

"Help us?" Spencer looked down at his feet. "Ma'am, it's been my experience that men you've shot at are usually unwilling to be helpful. Of their own free will."

"A misunderstanding." Elsie turned the chair to look out the window. "That's beside the point. It won't really be of his own free will. But he will help us nonetheless."

"I'll get it done, ma'am." Spencer looked at Barnes. "Do you have the details?"

"I do, Captain." Barnes pulled a few sheets of paper from his folio. "Her school. We think that might be a useful extraction point."

"She won't be at school."

"I'm sorry?"

"I just pointed a gun at her mother. She won't be at school."

"Hm." Sam considered the paper again. "You may need to use your intuition."

"She'll be with family or friends. I'll start there. I assume that Miss Kendrick and her daughter must be alive, but the other parameters of the mission are malleable?"

Elsie sighed. "Please, Captain. No details. Plausible deniability is hard to fake."

"As you say." Spencer took the papers from Barnes. "The workplace."

"Presence Unlisted?" Barnes nodded at the page. "She works nights and weekends, mostly."

"I'm not that unfamiliar with how bars work, sir." Spencer examined the paper. "It might be another avenue. We can apply leverage against Miss Kendrick through friends."

"Do what you think is most effective, Captain." Barnes looked at Elsie, then back to Spencer. "I don't need to remind you. We're running out of time."

As the captain turned to leave, Elsie spoke. "Captain?"

"Ms. Morgan?"

"Alive, Captain. They must be alive. I'd say that means you

should avoid a head on confrontation with Mr. Everard in the fore-seeable future."

Spencer nodded. "As you say." The door clicked closed behind him.

Elsie sighed again. She did hope that Mr. Everard would be willing to be reasonable. This is why she didn't like men in positions of power in the workplace; they could be so stubborn. They acted like they made all the rules.

Cancer didn't follow normal corporate rules. It was an important lesson to learn. Elsie nodded to herself; you could learn from your enemy. Break the rules.

And win.

TWENTY-SEVEN

When Valentine got back, he gave Danny a quick hug — short and fierce — before he walked into the lounge. She saw that his eyes were red. John followed him in, shrugging and mouthing, "I don't know," at her before following him.

Danny walked behind them both. She could see Val—

Valentine.

—was dusty, dust and flakes in his hair. His pants leg was torn, and there was a stain there, but he didn't seem to be limping. *What happened?* It was only supposed to be a doctor's visit. Valentine walked right up to where Adalia was painting, brown paper and brushes and paint scattered about, and crouched down beside her. He looked Danny's daughter in the face then gave her a quick hug.

She giggled. "Silly," she said. "You'll get paint on your shirt!" She brushed his nose with her brush, leaving a bright green stripe.

He laughed, and then tousled Adalia's hair. Still crouching, he looked at her, his face turning serious for a minute. "When's your birthday?"

"Soon," she said. "Are you going to get me a present?"

"Yes. But before then — well, I need to ask you a favor. Could look after something for me?" He held up a small toy. It looked like a My Little Pony, except it was broken — the head was turned at a crazy angle.

"What is it?" Adalia said. Her face also turned serious. "It looks broken."

"It's a little bit broken, but sometimes things with the best stories are."

"I like stories! What kind of story is it?"

Val turned the pony this way and that in his hands. "It's a story about a brave girl, who was in the wrong place at the wrong time."

Danny bit her lip. John opened his mouth to speak, then stopped.

Valentine continued. "She gave it to me, to give to you. It was a birthday present."

"Someone gave her a broken present?"

"It wasn't broken when she got it. It was broken when she was being brave. And ever since then, Prancer — that's her name — has had a little bit of magic inside. If you hold on to her, when things get really bad, and wish ... your wish can come true."

Adalia reached for the pony. "Her name is Prancer?"

"Yep."

"Thank you." She gave him another hug, getting some paint on his shirt. "I'll take care of her."

Valentine walked outside to where Carlisle was leaning on the balcony railing. Danny followed him, John a few steps behind. Valentine also leaned against the railing, shoulders hunched.

Danny slowly reached out, her hand touching his arm. "What happened?"

"They were there." Valentine stared out over the valley. "They knew I was coming." His hand covered hers. She could feel the heat in it.

"They?" Carlisle looked at him sideways. "Same as the station?"

"Looked like it."

John spoke from behind them. "I didn't see shit. Val comes running up to the car, all I hear is sirens. He wanted me to floor it."

"Did you?"

"Do I look retarded?"

Danny considered him. "A little."

He gave her the finger. "I drove out nice and steady. There were a lot of cops on their way there."

"Any white vans?" Carlisle was staring back out over the valley. The view up here was great. Danny loved living here; it was quiet, free of the usual detritus of the city.

"White vans?"

"Is there an echo? Yeah, white vans."

"Jesus. It's pick-on-John day." John leaned against the side of the house. "I wasn't looking for white vans. Could have been. I don't know."

"Every day is pick-on-John day." Danny looked at Carlisle. "What's the significance of white vans?"

"Tradesmen." Carlisle nodded down into the valley. "See down there, if we watch the road for a while? We'll see twenty white vans in as many minutes."

Valentine nodded. "I get it. Ordinary. Hiding in plain sight."

"It's how I'd do it. When they busted up the station they used white vans. The van at the Elephant Blues was white. Most commonly sold van color in the world." Carlisle breathed in, wincing. "God damn. I can't believe those fuckers shot me."

"What now?" Danny sighed. "I'm guessing you didn't get your tests."

"I got my tests. I wish that was all."

"What do you mean?" She searched his face. "What happened?"

"I..." Valentine faltered. "I'll tell you later. For now, I ... I'd really like to get Adalia somewhere safe."

"We were going out in a bit. We were just waiting for Carlisle to get more mobile."

"I'm mobile. I'm up. I just need more coffee." Carlisle gestured to the house. "Drugs are knocking me on my ass."

"Okay." Val thought for a moment. "I need to get a few things. From my place."

"No." Carlisle shook her head.

"What do you mean, 'No?'" Valentine tugged at his jeans. "I'm only packing the one pair of underwear here."

"Your house won't help you. The news." Carlisle shrugged. "There was a fire. Apparently you died inside."

"Wh..." Valentine looked at Carlisle, then back to the house. "What?"

"They're cleaning up, Everard." Carlisle's face turned grim. She rested her weight on her elbows. "No loose ends."

"I've got to go check. Baitain ... my cleaner—"

"I remember."

"You remember?"

"We interviewed her. When we were looking for you."

"She would have been cleaning today."

"Don't sweat it. You burned to your death last night. It was very sad."

"Christ. I mean—"

"What?"

"They found a body?"

"Yeah."

"Whose body?"

"I don't know." Carlisle stood up, arching her back. "It's the news. It's not forensics."

"But ... did they kill someone?"

"Seriously?" Carlisle looked at Valentine. "I doubt it. There's been enough bodies left lying around that one won't be missed. Not for a while."

"Jesus." John coughed out a little laugh. "I didn't ever dream I'd be having a conversation like this."

"There's more." Carlisle sighed. "The National Guard's been called out. At least, the TV says they're the National Guard."

"But you don't think they are." Danny looked at Carlisle, then at Valentine. "Why would they lie on TV?"

"I don't think they meant to. Let me see here." Carlisle held up a finger. "First, they're all wearing black. On the TV. Sound familiar? The National Guard ... well, they don't have that kind of fashion consultant."

"Like at the station?" Val frowned. "I'm not sure I understand."

"Someone very connected is pulling the strings, Everard. I tried the station. The switchboard ... well, it was someone I didn't know. And I think I know everyone there."

"Could have been a temp." Val's frown deepened. "I mean, there's a lot going on there."

"I thought so too, but on a hunch I asked for myself. I know from the news I'm already dead, right? They put me through to my partner. Vince."

"Really?" Val's frown eased a bit. "So you tracked him down?"

Carlisle sighed, and held up another finger. "That's the second thing. Sure, some guy answered the phone, said he was Vince Elliot. It wasn't Vince."

"What did you do?" said John.

"I hung up and tried his cell." Carlisle looked out the window.

"What did he say?"

"He didn't say anything. Some other guy answered the phone. Said he was Vince's son, and could he take a message." Carlisle shrugged. "Vince doesn't have kids." She broke off, swallowing a few times before saying, "I ... hell. I think he's dead."

They looked at each other in silence for a bit, then Val said, "I'm sorry, Melissa."

Carlisle nodded absently. "I appreciate that, Everard. I ... sorry." She tried a smile. "These damn drugs. They're making me all emotional."

"Like a girl?" John shrugged. "I can't tell. Really."

Carlisle punched him in the arm, but there wasn't a lot of enthusiasm in it. "Thanks, Miles. And by thanks, I mean fuck off."

"Come on." Danny tugged at Valentine's arm. "Let's get you cleaned up."

He followed her as she led the way through the house and into the bathroom. Danny turned the taps on the shower. The hot one was always a pain in the ass, a hair's breadth either way was the difference between the Arctic Circle and Mordor. She pointed to the shelf of towels. "Clean ones are up there. Help yourself to soap. But don't touch those." She pointed a couple bottles in a rack under the shower head.

"Why?" Valentine turned his head to the side. "Poison?"

Danny smiled. "Just very expensive. Girl stuff."

"Oh. Right." He looked around. "I guess this bathroom's a bit girly, isn't it?"

"What do you mean?"

"The pink inflatable sea horse is a bit of a giveaway."

"That's Adalia's!" She slapped him on the arm. "Christ. Look, get yourself scrubbed. I'll see you in a bit." She turned to the door.

"Don't..."

Danny paused. "Don't what?"

"Don't go." Valentine looked at his feet. "I don't want..." He stopped. "It doesn't matter. I'll see you in a bit."

"What is it?" Danny took a step closer to him. She put a hand on his arm.

"I..." He looked around the room. "Do my eyes look normal to you?"

"What?" She took a half step back and looked him in the eye. "Sure."

"Not like an evil yellow?"

"Did they give you drugs at the doctor's?"

"I'm being serious."

The smile fell from her face. "Your eyes look like eyes. My God. What happened today?"

217

"I don't want to … can we talk about it later?" He reached out and touched her face. "I don't want to be alone right now."

Kissing him was the most natural thing in the world. Danny kicked behind her to shut the door as the steam of the shower filled the room.

Valentine looked down at her, his eyes searching her face. "You okay with this? You want this?"

"I've wanted it since I met you." She kissed him again, her hand running over his chest.

"I guess I do need to get cleaned up." He pulled off his shirt, paint marks on the front. "I'll need a new shirt."

"We'll find you something." Her blouse joined his shirt on the ground. "I'm sure there's something around here from one of my many lovers."

"Christ, I've been in a queue?"

"Shut up and kiss me again."

So he did. It was wonderful.

DANNY WAS TOWELING off her hair in the lounge. John looked at her. "He must have been real dirty."

"Don't." Danny eyeballed him.

"Don't what? I'm happy for you."

"It was just a shower."

"I've had a lot of showers. There's long showers, short showers. But with two people? It's never just a shower." John chuckled. "Speaking of which, I could use one … but only if you two are finished. I hope you didn't use all the hot water."

"Help yourself." Danny smiled in spite of herself. "We'll probably be gone when you're out."

"Gone where?" Carlisle came back in off the balcony.

"We're going to drop Adalia off with a friend of mine."

"You trust her?"

"You don't have kids do you?"

"No." Carlisle shrugged. "Never really been the right time for it."

"If you had a kid, you wouldn't drop her anywhere you weren't sure she'd be safe."

"Fair enough." Carlisle nodded down towards the bathroom, a slight smile tugging at her mouth. "I take it, ah, the shower's free?"

"Don't think I won't smack an injured woman."

"I've got first dibs." John threw himself on the couch. "Assuming there's any hot water left."

"Christ." Carlisle shuffled into the kitchen. "I'll put on some coffee."

Valentine walked out wearing a tartan shirt. "Seriously?"

"It's Ralph Lauren." Danny looked him up and down. "Try not to get shit all over it."

"Hey." Carlisle's voice came out of the kitchen. "Want some company?"

"You're in no position to go anywhere." Valentine adjusted the collar of his shirt. "Damn, the last guy who owned this was a midget."

"God ... Christ." Something clattered into the sink. "You're probably right. I can't even stir sugar in like a real human. Just be careful." Carlisle came back out of the kitchen, carrying two cups. She handed one to John. "Watch out."

"Yeah." Danny nodded. "White vans, got it."

Carlisle nodded. "Get going. I'm going to make some calls."

"Still haven't found your partner?" Valentine kept fiddling with his collar.

"No." Carlisle shook her head. "I'm not trying ... I'm not going to call him anymore. I need to find out who these assholes are who keep shooting at my friends." She winced. "And me."

John sipped his coffee. "This is terrible." He sipped again, making a face. "Put Val back in the kitchen. He can make a decent brew."

"I'm licensed for firearms use."

"Great coffee." John took a big slurp. "Some of the best."

219

Danny took Valentine's hand. "Let's go."

"Sure." He tugged at his collar again. "Maybe on the way back we can get me a new shirt."

They walked out to the car, Adalia in tow. She had a small backpack of clothes, and carried a single toy. *Prancer.* Danny bundled Adalia into the backseat of her car.

Her daughter looked up at her. "How long will I be staying with Mandy?"

Danny made sure her belt was clipped in. "I thought you liked Mandy."

"I like Mandy. But I like Valentine too. He's nice." She held up the pony.

Valentine climbed into the passenger seat, turning to look back at them. "You can talk to Prancer. Tell her stuff you'd tell me."

Danny got into the driver's seat. "That's right sweetie. And we'll call you all the time."

"I know." Adalia pouted. "It's not as fun though."

Val looked out onto the street. "No white vans."

"No white vans." Danny put the car into drive, and pulled away from her house.

A few moments later, a black town car pulled out from the curb and followed them. They didn't notice — it wasn't a white van.

"THANK you so much for this, Mandy." Danny hugged her friend. "It means a lot."

Mandy looked at Valentine out of the corner of her eye. He was settling Adalia in; they were talking about something. "So I see."

Danny smacked Mandy on the arm. "Hands off. It's not a tag and release program."

Mandy gave a mock sigh. "So sad." She hefted Adalia's bag. "Anything I need to know about?"

Danny shook her head. "It's probably best if you don't."

"You in some kind of trouble?"

Danny looked at her daughter playing with Valentine. "Some kind, yeah. I'm not sure if it's good trouble, or bad trouble. Maybe a little of column A, a little of column B."

Mandy laughed. "Oh girl. That's bad trouble most definitely. Two columns of bad trouble."

"I guess." She reached for her purse. "You'll need some cash—"

"You know we don't work that way. There'll be some other favor. Later." She raised her eyebrows in Valentine's direction. "It'll be a big favor."

"I'd prefer to pay up front. That kind of favor sounds expensive." Danny eyed her in mock seriousness. "Do you take credit?"

"You said on the phone I shouldn't go to work for a couple days."

"You can manage that?"

"I got some time they owe me. You don't want Adalia in school?"

"No." Danny shrugged. "It's not really very safe."

"Since when is school not safe?"

"Since..." Danny gestured to Valentine. "Since bad trouble came knocking."

"He in the gangs?" Mandy looked at her over her glasses. "You can cut free now."

"It's not like that." Danny put her hand on Mandy's arm. "It's not him."

"You come in here with two black eyes, we'll be having this conversation again."

"Fair enough." Danny put her purse away. "And don't answer the door to people you don't know."

"Jesus. Can I order pizza?"

"No."

"I was joking."

"I wasn't."

The silence sat between them for a bit. Mandy spoke up. "Okay, no pizza."

"No pizza."

Val got up from where he was talking with Adalia and came over to them. "Thanks again for this, Mandy."

"Your girlfriend's gonna owe me, don't you worry."

"Girlf... right." Val looked back at Adalia. "Is there anything you need?"

"No. But thank you. You two best be getting back to whatever trouble you're in."

"I have one question." Val looked around the small apartment.

"You don't like my decorator?"

"What kind of parent names their child Mandy? In this day and age, I mean — really."

Mandy broke out laughing. "Oh, I see why you like this one, Danny. He's just like you."

Danny smiled. "He's not quite as smart."

"Hey." Valentine pointed at his chest. "Job in computers. That's pro levels of smart."

Danny nodded at Mandy. "Like I said. Not quite as smart."

Mandy chuckled. "It's short for Mandela."

"I..." Val adjusted his collar again. "That's a boy's name."

"Only child. Black rights activist parents. Do the math. You're apparently smart."

"Mandy it is. Actually, there's one thing I need."

"What's that?"

"You got a bigger shirt?"

"Go on. Get out of my house." Mandy hustled them to the door.

"Don't forget to lock it," said Danny from the other side.

"She seems nice." Val sat in the passenger seat next to her. "Where'd you meet her?"

"Work. She's a short order cook."

"That's what her job is. But what does she do?"

Danny looked out the window of the car, then started it up. "I don't know. She's my friend. That's enough."

"Don't forget."

"What?" The little car was picking up speed, the streets quiet at this time.

"Shirts."

"It's late. Nothing will be open."

"Ah, Christ. You're right. Well ... FUCK! STOP THE CAR!"

Danny slammed on the brakes. "What is it?"

But Valentine was already running. He'd kicked his door open before she'd come to a stop. She looked out the car as he sprinted up the street, back towards Mandy's place. He looked back over his shoulder. "Call the police! Tell them you heard gunshots!" Then he was gone, legs pumping as he ran.

Oh no, thought Danny. *My baby. My baby's up there.* She spun the wheel around hard and floored the gas. The little car's tires scudded on the tarmac as she drove back up the street, following Val.

TWENTY-EIGHT

Val heard the shot from behind him. He'd been saying something to Danny, but the memory of it was already gone. He hadn't stopped to think, he'd just—

The cub is in danger.

—kicked the door open, shouting something, then dropped out onto the street while the car was still moving. He'd seen the smoke coming off the tires as he'd come into a crouch, then turned away he sprinted up a street. Danny had called out after him, and he'd shouted something back at her.

He heard her car turning around, coming after him, but he was running now, pushing his body faster than he'd—

Tongue lolling, Pack hunts through the trees. Prey is close.

—run before. The two men in the black town car had started to get out as they saw him running towards them. Their dark suits were identical. They moved in tandem, driver and passenger doors opening at the same time. The passenger was dropping a — *radio? phone?* — device back into the car as he stepped out. The driver was pulling out a pistol as his foot touched the pavement. Val was on him before his gun had cleared the holster, dragging him from the car with one arm.

The man tried to bring the gun to bear on Val, but he clubbed the man's arm aside with his free hand. The gun spun across the hood of the car, clattering to the sidewalk. Val dragged the door open, first slamming the man's head through the window glass, then throwing him to the ground. Val held onto the back of his jacket, the man flailing and trying to rise on all fours; Val slammed the door into his head, once—

They think to hunt us?

—twice, the sound hollow. The body jerked with each slam—

They hunt our Pack? We are the Night.

—three times, then Val heaved with his arm still holding the back of the driver's jacket, dragging the man up and tossing him aside. The man's body fell to the road behind him. The passenger had freed his pistol from his jacket, was bringing it—

Move.

—around to bear on Val. Val slammed the driver's door closed —

Faster.

— and twisted his body sideways as the gun went off. Val could feel the kinetic wave of the bullet as it passed through the space where he'd been standing. His hands gripped the edge of the roof where it met the door, a hanging shard of glass crunching against his palm. The gun spoke again —

Strike from below.

—but he wasn't there anymore, tucking his feet up as he gripped the edge of the roof. He pushed his feet through the open driver's window, straightening his body as he arched through the interior of the town car. His shoes hit the man in the stomach on the other side, knocking the passenger off his feet and backwards onto the sidewalk. Val grabbed onto the passenger seat, scrambling out of the open passenger door.

The man had retained his gun, and was struggling to bring it around on Val. Val kicked it aside, the gun clattering to the curb. He reached down, pulling the man up by the front of his jacket with one hand. The man was babbling — *please no please don't please stop* — as Val grabbed him with his other hand. Using both hands, he leaned back for leverage and hurled the man into the side of the car. His body hit the rear passenger door, the metal deforming inward. The car rocked with the force of it, the man bouncing back towards Val. Val was already moving, his punch connecting with the man's head, the hit knocking him back into the car. The roof of the car buckled upwards as the man's body hit the side again, denting it further, the back window crumbling into small, granular chunks as the tempered glass broke.

Val was running again. He didn't try the buzzer for Mandy's apartment, throwing himself at the locked door of the brownstone with his full weight behind his shoulder. The hinges of the double doors popped clear of the frame, wooden splinters spraying into the lobby area. She was on—

Climb. Scramble against mud and stone. The prey is above us.

—the eighth floor. He hit the door of the stairway like he'd hit the main door, the wire mesh glass of the fire door popping free of the frame. Val hit the concrete wall opposite the door and looked around. A soldier was standing on the landing above him, rifle already firing. Val's feet slipped on the debris on the floor, a hand reaching out to snare the railing. A bullet hit him in the shoulder, and he yelled—

Clever monkey. Dead monkey.

—before he gained his feet. He launched himself up the stairs, taking the first three steps in one bound. The second bullet hit his chest, but he was still yelling, his feet taking himself up the wall as he got out of the way of the chattering of the gun. The soldier's eyes went wide behind the visor as Val ran against the wall, springing off at the top into a dive that slammed him against the soldier. The man's gun was still firing but Val was too close, the rounds chipping the concrete walls around them. Chunks shattered off the roof, a tiny cut appearing above Val's eye. He bashed the man's gun arm aside and brought his fist down into his visor, cracking the glass. The man's head bounced against the floor as Val hit him again and again. He stopped hitting when the gun stopped firing. He got up and ran again, up the stairs, the blood from his shoulder and chest making his shirt stick to him.

He checked the numbers written large against the doors as he ran up the stairwell. Val grabbed the railing as he rounded the flights of stairs, keeping up his speed by throwing his momentum around each bend. The building was silent above him as his breath ran ragged in his lungs. His throat burned, and he felt sick. Val remembered Amy at the—

No.

—at Doc Phillips' place, about how her—

It will not happen to Pack.

—life had fluttered out. She'd been alone, and hurting—

We will be make it in time.

—Val slammed the door of level eight open, then pulled his head back as bullets tore into the door frame. He panted in the stairwell. "Adalia!" Val's voice was hoarse, and he tried again. "Adalia! Can you hear me?"

"Val!" He could hear her voice from the corridor. He tried poking his head out again, but the chatter of bullets pushed him back.

He leaned against the cool concrete wall of the stairwell. *Why would they be going after Adalia?* "What do you want?"

There was no reply. He heard the chime of an elevator, and risked ducking his head back into the corridor. No shots came this time. He could see down the corridor, Mandy's door at the end standing open. There were two elevator doors; one was closed, the other just opening. He launched himself up the corridor, rounding on the open door as—

Pack mate.

—Danny stepped out. She started at the sight of him. He glanced at her, then at the closed elevator door.

"Val, where's—"

227

"They've taken her down!" He grabbed the edges of the elevator door, clawing at it. He heaved, the elevator doors sliding open, clanging into the frames. He jammed himself into the opening and risked a look down the shaft, the cables spooling out in front of him as the car descended. Val looked over his shoulder at Danny. "I'm sorry. I'll get her back." He looked into the elevator shaft, then back at her. "I love you." Her eyes widened, and she started to say something.

The cables stopped moving. The elevator had hit the ground. They had an eight-floor lead on him.

He dropped into the shaft, the doors sliding closed behind him. Whatever she'd been about to say was lost in the darkness as he fell down. The shaft was pitch black, occasional glimpses of light licking out as he fell past each floor's elevator door. Val felt the wind of the fall in his face.

When Val hit the top of the elevator, the shock ran through him and he lay stunned for a moment. The top of the elevator creaked then collapsed, dropping him into the floor of the car. He lay in a tumble of metal and wires, a fluorescent lighting tube dangling above him. It flickered, then went out. He had time to glance outside the car before the doors slid shut. He saw men—

Dead men walking.

—one of them dragging a small form—

Cub!

— to the door. As the elevator closed, he saw guns being raised towards him. Val crab-crawled sideways as the bullets shredded the metal of the car, the noise of it deafening inside the small space. Chips of veneer and plastic and metal rained down around him.

Silence.

Run.

His hands reached for the doors of the elevator, shafts of light coming in through the holes. His fingers caught and cut against the sharp metal of the holes, and he could feel something wet on his hands. Val's scrambling started to become—

They have cub!

—frantic before his hands found the edges of the doors. He yanked them open, seeing the last of the soldiers leaving through the main door of the foyer. Val was moving towards them as a small black — *what the fuck, a hockey puck?* — object slid across the floor towards him.

The flash grenade went off, the light activating all the photoreceptors in his eyes in single, brilliant instant. The sound was more force than noise, the pressure of it making him clamp his hands to his ears in pain. Val stumbled, falling to his knees, a hand flailing out for balance. He blinked — *God, I'm blind* — and a bullet took him in the side. He fell, crawling blind across the floor. Val's fingers felt the texture of the lobby floor, the tile edges under his fingertips.

Get up.

He heaved a leg under himself, getting into a half kneeling position. His vision started to clear, and he could see one of the soldiers yanking another back out onto the street. He started to push himself to his feet, his balance still off — *they had me dead in their sights, why didn't they shoot?* — and stumbled after them. He reached the street as a white van was pulling away from the curb. Danny's little car was still on the street, and he started towards it—

It can't dodge the antlers of the deer.

—before deciding against it, setting off in a jagged run after the van. Val touched his ear, feeling the blood from a burst eardrum. The pain in his side from the bullet was fading — *adrenaline* — and his gait eased. He started to get his balance back and picked up speed, arms and legs pumping as he ran after the van down the middle of the street. The van was pulling away from him as the driver floored it, jerking and swerving around traffic. Val's running took him past other cars — *it must be slow driver day* — and he followed the van through an intersection. Horns blared, the van's tires peeling off black smoke as it slid around a car. Val vaulted the same car, one hand on its roof, and landed in a dead run on the other side. He heard the horn as another car hit him from the side. He was knocked clear, landing in a roll; he clambered to his feet in the dirt and grit on the side of the road then powered into a sprint again.

Val looked up at the sound of a helicopter. It was black, running lights off as it flew over the top of him, then banked around to the east. The van swerved down a street ahead, following the flight path of the helicopter. Van saw an alley to the east, ducking into it. He ran past garbage cans, leaping onto a dumpster to vault a chain link fence. He landed on the other side, his feet slipping briefly in the muck before he caught himself and got up to speed again. A flash of color from a doorway caught his eye as he dodged around a woman carrying a — *pail? Bucket?* — the contents spilling into the alley. Her voice carried behind him, calling out in some Asian dialect. He didn't pause, breaking into the street on the other side of the alley.

A car's lights flashed to his right and Val held his hands out to the screech of tires. He looked up and saw the van crossing an intersection ahead of him. He ignored the incredulous look of the man behind the wheel in front of him, ducking around the side of the stopped car and sprinting off. He rounded the corner behind the van, seeing it slow for traffic ahead. Some kind of altercation at the intersection was snarling everything up. The van slewed to the side around the cars, mounting the sidewalk. Pedestrians yelled and screamed, one lady with a baby in a pushchair—

They do not hunt.

—Val turned his head away at the crash, and his eyes shut for a moment at the anguished scream that followed. He wanted to keep running, but the cars ahead of him were packed in—

Lambs in a pen.

—close, so he jumped onto the roof of a car. He used the new height to jump from roof to roof, ignoring the shouts and horns behind him as he leapt between the cars. His feet were slick against the metal and paint and he stumbled more than once. The van was pulling away again as he cleared the traffic snarl, the protagonists in the intersection altercation staring at him dumbfounded, their argument forgotten. He was past them, running—

Running free.

—down the street. His lungs heaved. Val could see a clear parkway ahead, the helicopter set on the ground, rotors thumping the air. The van's engine was screaming as the vehicle jolted this way and that before sliding to a stop by the helicopter. He ran up to the rear of it and grabbed one of the door handles, wrenching it—

End this.

—with all his strength. The door's bolt popped and it swung free. Val caught two gun shots in the chest, and fell backwards onto the ground with blood staining his shirt. He saw a glimpse—

Cub!

"—Adalia!" he shouted, and started to rise to his feet. One of the soldiers inside was braced and fired at him again. Val twisted aside, then grabbed the edge of the van's roof and jumped on top. He could see Adalia being dragged towards the helicopter, her tiny arm outstretched towards him. He bunched into a crouch, about to leap from the roof when he felt the bright sting of the bullets as they hit his legs from underneath. He stumbled, slipping on the roof, falling off the van over the front. Grabbing the grill, Val pulled himself up and looked the driver in the face. The man's eyes were wide with terror, and he jammed the accelerator down, the van collecting Val. He clawed at the grill, one hand reaching up towards the driver. Val's hand grabbed one of the wiper blades, and he held on as the rear tires screeched on the ground.

The impact knocked the breath from him. The driver had rammed the van against a parked car, Val wedged in between. The rear tires screeched, smoke starting to come off them as the driver held his foot down. Val looked aside and saw Adalia being loaded into the helicopter.

No!

"No!" His hands pressed against the front of the van, the engine screaming in front of him. He pressed—

Caught under the rock. Be free or die.

—against the front of the van. He yelled. The vehicle bucked and tossed like a living thing, the tires shrieking their way sideways across the pavement. Slowly, the van started to move backwards. He braced his legs against the car behind him, the pain so hot and real from the bullets that he wanted to vomit. He pressed—

Caught under the rock.

—harder, the veins standing out on his forearms. His muscles bunched under his shirt. He pushed again—

Be free. Or die.

The van skidded backwards as he heaved it away, the tires scribing a mark on the ground as they scudded back. He dodged to the side as the van roared forward again and crashed into the parked car, the driver frozen at the controls. One of the tires burst from the heat, smoke still pouring from the rims as metal started to grate against the ground. Val turned to the helicopter.

It had started to lift from the ground.

His legs weren't working right, the bullets had torn something inside, but he tried. The pain was ebbing, but not fast enough, as he pushed himself towards the rising helicopter. Bullets chattered into the ground around him, but he didn't hear them. The helicopter rose faster above him, and he crouched down, legs bunching up. He saw a face — *Adalia!* — above him. Someone was trying to drag her back from the edge, but she was fighting, biting and scratching. Time seemed to slow, and he saw her spitting and striking like a feral cat.

Val jumped.

His arm was stretched out above him. He reached for the skids of the helicopter. Val's hand grabbed the edge of it as a soldier stood out over the edge. He recognized the face—

Enemy.

—from the hospital, the man who'd smiled with dead eyes. He was holding a rifle, a fleck of red on the magazine catching Val's eye. Val could see Adalia screaming as she looked down at him. The man had that same dead smile as he pulled the trigger and fired a single shot. The pain was pure and bright, and smoke peeled from the bullet hole in his shoulder. He clawed at the skids with his other hand as the helicopter rose higher, pulling hard to gain altitude.

The man leaned down next to the edge of the open door. "Mr. Everard." His voice was raised over the sound of the rotors, almost a shout. He checked his weapon, then looked back down at Val. "Please, do us all a favor and just die." Then he pushed the rifle against Val's chest and squeezed the trigger, holding it down.

Val stretched a hand up to Adalia as he fell. The last thing he saw was her face, the tears leaving silver tracks in the night.

THE CREATURE HUNTED.

Blood tracked down from its throat and chest, flowing freely as it grabbed the driver of the van in one clawed hand. The rage burned inside it, bright as a new sun, brighter than the pain as it tore the man's body apart and tossed the pieces to the ground. It ripped the side off the van, grabbing the soldier from inside as if it were plucking a chocolate from a variety box. It swatted the rifle away, then slammed the man into the ground again and again. The man's body flopped like a wet noodle when it had finished with him. It arched its head back and howled its rage and loss at the sky.

Then it turned lambent, yellow eyes on the crowd.

Prey.

CHAPTER
TWENTY-NINE

Danny had lost sight of Val. A helicopter passed overhead, and on a hunch she turned her little car down a street in that general direction. Her knuckles were white on the steering wheel, fingers gripping so hard that the blood left them. The car's engine whined as she held the gas to the floor. She could smell something like smoke as she wrenched the wheel to avoid other cars. The brakes were getting spongy as she stamped the pedals like some bizarre game of whack-a-mole, trying to gain speed after each brake and dodge of traffic.

My baby. She had to catch up with Valentine. *My baby's been taken.*

The traffic was starting to thin. She wound down the window, slowing down for a moment. She thought she could hear the racket of gunfire — *there!* — and she floored the car again. The sounds overlaid each other through the open window, the car's engine, the chatter of the rifles, and the thumping of the helicopter as it blasted over the night sky. She couldn't see it anymore, but its pitch was changing. Danny didn't know much about helicopters except what she saw in movies, but she knew her city. A helicopter flying low and dark over the city streets was unheard of.

As unheard of as someone snatching her little girl. Or of—

Blood.

—she swallowed. Danny had ducked through the open door of Mandy's apartment after Val had—

He loves me.

—jumped down the elevator shaft, the doors sliding closed behind him. Mandy had been on the floor, blood staining her shirt, pooling underneath her. Danny had fumbled for her phone, making the emergency call. Mandy had whispered something she couldn't understand before slipping into unconsciousness. The guilt had sung inside her head, loud as the sound from the bottom of the hotel, and then she'd run. Run out the door of the apartment, and back down the stairs, taking them three at a time. She'd been able to follow Val's path — where Adalia was taken — by the stopped cars peppering the road. Danny was glad of her little car then; beat up as it was, its size let her move through intersections a larger car would have been snared in. She'd climbed the footpath, hand on the horn to warn pedestrians, as she'd tried to catch up, but she'd lost them.

The helicopter was all she had left.

It was as Danny was leaning forward, trying to catch another glimpse of the helicopter through the buildings around her, that she hit the man. The crump as he hit the front of her car jerked her back to the here and now as he tumbled up and onto the windshield. The hit hadn't been that hard — she'd just turned a corner — but it left a dent in the hood of the car. She slammed on the brakes, the man rolling off and landing on the street.

Danny grabbed for the door handle, yanking it and stumbling as she got out. "My God! I'm so sorry! Are you all right?" She stepped towards the man, who was scrambling to his feet. Why had he been on the road anyway? She was sure she hadn't skipped a red—

"Lady!" He grabbed her arm with both hands. "Run!" Then he was gone, stumbling back down the street the way she'd come.

She stared after him a few moments. He must be confused from the impact, dazed. Danny looked after him, then back the way he'd come. The way she was driving. She saw the smoke rising, and heard the sound of the helicopter fading as it pulled further away.

Where were all the other people?

Danny saw another man running for her. He was dressed in black. "What's happening?"

The man ignored the question, grabbing her and roughly shoving her away from the car. Then he jumped in the open driver's door, slamming it closed, and floored her car.

"Hey!" She waved her arms, but the man in her car ignored her, swerving the car in a U to go back the way she'd come. Come to think of it, he was dressed a lot like those soldiers from the hospital—

That was when she saw it. *My God.*

The creature loped up to the turning car, smoke pouring from the tires as the man inside tried to make her car go faster. The thing kept pace with the car, loping alongside as it gained speed down the street, then reached out one clawed arm and punched through the passenger window. It gripped onto the metal frame of the door and pulled, slowing the car. The wheels still spun, more and more smoke rising, as the creature hauled the car to a stop. The man inside was shouting, screaming something, as the creature lifted the car and tossed it into the wall of a building.

Her car landed on its roof, the man inside fumbling for the door. He stopped as he saw it coming towards the car, pacing—

Stalking.

—closer with slow measured steps. Danny watched, mouth open in a silent scream, as the creature tore the door off her car and snatched the man from inside. He was babbling now as the creature held him up in front of its face, turning him this way and that. Then it roared, grabbed the man with it's other arms, and—

She looked away, but couldn't stop hearing the sounds. The scream that stopped, the gristly tearing sound, the wet spatters.

The silence.

Danny looked back, then froze. The creature was standing in front of her, its head tipped to one side as it looked down on her. It ducked its head forward and sniffed, big chuffing sounds as it tasted the air around her with its nose. It panted, then paced a circle around her as she stood still. She could see the blood streaming down it, tears and holes in its neck and chest. A small whine escaped it. It stood between her and the smoke rising up ahead. She had to go that way, around the thing, to get to Adalia. To get to Valentine. She needed to find them both.

"Please don't kill me." It watched her again, its head tipped sideways again like a curious dog. "I ... I need to go that way. My little girl. I need to find my baby."

Oh God. What if Adalia was caught up in this, if this thing had—

It chuffed again at her, one clawed hand raking slowly against the tarmac, cutting grooves in the ground. She watched, fascinated, as the claws cut deep into the ground, little chunks of torn pavement bunching and clustering as little furrows were formed. The swipe was sideways, four lines — one for each claw — running perpendicular between her and the creature. It leaned back, staring at her again.

"I..." She looked down at the lines. "I don't know what that means. Please. I need to go that way."

It didn't do anything except look at her, breathing deep and low. Danny started to step sideways slow and careful; she walked to the left, trying to go around the thing. It watched her move, its head turning to follow her. As she made to step forward across the lines cutting through the ground it — quick as a fox — stepped sideways in front of her again. A low growl escaped it, lips pulled back from long white teeth.

"I can't stay here!" A sob escaped her. "If you're going to kill me, just do it! But you can't stop me getting to—"

Those I love.

"—my daughter!"

It looked from side to side, another whine escaping it. Then it leaned towards her, another growl escaping it.

I don't want to die. She reached into her pocket for her phone, holding it up in front of her. "Look, I'll show you." She swiped through her photos, pulling up one of Adalia. She'd taken it just a few weeks ago. She held the phone's tiny screen towards the thing. It looked at the phone, then at Danny.

The gunfire shocked her so much she dropped the phone, the screen going dark as it hit the ground. The creature was on her — *God oh God oh God oh* — before she could flinch. Danny squeezed her eyes shut, waiting for the pain. It grabbed her up, and she could smell the thing's closeness, an animal musk as it held her against its chest. She could hear the gunfire, and the thing roaring, so close and so loud that she was screaming, screaming with it and waiting to die—

The gunfire stopped, and she heard a click. The gun was empty.

It dropped her to the ground, and she landed awkwardly, her tail bone hitting the ground first. The pain of it made her feel sick, and she couldn't get up. Danny watched as the creature loped towards the soldier dressed in black, pushing another magazine into his weapon. The helicopter screamed into view from behind a building, the noise loud and sudden, rotors beating the air. It was turning in the air, tipping to bring its side to bear on the thing. The creature snatched the man in front of it off the ground, then hurled him at the helicopter. The turret that was about to fire on it sprayed bullets that cut and chipped a line up a building as the pilot wrenched the helicopter sideways. He wasn't fast enough, and the soldier's body hit the side of the helicopter, crumpling a side panel. A man fell from the open side, screaming as he fell to the street.

The creature bounded back towards her and grabbed a car from the side of the street. Its claws punched through the windshield and rear glass as it lifted it by the roof. Holding it over its head, it walked back over to her, holding the car above her. She tried to move, but she still couldn't use her legs properly. Looking up, saw the engine bay of the car above her.

The sound that hit her ears then was like a chainsaw, impossibly loud. Faster than she could imagine, holes appeared in the car above her, bullets from the helicopter's gun tearing into the car. Pieces of the vehicle were shearing off. The creature roared its defiance as it held the car above her. It fell to one knee, then shook its massive head. With a mighty shrug of its shoulders it flipped the car through the air at the helicopter. The pilot pulled the helicopter out of the way this time. The creature looked at her, then bounded off to the side of the street, ducking into an alley between buildings. Bullets tracked its progress across the ground, then chipped brickwork from the sides of the building where it crouched. It stepped out briefly, tearing a mailbox from the concrete ground and throwing that at the helicopter before ducking back between the buildings. The helicopter's main light lit up, and it banked so the pilot could see down the alley. The engine note of the helicopter changed, and the rotors chapped at the air as it gained height. Tipping forward, it tracked above the alley after the thing.

Adalia.

Danny clambered to her feet. She still felt unsteady from the pain in her coccyx. A quick glance told her that her car was a lost cause. She stared back down the street, towards the rising smoke. She needed to get down there. It didn't look far; she could walk it.

"Come on, Danny." She looked down on the ground, saw her dropped phone—

What the hell?

The ground around where she'd been sitting was torn, pitted, a hundred little craters from bullets marking the ground. There was a small patch of unmarked ground where she'd been sitting. Where the creature was, there were wet marks on the tarmac. She reached down and touched a spot with one hand; her hand came away red. Danny pocketed her phone and limped towards where the car had landed. It was shredded, holes through every part except the hood she'd been staring up at. The engine inside had stopped the rounds, protecting her from being riddled with bullets. The creature had wanted to stop her going back up the street, but then it had run off—

It held the engine above me.

She looked between the torn car and the alley, then back at the lines scored onto the ground.

It was leading the danger away.

Danny limped towards the smoke, taking the sidewalk. She passed bodies where they'd landed, saw a baby's pram out the corner of one eye — *don't look don't look don't look* — and made her way out to a clearing of sorts. A van was on the side of the road, the back torn off it. Flames licked out of the van's engine bay and dirty smoke rose to the sky above her. Street lights cast their orange glow across the scene. From far away she could hear sirens and the chatter of guns. Bodies were scattered around, dead soldiers torn and tossed aside. The occasional colorful splash of non-military clothing told the tale of a fallen civilian.

Valentine. Where was he?

She pulled out her phone. It still worked despite the crack in the phone's glass, and she pulled up Valentine's details. She dialed the number, and waited for it to be connected. The ringing surprised her; she could hear her phone's speakers ringing at the same time as the sound of a phone ringing nearby. She cut off the connection and the other phone stopped ringing.

Danny stared at the phone in her hand for a long time. She looked around her at the bodies. Then she redialed Valentine's number.

The other phone started ringing again. She walked slowly around a car and saw a pile on the ground. Scraps of bloody tartan, with a — she poked through the pile — Ralph Lauren label. What used to be some jeans, ripped and torn. And a phone. Her photo was flashing up on the screen, the caller ID identifying her not as Danny Kendrick but as *Drop everything and answer!*

A sad smile tugged at the corner of her mouth.

She crouched down, leaning her back against the car. She felt so tired. She looked through the tattered clothes again, her eyes spotting a glint of metal. She reached for it, pulling up a tiny cylinder with a domed head. It was a bullet.

A silver bullet.

She leaned forward, scrabbling through the bits of cloth. She found a handful of silver bullets, scattered and fallen in amongst Valentine's clothes.

No. Her hand covered her mouth. *It couldn't be.* Danny had been with Valentine at the hospital as that creature had torn up the place. He couldn't be that thing. Not unless—

Not unless what, Danielle? It was simple. It was impossible.

Not unless there were two. What had John said? *Are they hunting werewolves or something?*

They were trying to hunt Valentine. That thing in the street back there, it was Valentine, she was sure of it. It had tried to protect her, it had shielded her from being shot, before it — *Valentine*, she corrected herself — before Valentine had run off, drawing them away. He'd been so badly shot, the blood matting over his fur, covering the pavement beside her. It could only be Valentine. He was protecting her from them after he'd tried to get Adalia back.

She didn't know who *they* were yet, but she was sure that they had — *my baby* — her daughter.

Danny scooped up Valentine's phone, wallet, and after a moment's thought, the silver bullets. She needed to get out of here. She could still hear the sirens, and sooner or later she'd be caught up answering police questions. She didn't have the time for that, not with Adalia and Valentine out there. Danny needed help, but she couldn't get stuck inside an interrogation room. If she could get back to Carlisle, she was sure she could explain all this — *look, Carlisle, Valentine's a werewolf and mysterious black-suited soldiers have taken my daughter, could you make some calls?* — well. She could try.

Danny looked around, spotting a car with its door hanging open. The front was knocked in a little, and she saw that it had collided with another car. They were sitting in the intersection, but their occupants — and the story behind the crash — were long gone. She hopped inside, finding the keys in the ignition, and started it up. The fan belt screeched at her as she gunned the car down the street, heading for home.

~

DANNY SAT HUNCHED on her couch, the blanket pulled close around her. She gripped a mug of Scotch in her hands with the same white-knuckled intensity she'd held a steering wheel an hour ago, rocking back and forth a little.

"What?" John looked at her, then burst out laughing. The laughter faded as she didn't join in. "Holy shit. You're not joking."

"I'm not joking. And I wasn't talking to you."

Carlisle cleared her throat. "Let me try. What?"

"Like I said. It's too hard to explain any other way. Valentine's a werewolf. There's a bunch of soldiers out there. They've grabbed Adalia, and Valentine's caught up in it somehow. Melissa, *please*. They've got my baby. We've got to go get her!" Danny sipped at the scotch, the fire of the drink hitting her. She needed Dutch courage right now, something to stop her hands shaking.

"I..." Carlisle sat down. "Yes."

John did a double take with his head. "What? Look, Melissa, she's been knocked about, maybe a hit on the head. She's not making—"

"She's making perfect sense. And call me Carlisle." Carlisle reached for the bottle of Scotch, pouring herself a generous two fingers and slamming it back. "Vince showed me something. A surveillance tape of when you and Everard were..."

"You can say it."

"Mugged."

"Right. So what was on the tape?"

"Nothing I can explain. Not soldiers. But something."

"Something? What the fuck is something?"

"Okay, it's not something. It was definitely a werewolf. Huge. Fur. Claws."

"You didn't think to bring this up before?" John's voice was rising and he got out of his chair, pacing the room. "Why?"

"I didn't believe it myself. The tape was blurry."

"How blurry did it have to be to not make out a fucking werewolf?"

"Look, I..." Carlisle refilled her Scotch. Danny watched her, sipping from her own again. "He saved your life."

"What?"

"He killed the muggers."

"Val? Val wouldn't hurt a fly. He's not wired that way."

"It doesn't matter." Danny's voice was hoarse — *my baby, they've got Adalia, my little girl.* She looked at John. "We're wasting time. Do you want me to say you were right?"

"Right?" John ran a hand through his hair. "About what?"

"At the hospital. You said they were hurting werewolves."

"I was making a joke. I don't want to be right. I want you to make sense." He stuck a hand in his pocket for his phone. "I'm calling a taxi. Going to go down there, take a—"

The *plink* as the bullets hit the coffee table cut him off. Danny was dropping the silver bullets one after the other next to the bottle of Scotch. "I found these in his clothes." She tossed his wallet on the table after them, then Valentine's phone. "And his wallet. Phone. Just bloody clothes. They shot him with silver."

John looked at the small pile underneath her on the couch. "But..." He looked lost, his voice small. "They shot Val?"

"Yeah." *And took my little girl.*

"Christ." John looked at her, then at Carlisle. "Melissa. We've got to find him."

"It's Carlisle. You believe us now?"

"No. But Val? He's my friend. My best friend." John swallowed. "I remember what the silver did to his hand. Aller ... what was it?

243

"Allergic dermatitis." Danny nodded. "I think it's a bit worse than that."

"Whatever. Allergic dermatitis. I don't care if you crazy bitches think he's a werewolf or not. But if he's been shot? With these?" John shuffled a foot through the bullets on the ground. "We got to help him."

Scotch sloshed into Carlisle's glass again. John snagged the bottle from her.

Carlisle glared. "Hey."

"Focus. What do we do next, Melissa?"

"*Car*lisle. Car*lisle*. And I think it's obvious."

"For those of us without your excellent Police training." John crossed his arms. "Enlighten the masses."

"Sure." Carlisle tipped the last of the Scotch from her glass into her mouth. "They've taken Adalia because they want a hostage. We don't need to find your daughter. We need to wait for them to call."

No. "What about Valentine?" Danny's fingers whitened against the side of her glass.

"I don't think he needs our help." Carlisle picked up one of the bullets, turning it over in her hand. "Not yet, anyway."

"How come?"

"Because he's not here. And when I saw that thing—"

"Valentine."

"When I saw Everard on those tapes? He was pretty fast. We're not going to catch him until he wants to get caught. The one thing we got? He knows where we are. He'll come to us."

John looked at his watch. "It's three in the morning. How does this work, do we keep watch or something?"

Carlisle looked at him sideways. "You watch a lot of movies?"

"Some."

"Right. Sure. Okay, you can keep watch."

"Really?"

"Really."

"Do I get your gun?"

"What do you think?"

"Right." John looked at the door, then put the bottle down. "I'll be outside. On first watch." The door clicked shut behind him.

Carlisle reached for the Scotch. "Refill? Waiting's going to be hard, Kendrick. Really hard. This'll help."

"It will?" Danny met her eyes over the bottle.

"Yeah." Carlisle nodded. "A little."

Danny held her own glass up, her hand — *they've got my little girl!* — shaking. She'd take all the help she could right now; she was going to need more than a couple of glasses to get through the night.

THIRTY

Adalia's head felt fuzzy, like she'd had too much sleep. She tried to open her eyes, but they were very heavy. She caught a glimpse of a ceiling, plain and white, before letting her lids fall shut again. The bed she was in was soft and warm.

"She's coming around." It was a man, flat and mean. Something tugged at the edge of her memory, but she lost it, falling back to drifting.

"I don't understand why you felt the need to sedate the child, Captain." A woman, used to talking in the Mommy Voice. "She's hardly a danger to you or your men."

"It was for her own safety. There were ... complications." There was a pause. "It'll help a little as she wakes up. Soften the edges of last night for her."

"Propofol?"

"Amongst other things. A little cocktail we sometimes use."

"Hm. I wonder what else was in that cocktail, Captain. She's a bit young for an amnestic."

Adalia avoided thinking about the big words, and what they

might mean. It was nice just to lie here thinking about nothing much at all.

She heard steps coming closer to her bed and tried to open her eyes again. She saw a woman, tall and thin, standing over her bed.

"How are you feeling?"

"Mmm. My head feels funny." Adalia slurred a little, giggling. "I'm all floaty."

"I can imagine. My name's Elsie."

"I'm Adalia." Her mother told her not to talk to strangers, but she felt too relaxed to worry about that now.

"Do you know where you are?"

"I'm..." She thought about it. "I'm staying at Mandy's house."

"Hm. Mandy had an accident."

An accident? Adalia remembered something, a door crashing open, a loud noise. Mandy... "I remember. Mandy fell down."

"That's right. So we had to come in. You're in a hospital."

"A hospital?" Adalia hadn't been in a hospital since she broke her arm. She'd had to wear a cast for weeks, and it itched. "Will Mommy come to visit me?"

"Soon." Elsie paused for a minute, which was okay because it let Adalia float for a bit longer. "There's a young woman in here, a little like you. Just a bit older. Would you like to meet her?"

"Maybe. I think I should get up first."

"Yes, that's right. She's still having breakfast anyway. But after you get up, you can meet her. Her name is Birkita."

"Bir..." Adalia tried to get her tongue around that. "Birkita? I haven't heard that name before."

"It's a little unusual, you're right. You're very clever, Adalia." Elsie got up. "Rest now. Someone will be back later. When you're awake."

That sounded nice. Adalia let her eyes close again. The bed really was nice and warm.

∼

SHE WOKE WITH A START, scrambling inside the blankets. She felt trapped, and she had to get away. She had to run!

"It's okay, love. I've just brought some breakfast." An old woman wearing white closed the door behind her, carrying a tray to Adalia.

"What's happening? Where's Mom? Where's Val?"

"Oh, hush now. I don't know those people. But I've got your breakfast." The old woman put the tray down on a table next to Adalia's bed, then sat on the edge of the bed. She had an easy smile, her face wrinkling around surprisingly white teeth. She didn't smell bad like most old people. "Little one like you, you're too young to carry so many cares. A little chocolate milk will help with that, I think."

"Chocolate milk?"

"Just as I said. Some toast too, if you're wanting it." The woman nodded at the tray. "Or I can bring it back later."

"No!" Adalia bit her lip. "I mean, no thank you. I'm really hungry."

"Toast it is, then." The woman settled the tray in front of Adalia. "Don't go knocking this over on the ground. If you like, you can watch TV. The remote's here." She opened the top drawer on the bedside table, pulling out a rectangle of black.

"Thank you." Adalia chewed on some toast. "Where am I?"

"Here is where you are. Ain't no where else you could be right now. Oh! I almost forgot." The woman patted her gown, then pulled something out of a pocket. "You had this when you came in. Took it off you so I could get you cleaned up, but I was only minding it for you. She looks a little banged up. Like you." The old woman smiled again, brushing a lock of hair off Adalia's face.

Prancer. Adalia scooped up the toy, hugging it briefly to her chest. Then she put it on the bedside table, so Prancer could be part of the conversation.

"I'm Adalia. This is Prancer. Val gave her to me."

"Well how do you do. I'm Belle. Mr. Val is awful generous."

Adalia smiled. "He's nice. He was..." She wanted to remember something, but it wouldn't come. "Do you want some toast, Miss Belle?"

"Oh, it's just Belle, sweetie. And no thank you. I've had my breakfast. Been up a few hours now."

"What time is it?"

"It's time enough for you to eat your breakfast, and don't go minding about that. Time is as time does."

"I meant, have I been here long?" The chocolate milk was good, thick and creamy, not really a milkshake and not really plain milk either. It was a little cold. She'd never had chocolate milk for breakfast before.

"A little while. A night at least. You weren't here yesterday, and why, this morning here you are, bright as a button on Sunday."

"I ... I can't remember stuff." Adalia thought for a moment. "There was a woman here. She said her name was Elsie. And the captain."

"Ms. Morgan was here? Fancy. She usually comes here to visit her ... to see Birkita." The old woman sighed. "That poor girl. Never you mind about that though."

"She said I could meet her. Bir ... Birkita."

"Well, that would be a rare treat." The old woman stood up, taking the empty tray from Adalia. "I'll most likely see you at lunch."

"I'd like that. Thank you, Belle."

"You're most welcome, Adalia. Good to know you."

Belle walked out the door, leaving Adalia alone again. Where was she? There was a window with the blinds drawn, and her room had a big mirror in one wall. A black box with a white button and a grill was on the wall next to the mirror. The TV sat on the wall, but she didn't feel like watching TV. She checked the bedside table, and found her clothes there. She dressed, folding up the hospital gown she'd been wearing and placing it neatly at the foot of the bed. Walking up to the blinds, Adalia looked for a bit until she found a stick she could turn, opening the louvers.

Outside was lush and green, woods as far as she could see. There weren't any woods around where she lived. She was sure she hadn't seen that many trees in her life. There weren't any landmarks she could see that she knew.

"Are you awake?"

Adalia almost jumped out of her skin. There was no one in the room with her.

"You have to press the button. By the mirror." The voice sounded like a girl's. "If you're awake, that is. I can't tell."

Adalia moved to the black box with a white button, and pushed it down. "I'm awake."

The mirror lit up, then her reflection faded away into a view of another room. A girl was standing there, looking at her. When she saw Adalia, she smiled. "Oh great! You're up."

Adalia stepped back a few paces, looking up at the view into the other room. "This was a mirror before!" The room behind the other girl had a big bed, and toys scattered everywhere. It looked like a playground, not a bedroom.

"Yeah. It's a big TV. It lets you see me, and I can see you. So we can talk without you needing to put on a suit."

"A suit?"

"No one can come and see me without a suit." The other girl scratched her head, ruffling big locks of red hair. "It's because I'm sick."

"Oh." Adalia looked down at her feet. "I'm sorry."

"It's not your fault, silly. I've been sick for a while." The girl tipped her head sideways. "Do you like my hair?"

Adalia looked closer. "It's very nice."

"It itches." The other girl looked sad. "It was supposed to make me beautiful, but it just makes me itchy."

"Maybe it made you itchy and beautiful."

The other girl brightened. "You think?" She spun around, locks flying out a little ways. "I picked the color."

"Do you know where we are?" Adalia looked around her room, then pointed out the window. "There's a forest out there."

"We're in my hospital."

"Your ... you mean we're at the hospital."

"It's my hospital. Mom built it for me." The other girl looked at her feet. "My name's Birkita. But you can call me Scarlett, if you like."

"Because of the hair?"

Birkita paused. "Yeah, because of the hair. Is that okay?"

"Sure. Scarlett. I'm—"

"Adalia. I know. My Mom told me."

"Elsie?"

"Yes. She said I'm not going to die."

Adalia stared at Birkita through the glass. "Wow. You're going to die?"

"No, she said I wasn't."

"Scarlett, what are you sick with?"

"They say it's cancer."

Even Adalia had heard of cancer. It was on the TV all the time. "How does Elsie know you're going to live, Scarlett?"

"Mom said she's got a plan to get a man here who can help."

"A man? Like a doctor?"

"No." Birkita looked a little confused. "That's the super weird thing. He's just some guy."

"Well, how's he supposed to help then?"

"I don't know. She told me to look up," and Birkita's face scrunched up, "'lysogenic virus reproduction' on the Internet."

"What's that mean?"

"You know what a virus is?"

"Not really."

"Hm. Well, sometimes you get sick, right? Like with a cold?"

"Yeah. I get sick." Adalia thought about it for a moment. "I get to stay home from school."

"Lucky." Birkita frowned. "Going to school, I mean. I don't get to go to school."

"You're the lucky one!" Adalia laughed. "It's so boring! There's teachers and all they do is talk, blah blah blah, about stuff."

251

Birkita's mouth quirked. "I remember. I used to go to school. Before, I mean."

"You stopped? Because of the cancer?"

"I guess. My mom has a man who comes here and home schools me. And I have the Internet."

"Is the cancer caused by a ... by a virus?"

"No." Birkita shrugged. "But the man who's coming has a virus that's going to help."

"How?"

"Well, the virus is like a secret agent. And it's going to get inside the cancer, and take it over — bang!"

"Won't that make you sick?"

"I hope not. It takes me a long time to get better if I get sick."

"Is the man sick?"

"Mom said no. He's got this virus, but it makes people better."

"Really?" Adalia looked doubtful. "You think that'd have been on the TV or something. What's his name?"

"The man? It's a silly name. Valentine."

"Valentine?" Adalia's mouth fell open. "I know Valentine. He's super nice." She reached for Prancer on the table. "He gave me Prancer. She's a magic horse. But he never said anything about being able to make people better."

"Hm. It might be a different Valentine."

"I never met anyone named Valentine before." Adalia looked at Prancer. "It'd be funny if there were two Valentines."

Birkita looked at Prancer. "What happened to your pony?"

"Valentine said she belonged to a girl who had an accident. But she grants wishes."

"That's silly. Nothing grants wishes."

"I tell you what. I'll wish something for you."

"Like what?"

"I'll wish for Valentine. To come here."

The memory came sudden and sharp, and she gave a little cry

before sitting on the ground. Birkita rushed forward to her side of the glass, putting her hands on it. "What is it?"

"Valentine." Adalia started to cry. "I don't think he can come here."

"Why not?"

"He ... he was trying. To save me. Some men came. They ... Mandy ... oh." She stopped.

"Adalia?"

Adalia looked up, tears on her face. "I don't think Valentine's okay anymore, Scarlett. I don't think he's okay at all."

"Why? How?"

"Some men came, and, and, they used guns. They hurt Mandy, and they hurt Valentine, and he fell from the helicopter, and I'll never see him again."

Birkita stood on the other side of the glass as Adalia cried on the ground. "I'm sorry."

"It's not your fault. You've been stuck in here."

"I know. But I'm sorry anyway." Birkita took one of her hands away from the glass but left the one there. "Look, I can't go to where you are. I'll get sick. But ... if you touch the glass. It'll be like I'm there."

Adalia sniffed, but climbed to her feet. She walked up to the glass, and put her hand against the glass where Birkita's was. There was a chiming sound, and the glass lit briefly, freezing their pictures in place.

"There."

"What?" Adalia stepped back from the glass, looking up at it. "What just happened?"

"It took our photo. Even when we're asleep, you can press on the glass in the corner, and it will light up and show you the photo. If you ever need a friend, you can look at my picture there." Birkita looked down at her feet. "If you need a friend."

"I..." Adalia pressed the glass in the corner, and a picture popped up of Birkita, her hand on the glass. She saw that her eyes were sad, even though she had a small smile on her face. "Thank you, Scarlett. I need a friend."

"You should still do it."

"Do what?"

"Wish. For Valentine." Birkita nodded at Prancer. "I have a lot of toys, but I don't have a single magic one. If it really is magic, this is what it's for. Getting impossible things. Don't wish for him to come here for me. Get him to come here so you know he's okay."

"You don't want him here for you?"

Birkita sighed. She reached up, and pulled at her hair. The wig came off, showing her bald head. "I don't think there's any hope for me, Adalia. It's been a long time coming, but I'm just tired. I don't know if I can keep it up."

"What happened to your hair?"

"They give me drugs, to help fight the cancer. It made my hair fall out." Birkita gave a sad little smile. "My real hair was black. Not like this wig."

Adalia looked through the glass Birkita. "I don't think you need the hair, Scarlett. I think you look pretty just as you are."

"You think so?"

"I think so." Adalia held Prancer close to her chest. *I wish Valentine is okay. I wish he could come here. I wish he could take me away.* She looked up at Birkita, the sad lonely girl on the other side of the glass. *And I wish he can make Scarlett better. She doesn't want me to wish for that, but I want it anyway. She's my friend.*

"Are you okay?" Birkita looked concerned, a small frown crossing her face. "I didn't mean to get all heavy on you."

"I'm okay." Adalia looked around her room. "What's there to do here?"

"Not much. I watch a lot of TV and surf the Internet. We could watch TV together."

"I guess. What do you want to watch?"

"Whatever you like. You turn on your TV, and I'll turn on mine.

We'll watch the same channel, and we can talk about what's happening. We don't have to be in the same room."

Adalia smiled. "That's a good idea." She clicked on the TV, and started to flick through the channels. "I haven't seen this one before. It's called Dr. Phil."

"Ugh." Birkita shook her head. "He's not a doctor."

"He's not?"

"No. Well, he's got a PhD. But it's not in medicine."

"I don't know what that means."

Birkita laughed. "It's okay, I didn't either at first. But I have a lot of time to read in here."

Adalia stared at the face of Phil McGraw on the TV. "Doctors help people. Does Dr. Phil help people?"

"Sometimes. I dunno. I guess."

"That's what I want to do when I grow up."

"You want to be on TV?"

Adalia laughed. "No! I want to help people."

Birkita looked at her for a few moments. "I don't think you need to wait until you grow up, Adalia. I think you're doing it already. Okay … great. Dr. Phil it is."

They sat back on their individual beds, and talked, and laughed, and joked about the people on the Dr. Phil show. Prancer sat on the bedside table next to Adalia, keeping watch. Adalia really hoped Prancer could grant wishes. She didn't want her new friend to die.

CHAPTER
THIRTY-ONE

J ohn woke with a start in the predawn light. The chair he'd been sitting in had grown hard and cold overnight, it felt like the damn thing had fused to his spine. He was sitting on the porch of Danny's house, and the chair was some old torture device re-purposed as a rocking chair. He'd hated it almost instantly, and the feeling was obviously mutual: he'd barked his shins against it twice just trying to sit down, and when he managed to seat himself it had whacked him in the back of the head as the seat leapt forward. He'd have to talk to Danny about her choice in outdoor furniture when this was all over.

Sooner or later, this would all be behind them. He'd be able to get whatever was going on with Val straightened out, convince those two crazies inside he was just some guy, and they could go down and share some laughs over a brew. Everything was funny in hindsight.

John put his hands — carefully, or the damn thing would smack him again — on the arms of the rocking chair, and stretched forward. Getting to his feet, he arched his back. It popped a couple of times. He turned his head around to look at the chair. There were movies about possessed things, like that doll — what was it, *Child's*

Play? He wouldn't be surprised if there was a serial killer stuck inside the frame of that damn chair. It wasn't natural how sore he was. He turned back around and looked out over Danny's front lawn.

That's when he saw Val.

He was lying face down, buck naked, covered in blood. John hoped it was Val, because finding a strange naked guy on the lawn would just add too much weird to an already off-the-chain situation. John was running before he realized it, grabbing Val by the shoulder and turning him over. He looked a mess, some big wounds — *Christ, is that what bullet holes look like?* — in his neck and shoulders.

"It's me, buddy, it's John," he said. "Let's get you inside. Wouldn't do for either of us to be seen out here like this, what with you being naked." He tucked his arms under Val, and heaved him up. "Christ, you're heavy. Come on buddy. Let's get you up." John walked, stiff-legged, back up to the house, and kicked on the front door. "Hey! Open the door!"

There was no response. He kicked again. "C'mon guys! It's Val! He's hurt!"

John heard the scrabble of the lock being drawn, and Danny yanked the door open. She took one look at Val, then stepped aside. "In the lounge. Put him on the couch."

"Isn't Carlisle sleeping there?"

"She's awake. Been awake for hours." Danny shut the door behind him, then led him down the hallway to the lounge. "Here."

John laid Val down, then scrambled for a blanket, tucking it over his friend. "He's hurt pretty bad. I don't know what happened."

"They shot him." Danny stood with her arms crossed. "They shot him again and again, and they wouldn't stop." She reached out slowly, her hand touching the wound on his neck. Her hand came back wet and red.

John looked up at her, then stood up. He put his hands on her shoulders. "It'll be okay. He's here. We're here."

"It won't be okay. Look at him!" Danny stopped before the sob could come out. John looked away.

257

Carlisle came out of the kitchen with a pan filled with water. "Kendrick. Clean towels. Whatever you can get. Fast."

Danny nodded. "Right. Okay." She looked around the room, as if seeing it for the first time. "I can do that." She went back out to the hall.

John took the pan from Carlisle. "It'll be okay."

She gave him a flat look. "Right."

"He ... he made it here."

"Did you take a pulse?"

"Did I..? Uh."

Carlisle crouched down, pulling out one of Val's hands from underneath the blanket. "It's there. Strong, too."

"Is that good?"

"It's unbelievable." She pointed at Val's neck. "That should have killed him."

"You're sure?"

"This isn't the movies, Miles. One bullet's normally enough. Two's being sure. Three's showing off." She pulled the blankets back, showing the holes up and down Val's chest and stomach. "How many do you count?"

"There's more than three."

"Great. Head of the class." She sighed. "He should be dead, Miles. Do you believe in werewolves now?"

Danny came back in, carrying a load of blankets and towels of mixed sizes. "I didn't know what to bring, so I got everything."

"Perfect." Carlisle grabbed a towel from the top of the pile, swabbing it in the water. "We've got to get him cleaned up. See what the damage is."

"With water?" John looked at the pan. "Isn't that, uh, a bit septic?"

Carlisle gave him that flat stare again. "The bullets were a bit septic. Anyway, I've put some peroxide in the water."

"Peroxide?"

"Best stuff I could find under the sink." Carlisle continued to swab away the blood and grime. "Shit. He's been through the grinder."

"What can we do?" John stepped from foot to foot.

"Can you make coffee?"

"Coffee?"

"There's that echo again."

"Right. I can make coffee."

"Great. Make it strong and hot. Three spoons of sugar in the cup."

"I thought you cops were just into donuts. That's a lot of sugar."

"It's for him, not me." Carlisle squeezed out the cloth again, the water running red out of it. "Honey would be better."

"There's some in the pantry." Danny nodded to the kitchen. "Let's go. Leave her be."

"Sure." John followed Danny to the kitchen. He put his hands against the bench and breathed out. "Christ. Val's been shot."

"Yes." Danny's voice was small. "He's been shot. Trying to get my little girl back."

John shook his head. "This whole week has been crazy."

"What do you mean?"

"The last time Val got in a fight, we were in school. He's a lover, not a fighter."

"Mm." Danny put heaped spoons of coffee in the bottom of the press.

"I ... I didn't mean it like that."

"What? Oh." Danny nodded. "I wasn't thinking of that either. It's just ... it's like we know two different people."

John wrangled some cups out of the cupboard, thinking about that. "You're right." He put the cups down, and started spooning honey into the largest one. "I've known him since he was a kid."

"It's not that." She leaned her hip against the bench. "The way you tell it, he's a real gentle soul. Nice-guys-finish-last type."

"I didn't say that."

"Sure. But it's what you think."

259

"I…" John fiddled with the cups. "He's never been much into confrontation, no."

"See, the Val I met recently? He's always racing ahead. He was after armed men, trying to get to Adalia."

"Adrenaline."

She stared at him.

"Okay, maybe not adrenaline. I get your point, but…"

"But what?"

"Well." John coughed. "It might not be the best time, but he seems to really like you. Ever since…" He stopped.

"What?"

"No, it's nothing. Forget it." John reached for the coffee press.

Danny pulled it away. "It's not nothing."

John sighed. "Okay. Look. He's my friend, and I don't want to go all primal on you—"

"So don't."

"—But I don't want you to break his heart."

"Break? His heart? Why would I do that?" Danny's eyes were wide.

"Oh, hell. You wouldn't mean to. It's just … well, he hasn't been like this with anyone since Rebekah."

"Who's Rebekah?" She was using *the tone*. John hated it when chicks used *the tone*.

"It's—"

"Is he still pining after some woman who broke is heart?" Danny pushed the coffee press back towards John. "He doesn't seem like that."

"No, it's nothing like that. It's not really my place to say, but … Rebekah and he were college sweethearts. She fell for him in the final year, asked him to go to the prom. You got to understand, he was a little heavy even back then."

"He's not fat."

John thought back to Val, lying on the lawn. "No, no he's not. Not anymore, anyway. So Rebekah, she's sweet on him. Sees something no other girl in the school can see."

"Really?"

"Sure. Not a big ladies man, our Val. She chased him for a month before he realized she was after him."

Danny giggled. "You didn't say anything?"

"Hell no. You see a woman like that, it's a good sign you should be running. She'll want kids next."

"But he worked it out."

"Yeah." John ran a hand across his face, remembering. "God. He even wore a white tux to the prom."

"He didn't!"

"He did. I've got photos. He'll never let me show you."

Danny smiled down at one of the coffee cups. "It's okay. I believe you." She looked back up at John. "So ... where's Rebekah now?"

John's felt the smile fade from his face. "She died."

"Jesus!"

"Yeah."

"What ... what happened?"

"Usual thing. They got married."

"No ... how did she ... she died?"

"Yeah. Val, well, he likes to drink." John swallowed. "Hell, this'll come out anyway. You should probably hear it now."

Danny looked uncertain. "Know what?"

John stared out the kitchen window. "They got married right after school. Best damn advertisement for marriage I could think of." The megawatt smile teased at his face. "Almost converted me." He held up a hand. "Almost. Anyway, turns out she did want kids, and that cured me of marriage. They were trying to have a baby. Rebekah got pregnant pretty quickly."

"Val didn't say he had kids."

"He doesn't. You know, it's funny, thinking about this. It's been a long time since Val and I have talked about it at all. But I know ... well.

Rebekah and Val were always happy to put me up. Whenever I had a new girl, they welcomed her like she was The One. Rebekah treated me like one of her brothers. I guess that's a good thing, right?" John's shoulders slumped. "They were at a cabin, getting some space. In the woods. Don't worry, it's not a horror movie cliché. She still had a bit of time before the birth and wanted to blow off steam. Val wanted to stay in the city, just in case. She won the argument ... said that at least the place would be far enough away from a corner store she wouldn't keep asking for pickle juice." He shook his head. "Can you imagine that? Pickle juice. She just drank it straight out of the jar."

Danny reached out a hand to touch John's shoulder. He shook it off. "It's okay. Anyway, as Val tells it, she went into labor early. They're in this cabin, in bumfuck nowhere, can't get a phone signal. He'd had a couple of drinks. The police report said he was borderline." He shrugged. "Maybe not 'fine,' sure. I don't think that matters to him anymore.

"So — hospital's hours away, but they need to get her some medical help. They're packing shit into the car, but the contractions are coming on super fast. You know in the movies when a chick goes into labor and 20 minutes later a baby comes out? It's not like that. Takes hours, normally."

"I've got a daughter. You've met her."

"Oh. Sure. Right. Sorry." John fiddled with the coffee press, then pushed it aside. "He was driving her back into the city. They were pretty close to town, and their car stalls at an intersection. It's the middle of the night, not a star in the sky. Car's dead. Sitting in the middle of the road. So Val, he's trying to work out what's going on with the car, fiddling with the keys, whatever, and this other driver comes at them down the road. He's speeding, out of control, something like that." John looking out the window again, but he wasn't seeing Danny's yard. "Hits the side of the car where Rebekah is sitting. Kills her instantly. The baby too. Just like that, his wife and child were dead."

John started to pour the coffee.

"My God." Danny looked out the window.

"Police charged him with DUI, but not vehicular homicide. They said he was blameless for the deaths but shouldn't have been behind the wheel, like it's supposed to be some kind of runner-up prize. He's never acted blameless since then. Hasn't been a night since the accident he hasn't drunk himself unconscious." John looked up at Danny. "Until he met you."

"Me?"

"Sure. That night we were mugged? And he met you?"

"I remember."

"He wasn't drunk. It was like he'd been sipping water all night. Booze couldn't touch him. Haven't seen him drunk since." John nodded his head towards the lounge. "The man on that couch did not get drunk last night. That's a new Val." He sipped his cup.

"I ... I don't know what to say."

"You don't have to say anything." John tried on the megawatt smile again. "It doesn't change anything. He's still our friend, and he's still been shot by bad people."

A cry came from the lounge. Danny and John ducked out of the kitchen to see Carlisle wrestling with Val. She had a cloth in one hand, and he was holding that away. "What the fuck, Carlisle! It burns! Make it stop!"

Carlisle held up her free hand. "Okay. It's just to stop infection."

"God! It feels like my whole chest is on fire!"

"It's the silver." The words landed like pennies dropped into a pool, each one hitting distinctly. Danny stepped forward. "Valentine, do you remember last night?"

"God! It hurts!" Val's eyes were red. He flailed, kicking the blanket off, and lurched to his feet. He stared down at himself. "Which one of you assholes took my clothes?" He cried out again, a hand clawing at one of the marks —*Jesus, what the fuck*, thought John — on his chest, and he sank to one knee.

Carlisle stepped forward, drew one hand back, and slapped him across the face. "Get your shit together, Everard. There's nothing wrong with you."

"There's nothing ... are you crazy?"

John stepped forward, snaring the blanket from the ground. He draped it around Val's shoulders. "Hey. She's telling the truth. I pulled you off the front lawn no more than twenty minutes ago. You'd been shot, and were full of holes."

"I don't feel like I've been shot. I feel like I've been set on fire."

"You were covered in blood. I thought — well. The chicks thought you were going to die, but I knew you were fine. Right?"

"It's the silver." Danny went over to the mantelpiece and picked up a glass containing the silver bullets. "I think you were shot with these last night."

"Last night..." Val sank back onto the couch. "Where's Adalia?"

No one spoke for a moment. John looked at them all, then sighed. "Okay, let me see if I can get this right. Last night, you were dropping Adalia off."

"With Mandy, right." Val hunched forward again as a spasm shook took him.

"Is it the pain?

"Keep talking." Val's teeth were clenched. "It helps. Takes my mind ... my mind off it."

"Right." John started again. "You were dropping Adalia off. Then some guys snatched her. Danny says you went after them, but that's all we got. We don't know what happened then."

Val's eyes moved up and right as he tried to remember. "I was ... running." He clenched his teeth again, then held up a hand. "No, it's passing. God. I was running after them. They had a van."

"Do you remember Adalia?" Danny crouched in front of Val. "Did you catch up? Did you see? Did you see where they took my baby?"

"I..." Val reached a finger out and touched Danny's lips. "I can see her eyes. As I was falling."

Carlisle returned from the kitchen — *man, she moves quietly* — with the large cup of coffee. She handed it to Val. "Drink this."

"What is it?"

"What does it smell like?"

He looked at the cup. "Coffee."

"It's coffee, then. Drink it."

Val sipped from the cup, then gulped, his throat working as he emptied the cup. "God, I'm hungry."

John laughed. "Same old Val. I think I saw some cereal in the kitchen."

"Cereal? I could do a steak." Val looked at him, then at Danny. "What? What is it?"

John sat down on the couch. "How many unbelievable things have you heard this week?"

"I'm not sure." Val winced again, but it didn't look like he was in as much pain anymore. "A few?"

"Right. So. There's no easy way to say this."

"Say what?"

"You're a werewolf."

"Fuck off." No one said anything. Val looked at them all. "No really. Fuck off, I'm not in the mood."

Danny reached out a hand to him. "Let's get you that steak. Then we can talk."

Val grabbed her hand like a drowning man reaching for a rope. "Right. Thanks." They moved to the kitchen.

"Smooth, Miles, smooth." Carlisle frowned. "You could have been a bit more delicate."

"This? From you? I wasn't swabbing him with bleach."

"No." Carlisle sat on the couch next to him. "How are we going to convince him?"

"If he doesn't believe, I'm not sure there is any convincing him. Come on. I could do some steak too."

"So." Val chewed while he talked. "All y'all think I'm a werewolf."

"Yep." John sipped his coffee. They sat around the small kitchen table. A paint brush still sat in the middle, a reminder that Adalia wasn't with them.

"You know werewolves aren't real?"

"Yep." John sipped again.

"I don't bark at the moon."

"Full moon's not for a couple days. Give it time." Danny nodded at his plate. "I don't know many people who eat steak for breakfast."

"I do." John waved his cup. "Lots of bodybuilders do."

"You're not helping."

"Sorry."

Carlisle shifted in her chair, wincing. "I tell you what, Everard. You tell me about how I take one lousy bullet, and I'm still feeling like I've been kicked in the proverbial balls. You get shot five, six times and you're sitting pretty, eating your third steak."

"It's good steak."

"It could be pumpkin pie for all I care. Those weren't flesh wounds."

Val nodded. "Let's say I take this as true. I mean, I've been going through some weird shit lately."

"Like what?"

"Aside from the burning my hand thing yesterday with the waffle iron?"

"Aside from that, yes."

"I'm talking to myself."

"Lots of people do that."

"No, I mean, I'm really talking to myself. Like, I'm getting instructions or something. But it's really me."

"Okay. Usually only serial killers do that."

Danny leaned forward. "Now *you're* not helping."

"Sorry."

"Also," said Val around a mouthful of steak, "I'm pretty sure I killed more than ten people yesterday."

The table sat quiet between them. John tried first. "What?"

"You heard me."

"I'm going to pretend I didn't. Considering the circumstances." Carlisle reached for the coffee, pouring another hit. "Is it too early for Scotch in the coffee?"

"I'm saying it because you should know, Melissa." Val gestured at her with his fork. "You said something to me, that I didn't look like a murderer to you."

"Yeah."

"Well, what do you think now?"

"I still don't think you look like a murderer. Heck if I know what you are. But you're on our team." Carlisle sipped her coffee again. "Christ, Miles. I thought you said you could make coffee."

"I can."

"This is worse than the shit at the precinct."

Val put his knife and fork down. "Look, I don't care. All I want to know is, how can we use it?"

"What do you mean?"

"I mean, yesterday a little girl got taken because of me." Val stopped for a minute. "I'm sure of it. The 'biopsy.'" He gave air quotes around the words. "The hospital. It's all been a bit too right-place, right-time for it to be coincidence. So. They want me for something. Can we use that? To get Adalia back?"

"Maybe." Carlisle looked out over her coffee cup. "They need to let us know what they want first."

"You can't go." John looked at them each in turn. "Come on. There's no chance that's a two-way ticket. These guys have left a trail of bodies worse than an airline crash behind them. One more? It's not going to make a difference."

Danny didn't say anything. Val reached over and put his hand over hers. "It doesn't matter. It's my fault."

"It's hardly your fault."

"Semantics. I'm responsible."

John watched as Danny put her other hand over the top of Val's. "No, John's right. You can't go."

"She's your daughter."

"I—"

"Whatever." Carlisle cut across them both. "It doesn't matter yet. We don't know what they want. If they call — *if*, mind — then play along. Tell them what they need to hear. Set up a meeting. We can decide what to do after that."

"Won't we have decided?" John wiped a finger through the grease on his plate and licked it clean. "I mean, if we set up a meeting."

"They'll think so, sure." Carlisle nodded. "But what we've done is set up a place and time we'll know where they are. That gives us a bit of an advantage."

Val leaned forward. "It's not your daughter, though." He looked at Danny. "What do you want?"

"I want my little girl back. I want her home." Danny looked between Val and Carlisle. "We'll do what Melissa says. If they call. Then we can get them."

John nodded. "That's the spirit. A bit of payback is probably in order."

Val nodded. "I can be faster next time. They won't get away."

Carlisle held up her hands. "Whoa. Relax. This isn't some John Wayne shit here."

"Right." Val nodded again. "Sorry. It's just..." He looked at Danny.

"I know." Carlisle leaned forward. "They owe me one too. Vince — my partner — is still missing. No one's returning my calls. They killed a lot of my friends at the station."

"You've got friends here, Melissa." Val nodded at them all around the table. "Good friends."

John turned on the megawatt smile. "You know what they say. Friends help you move. Good friends help you move bodies."

That's when Val's phone rang.

CHAPTER
THIRTY-TWO

Elsie looked at Sam across the table. The grandfather clock ticked, a sound she usually wasn't aware of. Usually. The burner phone sat between them on the desk, the clean black plastic a contrast to what she was about to use it for. She'd had to do hard things before, but kidnapping — she stopped her thoughts in their tracks. *Get a hold of yourself*. This wasn't a kidnapping; she was saving a life. And if the science could be leveraged, exploited in the same way so many promising medicines were today, it would make more money for the company by saving more lives.

When that happened, all this would be a distant memory, a forgotten bout of teething pain. Birkita was worth any price and this would be transitory. Change and growth were always hard; her success secret was that she was not afraid to pay the full cost of change. When the boat man came, she paid in full, and enjoyed the trip. It's what made her better than most people, wealthier, and ultimately, more successful. Biomne was in the Fortune 100, a stock darling.

So why wasn't she smiling?

Elsie tapped the small square of paper in front of her with her glasses. It was bright pink, the Post-it staring up at her. A single number — no name — was written in precise numerals on it. Sam's handwriting, of course. Like the rest of his work, it was neat, meticulous, even the small details important. It didn't need a name — she knew who she was going to be calling.

"Would you like me to make the call?" Sam broke the silence. Despite his worth, he was still a man, and fell into the trap of needing to fill silence with action. Sometimes, silence was action.

"No." Elsie put her glasses on. "I'm not looking forward to this."

"I'm ... I'm happy to do it."

"I wouldn't think of asking you to. It's my daughter."

"We've shared the risk this far."

"Even so." Elsie pushed a button on the phone, the tone carrying over the sound of the clock — thank God. "This is his number?" She didn't really need to ask; if she was being honest, she was stalling.

"Yes." Sam sat still in his chair. A lesser man would have offered to leave.

Elsie tapped out the numbers written on the paper in front of her, fingers only touching the buttons on the phone. A sign of stress was to use force, to punch buttons or rush through the numbers. The ceremony of dialing was one she used to still her thoughts before these sorts of difficult calls. Hitting the phone didn't solve anything except make other people in the room with you concerned that you weren't capable of doing the job.

Not that Sam would think that. Even still. She turned the phone onto speaker.

The call connected on the second ring. "Caller ID blocked. Nice." The man's voice sounded confident. Strange. She thought he'd be less at ease.

"Mr. Everard?"

"What do you think? You dialed the number. Did you want a pizza?"

"How droll." A smile tugged at the corner of Elsie's mouth. In other circumstances, a man this punchy would be useful on her staff.

This wasn't other circumstances. "Pizza is not on the menu, however."

"Great. Who is this?"

"Names aren't important."

"Look lady — you're right. I'm not really interested in who you are. But I'm super interested in *what* you are." She heard the emphasis in his voice.

"Perhaps I'm being rude. You may call me Elsie." Everard's manner was making her punchy herself, her usual caution falling by the wayside. Sam's breath hissed across the table. He was right to be concerned, but it wasn't his risk.

"Hi. Look. Elsie. It's been great talking, but I'm expecting a super important call. Unless you're that call, I'm going to need to hang up. No offense."

"None taken." Elsie paused. "Mr. Everard, I have a young lady named Adalia in my care."

There was a pause, no sound coming down the line for a moment. "In your care? Can I speak to her?"

"No." Elsie pushed the scrap of paper around the desk in front of her. "I don't think that would be appropriate. But I think she misses her mother. We have her at one of my ... facilities. I'd like to return her to Ms. Kendrick as soon as possible. If you'd be willing."

"Sure. Drop her around. We'll be here all day."

"Ah. It's not quite that straightforward, I'm afraid."

"I figured." Everard paused again. "So do we have to pick her up, or what?"

Damn the man's pluck. How was she losing control of this conversation? "I think it would be best if you came to collect her, yes. But we'll need something from you."

"Okay. I'm listening."

"Listening? I hope that you're going to do more than listen."

"Sure. You've got some kid, you want something. We'll see where this goes."

"It's not just 'some kid,' Mr. Everard. Don't be coy." Elsie smiled at the phone. The man was overplaying his hand. "This is Ms. Kendrick's daughter. Her only daughter. As a mother, I understand what that means."

There was some kind of noise on the other end of the line, something muffled, and then a door closing. "Sorry about that. What was that?"

"I said, as a mother, I understand your children are the most important thing in the world."

"I don't think you get it. She's not my kid. Why do I care?"

Elsie leaned back in her chair, staring at the ceiling. "Mr. Everard, we know a great deal about you. I'm not a hundred percent sure why you might care, but I do know that you ran through eight city blocks after her, chasing men with guns, who were shooting at you. That shows an ... unusual level of commitment."

Another pause, but shorter this time. "Fair enough. Let's agree I have an interest in Adalia."

"I'm glad we agree on something. Perhaps we can work towards more mutual agreements."

"Keep talking."

"Mr. Everard, do you understand the gift you can give the world?" It was always good to deliver a solid teaser, to hint that there could be a greater win than just personal gain at stake. There wasn't, of course. At least, not for Valentine Everard. His fate was both certain and unfortunate.

"My good looks?"

"I'm thinking something longer term."

"You're referring to my recent feats of manly valor."

"Something like that. Mr. Everard — may I call you Valentine?"

"You can call me whatever you like. Valentine's not the worst thing people have called me."

"Quite. Valentine, you were exposed to a very rare, very special virus."

One heart beat. Two heart beats. Three. "A virus?"

"Yes."

"I'm not sure I follow. I'm just an IT guy."

"You graduated with a PhD in computer science from MIT."

"Like I said, I'm just an IT guy. I don't understand what's good about a virus. They're never good."

Elsie chewed that over. *Never good.* There was truth, and then there was truth. "I acquired a … sample from abroad. It was imported here recently, but the carrier fell outside my control."

"He escaped."

"Ah. You've met Volk?"

"I think so. We didn't talk much."

The hospital. Of course. "We believe that in Volk's escape attempt, he managed to infect you. There was a significant impact at a local bar where you might have been drinking."

One beat. Two. "The Elephant Blues?"

"The Elephant Blues." Elsie thought for a moment. "My adviser has suggested that in Volk's … state, that he might have infected you."

"I don't recall."

"Volk is a serial killer, Valentine."

One beat. Two. Three. Four. Five. "Mr. Everard?" She normally let a silence linger, but she thought the line had gone dead.

"I'm here."

"Did you hear what I said?"

"I heard you. I'm not sure I understand. How did you get … no, that's the wrong question. How the hell did you let a serial killer escape? That's a … that's cost a … People are *dead*."

Excellent. The man was finally flustered. "Volk was being detained in another country. We extradited him. He has exceptional value, value that was not well understood by his jailers."

"Because he has the virus."

"Yes. He has the virus. And now you have the virus."

"How do you know?"

"Valentine, I have received a video showing you being shot with an assault rifle." Elsie paused. How should she put this? "Our subcontractors try to keep detailed records of their activities."

"I hope you guys don't get audited by the IRS."

"I don't think the IRS is of great concern at this moment." The smile tugged at the corner of her mouth. She wished she didn't like Everard. It made a hard thing harder, in the end. "Do you know of many people being shot by an assault rifle and talking on the phone the next day?"

"Can I be honest with you, Elsie?"

"I'd prefer it if we could be completely honest."

"I've been around a bit, known a bunch of people. Drank a lot of booze. A lot, and I'm not just telling you that like it's some alcohol hero story. I meet people drinking, crazy people, clever people, even met an actuary once. That guy … well, that guy was more depressed than me. But never once have I known anyone who's been shot. Not with a BB gun, not with an assault rifle."

"Except you."

"I don't recall."

Was the man deliberately trying to rile her? "I said I preferred it if we could be honest."

"We are being honest. I don't recall. Elsie, I don't know what you think this virus can do. I don't know what you want it for. But I don't think it's what you think it is."

"My situation is bleak, I'm afraid. Without the virus … well, I've exhausted my options." Time to get this back on track. "I need the virus, Valentine."

"What do you think it does?"

"I think it transforms humans. Makes us stronger, smarter. Healthier."

"Ah."

"Ah?" Elsie stared down at the phone.

"Ah. You're sick."

"I'm not sick." Elsie tapped the square of paper. "But I need the virus nonetheless. The virus can be used to cure disease. Extend the human lifespan. Make us healthy, strong, slim, the dream of humanity."

"You want to market it as a weight loss drug?"

"That's one possibility. It's not without its merits." Elsie looked at Sam. "But I have a team of capable people who can bring this thing under control. In a few short years, strains of the virus will be out in the market in pill form. That is your value, Mr. Everard. You get to turn your ... condition into an asset. You'll cure diabetes and cancer overnight."

"You want the money."

Let him think that. It was as good a story as any. "I want the virus, Valentine. And for that, I need you."

"The truth at last. So you've already got my biopsy, I'm guessing."

"Yes. Unfortunately, that was unsuccessful."

One beat. Why was he pausing here? Two. It was unexpected. Three. "Unsuccessful?"

"Yes."

"Do you know a little girl named Amy?"

"No. Valentine, I really must insist that we bring you in. We haven't been able to identify the cofactor. There's something special about you, something different that—"

"How do I know that you'll return Adalia to me?"

"I thought we were being completely honest."

One beat. Two. "How do I know that you'll return Adalia to ... to Ms. Kendrick?"

Excellent. He understood the situation. "Valentine, you don't know. You can't know. But please understand, as a mother, I have no desire to hurt Adalia. But I will if I must, you must believe this."

"I believe you."

"Consider it an act of trust."

"I'm not sure we're real big on trust right now. Maybe I can make a suggestion."

"By all means." Elsie raised her eyebrows. It was unusual for takeover targets to be this open to discussion.

"Sweeten the deal. You say you're going to make big cash money on this. Make a deposit. A gesture of good faith."

"To you?"

"No. To Ms. Kendrick."

"Ah. To compensate her for her trouble."

"Yes. That'll buy some small measure of trust."

Sam shook his head at her over the table. He mouthed something at her, but she ignored it. Elsie chewed the proposal over in her head for a little while. "We can accommodate that."

"Great. You do that, and then I'll come to you."

"Of course."

"Elsie."

"Valentine."

"Don't fuck me around on this one. I'm not in the mood."

She stared at the phone. "I'm not sure if you're in the position to be in the mood or otherwise."

A laugh came down the line. "I really don't think you know what this virus does."

"I've seen the videos, Valentine. We believe we have a suitable ... suppressant."

"I'm sure you believe you do. Whatever. Where and when?"

"Do you know what GPS co-ordinates are?"

"I've got Google Maps."

"I have a set of co-ordinates here for you. Don't be panicked; it's a section of forest out of the city. There's nothing there."

"You want me to hike into the woods? I love the smell of nature and all, but it's hardly useful."

"One of my subcontractors will collect you and take you to my facility."

One beat. Two. "I think I've ... worked with your subcontractors before. They're not very friendly."

"Ah. I see your point. You're concerned that you will be harmed."

"I'm concerned that they're going to want to fuck up my shit, yes."

Elsie looked at Sam across the table. "I will send my assistant to liaise with you instead, then." Sam's eyes goggled at her.

"Your assistant. Does he wear black?"

Elsie looked at Sam across the table, eying him up and down. His mouth was open, but nothing came out. "He's wearing a fashionable blue suit right now, as it happens."

"Just him?"

"Just him."

"He doesn't have ninja skills or a concealed knife?"

"I don't believe so. He's handy with more administrative functions." Damn the man again. He *was* likable. Perhaps there was a way — no. There wasn't a way — they'd worked this out before.

"What's his name?"

"Sam."

"Sounds made up. Too boring to be real. Not like Elsie. That sounds like you could be on TV."

"I think my Hollywood career is behind me, Valentine. Be there. At the co-ordinates. Tomorrow. Ten AM."

"Why not today?"

"There are details I need to attend to."

"Details. Like silver bullets and soldiers."

"Like gene sequencing equipment and scientists."

"Ah. No bullets?"

"I regret that there will be bullets. Do you have a pen?"

"I can probably find one. Why, you want a love letter?'

"For the co-ordinates."

"Right." Everard was smart; he didn't try and talk her around. Elsie liked people who understood their position in things, the way the world worked, and how they needed to work together to get the right outcome. It was a shame they hadn't considered this earlier. She recited a set of numbers off to him from memory.

He read them back to her on the phone. "Got it. Right. Tomorrow. Ten. Okay." And like that, he hung up.

Elsie stared at the phone for a few moments longer, then pressed a button to turn it off.

"What!" said Sam.

"Relax, Sam."

"I — relax!"

"He's going to cooperate."

"That's easy for you to say. You're not going out there with, with a…"

"Say it."

"With a werewolf!"

Elsie sighed. "That's a little melodramatic."

"Like I said, that's easy for you to say."

"Sam." She looked at him over the table. He wasn't usually resistant to her ideas. "You'll be fine. We have Adalia."

"And he'll have me."

"He's a programmer, for pity's sake. He's not going to kidnap you in some freak revenge kick. The worst thing you've got to worry about is getting a cold in the woods."

Sam slumped back in his chair. "Can I take Spencer?"

"I think that would be a bad idea. I'm not confident that the good captain has been completely forthright with us."

"What do you mean?"

"I don't think he needed to shoot Mr. Everard."

"The man was hanging from his helicopter."

"So he says."

"You don't believe him?"

"I don't believe he's unmotivated by revenge. I believe that between Everard and Volk, a significant portion of Ebonlake has been put six feet under."

"It makes you wonder." Sam stared out the window. Elsie thought his expression was more glum than usual, but he'd get over it. He always did.

"About what?"

"Why haven't any of them turned?"

"They haven't been infected."

"Well, sure, but why not? Why just Everard?"

"We can postulate. The virus is most likely transmitted via body fluid, similar in nature to HIV. It's definitely not aerosolized transmission, or everyone would have it. Perhaps it's carried in the saliva, or perhaps it needs to be blood to blood. We need a specimen to test." Elsie pointed at the piece of paper in front of her. "We're about to get one."

"Everard's the only one that's been bitten?"

"Volk has a singular MO. He stacks his victims like cord wood."

"I read the report."

"I think he doesn't want to infect other people."

"He doesn't strike me as altruistic."

"I don't think he does it to save people, Sam. I think he doesn't want to share his power." Elsie looked out the window. "Soon, we'll have that power. And then we can tie up the loose ends at our leisure." She looked over at Sam. "Dress up warm. Like I said, you don't want to get a cold."

CHAPTER
THIRTY-THREE

Val knew what he had to do before he'd finished the call with Elsie. He'd taken the scrap of paper with GPS coordinates and pocketed it. The discussion with the rest of them had been — well. John had said he'd be crazy to go. Carlisle had echoed the sentiment — she'd gone further and said they should grab Sam in some sort of eye-for-an-eye vendetta. But it was Danny that had secured his course of action.

"Don't go," she'd said. But her eyes had pleaded with him to make the other choice.

As if there was any choice but one.

It'd been a long time since he'd felt in control. His body was changing — for the better, there was no denying it, but it was like a series of mystery presents. His life had been shifted off its reliable, predictable rails. First he'd been fired — or suspended, the words made no difference — and then by getting caught up in this, whatever this was. He'd made a new friend, grabbed a new life by the horns. He'd fallen in love.

Okay — that last wasn't so bad. Sometimes being out of control was a good thing.

Danny. She seemed tough and capable, in charge of her own life and living it her way — but when she'd told him not to go, he saw she was lost and alone. Her daughter had been snatched and no one could be tough enough for that. Val had looked her in the eyes and agreed not to go. The lie was the easier sin; he'd be able to live with it. If she hated him for it—

Pack would do it for us.

—then that was something he'd also be able to live with. It'd be hard, but not as hard as carrying the burden of another dead child. He'd do whatever it took to make sure Adalia came home.

They'd all agreed to sleep on it, but he'd already decided what to do. He'd got up earlier than the rest of them, stepping outside alone before dawn had had a chance to color the sky. He'd left Danny's house without looking back, his steps taking him through the quiet streets, the predawn light giving a not-quite-solid quality to the cars and buildings he walked past. Val felt like he wasn't there, that this wasn't real, except — well, he felt more *alive* than he had in years. Or ever.

The only people he passed were early morning joggers, trying to bounce away those calories. He'd never been a member of their religion, and — he looked down at himself — he knew he hadn't earned the body he walked in. It was a tremendous gift, but it wasn't his by any right or fairness. It was a currency, shored up against a debt. It was time to go pay up.

Volk — now there was a guy. Val didn't know why they'd leapt at each other, but something inside him had—

Maker. Father. Betrayer.

—twisted at the sight of him, and he knew the same was true of the other man. A common enemy had stopped them before, but next time — well. Val didn't like to fight. It used to make him feel sick and scared; even watching it on TV wasn't something he could do. None of that mattered when it came to Volk; something just took over.

His mouth twisted in a half-smile. When it came to Volk, it'd be on like Donkey Kong.

Not that it was going to matter. By the end of today, he didn't expect to be in a position to care. He didn't know where Volk had gone, but he was off the radar for now. There were bigger problems to solve. Val put his hand in his pocket, the paper crinkling against his fingertips. A month ago, he wouldn't have been able to tell crafted paper from regular run of the mill pulp, not by touch anyway. Now he could feel the texture of the paper, the fibers that had been pressed together to make it.

A diner up ahead was opening up for the day, light spilling out onto the sidewalk. He'd need some food to keep going — Val patted his stomach, flat and hard. A month ago, it'd been round, soft from long nights with a bottle for company. His new body wanted food, and lots of it. He pushed through the door to the diner, nodding to the girl behind the counter. "Yeah, look. Do you have a big breakfast?"

"Sure do. Eggs, bacon, hash browns, mushrooms, tomatoes—"

"Great. I'll have three."

"Three eggs?"

"No. Three breakfasts."

The girl behind the counter goggled at him. "Sir, they're quite big."

"How big?" Val tapped on the counter. "Like the size of a Labrador?"

She giggled, then caught herself. "More like the size of a cat."

"I could eat a horse. So best give me four."

She nodded. "Coffee with that?"

"As much as you've got. Keep it coming." Val pulled out some cash as she rang up the order, then went to grab a seat. The diner was empty aside from him, the newspapers on the tables crisp and unused. It wasn't often you got to read the newspaper first in a place like this — by the time he got out of bed and shook off the booze, they were folded inside out, a jumbled mess of articles and grease marks. Today he'd get to read the news in his own time. It'd be an hour or so to get to where he needed to be, which left plenty of time for breakfast.

John sat down in the seat opposite him. "This seat taken?"

"Fuck!"

"It's a bit early, and you're not that pretty."

"John! What are you doing here?"

"What I usually do." John waved at the girl behind the counter. She nodded, grabbing clean cups and the pot and heading over to their table. "Keeping you out of trouble."

The girl held up a pad. "Anything for you sir?"

"Sure." said John.

"He's not staying." Val's stare was flat.

"Ignore my friend, he's not really a morning person." That megawatt smile turned on, and the girl blushed. "Say. Do you do waffles?"

"Best in town."

"A bold statement, and one I'd like to verify. A stack."

"Bacon?"

"Is there any other way?" John pulled out some cash. "Keep the change."

She dimpled at him. "Thank you. I'll get the kitchen on it right away." John watched her go.

"She's no more than eighteen, John."

"What? Oh. Sure." John sipped his coffee. "So was I, once."

"Isn't she a little young, even for you?"

"I wasn't going to hop on that. I was just looking at her ass."

"You sure?"

"That's not fair."

Val sighed. "Sorry. My bad. It's just — seriously. What are you doing here?"

"Helping you." The megawatt smile came back. "Like always."

"I don't need help."

"That's the least true thing I've heard all year. Damn, this coffee's good."

"You should just go home. Get out of here."

John frowned. "Why would I do that?"

Val pushed his cup around in front of him. "They're going to kill me, John. There's nothing you can do about that."

"Sure there is. But you're forgetting something."

"What's that?"

"Someone's got to get Adalia out of there." John looked at his expression. "What, you think a little cash deposit makes us all friends? I keep telling people you're smart, but now I'm not so sure. No witnesses. They'll clean house."

"And you think you can do something I can't?"

John considered him across the table. "Yeah. I do."

"This isn't school anymore."

"You sure about that?" John took another sip. "Seriously. This is better than your coffee."

"What do you mean?"

"You put all kinds of cinnamon and shit in your coffee."

"Not about the coffee." Val sipped his own cup. John was right — it was pretty good. "About this not being school."

"Right." That damn megawatt smile again. "The thing about school was bullies. Some bigger kid beating up a littler kid. This is just like that. Biomne is a bigger kid. And you, my friend, are a littler kid."

"Biowhat?"

John tapped the headline of the paper in front of Val. The headline read *Biomne Stock Down 15 Percent*. The subtitle asked *Has CEO Elsie Morgan Lost Control?*

"Christ. She's the head of a pharmaceutical company." Val rubbed his face.

The girl returned with their plates, one of the kitchen staff behind her carrying some extras. "Jesus," said John, "What did you order?"

"One of everything, I think." Val smiled at the girl. "Thanks."

She nodded. "Sure thing. Sing out if you need anything else."

"More coffee? Just leave the pot."

"No problem." She bussed the coffee pot back to their table, and Val and John chewed in silence for a few minutes.

"These really are good waffles." John pointed a waffle-laden fork at Val. "But yours are better."

"Thanks." Val kept eating, speaking around his mouth of food. "It could be coincidence."

"Does it matter?" John tapped the paper again. "It doesn't matter if this Elsie is the same one on the phone or not. Whoever you talked to has resources. You, all you've got is your less than winning personality—"

"Thanks," said Val again.

"—And me," said John. "And those guns you didn't have last week."

"Guns?"

"Christ, man." John pointed at his biceps. "Those."

"Sure. Guns, right. The whole gym thing is a bit new to me."

"No kidding. I'm pretty glad you're diseased, actually."

"I'm not diseased."

"She said you had a virus, right?"

"Right."

"You're diseased." John stuffed another clump of waffle in his mouth. "Simple as that."

Val pushed his first plate away, pulling a second closer. "Fair enough."

John counted the plates on the table. "Did you really order four breakfasts?"

"Yeah. I'm pretty hungry these days."

"Getting shot up will do that to a guy. It's probably the whole werewolf thing."

"Shh!" Val held his hands up. "Not so loud. Not with the W word."

"What, werewolf?"

"Christ."

"Look, someone overhears us — and let's be honest, the girl behind the counter can't take her eyes off your biceps, she's not listening to a word you're saying — they'll think we're a couple talking about our kinky sex."

"She can't take her eyes off me?"

"Valentine. Focus." John pointed at Val's plate. "Don't look at her. You'll startle the poor thing. Eat your beans."

"I didn't know it came with beans. She didn't say."

"It's probably a bonus for ordering more food than a normal person eats in a week."

"I'm just having trouble getting used to it."

"Eating four breakfasts?"

"Being a..." Val waved his knife in the air. "C'mon. It's movie stuff. It's not real."

"So how would you describe it?"

"Forget about it. I'll handle it." Val took another bite of sausage. "Whatever. After breakfast, you need to get out of here."

"Not happening."

"You can't come, John. Not this time. You can't be there all the time."

John put down his knife and fork. "You need to listen, and listen good. I can, and I will."

"This isn't like the other times."

"It's exactly like the other times." John's eyes searched his face. "What, you think that just because the stakes are bigger, I'm going to run away? It doesn't work like that."

"They're going to kill you." Val leaned back in his seat. "I—"

"No. They're going to kill *you*."

"I thought you said you were going to help with that."

"Great, you're on board with the plan already."

"John—"

"Don't fight it."

"—People die around me. I—"

John waited.

"I don't want you to die." Val's shoulders slumped. "I don't want anyone to die because of me. Not anymore. Not ever again."

"It wasn't your fault."

"God damn it!" Val's hand hit the table, causing the plates to jump. "She's dead because of me!"

John waved the girl behind the counter away, showing a quick blast of the megawatt smile. "She's dead because life's shitty. It's not fair. Did you drive a car into her?"

"I—"

"Did you?"

"I put her there!"

John looked at Val's plate. "You carried her into the middle of the street?"

"Don't push this." Val's shoulders hunched.

"Or what?" John looked at him.

"I..." Val's finger's clenched in front of him.

He challenges us. We are alpha.

"He's my friend!" Val's teeth were clenched.

"What?" John's eyes widened.

"I'm not talking to you!" Val gripped the edge of the table in front of them, his fingers turning white. "Shut up! Just shut up!"

John paused, then nodded. "It's really fucking with you, isn't it?"

The air dragged in and out of Val in big gasping breaths. "It's so strong. John, I—"

"It doesn't matter, buddy." John picked up his knife and fork again. "I trust you. I've always got your back. And I know you've got mine. All I'm saying is — well. Rebekah was like a sister to me. I don't blame you at all. You can work out what that means for yourself. Eat your breakfast."

Pack.

Just like that, it was gone. Val let go of the edge of the table, looking at the cracked Formica where his fingers had been.

John looked at the cracks. "So. If you hadn't got a hold of it then. What would have happened?"

287

"I don't know." Val sighed. He grabbed up his fork and started eating again. "It's kind of new to me."

"Me too. You know, it's not all bad."

"How's that?" Val drained his cup, then topped them both up from the pot.

"After this is over? We'll get you into a circus."

"Go fuck yourself."

"Seriously. It'll pay well. Anyway. What's the play?"

"I don't know. I had it all worked out. But that was a solo job. How did you find me?"

"It was pretty easy. I didn't sleep last night. Followed you out this morning."

"Does ... did Danny—"

Pack mate.

"—know you were going? Carlisle?"

"No," said John.

"I guess that's something," said Val. "Okay. I like the beans."

"Good for you. So it's just you and me."

"Yeah. They're expecting me."

"Sure."

"They're not expecting you."

"Two for two." John looked at him over his fork.

"Let's keep it that way. Keep you out of sight. When I get a feel for it ... I'll signal you."

"How?"

"You got a phone?"

"Dial-a-Stud always has his phone." John snared his cup from in amongst the plates on the table. "It's like the Bat Signal."

"I won't be needing a male escort. I just need you to have your phone," said Val.

John nodded. "Fair enough. Your loss."

"Right. Sorted." Val let out a breath he didn't know he'd—

Pack stands with us.

—been holding. It was good to have John here. No matter how

crazy things got, he knew he could rely on John, even at the end of things.

"What do we do until then?" John pushed his plate away.

Val pushed his second empty plate away, pulling the third closer. "I say we keep eating."

~

"I USED to wonder how you became super-sized. I don't wonder anymore."

"Keep your voice down." Val looked at the map on his phone. "The place is just up ahead."

"Sure." John grinned at him. "This is just like playing spies and shit, back when we were kids."

"Okay, Bond. You keep your spy craft quiet, and wait here."

"Copy that, Gold Leader."

"That's Star Wars, not James Bond."

"Whatever."

The woods were cool, a quiet escape from the morning. The sun had come out, burning away Val's doubts. The day was hot already, climbing into shorts and T-shirt temperatures. He was sweating through his new clothing — John's idea — already.

"No, really. Army surplus." John had nodded to a store they'd walked past.

"What?"

"It's practical. Not like that shit you're wearing now."

"It's not like Danny has an extensive men's wardrobe at her place."

"I'm not saying it's her fault. I'm saying you look like a hobo."

Like that, they'd kitted themselves out with more rugged clothing. John was wearing a digital camo sleeveless vest — Guns, bro — chicks dig the guns — and Val had opted for a simple black T. John had wanted to get some weapons too, but Val had talked him down. The way Val saw things, if they needed weapons they'd need something bigger than whatever could be grabbed over the counter at an army surplus store.

If they needed weapons around Adalia, something had gone badly wrong, and that couldn't be allowed.

Google Maps showed him a generic forest — no Street View cars could get in here, that's for sure. Val walked on ahead through the woods, his feet crunching on the forest floor. He wasn't trying to keep his noise down — quite the opposite. Surprises were bad for everyone, and—

A flash of fire. He swatted the puny thing aside, grabbing the man —

—he didn't want to be shot again. It didn't matter what they'd said to him — being told you were a werewolf was one thing. Walking the walk was quite another.

Val stepped into a large clearing. A helicopter sat — *that might be a wee fly in the ointment* — silent and empty, in the center of the clearing. A man was seated on a fallen tree, wearing a cashmere sweater and slacks. He started upright as Val walked through the trees.

"Uh." The man swallowed a couple of times. "Mr. Everard?"

"Sam."

"Ah." Sam's forehead was sweaty. "Yes."

"I appreciate you doing this."

"You — you do?"

"Sure." Val smiled, showing teeth. "You've taken a hell of a risk."

Crush it. It has our cub—

"But," said Val, flexing his hands, "you know that already."

Sam swallowed again. "I assure you, Adalia is quite all right. For now."

"Now that's just plain nasty, Sam." Val let his teeth show some more, but it had stopped being a smile. "Why would you say something like that? We could have such a good thing going on here. You know, I get a bit unpredictable — jumpy, almost — when I get angry these days. I'm under a lot of stress."

"I only meant..." Sam started again. "I meant that we've taken good care of her."

"I'm glad to hear it." Val clapped a big hand on Sam's shoulder, hitting him a bit too hard. Then he looked at his hand, pulling it back. "I'm sorry, Sam. I hate bullies myself, and this situation's just bringing out the worst in me." He offered his hand.

Sam looked at it like it was a pit viper, then gingerly took it, returning the shake. "I'm pleased to meet you, Mr. Everard. I regret—"

"Look, save it. It's a shitty situation. I'm here for one thing, and I bet you are too."

"Yes." Sam nodded towards the helicopter. "Shall we?"

"Sure." Val walked towards the helicopter.

"Mr. Everard."

Val stopped, turning. "Yes?"

"I mean it." Sam looked at his hand, still held out. "I really am sorry."

Val nodded. "Sure, Sam. So am I. But I appreciate you saying that. I'll remember it."

"For what, Mr. Everard? I ... Elsie ... Ms. Morgan, that is—"

"I know, Sam." Val considered the man. "You're a very loyal man."

"Ms. Morgan and I go back a long way."

We will destroy their Pack, tear it down—

"Yeah." Val clenched his teeth. "Sometimes we don't get to choose, do we?"

Sam looked at the forest floor. "No, Mr. Everard. Sometimes there's no choice at all."

"I'm sorry, Sam."

Sam looked up at him. "What for, Mr. Everard?"

Val smiled, but there was no joy in it. "For the way the day is going to end. Come on. Let's get on. Got to pay the boat man."

Sam laughed. "You have no idea."

"What?"

"She says that same thing."

"Well, that's the only thing Elsie and I have in common." Val grabbed at the door of the helicopter. He checked his phone, then dropped it in his pocket before hopping in.

Sam took the pilot's seat, putting on a headset and handing a similar one to Val. "You're an honorable man, Mr. Everard. I'm sorry for the way the day is going to end too."

Val nodded, looking out at the forest edge. He couldn't see John anywhere. Exactly as planned.

CHAPTER
THIRTY-FOUR

John watched the helicopter take off through the trees, the beating of the rotors causing him to squint as bits of forest tried to get into his eyes. Despite having a physique that made heads turn, he never thought of himself as an outdoorsy type. There were insects and serial killers and, well, werewolves outside.

It was best to stay inside.

He fished his phone out of his pocket, tapping on Find My Friends. John had been nagging Val to get setup on the app for ages. It seemed all it took to get Val to do something was threaten the lives of people he cared about. Useful to know. The app tracked Val as the helicopter took him out over the forest.

John shut the app down, then started to dial. A crack off to his left made his hand freeze.

"Is not as planned?" The accent was thick, sounding like all the Russian mobster movie roles John had ever seen. John instinctively hunkered down against a tree.

"No." Spencer. John wouldn't forget that voice in a hurry. The captain followed the big Russian into the clearing, checking his watch. "It's not going according to plan. They were early."

293

"Ah. You should never trust a woman. I tell you this." The Russian was familiar, and John squinted at him, trying to pick where he'd seen him before. His walk was slow, and he winced before he spoke again. "The past is behind us. We are friends now, you and I. But you do not listen to your friends."

"It's fixable." Spencer spat into the grass of the clearing. "It's not good though. If she told me the wrong time, it means my position is compromised."

"What is this *compromised* word you use?"

"She doesn't trust me either."

"Ah. She is not your good friend, captain." The big man stretched his side, a grimace crossing his face.

"She's my employer. I don't know what it's like in mother Russia, but we don't usually get cozy with the boss."

The big man looked around the clearing, and John got a good look at his face. *Fuck*, he thought, *It's that janitor from the hospital. What are the odds?* "Is not so different."

"Figures. Volk." Spencer looked back at the big man — *Volk*. "You need to pay up."

Volk smiled. "Captain. It is not as simple. We are friends, of course. But we have deal."

"The deal was I help you kill Everard—"

"*Da*. I remember. In return..." The man trailed off, looking at the sky. "They really flew. Is amazing, this world."

Spencer looked at the sky. "You've never seen a helicopter?"

"Heli. Copter." Volk tried the word on for size. "*Angliyskiy* words. I know what helicopter is. I have been away long time. Not that long."

Spencer frowned. "Whatever. Volk, we have a deal. If you don't pay your half, I don't pay my half. It's as simple as that."

"Of course." Volk walked up to Spencer, clapping him on the shoulder. "But you haven't paid your half either. We are still even."

"I brought you to Everard."

Volk's smile faded. "Do you take me for simple man?"

"What?"

"Because of *Angliyskiy*. My English is bad, I know this."

"No." Spencer frowned. "Why do you ask?"

"*Xorošij*." Volk smiled again. "You brought me to here. To many trees."

"Forest?"

"*Da*. Forest." He beamed. "A new word. Is marvelous! But there is no one here."

"They just left!"

"*Da*." Volk nodded, gesturing around at the clearing. "No one here, no gift."

"Christ." Spencer rubbed his face. "I figured you'd do it here, and we could deal with Everard together."

"Together?" Volk seemed to think about this. "No. We are good friends, Captain. We are not good enough friends to hunt together."

John could see Spencer's jaw clench. "Christ. I don't want to go big game shooting. I want to put that rabid dog down. He's killed my men!"

"Rabid?" Volk frowned. "I do not know this word."

"A disease. Sickness. Dogs get it."

"Ah, Captain." Volk sighed. "This man you hunt—"

"Everard."

"This man you call Everard, he is not a dog."

Spencer shrugged. "Looked like a dog to me."

"Hah. Reminds me of funny joke." Volk cleared his throat. "Would you like to hear it?"

"How do you know any English jokes?" Spencer checked his watch again. "You've been in a hole in the ground since baby Jesus walked the Earth."

"*Da*." Volk grinned. "One of your men told it to me. On the way here." The grin faded. "I think he thought to take my mind off the pain. He was the first to die for it." The grin returned. "But I remember his joke."

John thought Spencer turned a little pale at that. "He died for it? The joke?"

"No. The pain." Volk shook his finger at Spencer. "You will understand, soon enough."

"When you turn me." Spencer nodded. "I get it. No more silver jewelery. It doesn't really go with the uniform."

"Turn?" Volk rubbed his chin. "I had not thought of it that way before."

"What would you call it?"

"*Bratstvo.*"

"What?"

"I do not know English. Is *bratstvo.*"

"Whatever. Call it what you like." Spencer checked his watch again.

"Why you check time? Is all same."

"In five minutes, it'll be time for us to be here. When Morgan told me to be here."

"So?"

"So. The bitch has probably set us up." Spencer checked his sidearm, cocking it before putting it back in his holster. "I figure they'll try and take us from up that hill." He nodded towards where John was hiding. *Christ,* thought John, *I'm going to have a bunch of soldiers up my ass. It'll be worse than a prison shower.*

"Ah. I must tell joke then."

"What?"

"Before they get here. Will spoil timing."

"Sure. Whatever." Spencer scanned the tree line of the clearing. "We should get out of here."

"Relax. Your men only expect you." Volk used a toothy grin. "*They* will be surprised."

"They'd be more surprised if I wasn't here."

Volk held up a hand. "No worry. No worry. Joke. During cold war, Mother Russia and America, not good friends. Not like you and me, *da?*"

"Sure."

"So, they decide on contest. To end war. Very brave men die on both sides. I know American mothers cry for their children. Russian mothers cry too. Is good idea, for contest, rather than all those brave men dying."

"What was the contest?"

"Ah. So contest was, find the best fighting dog. Put dog in ring, and best of three. Victor, they win." Volk nodded, a solemn expression on his face. "Mother Russia, we have many strong dogs. Our best men try to breed a wolf with a bear, and succeed. Strongest fighting dog ever. Ferocious animal. Cannot be controlled."

"I get it. Looks like a dog, fights like a bear."

"*Da*! Very good, captain. You know this joke?"

"No."

"Is good. Americans turn up for contest. Is held in neutral country. *Švejcarija*."

"Switzerland?"

"*Da. Švejcarija*. Americans bring out dog, is long like a sausage, but very big. Dachshund. Many Russians laugh, thinking big joke. Dogs go into ring, and Russian dog is fierce. It leaps at American dog, there is snarling, there is biting." Volk made slashing hand motions in the air. "In end, only one dog alive. First round, Russian dog is dead!"

Spencer laughed. "No best of three?"

"No best of three. So Russians say, 'Our best men! They take three years to breed this dog. How did you beat us?' And American man, he explain. Says that it took three years for their best plastic surgeons to make an alligator look like a dog."

Spencer snorted. "That sounds like us."

Volk frowned. "You do not get it."

"I get it. I'm just not laughing."

"No. You do not get why I tell joke. I tell joke because you say this man, Everard, he looks like a dog."

"Sure. Looked that way. Bigger, maybe."

"Ah. But on the inside? He is an alligator. If you try and fight him like a dog, you will die."

Spencer was silent for a few moments. "Fair enough." He checked his watch again. "We should get out of here."

Volk smiled. "We go to finish this?"

"Yes. I'll take you to Everard. And you'll give me..."

"A gift, yes. Good. We go to finish this." Volk gestured with an outstretched hand. "Lead. Slowly."

Spencer looked Volk up and down. "I thought you'd be over this already."

Volk's face twisted. "Is difficult. If I had been shot before the change, it would have been easier."

"Before?"

"*Da.*"

"Why?"

"Why is the sky blue?" Volk nodded up. "Is just blue."

"Could it kill you?"

"After change?"

"Yes. After the change."

Volk looked at Spencer, his mouth turning down. "Why would you ask such a thing? We are good friends, you and I."

"I'll take that as a yes." Spencer smiled a flat, dead smile. "We are very good friends, Volk. The best of friends. I want to know because soon I'll need to worry about these sorts of things."

"Ah." Volk sighed. "That is good, Captain. It would be bad if I had to kill you and leave your body here."

Spencer swallowed, the smile leaving his face. "We have a deal."

"*Da.* Do not be afraid. I am not hungry." Volk smiled again. "You will find out soon enough. But no, Captain. Just shooting after the change? Is very hard to kill that way."

"How are you going to deal with Everard then?"

Volk smiled, saying nothing.

Spencer looked out into the forest. "Fine. Let's get out of here."

"Good. Tonight it will be over."

"Yes. Tonight it will be over." Spencer led Volk out of the clearing, and John listened to their voices fade away through the trees. He checked his watch, then looked back the way he'd come. No going back that way. He moved away from the tree, then started to jog in the opposite direction to where Spencer and Volk were heading. It would be bad news running into them. Soldiers to the left, sociopaths to the right.

It was going to be a long day.

JOHN RESTED AGAINST A TREE. He'd been jogging for about fifteen minutes, enough to work up a sweat and put some distance from the clearing. Being alone in the forest complicated things a little — he had to get to where Val was. He pulled out his phone, checking the Find My Friends app. The little blue marker showing where Val was had stopped moving. A short chopper ride was still a hell of a long walk.

He dialed a number, waiting as it rung a couple times. A woman's voice answered. "Did you find him?"

"Jesus, Danny. What's this? No hello?"

There was a moment of silence from the other end. "Hello. John. How are you." Her voice was flat.

"That's better." John grinned to himself in the forest. "What are you wearing?" The line went dead. John looked at his phone, then dialed again.

"John."

"The one and only."

A sigh came down the line. "Did you find him?"

"Yeah." John nodded to himself. "I found him all right."

"But he didn't turn around." It was hard to tell what was going through Danny's mind without seeing her face, but if John had to pick it she sounded a little relieved.

"No, but we didn't expect him to. I've got the next best thing."

"What's that?"

"Wait. Is Melissa there?"

"Yeah."

"Put me on speaker." John waited as muffled sounds came down the line.

"You're on."

"Christ. I sound like I'm in a goldfish bowl."

"You wanted to be on speaker." John was sure Danny sounded exasperated.

"Miles." It was Carlisle's voice. "What's the situation?"

"Hi, Melissa. Look, the situation? It's a bit more complicated than we thought."

"It's Carlisle. How's that?"

"Well, there's good news, some more good news, and some bad news."

There was a pause, then Danny said, "What's the bad news?"

"Yeah, I always want the bad stuff up front too." John looked at his watch. "I couldn't follow Val to where he was going. There was a helicopter and they flew him off somewhere."

"Shit!"

"Yeah."

Carlisle spoke up. "What's the good news?"

"Good news piece number one. I know where Val is."

"What?" There was a rustling after Danny spoke. "I've got a piece of paper. Spill."

"Relax, there's no address. It's in the woods."

"The woods?"

"Well … it's not on Google Maps anyway. How cool is this? Val's been taken to a secret lair. In the forest." John checked his phone; the line was still open. "Hello? You guys don't think that's cool?"

"This isn't a movie, Miles," said Carlisle. "It's not cool."

"It's a little bit cool. How many people are villainous enough to have an actual lair?"

"Okay, okay, it's cool," said Danny. "You had some other good news?"

"Sure do. This is even better. The bad guys, right?"

"Bad guys?" said Carlisle.

"Yeah, guys in black."

"Right. We call them suspects."

"That's because you have no soul." John checked the forest around him. Still no company — *good*. "The suspects? There are now two warring factions."

"What?" Danny sounded surprised.

"Val and I think that the main party is Elsie Morgan, of Biomne fame. The guys in black? They're a second faction."

"How you figure?"

"Saw one of them arguing with the janitor from the hospital." After a moment, John checked the phone again. Coverage out here was a bitch. "Hello?"

"We're still here. I just want to check what you just said," said Carlisle. "You say you saw a soldier arguing with a janitor. In the woods."

"Yep." John grinned to himself again. "Except he's not a janitor."

"He's not?"

"No."

"Then who is he?"

"Some Russian guy." John cleared his throat. "God damn allergies."

"A Russian janitor?" said Carlisle.

"Look, the important thing is that he's a werewolf."

"What?" said Danny.

"Is the line bad?"

"The line's fine. You're not making sense."

"Okay." John rubbed his face. "They were talking. Sounds like the janitor is some guy named Volk, who's a Russian. He's made a deal with the boss military guy."

"Captain?"

"Yeah, captain. Sure. His name's Spencer."

"The guy from the hospital?" said Danny. "I thought you said it was a janitor."

"Spencer's a soldier. The janitor's Russian."

"Wait," said Carlisle. "Let me see if I've got this. There's a captain — Spencer — who's teamed up with a Russian werewolf named Volk."

"That's what I said." One of them sighed. John wasn't sure which one.

"So how do you know this Volk is a werewolf?" said Carlisle.

"Said he was going to turn Spencer."

"Christ."

"Yeah, just what we need." John stood up. "We need to get moving. I'm going to come to you, then we'll head out."

There was a pause on the line. "Does Val know we're coming?" said Danny.

"No." John sighed. "He wouldn't have gone along with it if he thought it was more than me."

"I know," said Danny. "I feel—"

"I know," said John. "I feel it too. But sometimes you need to stretch the truth to help people out."

"We're not stretching it," said Danny. "We're lying to him."

"Yeah." John scuffed his foot in the forest floor. "Don't sweat it. I'll tell him it was all my idea."

"It was!"

"Exactly," said John.

"Great," said Danny. "Hurry back."

"You didn't answer my question." John grinned again.

"What question?"

"What are you wearing?"

The line went dead again. John was still grinning as he pocketed the phone.

THIRTY-FIVE

The chopper chattered into land on a pad set in a wide clearing, leaves and dust scattering in the downdraft from its rotors. Sam flipped some switches in the cabin, then nodded to Val. "We're here."

"Great." Val swallowed, then opened the door hatch. He stepped out onto the landing pad, breathing in the air.

Same forest.

"We haven't gone far, have we?" he said.

"What?" said Sam. "No, not far. Just a little distance to make sure we weren't followed."

"Fair enough." Val took in a row of prefab buildings in the distance, then looked up at a larger, central building. It was tall, maybe eight or ten stories high, the entire exterior plated in dark glass. The forest had been cleared in every direction; the central building stood like a giant version of the monolith from *A Space Odyssey*. He whistled. "Nice place."

"Ms. Morgan spared no expense." Sam nodded at the larger building. "We're heading in there. Sorry, it's a bit of a walk."

"What is this place?" Val waved his phone. "It's not on Google Maps."

"No." Sam nodded at the phone. "You'll need to give that to me."

"Sure." Val handed it over. "You'd figure something like this was on Google Earth."

"Google are able to be appropriately incentivised."

"You paid Google to keep it off the map?"

"Not quite." Sam grabbed a folder from the helicopter. "One of their executives has a child with a rare condition. There's an experimental drug that hasn't passed clinical trials. You know how it is."

"I guess I do." Val cleared his throat. "Must be nice to have powerful friends. How do you deal with Bing?"

"We donate to the Gates Foundation."

"What about Yahoo?"

"No one uses Yahoo."

"You guys have it all covered." Val nodded at his phone. "Don't lose that. I'll be needing it later."

Sam gave a half smile. "Later?"

"Don't sweat it. Lead on."

"Of course." Sam lead away from the helicopter pad towards the main building. Val looked up at the building, trying to catch a glimpse of anything. Anyone. The glass tinting was good; he couldn't make anything out.

"Adalia's here?"

"Hm? Yes." Sam held the door open for him, and they walked into a spacious foyer. It was deserted.

"Where is everyone?"

"There's not many on staff here, Mr. Everard." Sam led the way to an elevator. "There is only one patient."

Val looked around the foyer. "One patient? For all this?"

"It's a very special patient. Ms. Morgan has spared no expense."

"Do I get to meet your patient?"

"I'm not sure that's a good idea." The elevator arrived, and Sam swiped his card over the panel. The doors closed silently, and they started to rise. The elevator was slow and smooth, without the usual lurch of motion.

"Man. This elevator's something."

"As I said, no expense was spared." A large display read the number 4, and the elevator stopped. "Here we are."

"What's here?"

"Mr. Everard, I appreciate you have questions. I'm going to take you to a ... holding facility for the moment, and then Ms. Morgan will speak with you directly." Sam led the way again, heading down a corridor. The white walls were featureless as they passed closed door after closed door.

"The queen herself?"

A smile tugged at Sam's face. "I'm sure she would be quite fond of that description. Yes, Ms. Morgan will speak with you."

"I wouldn't have thought she would be comfortable with that."

"Why not?"

"Because." Val gestured at himself. "Ah. My condition."

Sam stopped before a door, and passed his card in front of the lock. A light on the door lit green, and it opened with a click. "Ms. Morgan has an established history with confrontation."

"She's going to argue with me?"

"If I have this right," Sam said, "And I'm not sure that I do — well. If I understand Ms. Morgan at all, she believes the best approach to conflict is to be able to make an offer the other party can't refuse."

"That sounds very Corleone." Val pushed the door open to reveal a small room with a bed, table, and large mirror against one wall.

"It's more of a win-win. If both people get what they want, then it's an easy sale." Sam nodded. "Mr. Everard, I'll leave you here—"

"There's no signs."

"I'm sorry?"

"There's no signs. Usually a hospital has signs. Radiology, shit like that."

"Ah. There's no need for them. This is not a typical hospital.

People who work here … well, they know where they're going and why they're going there. We like them to think of it like a home away from home. You wouldn't have signs in your home, would you?"

"I guess not."

Sam hesitated, then held out his hand. "It's been a pleasure meeting you, Mr. Everard."

Val took the handshake. "And you, Sam. Can I make a suggestion?"

"Certainly."

"Get back in the helicopter and fly out of here."

Sam looked at his feet. "Why's that?"

"I don't think all of us are going to make it out here alive today, Sam."

Sam nodded at him. "I appreciate the concern, Mr. Everard, but it's misplaced. Good day to you."

He closed the door behind him and the lock clicked. Val stared at the door for a moment, then sat down on the bed. "It's like a gulag," he said to the empty room. They hadn't even left him with a TV.

VAL TRACED the line on the ceiling with his eyes for the hundredth time. It was hard to see, that line, a slight imperfection of the plaster. He'd had nothing to do but stare at the ceiling for an hour or so. Sam had taken his phone — he couldn't even play a shitty game.

"Mr. Everard." The voice startled him upright. He saw that the mirror had turned into a screen, an older woman — still fit and trim, but showing the marks of time — looking at him, larger than life. It was a head and shoulders anchor shot, like from a newsroom. He recognized the voice straight away.

"Neat trick." Val got off the bed and walked over to the screen. "I hadn't noticed it was a monitor, Elsie."

"Indeed." Elsie looked him up and down. "You're—"

"Don't say it." Val nodded at the mirror. "You can do better than that."

She smiled. To Val's eye, she looked more tired than happy. "Better than what, Mr. Everard?"

"You were about to say that you expected someone taller."

"I was about to say that you're looking well, for someone who's been shot. More than once, if reports are to be believed. I've even seen some video. It's ... it's more than we've hoped for. I hope you don't mind me saying that."

"You shouldn't believe everything you see on TV." Val nodded at the door. "Am I prisoner here?"

"I'm not sure. Are you?"

"Sam locked me in."

"I think we both know that door's not going to hold you. Sam's locked other people out."

Val nodded, thinking for a moment. "Where to from here? I've done as you've asked. I'm here."

"You're referring to Adalia."

"I am."

"Once we extract the virus—"

"You what?"

"Extract. The virus." Elsie looked down at something Val couldn't see. "You carry a very special, very unique pathogen."

"I don't really feel sick. I feel better than I ever have." Val breathed in deep, then let it out. "It's a funny virus, if that's what it is."

"How so?"

"Okay. First." Val ticked them off on his fingers. "It makes me faster and stronger."

"Yes."

"I haven't finished. Second." He held two fingers up to the glass. "It makes me hard to kill, in the traditional sense."

"What do you mean by traditional?"

"You're a clever lady. You've seen the videos, as you say. Three."

307

Val cleared his throat. "This one's the killer. It turns me into a monster."

"Yes. We're having trouble reconciling that one ourselves." Elsie tipped her head sideways slightly, studying him. "It doesn't make sense."

"You should try it from this side."

"Hm. Yes." Elsie smiled the tired smile again. "Unfortunately, we don't have a lot of time to puzzle through it. Our usual ... more scientific approach won't be useful here."

"How's that? You're the head of big pharma."

"Our ... client is on a tight schedule."

"Your client is dying." Val sighed. "That's what this is about, isn't it?"

Elsie's eyes flicked to his face. She was looking for something, Val wasn't sure what. "Yes."

"You could have just asked." Val walked over to the window, staring out at the forest. He nodded to himself. "Figures."

"What figures?"

"What? Oh. Nothing." Val turned back to Elsie. "Why didn't you ask? You've—"

No. That memory lives in darkness.

"—killed. People." He gritted his teeth. "Children."

"You must understand, Mr. Everard." Elsie fiddled with her glasses. "The loss of life is something I deeply regret."

"Hm."

"I'm sorry?"

"Are you?" Val gestured at the room. "Really sorry. You know, do you regret it? This facility. It speaks of a grand design. It's not on the Internet, for Christ's sake. Whatever's here, it's important to you. A couple of people, dead? Probably just a rounding error to someone like you."

Elsie sighed on the screen. "No."

"It's not a rounding error?"

"No. You're right. I don't regret it." Elsie looked off to the side at something Val couldn't see. "It's possible I've lost some perspective through all of this."

"Perspective?" Val cleared his throat. "It might be more than perspective."

"I'd do it again, you know." Elsie looked back at him. "If it works, it'll be worth it. The things we can do with it—"

"Yeah, I get it. You'll cure HIV and cancer." Val studied her. "Ah. Cancer."

"Our client—"

"Is dying." Val held his hands up like balance scales, tipping them one way and that. "You've put one client in this side. Wagered everything. Against this other side." He lifted his other hand. "Hundreds of people. They're all gone, Elsie. They can't come back. They'll get no benefit from this."

"No, Mr. Everard."

"And you're willing to pay."

"I'm willing to pay."

"At the cost of your soul."

That tired smile came back. "I don't believe in such things, Mr. Everard."

"Whether you believe or not, the cost is high." Val gestured out the window. "Not just money. There's things you can't come back from. If this ever gets out—"

"You think this is the worst thing that we've ever done? That I've ever done?" Elsie leaned forward. "The business of curing the sick is not a philanthropic one, Mr. Everard. It's exactly that — a business. Profit and loss. Curing people is incidental to the business of making the cures themselves. They don't need to work — people just need to buy them." She stopped for a moment. "But this is different. This virus you have? It's the real thing. It will cure people. If we corner the market, we'll have a drug people will pay any price for. And — finally — it'll be a real cure."

After a moment, Val nodded. "That's how you justify it."

"There's no need to justify it. It is what it is."

Val looked at his shoes. "You realize it's a curse, right?"

"I beg your pardon?"

"Your cure. It's a curse."

"Not wearing silver is hardly a curse, Mr. Everard. Perhaps one mining industry is adversely affected. A drop in the bucket."

"I'm not talking about miners out of jobs. I'm talking about a real, honest to God, actual curse."

"You're being melodramatic."

"Am I?" Val held his hands up to the screen. "Elsie, I've killed people. I can't remember doing it—"

Salty, hot spray. The hunt.

"—but I'm sure it's happened." Val swallowed. "I ... I see things. Memories. Flashbacks. I don't know ... something." He shrugged, sitting back down on the edge of the bed.

"A possible side effect of the virus. You may be running a fever, having hallucinations—"

No. We are the Night.

"No." Val shook his head. "It's nothing like that. When it takes over, I'm gone, and then..." His shoulders slumped. "It's why I'm here."

"You want a cure?" Elsie shook her head. "Anti viral meds are a long way—"

"I want an end." Val gestured at the window. "When it takes over, I'm not me. It—"

"It?"

"Whatever." Val thought for a moment. "How old is your kid?"

"I'm sorry?"

"Your kid. The one who's got cancer."

"Don't be—"

"Elsie. Remember, no lies. Not between us." Val looked at the screen. "You owe me that."

Elsie sighed, looking down off screen. "Birkita is her father's daughter, really."

"Ah. A daughter." Val's mouth quirked. "Birkita?"

Elsie smiled in return. "Her father's daughter, as I said. You'd like her, I'm sure. She's full of the small concerns for people that seem to plague you."

"I like her already." Val shook his head. He felt sad. "You want to give this to a kid?"

"She's going to die, Mr. Everard."

"She's dead either way, Elsie. You let her die now, it's the cancer. You give her this, it's her soul."

"I've already told you, I don't believe in such things."

"She will." Val shrugged. "In the end. Why haven't you just," and he waved his hands, "given it to her? I'm sure you've got my biopsy."

"Yes." Elsie tapped off screen. "Let me show you." A magnified view of a cell appeared in the corner of the screen. "Here's a cell of blood — not one of yours. It's healthy, normal blood, coming from a clean skin."

"Clean skin?"

"Ah. Yes, what we call people who go through life without getting a serious malaise. If we were insurance underwriters, we'd want this person as a client."

"Got it."

"Here is where we introduce some of the virus — courtesy of your blood — into the cell." The image showed the virus moving up to the cell. "It's lysogenic."

"Lysowhat?"

"It makes the host cell replicate for itself." Elsie cleared her throat. "You can see the virus invading the cell." The image showed the cell started to grow, then split. "Here we are. Two copies, each with the virus."

"It looks the same."

"It's lysogenic."

"You said that before. I work in computers."

"It'll become clear soon enough, Mr. Everard. Ah." Elsie nodded. The screen showed the cell break down, falling apart. "There."

"What just happened?" Val looked at the image on the screen. "It looked like it fell apart."

"Yes. Lysogenic replication usually involves a lytic cycle, and the cell breaks apart and releases new virus structures."

"I didn't see any new virus particles. I don't know what they'd look like, but that sucker just ... melted."

"Melted. Curious word." Elsie nodded, tapped something, and the image went away. "That's what seems to happen. Can I show you something else?"

"Sure. I don't have anywhere else to be."

Else typed some more off-screen and a new image came up. It showed a man strapped to a chair, metal restraints holding him down. A complicated set of machinery sat to the man's side, a drip going into his arm. "He seems quite relaxed," said Val. "Why are you chaining him to a chair?"

"In case we're successful." Elsie pressed a button, and the image started to play. A timer down the bottom of the screen started to count up the seconds. "Here, we inject the virus."

The timer showed five seconds. "He volunteered?"

"Yes."

Ten seconds. "Why would he do that?"

"You killed his friends."

Fifteen seconds. The man in the chair had started to sweat. "I did?"

"You, or Volk. It doesn't matter. He wanted revenge."

Val didn't ask what for. Twenty-five seconds. The man was pulling at the restraints. "He doesn't look happy."

"No." Elsie's mouth was pressed into a line. "Here."

Thirty seconds. The man said something, but Val couldn't make it out — there was no audio. "What did he say?"

"We think he said, 'Turn it off.'" Elsie shrugged. "It wouldn't have mattered. There's nothing to turn off. He's already infected."

Forty seconds. The man started to thrash in the chair, and his mouth opened. "My God," said Val. "He's screaming."

Elsie nodded. "You'll see the reason for his discomfort shortly."

Fifty seconds. A line appeared on the man's cheek, blood seeping out. Tears of blood started from his eyes. "Christ."

"It's not much longer now, Mr. Everard."

The man was thrashing his head about, blood and spittle leaving his mouth. He convulsed in the chair, back arching, the metal clamps biting into his wrists. Blood was streaming from his eyes and ears freely. He gave a massive convulsion, and one of his arms tore free from its socket. He thrashed for what seemed an age, then was still. Blood continued to flow, and his skin peeled off and sloughed to the ground. Big lumps of muscle and other tissue slid free.

One minute, ten seconds. The video stopped.

Val stumbled back, hitting the edge of the bed. He sat down hard. "Christ."

"Quite." Elsie tapped, and the image disappeared. "Simply injecting the virus into a host does not appear to have the desired result."

"Desired result?" Val wiped his face. "The man—"

"Melted. As you said before."

"His skin came off, for God's sake! He ... he ripped his own arm off!"

"Yes. The clean up was distressing for our staff. The tissue just wouldn't hold together. We have a theory that there's something unique about the way the virus spreads. Improper transmission of the virus leads to a flaw, and the host dies."

"But. But. Even I know viruses don't work that fast."

"We know. We don't understand. That's why you're here."

"You want to give this to your daughter?"

"Not quite, Mr. Everard. Obviously what we've tried is a death sentence. Oh, we're sure we can crack it, given time. But we don't have time."

"How long does she have?"

"My staff believe no more than a month. That's being optimistic. She's already on borrowed time."

Val sighed. "What's next?"

"You're familiar with the werewolf legend."

"I've seen movies. Barking at the moon. Shit like that."

"Barking at the moon. Yes." Elsie nodded. "It's a bit deeper than that. We had to find a carrier, first."

"Volk."

"The Russian, yes."

"We've met." Val flexed his left wrist. "He's not very nice."

"No. He wasn't as cooperative as we'd have hoped." Elsie smiled. "We'd have thought in exchange for his freedom—"

We will not be caged.

"Freedom?"

"Yes. He was in a dingy prison in Siberia. It took us a long time to find him. Most of his records weren't computerized."

"Russia, huh?"

"Oh, it's not because of their outdated technology in government." Elsie looked to the side again. "It's because he'd been there for a very, very long time."

"How long?"

"We're not sure."

"Ten years? Twenty? He didn't look that old to me."

"No." Elsie raised her hands upwards. "Think higher. Perhaps two hundred years."

"Two hundred!" Val leaned forward. "He looked in his twenties."

"The virus, Mr. Everard."

Oh God. I'm going to live for a hundred years, and kill everyone I love. The thought punched him hard, and he swallowed.

"Mr. Everard?"

"I'm okay, Elsie. Just ... acclimatising." Val ran his hand through his hair. "There's just one carrier?"

"Only one that we could find. The Russians were experimenting on him."

"They're trying to find the magic bullet too."

"Perhaps. They engineered this virus, with inconsistent results. But we have the edge in medical science."

"So you busted him out and shipped him here?" Val gestured around the room. "Where is he?"

"Containment is ... tricky. It's why we've adopted a different approach in your situation."

Val's stare went flat. "Adalia."

"Yes. I'm sorry about that. I have a daughter too."

"I know." Val felt tired more than anything else. "How is it done?"

"We're going to need you to bite Birkita."

"You're joking, of course."

"I'm quite serious, Mr. Everard. Saliva appears to be the universal carrier within all the werewolf legends." Elsie frowned. "I've read them all."

"All of them?"

"Aside from recent pulp literature, yes. Did you know many cultures had a shape shifting lore?"

"Like skinwalkers?"

"Ah. You're familiar with other sources of the truth."

"I wouldn't say that. I saw a really bad movie with the same title. I'd hardly call it historical canon." Val shrugged. "Rhona Mitra is fine."

"Regardless." Elsie waved a hand. "A bite that breaks the skin seems to be the necessary means of transmission."

"That's a little surreal. Have you briefed your daughter about this?"

"Not yet. I'll be talking to her shortly."

"Can I suggest an alternative? It seems a bit unhygienic to follow your path."

"I'm listening." Elsie crossed her arms on the screen.

"Why not give her a cut, and swab me for some spit. That way she doesn't have to have some scary man bite her arm."

"It might not work." Elsie took off her glasses, and tapped them against her hand. "The legends are all fairly specific."

"One second you say it's a virus. The next it's a legend. Can we at least try it my way first?"

Elsie seemed lost in thought, then said, "Yes. It'll need to be a fresh sample though. Mr. Everard, let me talk to my daughter, then we'll try it your way."

"You're forgetting something."

"Adalia?"

"Yes." Val shrugged. "That's why I'm here."

"If I may be blunt, you're here to die." Elsie shrugged. "That seems to be what you want."

"In the end, yes." Val looked at his hands, turning them over. "But first, I need to see she's safe."

"Once our business is done, I'll have Sam fly her to the city. Will that suffice?"

"I've a question first. Are you expecting company?"

"I'm sorry?"

"It's just that when I looked out the window before, I saw a couple guys creeping around at the edge of the forest."

"Two men?"

"Yes. One of them was your crazy Russian. The other was that soldier you sent after me."

"Spencer?"

"Spencer, that's the guy." Val sighed. "It figures. You're going to kill Adalia anyway."

Elsie looked off screen again, then back to Val. "You must believe me, Mr. Everard. Our agreement. I intend to honor it."

"Hm. Spencer still on the books?"

"The books?"

"Look." Val spread his hands. "You guys make me sick. This whole thing is a cluster fuck. You've killed people. You're threatening the people I love. You've brought my friends into danger. That's on you. Your methods are not exactly above board."

"I…" Elsie stopped, then looked off screen again. She tapped on her keyboard. "Mr. Everard, I need to go."

"Elsie—"

There was a muffled *whump*, and the building shook. Val stood. "That's not good news, is it?"

"Did you bring friends, Mr. Everard?"

"Do I look like I need backup?"

Elsie didn't answer. The screen faded back into being a mirror. *Shit*, thought Val. *This just got a little more complicated.* He wondered where John was. He looked at the door.

They kill within their own Pack.

It was time to find Adalia. He walked to the door, gripping the handle with one hand. He leaned back, pulling, and after a moment the handle popped free in his hand. He stared at it for a moment, then at the door. "No expense my ass. What kind of lousy workmanship is that?"

He shrugged. *Stop talking to yourself, Val. It's the first sign of madness.*

Val looked around the room, then backed away from the door. He braced himself, then charged the door with his shoulder. It crashed free of the frame, landing in the corridor outside. Val coughed at the dust, waving it from his face as he looked around. There were no damn signs.

There are no clever symbols that guide us to prey.

He looked left, then right, then closed his eyes, listening, his breathing and pulse slowing. *Yelling. A scream. Gunfire. An engine. A child's voice.*

It is not cub.

There. He'd bet dollars to donuts that was Birkita. Finding her was a step in the right direction. Hell, maybe he could even ask her what *she* wanted. Whatever — he'd need to head up to get there. He knew it wasn't Adalia, but—

Another explosion shook the building and he stumbled, a hand going to the wall to steady himself. A child's scream.

Cub!

"Wait!" He gritted his teeth, holding himself back. He wanted to run, to climb, to get to her, to—

Kill them all.

"I said wait!" A sliver of saliva ran down his chin. "No. Think."

They have cub.

"The explosions. Are down. Adalia. Is up." He breathed in and out, talking himself through it. "They want me. We need to get her out first. To safety. To John."

Kill.

"We need to be silent. Not draw … the hunt to us." Val swallowed. "We can't lead them to Adalia."

There was silence in his head. He swallowed again, relaxing a little. Slowly, he walked towards the elevators — there should be a stairwell up. Then — well, one step at a time. But there'd be no killing until she was safe. He needed to be discrete. After that—

They will die.

Val nodded. There'd be plenty of time later. For everything.

THIRTY-SIX

"I can tell that you work out." John leaned against the wall.

"Stow it, Miles." Carlisle didn't turn to look at him. Which was fine by John — she didn't look pretty when she was angry. She was on his left side, peering around the edge of one of the low prefab buildings of the complex. They'd run to the edge of the building; the prefabs were the only cover between the central building and the forest's edge.

"No, really. And your back especially." That earned him a glance over the shoulder.

"What?"

"Well, it's all I can see. Because you're in the way." John gestured at the building's corner. "What's the play?"

"I'm in the way because you're a civilian. Both of you are." Carlisle leaned back against the wall next to them. She pulled her sidearm out, checking it for the hundredth time. "You shouldn't even be here. The only reason you are is because I'm doped up on benzos and I'm not thinking straight. Pretty sure I've taken more than the recommended daily dose, if you get me."

"It's not your daughter in there." Danny was on the other side of

John, to his right. He was pretty sure Val was going to kill him for letting her come along. Still, it's not like he was in a position to stop her — the look on her face as he'd tried to start the conversation would have made Mike Tyson think twice about stepping in that ring.

John raised his hands up. "It's cool, you know. She's on our side."

"I'm just saying." Danny looked at her shoes.

"Well, this is uncomfortable." John leaned away from the wall, stretching. "Talk about a rose between two thorns."

"Sorry, Miles." Carlisle shrugged. "This isn't in the SOP."

"SOP?"

"Standard Operating — you know, never mind." Carlisle nodded to the large building in the middle of the compound. "That looks to be where the action happens."

"What tipped you off? That it's in the middle, that it's the biggest, or the legion of soldiers running in there?" John studied his nails.

"Christ. I don't know how you survived this long. I'd shoot you myself if I didn't need you to draw their fire." Carlisle's grin was wry.

Danny hefted the crossbow. "I'm not sure what I'm supposed to do with this."

"It was your idea." John shrugged. "Wave it at people if they look like they want to shoot you."

"I know that, it's just..." The crossbow twanged, the bolt skidding up and into the sky. It missed John's face by inches.

He pushed the front of the weapon away. "Easy, tiger."

"Sorry!" Danny lowered the crossbow down to her side. "I slipped."

"No, it's fine." Carlisle smiled. "You missed him though. Next time, a few more inches, and — pow."

John looked between them. "I'm not feeling loved." He rubbed his jaw. "That was pretty close. If she could aim, she'd be dangerous."

Danny grabbed another bolt from the quiver strapped to her leg, putting it in the crossbow. "It's lucky they don't know I can't aim."

"We know now." The voice was nasty, and all three of them spun. Two men dressed in black had walked around the corner, guns trained on them.

John heard a twang — *how'd she get it cocked so fast?* — as Danny fired her crossbow. The bolt went through the throat of the man who'd spoken. Carlisle was already moving, her left arm batting a rifle away as her right swung into a savage uppercut. The man stumbled back, but Carlisle held his rifle; she kicked down hard against his knee, and he fell forward again. The edge of her free hand speared into his throat below the helmet. She kicked him back with one foot, drawing her sidearm and firing into the man's visor three times. He jerked with each shot, then fell down.

"Christ." John looked behind him at Danny. "I thought you said you couldn't aim?"

Danny looked at the crossbow in her hands like it was a snake. "I … It went off."

Carlisle frowned at her. "It went off *right* this time." She turned to look at the two men on the ground. The one with the bolt protruding from his neck was clawing weakly at the shaft as red foam bubbled around the edges of the wound. She stepped over him and fired twice into his visor. The man was still. "That's probably our element of surprise gone."

John looked at the two dead men, then back to Carlisle. "I've seen that show *Cops*, on TV. Those guys don't fight like that."

"A girl has to have hobbies." Carlisle was searching the bodies.

"I play video games. That's a hobby." John gestured at the bodies on the ground. "This isn't a hobby. Unless it's the expert level of butterfly collecting."

"I study *Krav Maga*."

"What?"

"Israeli. Self defense." She stood up, and held a rifle out to John. "Do you know how to use this?"

He took the rifle from her. "Yeah, I guess. I've used one before."

"How long ago?" She checked her sidearm again, then holstered it.

"Actually, just a couple days. We were busting you out of the hospital." John went over to Danny, who was standing still, staring at the fallen men. "Hey. You okay?"

"I ... yeah." She swallowed. "These fuckers have Adalia, right?"

John looked back at the men. "Well, not these two specifically. But we think so."

An ugly expression crossed her face. "Then I'm just peachy." She hefted her crossbow — perhaps a little more confidently in John's eyes — and reloaded the weapon.

Carlisle hefted the other rifle. "Nice." She slung a belt across her shoulders.

"What's with the belt?" John eyed it carefully. He couldn't be sure, but those looked like —

"Grenades." Carlisle tapped some of the cylinders on the belt. "These guys are loaded for bear. This is not a hospital. At least, not one I want to stay at."

The explosion shook the ground, the sound of it terrible and sudden. John covered his head with his arms, falling backwards against the side of the building. "What the fuck!"

Carlisle ducked her head around the edge of the building. "Jesus."

"What?"

"Things just got complicated."

John put a hand on her shoulder and pulled himself around her to take a look. The main door of the building was a ruin, smoke and fire everywhere. A group of men in black were storming towards the hole, rifles firing into the breach. Return fire answered from inside. He pulled his head back. "I don't get it."

"It's a coup." Carlisle's mouth pulled into a savage grin. "Complicated is good for us. We get in, get the kid, and get out."

"Right." John looked around. "How do we get through that shit storm of fire?"

Carlisle's grin broadened. "We wait, Miles. They'll do the hard work for us."

"I don't want to wait," said Danny. "You guys can wait. I'm going in."

"It's a shooting gallery, Danny!" The sound of gunfire hammered the air, as if to support his point. John shrugged. "How do you think we're getting through that?"

"You're such a boy," said Danny. "Always thinking in straight lines. There'll be a back door." And just like that, she was off — running with the crossbow held in one hand as she made her way parallel to the action towards the rear of the large building.

"Well I'll be." John shrugged. "I guess we need to go back her up."

"I guess we do." Carlisle hefted her rifle, looking down the sights. "We're all going to be dead before the end of the day. You know that, don't you?"

"That's why I never joined the police," said John.

"Because it's a dangerous profession?"

"Because you're all sour, pessimistic fuckers." John clapped her on the shoulder. "Come on. We're leaving." He set off at a run, making it look easy. He liked to think he made everything look easy. He turned to make sure Carlisle was bringing up the rear — after all, she was the professional here — then turned his attention back to the front.

He was making it look dead easy right up until he drew fire. The bullets rattled along the building he was running beside, shards of plaster falling around him. John dropped into a crouch beside an air conditioning unit attached to the building, a big Panasonic unit with twin fans churning the air at a steady rate. It was a large industrial type, pipes and wires snaking from it into the building. It gave him a scrap of precious cover, wedged in the corner between it and the building, as he tried to get a view on who was shooting at him.

The goddamn building he huddled next to was between him and

the bad guys assaulting the front door, so where — *ah*. At the tree line he could see two men hunkered down. They were making hand signs at each other, and one of them pointed in his direction. The other nodded and started to move in a crouched run towards John, the first staying back to cover his comrade. John readied his rifle — *if I can just get the drop on these guys...*

The covering soldier at the tree line dropped like a stone. John scanned about, but couldn't see anyone. It could have been Danny or Carlisle or a random act of fate like a brain aneurysm. Hell, the guy could have been shot by Cupid's bow for all the obvious signs there were. John hunkered back down beside the air conditioner, keeping his arms and legs tucked in. He heard the other man come up close and felt the slight jar in the AC as the man set his weight against it. *The irony*. John moved his rifle slowly, so slowly, around the edge of the AC, the barrel creeping out.

A salvo of gunfire spat through the windows above them, showering them both with glass. There was a crunch followed by an explosion — *is that what a grenade sounds like?* — in the building they were next to. John and the soldier covered up, sheltering on opposite sides of the AC unit as the bullets cut into the building. Window glass exploded, wood chips and debris flying around them. John and the soldier both scuttled around the AC to sit next to each other, using the unit as mutual cover, an extra sliver of life between them and the chaos hammering into the building.

Silence. John and the other man looked at each other. *Alive!* They shared a grin, and John stood. "Shit man. That was intense." He held a hand out to the soldier on the ground.

The man looked at his hand. "What the hell," he said, and grabbed the offered hand. John helped him up, and they slouched against the AC unit.

"You do this often?" John checked his weapon.

The soldier did the same. "Yeah. Been a crazy few weeks."

John nodded. "So what now?"

"I dunno. I'm supposed to—"

"I know. Kill everyone you see, right?"

The helmet nodded. "Something like that. Aw, crap." The man stepped away from the unit, leveling his gun at John. "I'm real sorry about this."

"So am I." John nodded. "Say, save me a seat."

The helmet tipped sideways. "Seat?"

"Yeah. On the train to Hell."

Carlisle grabbed the soldier from behind, one hand on his chin and the other on his shoulder, and wrenched her hands apart. There was a crack as the man's neck broke, and he slumped to the ground, his useless rifle falling beside him. "You talk too much," she said.

"It's my thing." John turned on the megawatt smile. "That, and my handsome face."

Carlisle patted his cheek. "You're just too damn pretty to die, aren't you?"

"You know it. Where's Danny?"

"Up ahead. She's at the corner of the building. You think you can get there without being shot at?"

"Hey." John shrugged. "It's not like I'm wearing pink or something. This camo was expensive."

Carlisle snorted. "That vest was no more than ten bucks at a surplus store."

"You shop there too? I can tell."

She didn't say anything, jogging off towards the other side of the main building. They caught up with Danny as she waited at the rear of it, crouched low and leaning against the corner. John could appreciate what Val saw in her. She was a striking woman, come to think of it, in a fit sort of way—

"Christ, Miles." Carlisle coughed. "Stop ogling."

Danny turned around. "What?"

"It's nothing." John turned on the megawatt smile. "She's deeply, insanely jealous."

"Of what?" Danny looked between the two of them, then tried again. "Why?"

"That's what I said." John nodded at Carlisle. "For a detective, she's not very good at detecting."

Carlisle ignored him. "Kendrick, what've you seen?"

"Nothing. Not a goddamned thing." Danny smiled. "It's perfect. There's a door at the back, I think, there's a path that heads up to it. You can see it from here, and it leads off towards those helicopters back there."

"That'd be a perfect escape route, if one of us could fly a helicopter." Carlisle looked at both of them. "Guess not. Okay. We'll need the car then. Why don't I take the lead from here?"

"Who's going to watch my butt?" John jerked his head back the way they'd come.

"Trust me, it's not that riveting."

"Christ. There really is no love." John waved them forward. "You two go ahead. I'll hold here. Sing out when you're in."

He turned his back to the two women as they jogged off. John scanned back the way they'd come, but didn't see anyone. It really was a balls-deep invasion at the front of the building, that's for sure, but if he was a gambling man he'd send one or two to the back, just to make sure. That could have been the two that Carlisle had dropped earlier — *there*. He saw the movement as the soldiers — *what, four, five?* — scuttled along the path John had taken down the row of buildings. He slowly edged back around the edge of the building, using the line of the structure for cover. The soldiers had found the fallen man by the AC, and slowed their pace. *Shit*. They weren't going to be caught by surprise that easy. John turned back towards Carlisle. "What's keeping you guys?"

"It's locked." Danny sounded frustrated.

"Great. Say, Carlisle."

"Miles?"

"Can I have one of those grenades?"

"Do you know how to use them?"

"I'll work it out." He caught the thrown belt of grenades, fumbling along the line of cylinders. "Okay."

"What?" Carlisle sounded distracted.

"Can I phone a friend?"

"See the little metal ring?"

"Yeah."

"Pull that, and then throw it far away."

"Got it." John hefted the belt of grenades. How many grenades do you need to take out five guys? Probably one per guy, sure, that made sense. The belt held five grenades, which was super convenient, like a sign from God or something. He watched the men walk closer, edging along the line of the building towards him. *Fuck it.*

"Guys." John's head popped out, then he ducked back as bullets spattered the edge of the building. "Shit! I just want to talk!"

A moment passed, then, "About what?"

"I just want to go home!" John pulled the rings out of the grenades, one by one. "I'm coming out!"

"Sure. Put your hands in the air." John thought he could hear a grim chuckle, the sort any bully might make. He looked at the rings at his feet, then at the belt of now live grenades. How long did you wait before you threw them? That's probably important stuff to know. *Hell with it.* He whipped his hand around the edge of the building, tossing the belt, then pulling his hand back.

The explosion knocked a chunk of the building corner loose, the force throwing him back like he'd been kicked by a horse. He lay on the ground for a moment, seeing nothing but sky, his ears ringing. He drew a shuddering breath in, then levered himself up onto one elbow. The corner of the building was gone, a great crater blown into the side of it and into the ground. He couldn't see any sign of the five soldiers. He whooped, laughing out loud, then clambered to his feet.

Carlisle said something.

"What?" John gestured to his ears. "I can't hear so well right now. Speak up!"

"I said, are you fucking crazy?" Carlisle was shouting at him.

"Okay. Got it. Not quite so loud." John felt one of his ears, his hand coming away red. "Christ. I think I've burst an eardrum."

Carlisle's face was grim. "You could have been killed."

"Yeah, but I'm not. Dead, I mean." John turned on the megawatt smile. "And I'm up five."

"Five?"

"Yeah. The score. Danny has one, you've got two, and I've got five." He held up his hand, four fingers and thumb stretched out. "I'm winning."

Carlisle stared at him for a moment, then a grin cracked across her face. "Your five don't count. Grenades are a negative score."

"Says who?" John rotated his shoulder in the socket, wincing. "That was a hell of a blast. I should get a few style points at least."

"You get one point. One," she held up a hand, stopping him, "for killing something without dying yourself. You get another point for style. So we're even. Two for two."

"What are you guys talking about?" Danny said.

"We're keeping score." Carlisle walked back towards her. "Miles thought he was in the lead, but I've corrected him."

"Score?" Danny thought for a moment. "I'm guessing I've got just one point?"

"Yeah. Sorry."

"It's okay. The day is young." Danny nodded at the door. There was a woman in a lab coat on the other side, looking nervously through the glass. "She won't open the door."

John walked up to the glass, putting on his best megawatt smile. "Hello there!" he said. "Could you open the door?"

The woman looked at the gun in his hands, then shook her head.

John looked down at the gun, starting as if he'd seen it for the first time. He handed it to Danny. "Hey, look, my bad. See, no gun. You want to come out, right?"

The woman nodded, saying nothing.

"Okay. We want to come in! This is a great win-win. Say, can you fly a helicopter?"

She shook her head.

"Too bad. Look," and he peered at her name badge through the glass, "Millicent, could you open the door? There's a lot of guys out here who want to kill us, and, well, I haven't had lunch yet. I figure it's bad form to die on an empty stomach. What do you say?"

Millicent's face quirked. "I—"

"Look, take your time. Have a think about it." John shrugged at her.

"What?" Danny tugged at his vest. "We're—"

"Hey." John shushed her. "If she needs some time, she can take all the time she needs."

"Ma'am." Carlisle stepped up to the glass, pushing her ID up against it. "I'm a police officer."

Millicent looked at John and Danny. "Who are they, then?"

"These people?" Carlisle looked at them. "That's a good question, ma'am. They're ... they're, ah—"

"We're helping her with some inquiries," said John. "So, what about it?"

"I'm not supposed to—"

"Let anyone in?" John examined his hands.

"No. I mean, yes. I mean, that's right."

"I get it. But we're the good guys." John looked back up, beaming at her. Chicks couldn't resist the smile. "Seriously. Also, there's a bunch of assholes coming in the front who are going to kill everyone."

"Oh."

"Yeah. It's probably best if you just open the door."

Millicent nodded, swiping her card against the lock. It beeped, and the door opened. John smiled at her. "Thanks a bunch."

"You're not going to kill me, are you?"

John stared at her. "Shit no. Why would we do that?"

"It's just — the guns."

"I bet you didn't think today would be like this when you were having your morning coffee."

The woman cracked a nervous grin as the three of them filed in.

John held the door for her, and she took a cautious step outside. "Say, Millicent."

"Yes."

"Be careful, okay?" John nodded towards the forest at the back of the complex. "I'd make a bee line for those trees. Lose yourself in there for a while. It's not safe here."

Millicent looked at the trees, then back at John. "Thanks. Say."

"Yes?"

"It's about the girl, isn't it?"

"What girl?" John kept his voice casual.

"The little girl. They brought her here a couple days ago—"

Danny rushed forward, grabbing the woman by her lab coat, slamming her up against the wall. "Where is she!"

"I ... I—"

A snarl twisted Danny's face. "I swear to God, I will tear it from you!"

John put a hand on her shoulder, very gently. "Danny." She was panting, he could feel her shoulders heave with the force of it. "Danny. Put her down."

Danny turned her head back at him, her face still twisted, then she turned back towards Millicent. She was holding her up against the wall, the woman's shoes a good foot off the ground. Danny relaxed her shoulders slowly, Millicent sliding to the ground. "Sorry," she said.

John stepped between the two of them, hands out. "Say, that was intense." He beamed. "I'm real sorry about that, Milly. But the thing is, that little girl? Well, Danny here—"

"She's my daughter." Danny's voice was steady.

"I..." Millicent cleared her throat, then started again. "I'm sorry, I had no idea. She's on the top floor."

"You've seen her?" Carlisle's question was sharp, professional.

"Uh, no. But the other floors are empty. They always have been. It's just the top floor."

John nodded. "Thanks. Now get out of here." He nodded at the tree line. Millicent broke into a run, her lab coat flashing white behind her.

Carlisle shrugged. "That was unorthodox, but we got what we needed. Top floor it is."

"You think she's telling the truth?" John looked after the running woman. "I mean, you know. What's her motive?"

Danny sighed. "Does it matter? Top or bottom, we've got to start somewhere."

"You're right." John closed the door behind them. "I guess we'll start from the top."

He waited until Carlisle and Danny had walked into the back foyer, watching Danny. John sighed, then punched a button on the lock. It clicked, then lit red. If Val was here, he'd probably have thought to get the woman's card from her. That'd have made things easier.

Where was Val anyway? John was sure he should have seen some sign of him by now. He jogged after the women as they headed into the core of the building.

THIRTY-SEVEN

Spencer watched the battle unfold. He'd planned for this, but plans rarely survived contact with the enemy. Still, the ace in the hole for his side was Volk. The man stood to his side, grinning at the gunfire, and actually laughed out loud when a man screamed up ahead. He looked like a child, face alive with glee — he even clapped his hands like an excited schoolgirl at one point. Spencer would have tried to put him down already if he didn't need what he had.

That, and Spencer wasn't sure if he could put Volk down. He was aware of his many flaws, and self-delusion wasn't one of them.

Regardless, having a man without fear in a heated battle was a solid asset. He was confident Volk wouldn't fold under pressure. Hell, he'd seen the man provoke one of his soldiers into unloading a grenade into him. Spencer didn't care which side of the tracks you came from, that took balls. Even if you knew you couldn't die, there'd have to be some nagging doubt in a man's mind that this would be the last time.

Wouldn't there?

A bullet whispered past his face. That one almost had his name on it. Hunkering down, he shouldered his rifle, aimed through the scope, and fired three shots in quick succession. All three hit.

Of course.

He didn't notice the noise of battle anymore. You didn't get through two tours in Afghanistan without picking up a thicker skin. Weaker men, less deserving men, had cracked, gone back home with PTSD, crying to their mothers, unable to hold down a job. One of his comrades had even killed himself once he got back Stateside. That kind of weakness turned Spencer's stomach. It's what he admired most about Volk; the man was a force of nature, unshakable. He did what he wanted.

Spencer wanted a little piece of that. He'd not really done what he wanted for a long time; it was always at someone else's behest. This little engagement was a good example. If he had his way, his men would have the gift, and they'd be unstoppable. They wouldn't have all died, falling like tin soldiers as they'd thrown themselves against an enemy they couldn't be prepared for.

No use whining about it. Time to muscle up and take charge. That's what he'd done: take charge. After he'd run Volk to ground, he'd found the man bleeding out in a gutter and made him a deal, trading life for life. If there was one small wrinkle in the plan, a fly in the ointment, it was that he didn't trust Volk. Not one bit.

The schism at Ebonlake hadn't helped. He'd tried to explain the tremendous potential asset to the chain of command, but they simply weren't visionaries. They thought he'd cracked, for God's sake. It'd take more than an unexpected encounter to crack Tim Spencer; his mother hadn't raised a limp-wrist fagot. Ebonlake had told him to take some leave, get some distance, some *perspective* back.

He had all the distance he needed at the end of his rifle.

It was a shame, really — some of his men, aware of the rewards that Volk could give them, had left Ebonlake. They had his back, but Ebonlake was still cashing checks from Biomne and that bitch Morgan at the top. He'd wanted to throw her out a window the first time he'd met her; she was cosseted inside the cozy walls of law and rule and thought to give him commands. *No.* It wasn't commands he didn't like. He needed to be honest: he'd taken orders all his life from people he didn't much like, so that wasn't it. It was that she'd thought to play him. He couldn't abide that, that lack of respect.

His men — the ones still loyal to him and not to the pay check — were pushing into the facility. He knew the target would be at the top. Not Morgan's kid — but Everard. He'd be drawn up there like a bee to honey, and that's where they'd take him down. That was the deal.

"You want this, yes?" Volk had spat blood onto the ground. "The power. You need it."

"It gives a tactical advantage I can't ignore." Spencer had pushed the man with his boot, watching as the Russian had winced in pain. "Still, you're not invincible. I have to wonder if it's worth it."

"Worth it? You will see many things." Volk had coughed, red bubbles coming to his lips. His hand had reached up, clawing at Spencer's pants. "I promise you this. By tooth and claw, it will be done."

"What's the catch?" Spencer had adopted a bored expression, thumbing silver rounds into his pistol's magazine. He'd cocked the weapon, looking away from Volk. Waiting.

"Mistakes." Volk had levered himself up against the wall, and grinned through the pain. "You must help me. Erase mistakes."

"Mistakes?"

"The other wolf. He should not be alive."

Spencer couldn't have agreed more. Everard should be six feet under. "It sounds like we have a deal." He'd offered Volk a hand.

It was curious that Volk wanted Everard dead. He was sure they didn't know each other, and such passion — well, it was to be admired, certainly. But it could be a cause for concern. If it distracted them...

No, it wasn't a distraction, it was the price of the mission. Once Spencer had Volk's gift, he'd give it to his men, and they'd become an army. Perhaps they could challenge the natural order of things. He'd always wanted to run his own country; the people usually in charge were motivated by politics and petty ambition, rather than structure and order. He'd do a better job of it.

There was an explosion as his men breached the main door. He thumbed his radio, ordering a handful of troops to flank their approach and take the rear. They were a sacrificial pool, designed to draw enemy fire, but the distraction might buy him success. If the enemy thought that they were being attacked on two fronts, they'd have to divide their forces. The shame of all of this was the cost; soldiers on both sides were dying, good men he'd fought alongside before and hoped he would again. The extra sweetener here was the Ebonlake contract; the death payments to families could potentially bankrupt a company the size of Biomne.

Maybe that was wishful thinking.

"Volk. It's time to move." Spencer nodded at the front entrance. "We've got a breach."

"*Da*. So you do, Captain." Volk grinned. "This is fun, yes?"

Spencer eyed the man. "Let's just get it done."

"Of course." Volk hefted the baseball bat he carried. It was a signed José Canseco bat, an older Worth one by the looks of it. Spencer wasn't a fan of the game, but he recognized that bat.

"Why did you bring that? A gun would be more effective."

Volk shrugged. "This is very effective! Besides. Canseco was the first honest American I hear of in Russia."

"Honest?" Spencer spat on the ground. "Didn't he admit to doing steroids?"

"As I said. Honest." Volk started to jog towards the entrance, smoke pouring out of the breached doorway. "Come, Captain! There is much killing to be done."

Now that was a curious way of phrasing it. They were after Everard, for sure. Casualties would happen en route, that was a certainty, but Spencer took no special pleasure in it. It was like reaping wheat; it needed to be done to put food on the table, but that was all. Volk — well, the man seemed to relish it.

Spencer watched as Volk reached the front of the battle, three soldiers still at the doorway. God, but he was fast. As the Russian ran, he scooped up one of Spencer's loyal troops from behind, holding the man up as a shield. The surprised soldier had time to yell before the salvo of bullets hit his body. Volk had hunkered down behind his human shield, still running, until he was in amids the soldiers at the doorway. He threw the dead human shield at one man, then swung his bat into the helmet of another soldier. The man's head spun around, neck broken, his body tumbling into a patch of fire and smoke. Volk didn't stop to look at what he'd done — *he's damn sure that man's dead, isn't he* — just whipping the bat around over his head, gaining a revolution of momentum before releasing the bat into a throw. Spencer was sure he could hear the low *woosh* of it even over the noise of the battle around them.

It spun horizontally through the air, connecting with another man's helmet and bouncing off. The man fell, twitching, and Volk — *God damn, but he didn't just catch that bat did he?* That was an impressive thing to see. Another soldier fired at Volk, but he wasn't there anymore — he'd ducked into the smoke. The soldier took a cautious step forward before Volk lunged back out of the smoke, an overhead swing cracking the top of the man's helmet.

Spencer stepped through the doorway, looking at the bodies. "You're right."

"About what?" Volk was grinning like a happy dog.

"That bat. It's effective." Spencer waved his hands, and soldiers started to stream past them.

"I'm curious, Captain."

"About what?"

"All of you. You wear black. *Da?*" Volk picked up one of the bodies and shook it. It looked to Spencer for all the world like a cat trying to play some life back into a dead mouse.

"It's the uniform. Studies show black is intimidating." Spencer nudged a body with his foot, then fired once into the body's head and twice into the chest — you could never be too sure. Once when he'd been a rank and file grunt, his squad had been almost wiped out by an insurgent they'd presumed dead. Carelessness cost lives.

"I understand. What I wonder is, how you tell each other apart?"

"It doesn't seem to bother you." Spencer nodded at the torn body of the soldier Volk had used as a human shield. "That man was on our side."

"He was on *your* side, Captain." Volk showed his teeth. "He was not on *my* side."

"What—" But Volk was gone, loping off into the building. Damn it but the man was cryptic. Spencer assumed it was a language issue, or that Volk was simply crazy. Either way, he had solutions to those problems; once he had the gift, he could resolve the issues around Volk permanently. He patted the grenade harness around his body absently, feeling the dull metal of the silver. It'd been painted black so that Volk wouldn't notice, but the grenades were a complex mix of ingredients — a full silver casing with nano-particles of silver suspended in a gel at the core. Spencer was almost certain that one of those going off near you wouldn't make you happy. The metal shards would carry the silver into the blood, and then — well. The silver in the gel wasn't solid like a bullet that could be pulled out.

Spencer smiled a dead smile to himself. If what he'd seen when he shot Everard was anything to go by, a werewolf hit with one of these would burn alive from the inside out. Volk's untrustworthiness was a risk, and when you had risks you needed to carry insurance. If Volk tried to double cross him, the best the man could hope for was for them both to die. It seemed fair to Spencer.

It was as he was lost in thought that he almost died. It was a careless mistake — he'd assumed the squad he'd sent to the rear of the building would be effective. Most of his men were seasoned veterans, the odd new blood salted in for good measure. Spencer thought they'd breach the rear of the building and meet him here. What he didn't expect was the three civilians in their stead. *Civilians*, for God's sake, instead of his squad. Two of them looked familiar —

no, he corrected himself. All three were from the hospital — Everard's friends.

Spencer was so surprised to see them he failed to act, his gun resting in his hands while he stared.

One of them — *another woman, they show no damn respect* — drew a sidearm on him. She was pulling the trigger as Spencer's brain kicked in, and he rolled behind the reception desk in the lobby. It was a sidearm but still dangerous through the wood of the desk. He caught sight of Volk at the base of the stairwell, door held open as the big man looked at the action. He was grinning again.

Spencer lifted his rifle and fired blind over the top of the lobby desk. It wouldn't hit anything unless he was really lucky, but it'd keep their heads down. True to form, the shooting on his position stopped, and he risked a look around the edge of the desk. Large pillars touched the roof — they'd be hiding behind those. It didn't matter; he just needed to get to the top of the building.

"Volk!" Spencer said. The man's gaze swung briefly to him, then back into the room. "Give me a distraction!"

The big man looked at him again. "I think this is distracting enough—"

"Motherfu—" It was a woman's voice, and Spencer risked another look. His eyes widened. One of the other civilians — *a crossbow? Really?* — was trying to run towards Volk or the stairwell — it was one and the same. The third, a man, was wrestling with her, trying to get her behind a pillar.

Spencer grinned to himself, and stood up. He raised his rifle, but ducked back down as the first woman pulled out from behind a pillar and fired at him. He'd never have a better chance; Spencer ran towards the stairwell where Volk was waiting, bullets dogging his steps, the shots ringing loud and fierce in the lobby. He was almost there when Volk stepped back, letting the door close. Spencer slammed against the outside, then kicked it open, ducking into the dark beyond. The ceiling light was out but he saw Volk's teeth glinting in the dark.

"They a part of plan?" The Russian chuckled from the darkness.

"No." Spencer breathed heavily, then faced the door. He raised his rifle, shooting the door mechanism. That would slow them down some. Unless Everard had turned them — but no. They wouldn't have needed cover if they'd been turned, they were flesh and blood like he was. "Why'd you shut the door?"

"Is fun, this." Spencer saw the shadow of the man heading up the stairs. "Back home, I did not get much excitement."

Christ. It was all some big game to him. That's the last thing Spencer needed — some kind of goddamned Leeroy Jenkins on the battlefield. He'd need to bear that in mind, stay behind Volk and not rely on his support. It wasn't a mistake he'd make again. Spencer tasted dust in his mouth, spitting onto the ground.

"Excitement, huh." He checked his weapon again, then touched his grenade belt to make sure they were still there. "I guarantee you'll get all the excitement you need before the day is done."

There was no response. Spencer hurried up the stairs behind Volk, hearing noise from above — gunshots, then the sound of something heavy hitting flesh. He came to the second floor landing, finding black armored bodies. One man had been shoved through the stair rail, his head staring upwards as his chest faced down. Spencer looked away, then climbed higher.

More noises from above, and the sound of splintering wood. Spencer broke into a jog, double-timing up the steps. No telling how long those behind him would be held up at the door, and he hated having the enemy at his back. He came across another scene — three men, stacked in a small pile, with the broken haft of the José Canseco bat pinning all three together like some macabre shish kebab. He hadn't heard gunshots this time — Volk was moving to the top of the building, and killing everyone he came across. Spencer leaned down, checking a personal communicator on the chest of one man. The radio was set to Spencer's band.

Damn Volk all to hell.

Their target was going to be on the eighth floor, assuming

Morgan had been straight with him about that. It didn't much matter either way; everyone in this facility was fair collateral damage. All he needed was Everard dead, and then he could claim the gift. He passed the fifth floor marker, and more dead soldiers.

The door to the stair well slammed open, and Spencer was pushed back violently. *Everard!*

The man was fast, grabbing Spencer's rifle and tossing it away. Spencer dropped into a fighting crouch, pulling a combat knife from his belt. Everard's eyes narrowed, but he didn't back off.

"You know what this is, don't you?" Spencer waved the knife between them. "Silver blade. I'm sure I don't have to tell you what that feels like."

Everard didn't say anything, watching the edge of the knife, his hands clenched. Spencer would need to be careful here — Everard was strong and fast despite his lack of experience. No IT programmer in the world could stand up to battlefield experience, no matter what roids they were taking. Spencer feinted with the blade, and Everard flinched back. Spencer caught the other man in the groin with the tip of his boot, felt the steel toe go into something soft, and brought his fist around into a teeth-crunching blow to the jaw. His knife whipped in to cut his throat, finishing the job—

But Everard wasn't there. He'd danced back, grabbing the fire extinguisher bolted to the wall. Everard held the red cylinder in front of him like a shield.

"You're right." Everard spat out a bloody tooth. "You don't have to tell me what it feels like. There's no words. But I don't think you understand."

"Understand what?" Spencer moved the knife back and forth, light from the window catching the blade. He'd had the silver etched into it by a man who did all his work for him. The man hadn't asked questions, doing what he was asked. Spencer could see the lines of silver on the blade, almost like writing. Beautiful, in a way.

Everard swung the cylinder, hard and fast. It caught Spencer in the shin, and the pain was blinding. He went down on one knee, but brought the knife in an overhand strike to —

A hand closed around his wrist as Everard caught the swing. He let the extinguisher fall beside them, then lifted up Spencer with the one hand around his wrist. *Such strength!* They were face to face now, Spencer breathing heavily, Everard not at all.

"You don't understand — that first hit was free. We're not in the same game, you and I. I'm done playing."

Everard's fist caught him in the stomach, and the air rushed out of him. Spencer felt himself tossed against the wall, bouncing off like a Raggedy Andy doll. He tried to block, hands in the way as Everard's kick caught him in the stomach. He went down on all fours, and felt a hand grab the back of his jacket. Everard hauled him up again.

"You hurt my friends. By God, if you've hurt that little girl — but no more." The man spat out more blood. "I can't change what I am, but I can stop you."

Everard tossed him over the side of the railing, watching as he fell into the darkness at the bottom. Spencer thought hitting the ground would be the worst, but he was wrong. Hitting the ground didn't hurt at all. But the fall — that lasted a lifetime.

CHAPTER

THIRTY-EIGHT

Elsie hurried. It wasn't something she was used to; that's what staff were for. People like Sam existed to make sure she didn't have to hurry. But Sam wasn't here — God only knew where he was; he hadn't responded to her call.

She reached the door leading to where the girl was. She needed to grab Adalia and — *again* — rush. If Elsie was a judge of character — and that was something she prided herself on — Valentine Everard would be on his way. That was all part of the plan. What wasn't part of the plan was Sam dropping out of contact; he was supposed deal with Adalia while she gathered up Birkita. Putting on a hazmat suit took precious time, and time was something she didn't have right now.

Her card opened the locked door, and she opened it to see Adalia on the bed, speaking through the mirror to Birkita. Her daughter saw her come through the door, and waved.

"Hi, Mom."

"Hello." Elsie smiled, but felt it tight and stretched on her face. "I'm here to get Adalia. We're going to come meet you."

The girl — Adalia — was looking up at her. "We're going to meet Scarlett?"

"That's right." Elsie walked shut the door behind her, then walked over to Adalia. "You haven't been too worried, have you?"

"At the noises?" Birkita looked paler than usual. "I can't make the cameras outside show me what's going on."

"There's been a bit of a complication. Some of the staff have ... well, they've resigned."

"So what's with the explosions?" Birkita pulled her wig off, scratching her scalp. "That's what they are, aren't they?"

"Yes." Elsie never lied to her daughter. Or rather, she tried not to. Some things were not worth concerning her with. Like the late stage of the cancer. *Or how you're going to make her well again and what the cost will be.* "There's some people trying to stop you getting better." That much was true, at least.

"Why would they do that?" Adalia's forehead was wrinkled in confusion. "If anyone met Scarlett, they'd want her to get better."

"Of course they would. And on that — would you like to go see Birkita? You must be dying to meet her in person."

"I thought I wasn't supposed to have visitors." Birkita watched them both through the glass. "Won't I get sick?"

Elsie smiled, this time some genuine warmth seeping through. "Well, that's why we're coming to see you. That very special man I told you about is here."

"Valentine!" squealed Adalia. "He's here?"

"Mr. Everard is on his way up as we speak." Elsie saw Adalia snatch up a damaged toy of some kind. It might have been a dog or a pony at one stage. She held it up to the glass.

"See? I told you it was magic." She was grinning with the naive enthusiasm of youth.

Birkita was grinning back. "You did. It looks like your wish worked."

"Wish?" Elsie looked back and forth between the two of them,

Adalia here and Birkita's image on the screen. "What did you wish for?"

"Don't say!" say Birkita. "If you say, it won't come true."

"It's okay." Adalia was still grinning, happy and ignorant of her future. "My wish came true. I wished for Valentine to come and save you, Scarlett. Birkita, I mean."

How curious, thought Elsie. "You wished for Valentine to save … to save Birkita?"

"Yes." Adalia stroked the toy's mane. So — it *was* a horse. "Because she's sick."

"You didn't wish for someone to come get you?" Elsie looked down at the girl, so small and fragile on the bed.

"No." Adalia got off the bed. "They'll come and get me whether I use a wish or not." And with that, she headed towards the door. "Can we go? I want to see Scarlett! Maybe she can make a wish on Prancer."

"Maybe she can." Elsie took Adalia's hand, swiping her card across the door lock. It clicked green and opened. They stepped out into the plain corridor. When she'd had the hospital designed, she wanted no confusion — *no distractions* — from the primary purpose of the facility, which was her daughter's life. All things here focused on that one outcome and the small staff on premises knew their way around. It helped that most of the facility was just empty rooms — when her daughter was better, Elsie would re-purpose it into something finer, perhaps a school.

"How far is it?" Adalia didn't pull away from her hand. The child was so trusting. Elsie was sure she'd never been that trusting — it was a mistake you could never recover from.

"Not far. We'll go to a room up here, where we're going to get ready to make Birkita better. You can wait there as I go get her."

"Okay." Adalia skipped along, her pony in one hand. Something small and lost inside Elsie tugged at her. *This is wrong, and you know it.*

She crushed the thought, before it could grow into a worm of

344

doubt. Doubt was worthless — second-guessing yourself made you fall before your weakest enemy. There was no time for these sorts of concerns, not now and not here, of all times and places. In a few minutes her daughter would be fighting off the cancer, the virus in her body making her strong, and in a few weeks she would be well. Elsie would look back on this and know it was all worthwhile.

"It's just here." Elsie tapped her card against the lock of another featureless door, and it swung open to show a stark medical theater. A metal chair sat near the door, away from the tall floor to ceiling windows, and a surgical table took up the middle of a room. The metal chair had a set of drips and bags hooked up to it. One of her staff was already here; he'd obviously prepared the room. "You're alone?"

The man looked up, surgical mask covering his mouth. It didn't matter — all the worthy expressions were in the eyes. "My assistant left with the, ah—"

"Explosions, yes." Elsie looked down at Adalia. "This girl isn't afraid of those explosions. I need more like her on staff."

"Ah hah. Yes." The man's laugh was forced, and he took a cautious step back. "Is she..?"

"No." Elsie pushed Adalia towards the metal chair. The girl trotted over and sat down. "She's insurance."

The man looked between Elsie and Adalia. "I'm not sure I understand."

Elsie walked to the door, opening it. She looked back over her shoulder at the man. "You don't need to understand. Prep the chair."

"Prep ... she's a little girl!" The man's eyes were open wide.

"Oh, come now, doctor. You're on my staff because you're willing to go to exceptional lengths for science."

"She'll die!"

"She'll do no such thing," said Elsie. "That wouldn't be useful. But there's someone coming who may need ... extra encouragement. It must look authentic, Doctor."

She shut the door without looking back. The man would do as he was asked — she'd seen it in his eyes. He'd had the opportunity to sign on to cutting edge research and knew the stakes. A man like that wouldn't back away now; he needed to know the answer. That kind of enthusiasm was a resource to be tapped; such men were largely ignorant of how easily they could be played, of how their moral compass spun, unable to find North, when presented with any kind of academic accolade.

Biomne was built using such men.

She'd arrived at the vaulted door leading to Birkita's room, her feet walking the path without her noticing. She placed her hand against the door, then stopped. The chatter of gunfire was clear, forces storming the building against the Ebonlake team she controlled. Spencer had been an asset, but she'd miscalculated his allegiance. She'd figured him as a straight mercenary without ideals; she'd been wrong about that. Elsie frowned — she was so rarely wrong about the motivations of men. She'd cut him loose, but not before he'd managed to fracture the Ebonlake company from within. They'd offered her a discount.

As if a discount would make up for the death of her daughter — if it came to that.

No time for the hazmat suit. It was too late for that anyway — today Birkita would live free, or … she stamped down on that thought as well. There was only one outcome Elsie would allow. She swiped her card across the lock.

"Please identify yourself." The recorded voice was male; she detested computer systems with female voices. As if women were somehow easier to talk to, weaker, more pliable. The softly cultured tones from the machine were British.

"Elsie Morgan."

"Welcome, Ms. Morgan. I have detected stress anchors in your voice."

"It's been a busy day."

"Duress avoidance phrase recognized." The door locks disengaged with a soft hiss of air, and the heavy door eased open on hydraulic lifters. "Enjoy your stay."

She walked into the dark airlock, orange hazmat suits lining the walls. She faced a door, a small screen mounted beside it showing Birkita's life support signs. Her daughter's cortisol was elevated, as was her heart rate — normal reactions, considering the circumstances. She placed her palm against the screen, and the interior door clicked open.

"Mom! You're not wearing a suit!" Birkita looked at her, half in alarm and half in excitement. "Is it ... is he here? Is it time?"

"Soon." Elsie held out her hand. "Let's go."

Birkita looked around her at the room where she'd spent the last year, eyes drifting past the toys, the television, and lingering on the bed. "I'm not coming back here, am I?"

"We've got to hurry." Elsie tried to keep the anxiety from her voice. "There's not much time."

Birkita ignored her — *her*, of all people — and walked slowly to the bed. She touched one of the posts, hand lingering against it. Something fierce crept into her voice. "Good. I hate it. I hate it all, and I just want to leave." She turned, grabbing for something on the floor — the wig. Birkita jammed it on her head, red curls slightly lopsided. "I'm ready."

Elsie nodded at her daughter. "It's good you want to leave, for what's to come."

They walked through the door, past the orange suits, and into the corridor. Birkita's bare feet whispered across the tiles. "What do you mean?"

"You'll see." Elsie walked beside her daughter, but didn't hold her hand. *She's too old for such things.* "You'll need that fire before the day is done."

"This man."

"Mr. Everard?"

"Yes, Valentine. Adalia talks about him all the time."

"She does? That's nice." Elsie was distracted by the sounds from

347

the direction of the elevator. She hadn't fired a gun in her life, and had seen no more than a couple of poorly acted action movies — *enough for a lifetime* — but instinct told her violence was approaching.

"Is he a nice man?"

"What?" Elsie stopped, looking at her daughter as Birkita walked forward a few more steps.

Birkita slowed, then looked back at her. "I asked whether he's a nice man."

"Does it matter?"

"It matters to Adalia."

"Then it doesn't matter." Elsie started walking again, the briskness in her stride matching her tone. "Ah, here we are." She swiped the card against the door lock, opening the door. Her daughter stepped through.

"What's going on?" she asked, a hand covering her mouth.

"What is necessary." Elsie closed the door behind them. The doctor had put Adalia in the chair, the metal clamps on her wrists hunching her forward slightly. The girl was sniveling.

Birkita rushed towards her. "Take these off!" She grabbed at the metal clamps, trying to remove them.

"Doctor." Elsie waved a hand. The man grabbed Birkita's shoulders, pulling her back.

"No! What are you doing?" Birkita tried to struggle against the man. It was comical in a way, thought Elsie. Her daughter had wasted away in that room, all skin and bones, and thought to wrestle with a grown man. She'd learn over time which fights were worth fighting. Elsie had learned those lessons; if you only fought when you could win, you got a reputation for winning.

"It's okay." Adalia sniffed. "Scarlett, it doesn't hurt much. The man said that I needed to sit like this for you to get better."

"What about those?" Birkita was still struggling, but the fight had gone out of her. Perhaps she was just tired — Elsie wasn't sure.

"The drip?" The doctor looked at Elsie. "It's medicine."

Birkita looked between them. "Medicine? She's not sick."

Elsie frowned. "Birkita. Do you want to get better or not?"

"I ... I do."

"Then this is necessary."

The door thudded as something heavy hit the outside of it. *Perfect.* The handle clicked and rattled as someone tried to open it from the outside. Everard had arrived, and soon—

The lock splintered, the door crashing inward and one hinge giving way. Adalia screamed, and Birkita and the doctor stumbled back towards the window, knocking the table aside. Surgical tools clattered in a stainless heap onto the floor. The door hung at a crazy angle; Volk pushed it aside, wrenching it off the remaining hinge, and tossing the door across the room. It bounced against the plate glass, the windows bulging a little as they held.

Oh no. "What are you doing here!"

The Russian smiled an ugly smile that went all the way to his eyes. His hands and face were covered in blood, big red streaks flowing down from his mouth, and more was matted in his hair. He walked over to where the doctor was holding Birkita.

"*Deti?*" He looked Birkita up and down, one hand reaching up to touch one of the red locks of the wig. "You keep children here?"

Birkita trembled, hunching back into the doctor, trying to get away from Volk's blood-stained hand. The doctor was scrambling back and he let Birkita go. His heel caught against the floor and he fell to the ground. Volk shoved Birkita aside, and Elsie's daughter stumbled against a wall, hitting her head and slumping to the ground.

Volk had picked up the doctor in one hand. The doctor — to his credit — had grabbed one of the scalpels from the ground in his fall, and was cutting at Volk's arm. The Russian didn't seem to notice, each cut leaving a gash that healed over within seconds.

"It's not possible!" The doctor's eyes were wide.

"*Da.* Is very possible." Volk shrugged, then grabbed the doctor with his other hand. He hefted the man above his head, then dropped him down onto a bent knee, breaking the man's spine. Adalia screamed, and Volk turned as if seeing her for the first time.

"Two children? For me?" He licked his lips, then grinned. "This is good day. Very good day."

"You will not!" said Elsie.

Volk stopped, eyes wide in surprise. "I'm sorry. I'm not sure I hear. Many guns." He gestured at his ears. "I think you tell me to stop."

"Yes." Elsie almost crossed her arms across her chest, but stopped herself in time. Such a defensive stance wouldn't be helpful here. "I told you to stop."

Volk walked over to her. "Ah. You are the one Spencer speaks of."

"Spencer?" Elsie looked Volk in the eyes. "You've seen the traitor?"

Volk's head went back as he laughed, the sound coming from his belly. "Traitor. *Da.* I have seen him. He thinks to have the gift."

"As do I."

"So. We all want gift. Reminds me of old saying."

"What saying is that?" Elsie jutted her chin at him.

Volk stepped closer as he spoke. "Everyone want go Heaven. No one wants dead."

She snorted. "You don't have to die. It's just a virus."

"Is that so?" His eyebrows arched. "You *Amerikantsy*. You think you have all the answers."

Elsie waved at the chair where Adalia was. "We've got it. Extracted it from blood. We just haven't quite refined the transmission route."

"'Transmission route,'" he said, making air quotes. "You try to inject it, yes?" He mimed pumping a syringe with his thumb and fingers.

Elsie looked him up and down. "What of it?"

"Is old news. Has been tried." Volk shrugged. "Is not virus."

"It is a virus!" Elsie gestured at the chair again. "We've got it right there!"

"No. Gift is not virus. Virus you find? It was made by our doctors." Volk shook his head. "In Soviet Russia, we have many smart men. They try to control. Want to make many soldiers, strong as others. But you need leash. Before giving gift to others, *da*? It is a poison." He spat.

"They don't have our science."

"No. Science no help."

Could it be true? If it wasn't a virus, then what? "You're mistaken. You've infected another."

"*Da*. My mistake." Volk grinned. "Usually I am more careful. It was the silver, yes? Hurt my head. I could not think straight."

"But you're thinking straight now?" Elsie looked around the room. Birkita was coming around, shaking her head, still woozy from the hit. "Perhaps we can come to an arrangement? If you would just—"

"No. No arrangement." Volk ran his finger across his throat. "You bind me with silver, try to kill me. The pain, it is terrible. For that, you will die. You," and here he gestured at Birkita and Adalia, "And all you love. I will kill you all. You will not get the gift. I will not bite. I will tear." He made twisting motions in the air with his hands. "Then I stack you. Is neat. Is orderly. Then ... I think I will go see a movie."

"No." Valentine Everard stood in the doorway. "Not today."

Elsie looked down at Adalia's toy, the pony partially hidden under the metal chair. *Sometimes wishes do come true.*

The door slammed shut, Carlisle's bullets thudding into the frame. A moment of quiet sat in the air, thin and tentative like morning mist.

"Wait!" Carlisle coughed in the cordite smoke. She saw Kendrick stop struggling — no, *Miles* stopped struggling: Kendrick had been dragging him slowly across the lobby before Carlisle's shout. Kendrick's fear had made her reckless and strong, which was a bad combination. Carlisle had seen too many cops go down in a hail of gunfire because they'd been too careless, thinking they were bullet-proof. Heck, some of them had even had a vest. Against sustained fire, Carlisle's experience was it made little difference.

Carlisle wore a vest anyway. A little difference was better than no difference.

The magazine spat out of her sidearm, clattering against the floor of the lobby. It spun away as she locked another one in place. The handle was warm against her hand; she'd fired it more times today than she remembered firing in the rest of the time she'd owned it.

The quiet was broken by a couple of answering rounds from the other side of the door. The handle blew out, metal fragments scattering across the lobby.

Kendrick shoved Miles off her; they were to Carlisle's right. His hands were held up, palms out. "Hey, I'm just—"

"I know." Kendrick was watching Carlisle, not paying attention to Miles. "You don't need to."

Carlisle reached the door, putting her back to the wall next to it. She didn't look at either of them as she spoke. "Yeah. Yeah he did."

"What?" They both spoke at the same time.

She glanced at Kendrick, then back at the door. The handle had been blown clear out. It was a heavy door, designed to stop fires and God only knew what else. She tested it with her hand a couple times; it didn't budge. Carlisle looked at the sidearm she carried. Maybe she could shoot the bolt out? "These soldiers aren't fooling around. You guys need to get it in your heads. This isn't some movie. Bullets kill."

"Hey." John was smiling at her. The man was impossible, of course. "She was just trying—"

"I know what she was trying to do." Carlisle stepped back from the door, then gave it a good kick. It didn't even shift in the frame. Damn.

"*Your* daughter's not up there. Your..." Kendrick trailed off.

"My friend?" Carlisle cocked her head to the side. "Yeah, my friend's up there too. And your girl. We're going to get them both. I promise. But you know what? It's going to be a shitty rescue if I have to leave you two dead in the lobby."

Miles laughed. "I didn't know you cared, Melissa."

"I don't. It's the paperwork."

Kendrick nodded, a tentative grin tugging her face. "You guys are still using paper, right? Triplicate?"

"Triplicate." Carlisle looked around the lobby. There was another set of stairs on the opposite side of the elevator. "Let's try the other stairwell."

"That one locked?" Miles walked over to her, taking in the holes in the lock.

"No, I just don't think the door's the right shade of beige."

John just smiled at her. "Fair enough. What about—"

The other stairwell door crashed open, gunfire and the promise of death coming from it. Carlisle saw Kendrick *move*, duck fast and quick behind a pillar as the bullets tore around her. Chips of plaster were flying through the air. Carlisle could see Kendrick's mouth open in a scream that was drowned out by the hammer of guns. Her own sidearm was already up. Carlisle saw the lobby desk that Spencer had been behind; she pushed Miles towards it as she strode towards the other doorway, gun held in front of her as she fired.

The brass shells spun as they ejected from the side of her gun, the sound of it firing lost over the larger automatic weapons firing from the stairwell. It'd be lucky if she hit anything.

A man stepped through, and one of her rounds caught him in the side of the neck. She followed the body down with her gun, still firing until the weapon clicked empty. Carlisle ejected the magazine, still walking forward, pulling another from her belt and slapping it *in*, and she was firing again. Another man — *this one's a bit more cautious* — pointed the barrel of his rifle out and fired in her direction. She didn't slow her momentum, just changed direction to push herself up against the wall. The muzzle flash of the soldier's weapon was bright as a sun, the star burst pattern etching on her retina. His weapon clicked empty, and she ducked through the door of the stairwell.

Carlisle's free hand grabbed the fore grip of his weapon, pushing it against the face of another man to her left. Her sidearm came up under the first soldier's helmet and fired twice, then she kicked the body away. Another man — *that's three* — was crouched on the stairs, a fresh magazine almost in his weapon. Carlisle put her right foot on the man's knee to her left, using it to boost herself up, her left knee cracking into the man's helmet. He fell backwards into the wall, and the man on the stairs fired, but she was already moving past the line of fire, her sidearm swinging through the air over the top of the man's rifle and clocking him in the helmet.

The man jerked, his rifle firing wild, and she knocked it further clear with her other hand. Carlisle pulled her own gun back and fired point blank into the man's helmet three times. Without pausing, she spun on the man she'd knocked into the wall, and emptied the rest of her magazine into him. Her weapon clicked empty, and she ejected the magazine. Smoke curled from the barrel of her sidearm, a lazy haze rising up into the air of the stairwell.

She stood still for a few moments, listening. Her hearing was probably shot to hell, but you had to try, right? Her hand found another magazine from her belt, pushing it into her sidearm.

"You good?" It was Miles from outside the stairwell.

"I'm good." Carlisle looked at the men around her. "It's clear."

"Jesus fucking Christ." Miles coughed at the smoke. "You are your own team, you know that?"

"What?"

"Three on one. And they had guns. Big guns! I've heard that size matters." He nudged a rifle with his foot, as if it was a snake, then grinned at her. "Not that that I've had any complaints, you know?"

Carlisle sighed. "Big guns have no class."

"No class?"

"None. Also, fighting house to house, like this? You can't swing it around worth a damn. These guys couldn't get a bead on me."

"It's not because you're awesome?" Miles looked around her. "Not just a little bit?"

That coaxed a grin from her. "Like I said. *Krav Maga*—"

"Yeah, yeah. *Kung fu.* I get it." Miles looked back through the door. "Danny? You okay?"

"I..." Kendrick's hand came around the edge of the pillar, feeling its way up the cracked edge. "Yeah." She stood up, walking towards them.

Carlisle nodded. She was lucky — she knew that. In this situation, a couple of civilians was bad news. It was the sort of thing likely to get you killed. These two, though — well, they had it together.

They hadn't cracked. No one had even thrown up at the sight of a body, which had to be a first.

Kendrick was kneeling down by one of the bodies, unstrapping the helmet. It was the one Carlisle had shot under the chin.

"Uh, I wouldn't do that." Carlisle reached down, but Miles' hand stopped hers. He shook his head.

The helmet came free. What came out was messy but still recognizable. Kendrick was turning the man's face this way and that. She said, "What do you suppose made him want to do this?"

"Do what?" Miles had taken a step closer, then stopped.

"Try to kill us. Why are they shooting at us?" Kendrick was still staring at the man's face. "I didn't know this man. I didn't do anything to him."

"No." Carlisle looked up the stairwell. "But he did something to you, didn't he?"

"Yeah." She stood up, her face grim. "And I'll kill them all for it."

Miles threw a glance sideways at her. It said, *What the fuck?*

Carlisle stood still for moment. "Why do you say that?"

"Come on." Kendrick nodded around her at the bodies. "You're in the same boat. I don't know any cops who go in firing. You're like Chuck Norris or something."

"No one can be like Chuck Norris." Miles shook his head. "One day Norris was vacationing in Hawaii, right? Did a light workout. A couple guys followed him. It's now called the Ironman Triathlon."

"I'm serious." Kendrick looked between them both. "That's what we're doing, isn't it? We're here to kill them all."

Carlisle stared at her, then nodded slowly. "Yeah."

Miles looked at Kendrick, then at Carlisle. "Wait. What?"

Kendrick touched his elbow. "You know it's true, John. They've got your friend up there. Valentine." She paused on the name, swallowing. "Whatever it takes."

Carlisle looked at her sidearm. "I'm pretty sure they've killed Vince. My partner. He was a ... well. He was an adequate cop at best, but he was my partner. And he was a good man. He tried his best to speak for the dead."

"They've got Adalia. And my..." Kendrick swallowed again. "My Valentine."

Miles leaned against the wall. "Okay." He leaned down, snaring a rifle from the floor. "They've got my friend. But you know what?"

Carlisle shook her head. "No. What?"

He checked the weapon, clearing the breach. "I know they'll keep coming until they get what they want. And that shit's just got to stop. So I'm with you guys." He held his hand out, palm down.

Carlisle put hers on top of his. Kendrick put hers on Carlisle's. John said, "Hut."

"What?" Kendrick looked at him.

"Don't tell me you don't watch TV." Their hands fell awkwardly apart.

"I watch TV. I don't watch bad TV."

"Oh, it's like that, is it?" John shook his head. "It's football. It's what they say. You know. Hut-hut-hut."

"It's older than that." Carlisle started up the stairs, holding her sidearm pointed up. "It's from the Roman legions. It means, 'to execute.'"

"You watch the History Channel, don't you?" Miles talking from the bottom of the stairs still, checking the dead men for something. Carlisle looked back and saw Kendrick following close, the crossbow held at the ready.

"No." Carlisle fired her weapon twice as a head looked out and over the railing above her. There was a clatter and a rifle spun past her down to the bottom.

"Christ!" Miles looked after them. "Stop dropping shit. That one almost hit me. What do you mean, 'No?'"

"I mean no." Carlisle looked at the landing number — 3. Five floors to go. "My father was in the military. Loved all that stuff."

"I'm not surprised." Miles had started up after them but his voice still sounded distant a couple of floor behind.

Carlisle ducked back from the railing as a salvo of fire rained down. The bullets from above pocked the metal stairs. She held her hands up over her head as bits of metal and concrete spat about them. The guy almost had a bead on her, and she clambered up the stairs, falling to all fours as the bullets hit around her. Carlisle felt a tug as a round pegged her vest — *too close, too damn close* — and she scrambled up faster. She needed cover, had to get to a corner to get out of this shit storm coming down—

There was a twang close by, and the firing stopped. Carlisle opened her eyes to see Kendrick pulling the crossbow's bowstring back. After a moment, a black clothed body fell tumbled past them down the stairwell.

"Jesus!" Miles' voice was still a little below them. "Can you guys cool it for a second?"

"Not unless you want to die." Kendrick put a bolt in the crossbow.

Miles rounded the stairwell. "Okay, fair enough."

"What kept you?" Kendrick eyed him up and down.

"Last minute shopping. Let's go." He patted his pocket.

"We were waiting for you." Kendrick nodded at Carlisle. "You good?"

"Thanks." Carlisle checked the hole in her vest. A little red was seeping through — the round had done more than hit the vest. There wasn't any pain, and she was damn sure there wasn't enough time to take the vest off to check the damage. It didn't feel bad, not like the shot at the station.

Miles looked at her. Was that genuine concern in his face? "Did you get hit? Look, you stay here—"

"And what?" Carlisle gestured with her sidearm. "My score's a lot higher than yours. You're not doing a great job of convincing me you can handle yourself." She patted the number 4 on the stairwell door next to her. "Four more floors, Miles. You get four floors to catch up."

He held out a hand to her. "Fair enough. But you'll need to stand back. Let me work my magic."

Carlisle used his hand to get to her feet. She swayed a bit, putting her hand on the wall. "You know—"

"Save it. See if you can keep up." He turned that smile on her again, but it was dimmed a shade by concern. She wondered what he could see in her face.

"Really. I'm fine." Carlisle stumbled, and Kendrick caught her.

"Sure." Miles nodded to Kendrick. "I know what chicks mean when they use the word, 'fine.' It's one of those words that doesn't mean what you think it means." He hefted his rifle, then started up the stairs ahead of them.

Carlisle's felt a burning from her side, like a road rash from a bike accident she'd had years ago. Her hand came away sticky and red. She switched her sidearm to her left hand as they climbed higher.

"How you holding—" Whatever Miles was saying was lost in the confusion as a soldier walked out onto the stairwell in front of them. The man was as surprised as they were. No one moved for a couple of heart beats.

"Hey." Miles nodded at the man. "Where's the medic?"

"The what?"

"The medic." Miles' tone was exasperated. "We've got an injured man here." He pointed down at Carlisle and Kendrick.

"Uh—"

"Look. What's your name, son?" Miles walked higher on the stairs to stand next to the other man.

"Uh—"

"Private Uh, is it?"

"No sir!" The man snapped straight, clearly deciding that whomever Miles was, he knew what he was about, and that meant *officer*. "Private Witherling, sir!"

"Witherling." Miles sniffed at the man's name. Carlisle could only watch, her pulse pounding in her temple, as Miles clapped the man on the shoulder. "Witherling, we've got an injured man."

"I'm not sure—"

"I haven't finished." Miles stared the other man in the eye. "Did I sound like I was finished?"

"No, sir. I'm sorry, sir. It's just that—"

"Witherling."

"Sir."

"Witherling, I'd like you to do me a favor."

"What's that, sir?"

"I'd like you to look that woman in the eye, and tell her that she's going to die. Because if you keep standing there, she's going to. And it'll be on you."

"I — uh." They were standing quite close now, but Miles broke off, going to lean against the railing. The other man followed him. They both looked down over the edge.

"Tell me what you see down there."

Witherling looked over the edge, then looked back at Miles. "I"m not sure—"

"That's right, private. You're not sure. Which is a shame. You seem a decent sort." Miles clapped the other man on the shoulder again, then gave a heave. Witherling gave a startled yell, tumbling over the side. Miles watched him fall for a few seconds, wincing at the thud that came from below. "They're not really very clever, these military types."

Kendrick helped Carlisle climb higher. "How do you do that?"

"Do what?"

Carlisle winced. "Yeah. How do you do that? Getting people to do, well, whatever."

"Trademark secret." Miles tapped the side of his nose.

"No, really. I need to know." Carlisle coughed. "I'm probably going to die here, right? Your secret is safe with me."

"Right, fine." Miles gestured over the rail where the other man had gone. "You just need to know you're in control."

"Like the voice of authority?"

"It's not a voice, baby." Miles winked at her. "You need to *know*."

"Christ." Carlisle looked at the gun in her hand. "I might just shoot you myself."

They arrived at the level eight doorway. Miles rattled it, but it was locked. Carlisle waved with her gun. "Let me blow the lock out."

"Please." Miles looked down on her, then fished something out of his pocket. He held up a key card. "Last minute shopping, remember?" He swiped the card over the lock, and the door beeped green and clicked. He pulled it open a crack, then looked back at them. "You guys ready for this?"

Kendrick's arm was solid around her. She felt the other woman nod; Carlisle nodded too. "You still haven't caught up."

Miles' hand was on the door. "What?"

"Your score. You only got one on the way up."

"Oh come *on*. Style points."

"Style's only good at the rodeo, Miles." Carlisle pushed Kendrick away, taking a few deep breaths. "Stand back. It's probably best if I—"

"You can barely stand." Kendrick nodded at Miles. "John or I should go first."

"I'll be fine. I'm feeling much better." The lie was salty in Carlisle's mouth. But to hell with it if she was going to let civilians ahead of her. It's what the police were *for*. She shouldered Miles aside, and walked into the lobby of level eight. It was featureless, like the rest of the building. Carlisle held up a hand. "Quiet."

"What is it?" Miles was close behind her.

"Didn't I just say quiet?" Carlisle strained to her. There — down that corridor. She could hear voices, an argument breaking out. She led the other two around a corner, and caught a glimpse of Everard.

"It's—" said Kendrick.

Miles' hand clamped over Kendrick's mouth. "*Shhhh,*" he mouthed at her. It was good thinking for a civilian — there wasn't any need for anyone but them to know help was on the way. It wouldn't change what Everard was going to do — he was committed

— and it would give them the element of surprise in whatever he was facing.

Carlisle nodded. She picked up the pace. Everard was standing in the doorway ahead of them. Carlisle heard him say, "Not today," before walking into the room. She broke into a jog, rounding the corner moments behind him. Her gun was up ahead of her, pointing into the room.

She saw two girls — one of them was Adalia, locked into a crazy metal chair, the other on the ground. A older woman was standing by a man on the ground, his back at a crazy angle. And Everard, who was locked in a wrestle with Volk. A surgical table was on the ground.

"Freeze!" She pointed her sidearm at Volk, but couldn't get a clear shot. Neither Volk nor Everard paid her the slightest attention.

Kendrick rushed behind her to Adalia, trying to free her from a chair. Miles moved to help her. They were struggling with the clamps on it. Carlisle looked at her sidearm, then back to Volk and Everard. The bluff would need to be good.

"You want a silver round in the head? I said, freeze!" Carlisle shouted it this time, then pointed her sidearm at the roof and fired a round. Neither Volk nor Everard looked at her, but they stopped moving. "That's right. Silver. Got your attention?"

The girl on the ground got up and moved to help Kendrick and Miles. Kendrick eyed the other girl, but Adalia said something to her mother and she moved aside, letting the girl help. Kendrick's attention seemed to be pulled towards Volk.

"Detective Carlisle?" It was the woman. "I'm Elsie Morgan."

"Ms. Morgan? You're under arrest." Carlisle didn't look away from Volk. "And you. Asshole. Step the fuck away. Over there." She waved her gun at the wall furthest from Adalia.

Volk showed his teeth. *Was that a smile?* "Of course. There will be another time."

Carlisle was sure that Volk wasn't speaking to her. Everard spoke up. "Another time." They stepped away from each other, walking a step at a time backward. Like dogs, circling each other. Not dogs, she corrected herself — *wolves*.

"You too. Move the fuck over there." Carlisle nodded at Morgan. "Next to the big man."

Volk leered at Elsie. "Is good. We can continue conversation, *da*?"

Carlisle nodded to herself. It was good partitioning. Dead guy on the floor — he wasn't bothering anybody. Morgan and Volk — *the bad guys* — over by the other wall. Her friends behind her. And she was guarding the door. It'd do for a rush job.

"There, honey." Miles spoke from behind her. "What the hell do these needles do? I've pulled the drip out of Adalia's arm, but—"

"Ah." It was Morgan. "I wouldn't touch those if I was you."

"No shit. John, put that needle down." Everard's voice was calm. "Don't even touch what comes out of it."

"It's bad?"

"Your face will melt off."

"Really?" Miles sounded doubtful. "Why'd they have Adalia hooked up to it?"

"Because that bitch wanted something from me."

"*Da*. She can be very persuasive."

"Shut it, Ivan." Carlisle waved the gun at the Russian. "Anything you say can and will be—"

"I know Miranda. But I do not think you know me." Volk sniffed the air. "I do not smell *serebrom*."

"Feel free to test it out for yourself." Carlisle's gun moved back to cover Volk as she turned partially towards Miles. She was about to ask him to get the girl out of here. She never got the chance.

Tim Spencer stood in the doorway, a pistol in one hand. "Isn't this cozy." He looked around the room. "Police. That complicates things a little." He shrugged, then leveled his pistol and shot Carlisle four times with it. She felt the bullets hit home, falling back, a spray of blood against the clear glass window at the back of the room. She was lucky, in a way, that the man was injured — his shots were low. Two bullets hit her legs. Only two bullets for her chest. The vest took the worst of it, but she went down, the scream coming from her as the pain rose up.

Hell of a way to be lucky.

CHAPTER
FORTY

Val didn't take his eyes off Volk. He hadn't stopped watching the man when Carlisle and John and — *God, what's she doing here, she can't be here, she can't* — Danny walked through the door. He didn't want them here. Despite that, he felt the comfortable warmth of their presence in the room. The other—

Brother / Father / Saviour / Killer / Sickness / Enemy / It must die.

—man stood across from Val. He was next to Elsie Morgan, the woman who'd brought him here. Val felt the irony of Birkita being with his—

Pack.

—friends behind him, rather than with her mother and the Russian. Val could smell the cordite in the air; the smell clung to Carlisle, standing tall at his side, like a coat she'd thrown on against the winter. Thick and strong, it spoke of passage through enemies. He could smell the blood too, the metal tang of it sharp in the back of his throat. His lips pulled apart, teeth showing.

Carlisle was herding the room, organizing people like she'd done this a hundred times. Val heard a new voice — *Spencer* — and felt

365

Carlisle's attention swing to the door. The shots rang out hard and fast. Just for a second, Val's attention wavered from Volk, his eyes pulled to Carlisle as she stumbled back, red splashes coming from her, through her, and she was down.

It was only for a second.

Volk pounced, grabbing Carlisle's gun from the floor. Val tensed to spring — *it's only a gun* — but held back. Volk wasn't pointing the gun at him. The gun was pointed to Val's right, towards his friends. Val was sure he could deal with just one shooter, and edged in front of the chair, keeping—

Cub.

—Adalia at his back.

Spencer smiled a tired, dead smile and limped over to join Volk and Elsie. The man raised his rifle and pointed it in their direction. "Everard. You're a hard man to *put down*." The emphasis on the last two words was unmistakable. "Isn't that what we're supposed to do with rabid dogs?"

Val saw the slight tightening of Elsie's eyes. She was looking behind Val. "Birkita. Come over here. You'll be safer."

"Safer?" There were tears in the girl's — Birkita's — voice. "You tried to kill my friend!"

"It was make-believe. A trick." Elsie lied like a pro — something to remember for later, if later ever came. "Now come over here."

"It's okay." Val nodded, sparing the girl a glance. "Birkita? Go to your mother if you want. You should make up your own mind."

"My own mind?" She seemed uncertain. "Why?"

Val swiveled back to Volk, clenching his teeth. "I — I'm pretty sure that today's not going to have a happy ending." He thought of a girl named Amy. "You should choose who you want to end it with. John?"

"I'm here."

"I know. You're always there." The half-smile pulled at Val's face. He hadn't done anything to deserve such a friend. "Can you check Carlisle?"

"I don't think so." Spencer looked between them. "I think we're just going to—"

"No." Elsie interrupted Spencer with the ease of a person used to giving the orders. She held her hand out, and Birkita started to walk to them. "We don't have what we want."

"Yeah. Yeah we do." Spencer's head nodded towards Volk. "I've made a deal. We finish with Everard, and Volk will give us the gift."

"Is this true?" Elsie turned to Volk, her eyes searching for something.

"*Da.*" The Russian was holding Carlisle's sidearm like it was a water pistol. "The mistake must be fixed. Then we can go see movie."

She turned back to Spencer. "He's lying to you."

"Of course he is." Spencer tapped a belt around his body, studded with grenades. "That's why I brought these."

"My friend." Volk's teeth were showing. "What did you bring? Not something made with silver. We have had that talk."

"These grenades are filled with silver nano particles. They're linked to my vital signs." Spencer tapped a small box at his waist. "If I go down — well, whoever kills me is going to get a silver enema."

"I am hurt you do not trust me."

"You should be thankful I've been this ... thoughtful. It's how we can be sure that Everard won't kill us. And — naturally — that I get the gift without you taking a little too much."

"*Da.*" Volk seemed thoughtful. "Silver particles? What are particles?"

"I don't have time for a chemistry lesson. But I do have time for a lesson in human nature." That dead smile crossed Spencer's face again. "Everard, you have to choose. Who dies first? It's going to be one of the girls."

The rifle in Spencer's hands moved back and forth. Danny stood next to Val. "Me. I go first."

"What?" Val looked at Danny. "No. Please."

Pack mate!

She put a finger on his lips. "Shhh. You can't do what you need to do if you're thinking about me. Save my baby." She leaned in close to his ear. "I love you too." Then she turned and ran at Spencer.

Val's hand was reaching for her back as the shots spoke hard and true. He didn't feel the bullets, and looked at Spencer's rifle, seeing the curl of smoke rising from the barrel. His eyes followed the line of the shot, back to—

No.

His eyes wouldn't see. It couldn't be. There was blood, so much blood, and she was—

No!

Volk was laughing from the other side of the room, then pointed Carlisle's gun at Val. "Here. I help." He pulled the trigger, the shot slapping into Val's arm. Val didn't notice, all he could see was—

He held the elevator doors open. He'd wanted to tell her since the day he'd seen her. "I love you." Then he dropped into darkness.

—her hair, the crimson spreading out below her, as her dead eyes—

NO!

John was shouting something, but Val couldn't hear it. Elsie was grabbing for Birkita's arm, trying to pull the girl away from the middle of the room, but Val ignored it all. Another shot hit his chest, but he felt nothing, all he could feel was—

Danny leaned in close, the heat of her finger still on his lips. She whispered, "I love you too."

—the pounding pressure in his head, the feeling rising through him like a wave, the force of it too much to hold. No one should have to feel this, not again, not ever, not anymore — *please God no, not Danny, no—*

The beast broke from within him as his useless humanity fell from him like his flesh, thrown aside like old rags. The rage tore through, and he roared his loss and hate.

THEY WILL ALL DIE.

FORTY-ONE

John scrambled across the floor, pulling Adalia close to his chest. "Don't look honey. Don't look. Close your eyes." He held the girl close to him, hunching to create a shield with his body.

She was crying against him, the sobs wracking her little frame. John heard the shot and held Adalia tighter. He could see the patch of red on Val's arm. His friend's face was stricken, one arm held out towards Danny. He didn't look to be taking any notice.

"Val! Get down!" John shouted it, but the second gunshot came anyway. It hit Val's body, but the man didn't even move.

Volk was looking at the pistol in his hand, then back at Val. His eyes widened. John looked, and saw—

My God. My God. My God.

Val stood, a scream of rage coming from him. He spread his arms wide, then clawed at his chest, big hunks of skin sloughing off. Val grew, his body twisting, becoming more massive, his face twisting, his teeth—

John blinked, and saw the creature. The change hadn't taken more than a count of three. The creature — *Val, my God, it's Val* — stood over them all, then walked towards Danny's fallen body. The weight of it cracked the floor tiles; John could feel the *size* of it as the floor moved under him.

Volk spoke into the silence. "No. Is not possible. To change, you must die."

Val nuzzled Danny's body. A little blood was left on his snout, and he licked his nose. A low whine escaped him, turning into a low growl.

"Ah." Volk showed his teeth at Spencer. "You have done a very stupid thing."

Spencer had turned pale, his hands shaking as he tried to put a new magazine into his weapon, a red one. "For Christ's sake, do something!" His fingers fumbled, the magazine dropping to the floor. Spencer dropped to his knees, scrabbling for the lost magazine.

"Okay. So is not *serebrom*." Volk sighed, then inverted Carlisle's sidearm, pointing the muzzle at his chest. He breathed in once, twice, then pulled the trigger. Elsie screamed as the shot sprayed red out the back of the man, and Volk's body tumbled to the ground.

John looked over at Elsie. "Get her out of here!" He nodded at Birkita, who was hunched next to the wall, saying something over and over. She held a — *what the hell?* — small toy in her hand. It looked like a pony.

"No!" Elsie stood. "She needs it! She'll die without it!"

"She'll die if you stay!" John looked around. He'd dropped his gun, it had to be here somewhere—

Val broke off from Danny's body, crossing the room in two strides. He stood over Spencer, his head touching the ceiling, looking down at the man. Spencer managed to get the magazine into his rifle, bringing the weapon up, but it was too late. Val grabbed the man in one clawed hand and flung him across the room. Spencer landed next to John and Adalia, scrambling to his feet, and leveled the rifle at John.

"Don't fucking move! You touch me again, I'll execute these two!" The words were tumbling from Spencer, his rifle shaking slightly as he jabbed it at John.

John moved — *slowly, Miles, slowly* — and put Adalia behind him. She'd gone quiet — *God, she shouldn't have seen this, she shouldn't be here* — and limp. He stood, facing Spencer. "You piece of shit."

Val moved a step forward, but John held up his hand. "No, buddy. Not this time. You can't carry anymore. It's too heavy."

Spencer squinted at John. "What?"

"It's none of your business." John saw what was behind Spencer, and kept talking, moving closer. He stepped up until the barrel of Spencer's rifle was pushed into his chest. "You want to kill me? Then kill me."

Spencer was looking right in his face, and John saw it — that moment that the man switched, and decided to pull the trigger. John was waiting for that moment, that impossibly thin slice of time when action was about to start. Right there? That moment was when your guard was down.

Needs must, when the devil rides.

John slapped Spencer's barrel aside with one hand and shoved him backwards. The gun went off as the man stumbled, but that was always going to happen — this way the round took John in the shoulder instead of the heart. He fell back — *Jesus Christ, the pain* — as Spencer tripped. Right into the metal chair. One of the IV packs ruptured, clear fluid spraying over Spencer.

Spencer wiped the fluid off his head, looking at his hand. "This was your big play?" He looked down at John. "Pathetic." He raised his rifle again.

John chuckled. He knew it sounded weak, but damn his shoulder hurt, his entire side felt like he'd been hit by a truck. It made Spencer pause. "You ever wonder?"

Spencer looked blank. "Wonder?"

John jerked his head towards Val. "He hasn't torn you to shreds. Why is that?"

"I'm not sure—"

"It's because you're a dead man walking." John pulled himself upright, pulling Adalia close. "Come on honey. Let's get you out of here."

"I'm not done with you!" The rifle swung back up to John.

"No, I guess not." John sighed. "But I think they're about done with you."

"They?" Spencer looked around the room, and saw it. Volk's body was changing, twisting, growing. It jerked upright like it was on marionette strings as it changed, life coming back into the dead eyes, the smile returning just a moment before the face turned into a muzzle, the fangs growing—

Val roared at it, stepping forward. Volk rose to meet him, the two beasts grappling. Their moves were fast and powerful, claws and fangs flashing. Spencer raised his rifle to fire, then swayed. "I—"

John stepped carefully across the floor towards Carlisle. She was out cold, her lips blue. "Aw. Shit." He'd read somewhere you shouldn't move someone with a knife in them, but what about a gunshot? It probably didn't matter, not here, because if they didn't get clear they'd all be dead. He put Adalia down, then lifted Carlisle into a fireman's carry. He grabbed Adalia's hand, pulling the girl close. He spared a glance for Spencer.

The man's hand had came away from his bloody nose. "What the hell?"

"Beats me, pal." John paused, then looked back over at Elsie. "Elsie! It's over. Get her out!"

Elsie was ignoring him. She pulled Birkita away from the wall, and held her forward towards the two creatures. "Do it! Do it!" she screamed at the beasts as the tears tracked down her face.

Both Val and Volk paused, looking at her. Val's head turned on its side — *just like a curious dog, Christ, just wait till I tell him about this shit* — but Volk stepped forward. It snatched Birkita from Elsie. Val tried to step forward.

But it *was* too late.

Volk threw the girl at the window, her head leaving a bloody mark against the glass as she bounced off. She slid to the ground, lifeless. A keening started low and desperate in Elsie Morgan's throat, and she scrambled towards her fallen daughter.

Adalia watched it all with big eyes, seeing nothing.

Spencer coughed, blood coming out of his mouth. A bloody grin split his face, and he patted the grenade belt. "You're all coming with me. It doesn't matter. If I don't get the gift, none of you will."

John didn't see the change, didn't even notice until the third werewolf roared. Volk and Val stopped their fighting briefly — *just a second, God they're fast* — and then started to claw and rend at each other again. The new wolf was—

Danny's body was gone. Jesus Christ. How did that—

—tearing and slashing at Volk. John watched, his mouth open, as Val and Danny fought against Volk. He couldn't tell where one started and the other finished. Danny clawed at Volk's face, and Volk ducked back from that, but Val was there and waiting, his strike hitting low. Volk clawed back, but Val pulled away, Danny's slashing claws raking Volk's muzzle. They pushed Volk this way and that, striking, circling, never giving quarter.

It didn't matter. Each strike they delivered healed over as if it had never happened. No one could win this fight. Unless—

John turned to Spencer. "You want to be famous?"

Spencer had got back to his feet, and stumbled around to face John. Blood drooled out of the man's mouth. "Whaaaa?"

John turned back to the fight. He raised his voice. "Val. I know you're in there. I can't do this by myself. I'm going to get Adalia out, but you need to deal with Spencer!" John's boot caught the man in the stomach. It was a push, not a kick — he used his foot because he didn't want any of that stuff on his skin. That, and it'd be damn hard to push the man with Carlisle over his shoulder, but her weight helped the shove.

Spencer stumbled back, tumbling into Val. The three beasts looked at the man, their fighting forgotten for a second. Val stared down at the man, then looked up at Danny. He gazed at Volk, then back to Danny.

"No." John took a step forward. "Val, not like—"

Val grabbed up Spencer, patches of the man's skin falling off. He charged at Volk, shoulder catching the other creature, and they hit the plate window. It shattered outward, a star burst of a thousand shards of glass, sunlight catching them and scattering tiny rainbows of light. Val had grabbed onto Volk's back, Spencer's body held around Volk's front. The two of them tumbled out of sight, and were gone.

The explosion of the grenade belt was sudden and vast, the blast kicking the remaining windows in. John was hunkered over Adalia, squeezing his eyes shut — *at least Carlisle's got a vest* — as the shards of glass spun about them.

He opened his eyes into the silence. Birkita's body had been thrown away from the edge of the windows. John saw that Elsie Morgan sobbing, her eyes now blind ruins from the explosion of glass. She was moving bloody hands through the glass strewn floor, feeling for her daughter. John looked back to Danny, saw her sniff at Elsie, then growl low as she stalked forward. She loomed large above Elsie, one clawed arm coming up. John saw it clear in his head — Danny was going to tear Elsie apart. She'd die in pain and fear. It was what she deserved, wasn't it? He looked back down at Birkita's body. *No, John — no one deserves that.* He stepped forward.

"I've got this." John coughed. "Please. I need you to check. My friend. Valentine. Is he..?"

Danny turned her muzzle back towards Elsie, the woman's hands still shuffling through the glass of the floor.

"I know. I'll handle it." John swallowed. "Hut-hut-hut. Remember? I promise."

Danny moved to the window, one clawed hand on the edge as she looking down. She turned back and looked at Adalia. Danny growled at him, then turned and jumped out the window. Like that, she was gone.

John walked into the corridor, setting Carlisle down. He patted next to the woman, and Adalia sat, wide eyes still seeing nothing.

"Wait here honey. I'll be right back." He walked back into the room, moving through the debris until he found what he was looking for. He picked up Carlisle's sidearm, checking the weapon, and walked over to Elsie Morgan.

"I can't find her." The sobs shook the woman. "I can't find my little girl."

"She's safe now." John looked back at Birkita's body. "She's not in any more pain."

"She got the gift?" Elsie's sightless eyes looked up at him. "She's running free?"

"Yeah." John sighed. "She's running free. You know—"

"I need to pay the boat man?" Elsie stopped shuffling through the glass on the floor, sitting back on her heels. She looked at him with those sightless eyes. "I know."

"I..." John looked at the gun in his hand. *Mercy — you can give her that at least. There's no happy ending for her any other way.* "Yeah." He raised the gun towards her. The barrel shook a little in his hand. He shut his eyes and squeezed the trigger.

CHAPTER
FORTY-TWO

Carlisle drifted in and out of consciousness. She felt cold all over, her arms and legs heavy.

"Stay with me. Melissa! Christ." Someone slapped her face. Miles — damn it, couldn't he leave well enough alone?

Blackness.

~

SHE WOKE AGAIN to a stranger's voice. Carlisle tried to crack her eyes open, but they wouldn't budge. She felt warm and cold at the same time.

"Mr. Miles. What a pleasant surprise." It was a voice that sounded at home over an English breakfast tea. "It's odd, I was waiting for Mr. Everard, but..."

"Val can't make it right now." Miles' voice was right next to her. She felt strange, like she was the wrong way up to be having a conversation. "You were expecting him, weren't you?"

"Yes." The other man cleared his throat. "You don't know me. My name is Barnes. Sam Barnes."

"Hi, Sam." She felt a subtle shift under her as Miles spoke again. Maybe she was in a stretcher? "Look, this is a little weird."

"Ms. Morgan?"

There was a long silence, and Carlisle almost fell asleep again. It would have been easy, but something was hurting deep inside.

Miles broke the silence. "She's upstairs."

"I see." Barnes' voice was moving. "And Miss Morgan?"

"The girl?"

"Yes."

"She's upstairs too."

Another silence. Carlisle's pain was fading, but something trickled into her throat, making her cough.

"Melissa? Stay with me." Why did Miles keep saying that? She was right here. She couldn't walk, anyway — it's not like she was going anywhere. She wished he would call her Carlisle.

"Was it quick?" Barnes' voice was hollow. "Tell me it was quick."

"It was quick. Are you going to..?" She could feel Miles tense. Why was that — was he in the stretcher too? She would have giggled if she'd had the strength, the thought was preposterous.

"No." Barnes cleared his throat. "Mr. Everard was ... that is, Ms. Morgan ... well, Mr. Everard was most helpful earlier. He gave me some advice, advice that saved my life."

"Yeah?" Miles sounded dubious.

"But I couldn't ... I've waited, in the trees. For this to end."

"I'd say it's at an end. Look, I don't want to rush you, but—"

"Of course. Detective Carlisle."

"Isn't this some kind of hospital?"

"It's not that kind of hospital. And I think you'll find the staff have long gone."

"You stayed." Miles' voice was flat.

"Yes. I stayed."

Carlisle finally cracked her eyes open. She could see the ground, and the back of Miles' feet. *Damn the man* — he had her slung over his shoulders like a sack of grain. She could see blood on his clothes, and wondered whose it was.

"For Elsie? Did you stay to help her?"

"Not as such. I stayed to see if Mr. Everard — if Valentine needed a ride."

"A ride? We're in the woods."

"Yes."

"You can fly." Miles wasn't asking. He might make a half decent officer, if he could just keep his attitude in his pants. Carlisle wished she had the strength to smile.

"I think that's lucky for you, as Detective Carlisle needs a hospital."

"What's the catch?"

"The catch is that we need to go soon. This is a one-time offer. There will be people coming here with questions, questions I'd rather not answer."

"You realize this doesn't fix things."

Barnes sighed. "No, I imagine it doesn't. But I hope that ... well. Let's worry about tomorrow when it comes, shall we?"

Carlisle faded out again.

SHE WAS FLYING. Carlisle could feel it. There was light around her. Didn't they say not to go into the light?

THE ROOM she opened her eyes into was dark. The beep of a cardiac monitor sounded to her left, subdued into white noise against the backdrop of the morphine haze. Her tongue felt thick in her mouth. She looked around the room, eyes picking out the little details. No flowers next to the bed. Curtains for privacy, but pulled back. An empty ward, apart from her bed. And one other person.

Miles was sprawled backward in a chair, sitting at the end of the bed. He was snoring quietly. He wore a hospital gown, bandages creeping out from under it near his shoulder.

She slept again.

CARLISLE WOKE TO LIGHT. Miles was gone. Flowers had been put in a vase on the small table next to her. She pulled herself up slowly, wincing through the morphine. Carlisle groped for the glass of water next to the bed, gulping at the tepid water. An envelope fell from the table next to the bed — she hadn't noticed it when she woke, knocking it off as she'd grabbed at the water.

The ward was really empty — Miles was gone.

Carlisle looked down at the envelope, the cream paper contrasting with the speckled tiles of the hospital floor. It was a long way down to that floor. She — *slowly, Carlisle, Christ that hurts* — rolled onto her side and reached an arm down, grasping for the edges of the envelope. Prize in hand, she rolled back onto her back.

The envelope was blank except for a neatly lettered, "MC," on the front. She flipped it over, tearing at the seal, and pulling out the single sheet of paper inside. The letter was written in a neat, meticulous hand.

DETECTIVE CARLISLE—

I appreciate you have many questions.

Ms. Morgan is no longer with us to assist in your inquiries. I hope that whatever information I hold will be able to help in her absence. Based on events at our medical facility, we believe the virus angle is a red herring, some kind of control mechanism that never worked properly. It seems ironic: with our science, we might have fixed that, given time.

When you are better, have someone from your office arrange a meeting with me. I'll be happy to answer any questions.

Regards,
Sam Barnes
Acting Chief Executive Officer
Biomne
PS: Are you familiar with the Moon's synodic cycle?

CARLISLE FOLDED the letter back up. What the hell was a synodic cycle? She hated science back in school, and being shot didn't make her feel much better about it now.

She turned to the table next to her, opening the drawer. Some clothes were there, and — *so they haven't suspended me* — her gun and her badge. The gun sat black and heavy against a pair of pale blue jeans. She pulled herself upright, gritting her teeth against the pain. Enough lying around. She wasn't dead yet. The bandages around her leg and torso were clean and white, no blood staining through. *Good enough.*

Carlisle pulled on her clothes. A standing rack near the door held her jacket. She pulled it on, needing to use her teeth as one of her arms didn't work right. Her sidearm went into her shoulder holster. She looked at her badge for a few moments, turning it over in her hands, then put it in her pocket. Finally, Carlisle checked the card with the flowers, a smile tugging at her face. The card said, *"Shaggy! Mystery, Inc. needs you back! Meet back at the lair. Yours, Scooby."*

"Detective Carlisle." She spun at the voice from the door, a hand reaching into her jacket to hold her sidearm. An officer stood, uncertain in the open doorway. "You're not supposed to be up."

"I'm not in the mood." Carlisle relaxed her hand and pushed past the officer, making the corridor. Another cop was stationed outside. So — she'd been under protective custody. "There's more important things you two should be doing than looking after me. Or did you catch all the bad guys?"

"I..." The man tried again. "The Superintendent would like to see you when you're able. To move."

"Do I look like I'm able to move?" Hey eyes went between the two men. "I look pretty shitty and sickly, don't I?"

The other man's lips quirked. "You look almost dead, Detective."

"That's what I thought. Go grab a coffee. I'll report in a bit later. There's something I need to do first."

"Yes, ma'am." The men walked off down the hospital corridor, lost amongst the bustle of the place. After they'd gone out of sight, she leaned against the door frame for a moment. She really was almost dead. Nothing that some pain killers wouldn't fix.

She needed a car. Time to get a Mystery Machine.

THE PLACE WAS foreign to her, full of unfamiliar smells. The smell of dust underlaid it all, but there were children laughing and mothers having coffee and cake. It'd been a long time since Carlisle had been in a library, but the rules had obviously changed from "make no noise" to "have a party."

She shuffled amongst the aisles of books, not quite sure what to look for. A thin man with glasses approached her. "Need some help?"

"Like you wouldn't believe. Do you know what the Moon is?" The man blinked at her. Some things never changed — back when she was in school librarians didn't have a sense of humor either. "Never mind. Look. I'm trying to find out about the Moon's synodic cycle. Astrology or something."

"Oh right. Astronomy." The man pushed his glasses up his nose. "The synodic cycle is just a fancy way of saying the cycle as the Moon goes around the Earth."

"The Earth? Right."

"Sure. Why, you looking something up for the full moon?" The man's head cocked sideways.

The full moon. *What if...* "When's the next full moon?"

"Hell if I know. Sorry. Maybe tonight? The moon's pretty big at the moment."

"You a stargazer?" The professional detective inside Carlisle took over, asking questions from habit.

"I was at a rave last night." The man was losing interest, his eyes tracking a young — and attractive — woman with a toddler in tow. "Look, you need anything else?"

"No. Thanks. Happy fishing." The man was already gone, ignoring her.

Synodic cycle. *Well how about that.* She turned around, looking at some of the other shelves. Where was she going to find a book on werewolves in the non-fiction section?

SHE KNOCKED on the door of Danny's home. The day was wearing on, the afternoon sun shifting towards evening.

"Who is it?"

"Open the door, Miles."

"Christ!" The door yanked open, Miles standing there in a towel. The bandage on his shoulder was freshly pressed on. "You got out."

"I wasn't in jail, Miles." Carlisle pushed past him, going to the kitchen. Adalia was back at the table, painting. Her face was serious, full of childish focus. Carlisle walked up to her, putting her hand on the girl's shoulder. "What are you painting, sweetie?"

"Mom and Valentine." Adalia turned the painting towards Carlisle. There were two dogs on it.

Carlisle turned to Miles. "Is this..?"

"C'mon." He was tugging on a shirt. "She saw enough by herself."

"Right." Carlisle walked to the windows, looking out. "They haven't come back, have they."

"Melissa—"

"Call me Carlisle."

"Melissa, they're not coming back." Miles sounded strained. "They're de..." He stopped, looking at Adalia.

Adalia looked back at him. "They're not dead, silly."

"I ... of course not, honey." Miles looked stricken.

"She's right, you know." Carlisle turned back to the window.

"What? The grenades. There was a lot of silver." Miles started tying his shoes. "I want them to be okay, too, but—"

"They're not dead. I told you." Adalia's face was stern. "Scarlett told me—"

"Who's Scarlett?" said Carlisle.

"Oh. Scarlett's her made up name. Birkita."

"Elsie's daughter?"

"Yes. Anyway. Scarlett told me. She made a wish on Prancer. She wished that Danny and Val and all of us would be okay."

"All of us?" Miles looked at his feet. "I wonder if she knew what that wish would cost her."

"Do you know about the synodic cycle?" Carlisle looked around the room. "And you got any coffee on? It's going to be a long wait."

"Do I look like a plumber?"

"A little. But it's the Moon."

"The Moon?"

"There's that echo again."

"You're not making a lot of sense."

"I know. Put on the coffee. I'll take first watch."

SHE'D FALLEN ASLEEP ANYWAY, despite the uncomfortable chair digging into her bruises. She didn't know how Miles had handled it when he'd been out here last. Carlisle had left him inside, reading a book to Adalia. He'd done enough work for a while, and needed sleep more than her. At least that's what she'd thought, before dropping off.

She woke with a start, the predawn light giving the porch a ghostly feel. Kendrick stood in front of her, yellow eyes staring from her face. The woman was naked, and she was carrying Everard. One of his arms was burned, wasted at his side, and he was unconscious.

Carlisle blinked at her a couple of times then grabbed her blanket, tossing it around the two of them.

"Don't talk. Just come inside." Carlisle opened the door. Kendrick hesitated, the yellow eyes darting at the doorway and back to Carlisle.

"It's okay. She's safe." Carlisle grinned. "At least, she was. Miles was reading her, 'All My Friends Are Dead.' That man is warped."

Kendrick didn't smile. The yellow was still wild in her eyes. Maybe she wasn't ready to be human again.

"I know. It's a long way back, right?" Carlisle stood inside, holding the door open. "Maybe you should just think about it. Do you remember Adalia?"

Kendrick nodded, slowly.

"Good. Do you remember Everard's coffee? With cinnamon."

Kendrick's gaze went down slowly to the man she carried, then back up. A tear fell from her face. She nodded again.

"He's going to be okay. You'll see. Bring him in."

Kendrick did, then, walking past Carlisle on silent feet. Carlisle shut the door. "You should grab a seat. There, on the couch. I'll make some coffee. It's not like his, but maybe it'll help you remember."

CHAPTER
FORTY-THREE

Val held Danny close. He hadn't been able to stop touching her since he woke up. He'd felt weak as a kitten, and something under his skin itched, but he felt happy. Alive.

Adalia was playing at the table. She'd apologized for losing Prancer. He'd laughed, and said it was okay, telling her that magic wishing ponies were not supposed to last forever.

Danny leaned back into him, making a contented noise low in her throat. "I—"

"I know."

"Yes. You know." Danny snuggled against him. She smelled good.

"Christ, can you two get a room?" John handed them another cup of coffee each. "It's disgusting."

"It's my house." Danny sniffed at the coffee. "You're not getting better at this, are you?"

"Die in a carpet fire." John walked back into the kitchen.

"I can feel you smiling." Danny nuzzled his neck, and he stroked her hair. "What happened? I don't remember."

"I don't think we're supposed to." Val sipped the coffee. It really sucked. He laughed out loud.

"What?" She looked up at him.

"I love that guy." Val nodded towards the kitchen.

"He's all right." But the smile tugged at her mouth.

Carlisle came back in the front door carrying a couple of large brown paper bags. "Thank God. Food." Val stood, unwrapping himself from Danny. "Let me."

"It's okay." Carlisle pushed him aside, heading for the kitchen.

"It's really not. He's a terrible cook." Val grabbed one of the bags, sticking his nose inside. "What the hell is this?"

"Fruit. Vegetables."

"Where's the steak?"

"I got steak. That little girl," and Carlisle nodded at Adalia, "Cannot live on steak alone."

"Could she at least try?" Val put on his best I'm-hurt voice. "For me."

THEY SAT AROUND THE TABLE, plates cleaned, a fresh round of coffee in front of them.

"How did you know?" John sat opposite Val.

"Know what?" Carlisle sipped at her cup. "Thank God you're alive, Val. I don't think I could handle more of his coffee."

"I hope you choke on it," said John. "But — how *did* you know he was alive?"

Danny leaned forward, touching Val's wasted arm. She looked at Carlisle. "Yes. How did you know?"

"A hunch."

"Come on." John tried the coffee. "Actually, this isn't bad."

"All right. It was Barnes."

"Who?" Danny looked between them.

"Elsie Morgan's assistant. I know him." Val looked into his coffee cup. "What's he got to do with this?"

"He wrote me a letter."

386

Val tried to hold his coffee in his wasted arm, but it felt too weak. Still, he hadn't been able to move it this morning, and now he'd finished breakfast he could wriggle his fingers. "What'd it say?"

"Not much." Carlisle looked into her own cup. "It was a foolish hope."

"What was?" Val flexed the fingers of his hand. Definitely getting better.

"The Moon. That you'd—"

"That we'd change." Val nodded. "We'd be strongest when the moon was full."

"Yeah. And that..."

"What?"

"You held Volk between you and the grenades as you went over the side. I hoped you hadn't got the full blast." Carlisle put her cup down. "There's no way I can write up a report on this."

"I went over the side? The side of what? There's so much I don't remember..." Val sighed. "Did we get him?"

"Who?"

Maker. Father. Betrayer.

"Volk. The ... my maker." Val realized he was clenching his good hand into a fist. "I don't remember."

Danny's voice was soft. "I remember. A little." She looked down. "I can still..."

"What?" Carlisle had leaned forward. "Did he get away?"

"I'm not sure." Danny swallowed. "I don't think so. I can still taste his blood."

Everyone sat silent for a few moments. John tried first, the megawatt smile coming out. "There's one thing I don't get."

"Just one thing?" Val's smile was lopsided. "What is it?"

"How did Danny ... I dunno. What's the word for it?" John looked at the ceiling. "How'd she turn? You didn't bite her in the shower or ... oh. The *shower*." He put air quotes around the last word.

Danny snorted. "Now it's some sort of STD?"

Val snorted. "Heck if I know. I'm new at this. If we had Volk we

387

might be able to get some answers." He tapped his cup, then looked at Danny — *alive!* — at his side. His gaze drifted across each of them around the table. "Thank you. You guys, you're..."

Pack.

"It's okay." John looked at him. "Just remember this next time I ask you to help move my house, okay?"

Val laughed. It *was* okay. He was—

Running free.

THE END.

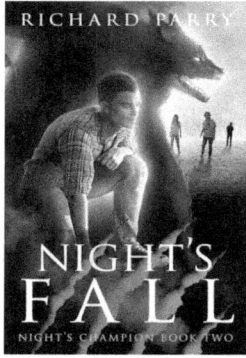

YOU SURVIVED THE NIGHT... But you might not survive what comes next.

Val thought he had outrun the worst of it. **He was wrong.**

Danny and Adalia are gone—fled to Alaska, trying to outrun the danger that follows them all. But there's no outrunning the past. **The dead are stirring, and something is hunting them.**

Val has fought monsters before, but this time, he's not the target. **They are.**

If he can't master the thing inside him, he won't just lose himself —he'll lose them, too.

Turn the page for a glimpse of what comes next.

Because staying away won't keep them safe.

NIGHT'S FALL

A WEREWOLF SUPERNATURAL
THRILLER ADVENTURE

CHAPTER
ONE

"What I'm thinking," said Carlisle to the barman, "is that you're a thief."

The barman blinked at her. "Say what?"

"Because I know a thief when I see one," she said, her words slurring just a little. She leaned forward over the bar. "Serious ... seriously? Twenty bucks for a shot of Jack is *theft*."

"You could drink somewhere else," said the barman. "Free country."

Carlisle gave a long, lazy smile. "Free country." *Only bar in this town. If you can call it a town.* She'd heard of one-horse towns, and this place was a horse short. No one else was in the bar tonight, the broken-down old jukebox spitting out the same two songs on repeat. She'd had about as much Johnny Cash as she could take. The door to the bar opened behind her, and she felt a gust of cold chase someone inside. She didn't turn to look, still holding her glass of Jack.

"That's right," said the bartender, his eyes lighting up a little as he saw a new potential customer. He started to clean a glass — Carlisle was about to say something else when a man slipped into the seat beside her.

She knew it was a man before she turned, the way he put himself in that chair like he had sovereign land rights. Carlisle spent some time taking him in. Close cut hair, ebony skin, stacked like a Vegas deck of cards inside a suit worth north of a couple grand. *Like.* She kept the lazy smile on. "Well hello, sailor."

"I'm not really a sailor," said the man. "But I'm impressed you guessed that I came here in a ship."

Carlisle let the smile fade away into a frown. His accent was strange. "Where you from?"

"The Caribbean, originally," he said. "More recently, Queens." The man gave the barman a nod. "Rum and Coke. Easy on the Coke."

"Starting hard, or..." Carlisle let herself trail off. *Something isn't right.* That old instinct came back, the cop inside her refusing to die like it should. *Too much damn alcohol, that's your problem. Thought you'd come out, get lucky, and here you are talking to a — a something.* "You some kind of soldier?"

"Not really," said the man, lifting his rum and Coke, breathing in the aroma. He smiled, his eyes closed. "More of a problem-solver."

Carlisle pushed her barstool back a little. "What kinds of problems you looking to solve tonight?"

The man laughed, something easy in it, and turned to look at Carlisle properly for what seemed like the first time. "That depends. You bring any trouble with you?"

"Left all my problems behind," she said, the lie coming easy. "Why else come to a shit hole like this?"

"Hey," said the bartender.

"Maybe your problems are trying to catch up," said Caribbean. "Maybe your problems are only just starting." He gestured with a hand to the air around her. "I can see your problems. They tug at you like needy children."

The bartender took a look around the bar, then moved through a grimy door to the kitchen. It was old and stuck just before it was fully closed. It was funny the things you noticed, just before everything went to hell. "So look," said Carlisle. "I'm here to have some drinks. Maybe get laid. Can you help with any of that?"

Caribbean downed the last of his drink in a long swallow, then turned the glass over in his hand. "Detective Carlisle?"

Fuck. "Not anymore."

"Detective Carlisle, we're trying to track down some friends of yours. Do you know a—"

"No."

"What?"

"No, I don't know anyone. Not who you're looking for. And," she said, as the man's eyes widened slightly, "not her either. And definitely not the next person you're going to ask about."

"That's a shame," said Caribbean. "That's what we call a 'crying shame.' Do you know why it's called that?"

Carlisle tipped her head from side to side, loosening up her shoulders, just getting the kinks out. "Because someone always ends up crying."

He nodded. "Do I look like the crying sort to you?"

Carlisle laughed, and Caribbean looked startled. "No," she said, "but you've made a huge mistake — and I mean, a massive, colossal fuck-up — if you think *I'm* the crying type."

"The name I was going to ask you about," said Caribbean, "was Elliot."

Carlisle blinked at him in the silence left between the tracks changing on the jukebox. Her veins felt like they'd just started running ice instead of blood, her head clearing from the fuzz of the alcohol. She could hear the machine catch, clicking as it tried to drop another disc in. She swallowed. "What did you say?"

"I thought that might get your attention," said Caribbean. "What would it be worth to you if you could see him again?"

"Elliot's dead," said Carlisle.

"Is he, now?" Caribbean reached behind the bar, snagging out the bottle of rum. "I wonder about that."

"I don't."

"Let me ask you something," said Caribbean. "Let's assume he's dead. What if I said I could bring him back to life?"

"I'd say you were crazy in the coconut," she said.

"Well," said Caribbean, "that's not an unusual reaction to get."

"You ask people about their dead friends often?"

"Often enough," he said. "It's a growth industry, in my line of work."

"Right," said Carlisle. *Here's a good one. Guy walks into a bar, asks about your dead friend Elliot...* "What exactly *is* your line of work?"

"I get things done," he said. "The job title changes week to week."

"First you said you were a problem solver. Now you say you can raise the dead."

"They don't have to be different things," said the man. "And I don't raise the dead. I'm more of an intermediary. The woman who stands behind me is the one who can raise the dead."

"Fancy trick," said Carlisle, turning on her stool to lean back against the bar. She took in the room — no one else here, clear exits, she should just get out. This kind of crazy talk wouldn't lead to any good.

"I can tell," said Caribbean, the soft touch of his accent making him easy to listen to, "that you're having trouble believing me."

"You think?"

"Here's a little taste," he said, reaching — slowly, Carlisle noticed — into the breast pocket of his jacket. He pulled out a few items — a small vial of clear liquid, a hand-rolled cigar, an old-style lighter. He placed these on the bar, then splashed a generous portion of rum into his glass. He emptied in the clear liquid, then raised the cigar.

"There's no smoking in here," said Carlisle. "Not that I give a shit, but you know." She pointed at the sign on the bar top, right next to the lighter. *Thank you for not smoking.*

"I see it," said Caribbean. "I don't think they mean this kind of smoke." He picked up the lighter, flicking it open, a long tongue of flame kissing the end of the cigar. He drew big puffs, then blew a stream of smoke towards the ceiling. "That feels right." He puffed a few more times, then blew another stream of smoke over the top of his glass. Instead of the smoke flowing past, it clustered and gathered at the top of the rum. Small eddies pulled the tiny cloud about, which then seemed to be drawn into the dark liquid.

"There's a thing you don't see every day," said Carlisle. "But if you think I'm drinking that, you've got another thing coming."

"Just watch," said Caribbean. He pushed the glass closer to her. Carlisle noticed he seemed ... *drained*, tired around the edges. "It won't be long now."

Despite herself, Carlisle looked into the liquid. She knew it would be some parlor trick, but she had to look anyway. The smoke seemed to bunch just under the surface of the liquid, a small storm in silent motion, then cleared, the liquid reflecting the room. *No. The liquid can't reflect the room, I should be seeing the ceiling in there, if anything.* She could see a room in the liquid, drawn out in shades of brown, and a man stepped into view. It was like she was looking through a peep hole and seeing—

"Jesus fuck," said Carlisle. It was Elliot, standing in there, picked out like she remembered him, even the gut. "Jesus fuck," she said again.

The image of Elliot walked closer, and his voice came out of the glass, blurred, like if it were a picture someone had colored outside the lines. She was hearing him from a long way away. "Carlisle?"

"Elliot," she said. "Is that you?"

"It's me," he said. "It's—"

"What was the last thing you said to me?"

"Hell if I know," said Elliot. "That was a long time ago."

"Take a guess," she said.

"I think we were talking about... It's so hard to remember, Carlisle. I think we were looking at some footage of something—" his face scrunched up as he tried to remember, and the surface of the liquid shimmered. "I can't remember. I'd started smoking again. Can you believe that? Praise no day until it's ended, that's what I always say."

"I can believe that," she said. "I can't believe *this*, though. What is this?"

"It's—" he was cut off as Caribbean knocked the glass over, the rum spilling out.

"What the hell did you do that for?" Carlisle said.

"Just a taste," said Caribbean. "Now we need to make a deal."

Carlisle looked at him, then at the splash of liquid on the bar. *That ... that was Elliot. But Elliot's* dead. "No deal," she said. She pushed off from the bar, jacket already in hand, and turned towards the door.

"Just remember," said Caribbean's voice behind her, "that we offered you a deal. You can still take it."

"Ain't no way," said Carlisle, "that I'm taking a deal like that."

"But you don't know what the trade is," said the voice at her back.

She paused, her hand on the door outside to the street. "I know well enough," she said. She reached up and brushed the tears from the corners of her eyes before she stepped out into the snow.

THE CARIBBEAN WATCHED her step out into the cold and the night and the loneliness of the world, then looked down at the bar. The spilled rum sat there, empty of purpose, but not of power. Not of faith.

He traced a finger through it. He felt the warmth of that power, a spill that had held — just for a moment — the captured soul of a man. He tugged on that faith, scooped his hand through the rum and closed his fist around it.

Liquid leaked and dripped around his fingers, and he looked at the door where Detective Carlisle had gone. What was it that she had said?

I'm here to have some drinks. Maybe get laid. Can you help with any of that?

He breathed deep, opened his hand as he closed his eyes, and blew air through his fingers, spraying rum into the room. Sending it on a path after her.

Maybe get laid.

So lonely, hidden behind that facade. She needed, *longed* with a will. All that she lacked was direction.

Can you help with any of that?

The rum floated in the air, slipped around a table, crossed over the top of a chair, and misted under the door after her.

"Yes, Detective," said the Caribbean. "I can help you with that. And you *will* help me."

Bound. Her need, balanced against the soul of a dead man. He felt the ties as they found their mark. Carlisle would want him. Follow him. Do what he needed, for as long as he needed.

So they could catch a monster, and save the world.

THEY RAN. IT DIDN'T MATTER.

THE HUNT HAS BEGUN.

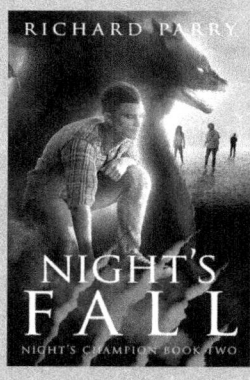

Val thought leaving Danny and Adalia behind would keep them safe. But **monsters don't care about distance**—and the dead are already closing in.

Now, Val has to face what's inside him before it consumes him completely. Because if he fails? **He won't be the one who pays the price.**

Grab *Night's Fall* now!

https://www.books2read.com/NightsFall

The fight isn't over. It's only getting darker.

ACKNOWLEDGMENTS

This isn't quite the first book I've tried to write, but it's the first one I've finished. That first book was a far fetched tale I'd started tapping out on a Commodore 64 with my mother's help, back when I was closer to being a zygote than an adult. I don't remember too much about that story — some high plot points maybe — but it's probably best that the tape holding it got lost somewhere. You get a lucky break like that sometimes.

Here I am at the end of this book, and — well, *shit*. There's a lot of people who helped get me here.

First thanks go to Mum — not for the obvious mechanical reasons of birth, but because she started to help me write that first story.

Second thanks go to Pamela Sharp, an English teacher of mine at school. She reviewed my nasty scribblings with a fairness that they didn't deserve, and was a good critic. I'm pretty sure she saved me from a life of romance writing, and I'm in debt to her. Her secret identity is The Electric Blue Pedagogue.

Third, but perhaps first after all, is my brother Jonathan, without whom you wouldn't be reading this. He bundled me off to a writer's group as a birthday present, and that group provided skills and insight I lacked in equal portions. Thanks bro.

On that note, my first writing group's advice carried the first parts of this book from fairly nasty prose to what's easier to digest. Thank you for your support — Frances Cherry, of course, but also Dot, Pru, Paul, Ana, the other Frances, and Sally. God — Sally, you still make me shudder to put this work out there; if I could be half the writer you are — well, it's probably a mercy. There's already one Stephen King, the Earth wouldn't take two.

I'm blessed with a life rich in friends who've given me encouragement along the way. I'd like to tip my hat to the people who believed in me — Greg, Gisela, Matt, Arran, and Arun to name a few. They wouldn't leave me alone, so you can blame them if you don't like what I've written because it's ultimately their fault. You guys. Whilst we're speaking of friends, it's worth mentioning my legion of beta readers - some previously mentioned but I'll go over them again, because they had to suffer. A lot. Raelene, Arran, Greg, Cheryl, Paula, Lynda, Michelle, Anthony, Jane, Stephen, Gerard, Erin, J, and Nerys — you guys rock.

Anthony deserves another special mention because not only is he a wizard with punctuation, but he also understands science. This makes him different to me, because I am into science fiction. The only reason the stuff on viruses in here makes any sense at all is because of him. If it still doesn't make sense, it's not his fault: he tried. Really, he did.

Kerry: thanks for the help to get me familiar with gun lingo. I always appreciate looking less like a fool than I otherwise would.

Last, but not least — my Rae. You have been at my side through it all, and carried me at times when you were already carrying too much. I'm humbled by you, and consider myself a very lucky Parry to have found you. This book is for you.

— R. P.
August 2013, Wellington

ABOUT THE AUTHOR

Richard Parry worked as a senior marketing manager in one of the world's top tech companies. It sounds cool, but it wasn't all cocaine parties. He lives in Wellington with the love of his life, Rae. They have two cats, Harry and Friday, who chase birds. The birds, who have the power of flight, don't seem to mind.

WAIT. DON'T GO!

Thanks for reading my book. If you enjoyed it, let's keep the party going:

📖 Join *Roll for Narrative* for reviews, storytelling breakdowns, and writing misadventures:

https://rollfornarrative.parrydox.com

✉ Lurk, judge, or say hi:

https://www.parrydox.com

P.S. An angel still gets its wings for every five-star review, but I'm told they're on backorder.

- ⓐ amazon.com/author/richard.parry
- ⓖ goodreads.com/richard_parry
- ⒝⒝ bookbub.com/authors/richard-parry-6ffc3911-9f2c-43ef-8ab4-13dc-cd7f5874
- ▶ youtube.com/@parrydigm
- 🦋 bsky.app/profile/parrydox.com
- in linkedin.com/in/therealrichardparry

ALSO BY RICHARD PARRY

DAWN'S WARDEN

The Three Faces of Fate

The Undefeated Throne

The Fury of the Betrayed

THE SPLINTERED LAND

Tomb of the Six

Blade of Glass

The Storm Within

Requiem's Justice

The Copper Bard

Heartsong

The Hymn of All

THE EZEROC WARS

The Ezeroc Wars universe is big (and growing!). Get the reading guide here:
https://www.parrydox.com/ezeroc-wars-reading-guide/

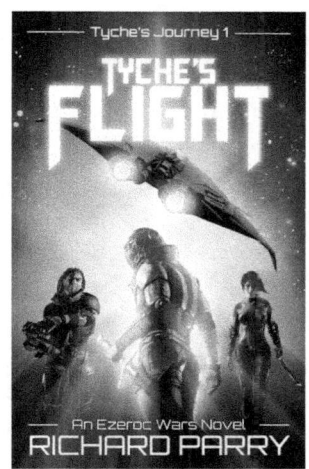

Tyche's Journey

The Empire's Rogues: Volume 1

FUTURE FORFEIT

Not sure where to start? Get the reading guide here: https://www.parrydox.com/future-forfeit-reading-guide/

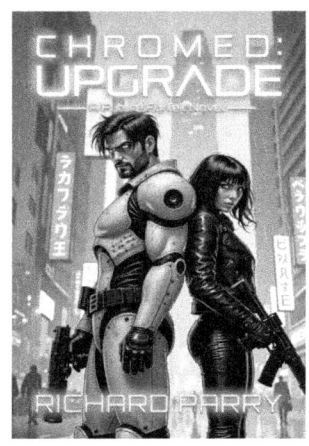

Chromed: Upgrade

Chromed: Rogue

Chromed: Restore

City Stories

Chromed: Consensus

Chromed: Delilah

Chromed: Meltdown

NIGHT'S CHAMPION

Night's Favor

Night's Fall

Night's End

www.ingramcontent.com/pod-product-compliance
Lightning Source LLC
Chambersburg PA
CBHW061509020726
47502CB00006B/1998